Beauty

Sarah Pinborough

Copyright © Sarah Pinborough 2013
Interior illustrations copyright © Les Edwards 2013
All rights reserved

The right of Sarah Pinborough to be identified as the author
of this work has been asserted by her in accordance with
the Copyright, Designs and Patents Act 1988.

First published in Great Britain in 2013
by Gollancz
An imprint of the Orion Publishing Group
Orion House, 5 Upper St Martin's Lane, London WC2H 9EA
An Hachette UK Company

This edition published in Great Britain in 2014 by Gollancz

1 3 5 7 9 10 8 6 4 2

A CIP catalogue record for this book
is available from the British Library.

ISBN 978 0 575 09307 2

Typeset by Input Data Services Ltd, Bridgwater, Somerset

Printed in Great Britain by Clays Ltd, St Ives plc

The Orion Publishing Group's policy is to use papers
that are natural, renewable and recyclable products and
made from wood grown in sustainable forests. The logging
and manufacturing processes are expected to conform to
the environmental regulations of the country of origin.

www.sarahpinborough.com
www.orionbooks.co.uk
www.gollancz.co.uk

For Lou and Joe Abercrombie.
Great friends and great people. With love.

1

'He needs an adventure...'

It was a warm spring and the king and queen took their breakfast on the balcony outside their private apartments, enjoying the fresh air without the burden of any sort of protocol. The sun was warm without burning and the sky was bright without making them squint. For the queen it was almost perfect. The only thing spoiling the moment was the subject of their conversation. It was, however, a talk they both knew was overdue.

'He needs to grow up,' she said, sipping her tea. 'We've spoiled him, I fear.'

'It's very hard not to spoil a prince,' her husband, the king replied gruffly. 'No doubt my father spoiled me. A prince must feel superior. How else can they ever become a good king?'

Beauty

The king's stomach was bursting free of his thick white dressing-gown and as he reached for another pastry the queen marvelled at how time changed them all. The handsome young prince she'd married had disappeared, swallowed up by this bear of a man. It had been a good marriage though, difficult as she found the endless pressures of royalty, and in the main he had been a good husband as well as a good king.

'Still,' she added. 'He's our only child. I think perhaps we've been too soft on him.'

'Perhaps you're right,' he grunted. 'He must soon marry and start a family of his own. He should attend more council meetings. Undertake more training with the generals for when he must lead the army. Learn to understand the revenue as he promised to.' He paused and frowned. 'What does he do with his time anyway?'

The conversation wouldn't have started if they hadn't seen their only child, the hope of the kingdom, their handsome golden boy, staggering up the castle steps in a wine soaked shirt as they'd taken their seats on the balcony that morning. It had become something of a habit, as a quick chat with the servants had revealed. Being out all night at inns and houses of ill-repute with various other young men of noble birth, then sleeping most of the day away. Occasionally riding out with the hunt, but too often not.

It was all, perhaps, to be expected of a young man, but it was becoming a lifestyle and that would not do. Their boy was going to be a king one day, and that would require a level of gravitas and respect that he currently did not have. The queen looked at her husband again. He was no longer a fit ox of a man. His face was red and veins had burst on his cheeks. He was carrying far too much weight. Her son's destiny might be closer to hand than any of them liked to think – and although no parent liked to think it of their own flesh and blood, the queen had become concerned of late that her boy would not rise to the challenge.

'We need to find him a good woman,' she said. 'Someone with a calm temperament and a clever brain.' It was easier to consider the qualities of a future wife than to discuss the flaws in the prince.

'He'll want a pretty wife,' the king muttered and then smiled at his queen. 'I was lucky. I found that truly rare creature: a woman with both beauty and brains.'

The queen said nothing but shared a contented

3

moment with him, knowing that the king too felt they had spent their years together well. Yes, she suffered from terrible headaches and various forms of anxiety, but she had been a good advisor to him behind the closed doors of their rooms and when he'd strayed, as kings, the most spoiled of all men, were wont to do, she had shrugged it away and known that he would be back in her bed before long. It was a royal marriage after all, and she'd had romance before it, a long time ago. Romance and—

'He needs an adventure,' she said, the words out before she'd really thought it through. 'All these wild nights; they're not good for him. He needs a proper adventure.'

'Hmmm,' the king said. 'The thought had occurred to me. But to send him from the kingdom? Our only son?'

'A king needs to know the outside world,' the queen said. 'He needs to understand how the nine kingdoms are different. Why they are at war. Perhaps find a way to make peace with an enemy. He can't do any of that here.'

The king knew the wisdom of his wife's words and somewhere in the recesses of his mind a memory stirred. 'My grandfather had such adventures, you know. When I was a child he told stories of visiting a faraway land and rescuing a girl from a tower by climbing her hair.'

They both laughed at that and the queen's eyes twinkled. 'I hope he was a slim man at the time.'

'I'd break your neck before I'd got one foot on the wall, wouldn't I?' The king shook his head. 'A crazy story from a crazy old man. But still, I think there is something to this adventure idea.'

The queen watched as her husband slipped off into his own thoughts. His eyes were narrowed and she knew better than to speak and interrupt him. Her seed was sown and now he'd be trying to determine the best kind of adventure for their son to have. One that was important enough, not too dangerous, but which might benefit the kingdom. After all, the kingdom was the only thing that mattered when everything was said and done.

She sipped her tea and leaned back in her chair, gazing up at the turrets far above her and the many, many windows that glinted brightly in the sunshine. Her head was mercifully free of pain and today there were no official engagements or lunches with noble women for her to attend. Birds sang in the trees. Below them the city rumbled into life. She felt content with her lot.

5

'I think I have it,' her husband said eventually. 'I think I have the very thing.'

The king spoke to his son about it over dinner. Being a relatively wise king he invited several influential noblemen to dine with them, along with their sons. A prince was as likely to bow to peer pressure as any other young man, and now that the king and queen had made their decision he would brook no arguments from his son about the task he was about to set him.

'Plague?' the prince said after his father had started speaking. 'What kind of plague?'

'I don't know,' the king answered. 'It might just be a legend. All anyone knows is that deep in the heart of the forest, near the base of the Far Mountain, there was once a wealthy city. A tenth kingdom. The story goes that nearly a hundred years ago a terrible plague struck the city. The forest, rich with magic so close to the mountain's edge, closed in around it, the trees and brambles growing so high and thick that the city and all its people were sealed off and lost forever.'

'And no one looked for them?' the prince asked.

His venison sat untouched on his plate and the king was pleased to see the story had his son's attention. But then the boy had always chosen romanticism over practicality.

'Perhaps they did, but the forest didn't allow them to be found.'

'Surely they could have cut themselves free from the other side?'

'But they didn't. Which leads me to believe that the entire population died very quickly.' The king paused. 'But of course, all the treasures will still be there. And if the city could be found, it would make a welcome addition to our kingdom. A lucrative discovery, a useful outpost for keeping an eye on our enemies or a perfect place to host peace talks between warring kings.'

'And you want to find it?' the prince asked.

The king smiled and sipped his wine. 'No, my son. I want *you* to find it. Every prince should go out into the world and have an adventure before settling down. This will be yours.'

Several of the young men around the table burst into excited chatter and the prince, the jewel at their centre, grinned. 'Then I shall find it for you, father! I promise you I shall!'

7

The huntsman had been lost in the dream when his father woke him. It was the same dream he'd had for several nights and it was so powerful that the echo of it stayed with him during the days. There was a girl with hair that tumbled in thick curls down her back, as red as autumn leaves. She was running through the forest and he was chasing her, following the flashes of her hair and the echo of her laughter, but all the time her face was out of sight. He ran as he had as a child, with no sense of awareness of the changing shape of the forest around him and without the tracking skills that had become second nature to him as a man. Nature didn't matter. The beasts that lived around him didn't matter. The forest itself, so much a part of him, no longer mattered in his dream. All he cared about was finding the girl who stayed so elusive ahead of him. His breath rushed in his ears and his heart raced.

He sat up with a start, for a moment confused by his surroundings. His father grinned at him. 'The girl again?'

He nodded.

8

'I told you. She's your true love. You're lucky; not many get the dreams. But if you do, you have to find her.'

'Well, she's not in the village, that's for sure.' The huntsman stretched and yawned.

'And a good thing too. You've had most of the girls here. Or they've had you.'

They smiled at each other, good-natured, easy with the natural way of men and women, and how frequently they tumbled into bed with each other until wedding vows claimed them. Men and women both were just animals after all, and life in the forest could be hard. Comforts had to be taken where you could get them.

'Why did you wake me?' The huntsman, said as he shook away his sleepiness and pulled on his shirt. Beyond the glow of his father's torch, he could tell it was still dark outside and the air held the crisp scent of a chill spring night. It wasn't dawn, but maybe two or three in the morning.

'The king's men want you.' His father held up a hand. 'It's nothing bad. They want the best young huntsman and the elders have all chosen you.'

'I *am* the best,' the huntsman muttered. 'But what do they want me to hunt?'

He peered out the window and saw several soldiers

in shining uniforms, sitting high on thoroughbred horses.

'They want you to babysit the prince. Be his companion on a trip to the edge of the Far Mountain.'

The huntsman's heart fell. He had no time for kings or princes. From what he'd heard around the campfires on the long winter hunts, nothing good ever came from their company. 'Can't he take care of himself?' he asked.

His father snorted with laughter. 'He's a prince. He's no match for the forest. He'll be lost within a day. Starving within two—'

'—and eaten within three,' the huntsman finished.

The horses outside pawed at the ground, picking up on their riders' impatience.

'I don't have a choice, do I?' he said, reaching for his knife and his axe and his old leather bag for carrying food and water.

'No, son, you don't. The king's decided his boy needs an adventure.' His father's tanned, wrinkled face looked like a craggy rock face in the gloomy light. 'But maybe you do too.' He smiled. 'Maybe you'll find that redhead of yours out there.'

'The girl of my dreams?' the huntsman said, wryly.

'Stranger things have happened.'

'If this prince doesn't get me killed first,' he said and stepped out into the night. He didn't look back at his father, or at any of the huntsmen and women who had gathered in front of their small cottages and huts to watch him leave. Long farewells weren't their way. He'd either come home or he wouldn't. Huntsmen knew each other well enough to know the things that were so often said by other men – and to know how rarely they were meant. He climbed up on the back of a waiting horse and patted its neck. The beast whinnied as nature recognised nature, and then they were gone, leaving the the village behind in the pale pre-dawn light.

The huntsman had been to the city before but had only visited the markets on its edges. The castle at its heart glittered like a diamond when the sun hit the banks of sparkling windows, but it had always seemed like an illusion in the distance. It was beyond him how men could build such edifices and he wondered how many ordinary people had died cutting, dragging and lifting the thousands of quarried stones that made up its smooth, perfect surface. He wondered if the king ever wondered that.

Now that he was standing in front of the man, he doubted it. Gruff and ageing as the king was, he had sharp, cool eyes within his fattening face.

'They say you're the best of the huntsmen,' the king said as he studied the man before him. 'That no one knows the forest as well as you.'

'I know the forest, that's true,' the huntsman answered. He had no intention of expounding upon his own skills. The king had already formed his opinion, otherwise they wouldn't be face to face. Boasting just set a man up for a fall, and the only reason to boast would be to somehow ingratiate himself with the king for personal favour or political gain. The huntsman wanted nothing from the king for, unlike so many, the glittering life did not appeal to him. He neither understood nor trusted it.

'And you're good with a knife? And a bow?'

The huntsman shrugged. 'I'm a huntsman. Those are my tools.'

'You don't say much,' the king said, smiling as he leaned back in his vast, ornate throne, inlaid with rubies and emeralds so large that the huntsman could almost see his reflection in them. 'I like that.' He waited for a moment as if expecting the huntsman to respond to his praise, and then his smile fell to seriousness and he continued.

'The prince is my only son. He needs an adventure. He also needs to come back alive. He is my heir and the kingdom needs him.'

'I'll do my best,' the huntsman said. 'But I am only one man.'

'If you were to return without him, it would not end well for you.' Any pretence at warmth had vanished from the king's face. 'Or for your village.'

His father, not without an adventure or two of his own below his belt, had warned him about the merciless ways of the rich and royal, and the king's threat came as no surprise. 'As I said: I'll do my best, your majesty. My best is all I have to offer.'

The king frowned for a moment as he tried to work out whether the huntsman was being ignorant, obtuse or just speaking plainly in a place where every sentence was normally laden with subtext, but eventually nodded and grunted.

'Good.' He ran thick fingers over his ruddy cheek. 'The prince must never know about this conversation. He knows you are to be his guide, and that your skills will be needed to pass through the forest, but he must believe that he's the hero in this tale, do you understand? Your role in protecting him must never be spoken of.'

The huntsman nodded. He had no time for heroes or stories or tales of true love, despite his own dreams.

'Good,' the king said again. 'Good.'

The huntsman met the prince down by the stables where he was choosing their horses, fine steeds whose muscles rippled under their glossy dark hides. The prince was as blond as the huntsman was dark and his easy smile charmed all those around him. At least he looked fit, the huntsman thought, and they were of a similar age. Perhaps it wouldn't be such a bad journey. The prince shook his hand vigorously and then pulled him close, patting the huntsman heartily on the back.

'We leave at first light,' he said and then winked. 'Which gives us all night in the taverns to give this city – and its maidens – our farewells! There will be wine and women for us, my new friend, before we leave to find a new castle for the kingdom!'

The huntsman forced a smile as his heart sank. He had no problem with wine and women – especially not with the women – but it appeared the prince was in danger of believing the legends of his princely deeds even before he had done any. That was never good. When huntsmen got too cocky they normally ended up gored. What would happen to this fine, handsome prince, he wondered. And how on earth was he going to save him from it?

2

'Bloody bastard wolves...'

She hadn't meant to come back this way but when her feet had turned her down the path she had followed them. Her basket was full and heavy and she should have gone straight to granny's cottage, but the forest came alive in the spring and nowhere were the scents more alive than at the edge of the impenetrable wall of briars and bushes and, as usual, she couldn't resist their lure.

None of the villagers ever came here. They spoke in whispers about it and the noises that could sometimes be heard in the night, and children stayed away, but Petra had always been drawn to it. She placed her basket on the rich long grass and pushed back the hood of her red cape so that she could gaze upwards. The dark green wall stretched up as high as she could see, blocking out any sight of the mountain, coloured here and there by small bursts of flowers poking through the brambles.

As she did every time, she wrapped her hands in her cloak to protect her from hidden thorns and tried to pull a few branches apart to see what lay on the other side, but it was a fruitless task and all she could make out were more twigs and vines, all locking together. She held her breath and listened, but there was only birdsong and the rustle of the forest. That was *all* there ever was in the daylight and she couldn't fight the disappointment she felt. Perhaps she'd sneak out again tonight and see if she could hear the plaintive howling that sometimes carried quietly over the briar wall on the breeze. The sound might have terrified men and children alike, but something in it called to Petra and made her heart ache. For a while she had just listened, but then one night she'd thrown her hood back and howled in response and the forest wall itself had trembled as their two voices became one. It had become a song between them, a delicious, private secret that made her shiver in ways she didn't really understand. But she longed to see beyond the wall and find the other half of her duet. What manner of beast was trapped there? Why did it sound so lonely? And what had made the forest create such a daunting, impenetrable fortress that no man had tried to break through it?

'I thought I'd find you here.'

Petra jumped slightly at the soft voice and turned. 'Sorry, granny. I just ...'

'I know,' her grandmother said. 'You just wandered here by accident.' She was a short, stout woman whose face was rosy with both good humour and good nature. Here and there a grey curl sprung out from under her cap. Petra loved her very, very much. 'The forest can be like that with places and people. When your mother, may she rest in peace, was little she was always up at the emerald pond. She'd stare into it for hours, hoping to see a water witch or some such foolishness.' She smiled and Petra smiled back, picking up her basket and turning her back on the lush vegetation that grew so unnaturally and fascinated her. She'd heard her mother's story many times before but she never tired of it and she knew it cheered her grandmother, although by nature a happy soul, to talk about her.

'I've put some soup on for lunch,' her granny said. 'Let's go home.'

They chatted about their mornings as they walked, the route second nature to them both even though the tiny paths that cut through the dense woodland would barely be noticeable to a stranger. The stream somewhere to their left finally joined them, babbling into their conversation as they walked alongside the flowing water, and finally came to the clearing where granny's cottage sat. Smoke rose from the chimney and flowers were starting to bloom in the borders that ran in front of the small house. It should have been a beautiful sight but today, as had happened on too many days recently, it was marred by a bloody trail of innards that emerged from behind the house and vanished at the edge of the forest.

'Oh, not again!' Granny gasped and the two women, age being no impediment to panic, ran to the small enclosure behind the cottage where granny kept her precious goats. It was as Petra feared. The gate had been broken through yet again. From somewhere deep in the trees a low howl of victory drifted towards them. It had none of the plaintive texture of the sound that drew Petra to the mysterious forest wall; this was all animal, fierce and hungry.

'Bloody wolves,' her granny swore. 'Bloody bastard wolves.'

'I'll mend it again,' she said, quietly. 'Make it stronger.'

Her grandmother was moving through the rest of

the scared goats who had huddled at the far corner of the pen. 'Adolpho. It's taken Adolpho.'

Petra had never tried to persuade her grandmother to move to one of the houses in the village as she grew older – she knew how much the old lady loved the peace and quiet of the forest – but recently she'd started to think it might be a good idea. It had been a hard winter and the wolves, normally a rarity in this part of the forest, had arrived as a hungry pack and, when the weather broke, they'd stayed. Where foxes were a menace they'd learned to deal with, the winter wolves were braver and stronger. Men in the village talked of cattle lost in the night to the wolves working in twos and threes, and although they had tried to hunt them, the pack was elusive.

'Go inside, Granny,' Petra said, knowing that the old woman would want a quiet moment to mourn the loss of the animal. 'I'll clean up out here.' The wolves would be back, that she knew for certain, and she couldn't help but wonder how long it would be before they saw the stout old woman as an easy meal. Especially if they couldn't get to the goats. She needed a fence as high as that wall of greenery around her granny's cottage. She needed to protect her. The wolf's gruff howl was joined by another and she was sure they were mocking her. She cursed them silently, then went to the shed and pulled out more planks of wood and rolls of wire. She would not give up. The wolves would not win. Her hair fell into her eyes as she worked, angrily focused on her task and wishing that the wolf from far away would come and scare these rough relatives away for her. At least then her fingers wouldn't be full of splinters and her skin slick with sweat.

She was halfway through the job when there was a crash from inside the cottage, a scream, and the sound of plates being dropped.

'Granny!' Her heart in her mouth, she turned and ran.

They had been travelling through the forest for several days before the two men eased into a comfortable silence. The first day, once out of sight of the fanfare and grand send-off the king had arranged for his son, had been a relatively slow one given the prince's hangover. The huntsman's own head was clear having been on the outskirts of the group for the night, gritting his teeth every time the prince introduced him to some new dandy as his servant. Huntsmen served no one but nature. He'd drunk one or two cups of beer but the group of rowdy young men hadn't impressed him and neither had they particularly encouraged him to join them, which suited him just fine. He was glad when dawn broke and he could wake the prince and prepare to get out of the city. He'd had enough. He wanted their 'adventure' over so he could return to his people, and at least in the forest he would feel that he was almost home.

By the time they'd made camp, the fresh air had revived the prince's spirits enough for him to make a fire while the huntsman fetched water and killed a rabbit for their dinner. At first the prince had been determined to prove his superiority by trying to impress the huntsman with tales of castle living, but after a while he'd become curious about his companion's way of life. The huntsman answered his questions as best he could as he skinned and cooked the animal, and it was clear that the prince, away from the peer pressure of his cohort, was begrudgingly beginning to admire his companion. The huntsman relaxed his own judgement on the royal in return.

The next few days passed well and they even laughed together occasionally at some joke or story one or other would tell. They might not have been a natural pairing for a friendship, but it wasn't the prince's fault that the king had dragged the huntsman from his home and rested this burden – and the fate of his village – on his shoulders. He would make the best of it and perhaps they would both come out of the experience better and wiser men.

After ten days of travelling the Far Mountain had grown taller in the skyline and the forest thicker; green and lush and rich with life. The light scent of spring in the air became tinged with something heavier, and when they finally found a large pond to drink from the water was bitter and they had to spit it out. The prince declared it was magic they could taste and shuddered slightly, afraid. The huntsman pointed out that magic was simply nature in another guise and nothing to be either feared or courted, but before they could get into an argument about it he saw chimney smoke drifting up from behind some trees to their right.

'They'll know where there's good water,' the huntsman said.

'Isn't it your job to find it?' the prince shot back.

The huntsman ignored him and found an almost invisible path through the trees that led to a small clearing at the heart of which sat a cottage surrounded by pretty flowers ... and by the faintest blood-stained trail through the grass that none other than an animal or a huntsman would be likely to spot. He frowned slightly; there had been trouble here. He paused and looked up. The door was open and from inside came the crashing of plates and a short scream. He gripped the hilt of his knife and ran forward.

'Granny!' A girl's shout came from somewhere behind the cottage but the huntsman and the prince didn't pause. They ran straight inside.

A low growl came from beyond the cosy main room and the two men knocked over a side table as they followed it, the prince with his sword drawn and the huntsman with his knife.

A large grey wolf, teeth bared, was scrabbling and scratching at a tall cupboard door in the corner. It suddenly jerked open an inch and a broom handle poked out sharply and jabbed at the beast. 'Shoo! Shoo!'

The prince, clearly nervous, was waving his sword so high in the small room that the huntsman had to duck to avoid losing an ear.

'Watch what you're doing with that thing,' he muttered, as the wolf turned to face them. It snarled, ready to pounce. Faced with the full sight of its bloody mouth and sharp teeth, the prince paled. 'Perhaps we should run.'

'We can't outrun it,' the huntsman said, his voice

low. The wolf growled again, and the prince trembled slightly, grabbing at the huntsman's arm and tugging him backwards – and off balance – ruining any chance he had of defending them.

Sensing their fear, the wolf leapt, across the table at them, all raging heat and hunger. The huntsman shoved the clinging prince away, sending him flying into a dresser and breaking more crockery, but as the beast loomed over him his own balance was gone and he cursed under his breath, preparing to feel the sharp thick claws and heavy teeth tearing into his skin.

An arrow whistled past him, straight and true, and struck firmly lodging several inches deep in the wolf's chest. All momentum suddenly lost, it mewled and dropped, crashing onto the table. It shuddered for a second and then was gone. As the prince got to his feet, the huntsman stared at the dead beast, and then turned to look behind him at the girl holding the bow.

'You can come out now, Granny,' she said, softly. 'It's dead.'

The girl stared at the wolf with a mixture of loathing and sadness and then turned her eyes to the men; one dressed in the finest clothes with royal insignia on his red cloak and sword, and the other in the rough green fabrics and tan leathers of a working huntsman.

'Can I help you?' she asked.

'We heard the scream,' the huntsman said. 'And came to help. But it seems you had it all under control.'

'We were hoping you could direct us to the nearest stream,' the prince said, as if he hadn't been trembling in fear only seconds before and there was no dead wolf bleeding over the kitchen table. 'We've been travelling for days and this part of the forest is strange to us. We found a pond, but the water was undrinkable. And then we heard the crash and saw the door was open, and came inside.'

'Oh, they say that pond's cursed. But that can wait until we've had our somewhat late lunch. The wolves have ruined our day.'

A small, stout woman with a cheerful face lent character by a life in the forest, stepped out of the cupboard, put the broom she was holding away, and then smiled at them. 'You will be staying for some food, I presume? The stew's nearly done and there's plenty to go round.'

The girl sighed and put her hands on her hips. 'We don't know them, granny. They could be anyone.'

Her grandmother peered over her glasses and looked the men up and down.

'Everyone's someone, Petra dear, and that one has the manners of royalty about him, and the other looks like a huntsman to me. You can always trust a huntsman, that's what my mother told me. Now, come on, having visitors will be nice.' She smiled warmly. 'I'm always curious when strangers from distant places turn up at my door, and so should you be.'

'They can help me clear up first then.' The girl didn't look as convinced as her grandmother.

'We'll be more than happy to help,' the prince said, and gave the girl a curt bow. She didn't look too impressed, but instead grabbed the wolf's fore-legs. 'Then one of you give me a hand getting this outside.'

As Petra and her granny cleaned the cottage, the huntsman and the prince worked hard to make the goat pen secure. When they were done, the huntsman smeared the wolf's blood on all the posts until they looked almost painted red. The goats shuffled nervously inside.

'It'll help keep the wolves away,' he said, as Petra came and inspected their work. 'And better the goats are nervous than dead.' She didn't disagree, and he saw a little of the tension escaping her shoulders. They might not be friends yet, but perhaps they were no longer irritating strangers.

The cottage was warm and cosy and it was good to spend a night inside. Petra fetched them some wine and there was bread and stew enough for them all to be full and have some left over. The huntsman was pleased when he saw the young prince leave a few gold coins on the dresser when he thought no one was looking. By the time they'd eaten night had fallen and they sat gathered round the comforting warmth and light of the large fire in the grate.

'So,' Granny said, her knitting needles clicking together and her chair rocking slightly under her. 'What brings you to this corner of the kingdoms?'

'We're in search of a legend,' the prince said. 'My father has sent me to find a lost castle, vanished for nearly a hundred years. Apparently it's hidden behind a forest wall of some kind—'

'A wall of forest?' Petra sat upright in her chair. 'I know where—'

'Shhh dear,' her granny patted her knee. 'All in good time.'

It was the most animated the girl had been since their arrival, and that intrigued the huntsman. Unlike the city girls she seemed unimpressed by the handsome prince, and he liked her all the more for that.

'Why does your father send you to find it?' the old lady asked.

'He thinks all young men should have an adventure,' the huntsman cut in, before the prince could muddy the waters of their travel with talk of outposts and amassing land.

'And that's a good enough reason,' Granny said and she smiled, nodded and put down her knitting.

'Have you heard of this place?' the prince asked.

'Oh yes.' Granny's eyes twinkled. 'My mother would speak of it sometimes. Mainly when she was older than I am now, and her mind was not always as it should have been. It sounded a strange place, from her tales. But then most cities are strange and, to be fair, she was always full of fancy stories which no one knew the truth of.'

'I go to the wall,' Petra said suddenly. Her face was flushed and alive. 'Sometimes I hear a sound from the other side. A lonely, echoing cry. It haunts me.'

'I think it's more than that, dear,' her grandmother's

eyes twinkled fondly as she looked at her. 'You should go with them.'

'Oh no,' Petra said, holding her granny's arm. 'I'll stay here with you. I need to keep you safe.'

'Don't be silly, dear. It's not just men who need adventures, you know. Everyone has their own destiny to find. And if there's something over that wall that's calling to you, you have to find it. That's the way of things.'

'No,' Petra said, although it was clear in her eyes that she was desperate to go. 'There are still too many wolves in the forest. If the pen holds and they can't get to the goats, what if they come for you again? Like today?'

The huntsman looked thoughtfully at the two women and then left them by the fire with the prince and went outside. He dragged the wolf's body into the forest to work on it and then took the result to the pond to wash it clean, relying on his forest instincts to lead him where he needed to go. By the time he was done he was sweating but pleased.

'Here,' he said, and held up his completed work. 'This will keep them away. They'll smell one of their own instead of you.'

'What *is* that?' Petra asked.

'A wolf wrap,' the huntsman said. He helped the old lady put the wolf's skin on, and then wrapped her own blanket round her shoulders and placed her cap back on top.

'It's lovely and cosy,' she said from somewhere under the wolf's snout. Her hands, under the wolf's claws, looked strange as she continued her knitting.

'You look so peculiar,' Petra giggled. 'Like a wolf has dressed up in your clothes!' They all laughed aloud as the old lady rocked her chair backwards and forwards. 'Well, I quite like it,' she said. 'I can save on wood for the fire if I have this keeping me toasty. And you,' she turned to her grand-daughter and lifted her head so her own face was visible beneath the wolf's, 'Can now go on your adventure.'

And so it was decided. They would leave their horses in Granny's care and Petra would join them.

The next morning they ate a hearty breakfast of eggs and bacon and forest mushrooms, and Petra's granny packed some bread and cheese for them which she loaded up in the huntsman's knapsack, before fixing Petra's red cloak over her shoulders. She smiled and her eyes twinkled but the girl looked as if she was about to burst into tears.

'I love you, Granny,' she said.

'I love you too, Petra.' She squeezed the girl tight.

'But your life is out there, not here with me. And I shall be just fine.'

She waved them off from the doorway, and then the girl led them towards the forest wall and whatever lay beyond it.

3

'Once upon a time...'

Once upon a time a young king was out hunting in the forest that lay at the edge of his city. He had not long come to the throne, but he was a good man and was mourning the loss of his father rather than relishing his new power and preferred to hunt alone as it gave him some private time away from the rigours of court life and kingship.

It was a warm day and, with his enthusiasm to chase and kill a living creature dampened by his recent loss, he dismounted and walked his horse to a large pond of sparkling blue water that was so cold and deep that it must have been home to a natural spring beneath its bed.

The young king sat by the pool as his mount drank

and stared into the surface of the water, lost in his own thoughts. Now it is said that deep in the heart of the pond that rarest of creatures, a water witch, sensed the young king's distress and looked up. She saw his handsome face, so weighed down with grief and responsibility, and it touched something inside her. She immediately came to the surface, unable to stop herself.

The young king and the young water witch fell almost instantly in love and in order to be wed she sacrificed her watery home and went back to the city to become his queen.

At first the king's advisors and, indeed, many of the ordinary people, had reservations about their match, but the new queen kept her magic locked away inside her and she was always so kind and ethereal that soon, despite her icy beauty and eyes that changed colour as water does when the sun hits it, they grew to love her almost as much as the king himself did and the kingdom was content.

For the queen's part, sometimes the wild call of the water and the pull of her old solitary life tugged at her, but she hid that longing away with her magic because in the main she was happy and she loved her king so very, very much. Occasionally, when the yearning became too great, she would return and secretly allow her magic a release, diving deep into the water and feeling the cool aching caress on her skin. But the visits were not often, and she never looked back when she walked away from the pool. Her husband was waiting for her, after all.

Only one thing blighted their bliss. The lack of a son or daughter to make their union complete and secure the future of their kingdom. Eventually, as months passed and no sign of a child was to be had, the king, sensing his beautiful wife's growing sadness, asked the advice of a witch who lived in a tower far, far away. He begged her to help them and, after a few minutes reflection, she smiled and said she would. She told the king that he would be blessed with a daughter. She would be graceful, she would be intelligent and she would be kind. The king smiled and laughed and offered the witch gold and jewels in reward, but she shook her head and raised her hand and said she hadn't finished. There was something more. He should know that the princess would be happy, but one day she would prick herself on a spindle and would sleep for a hundred years. The king was aghast at her words and demanded that it not be so, but the witch disappeared in a cloud of sparkling dust and his words were spoken to an empty room.

Within a year, they learned that the queen was with child. There was much pageantry and the kingdom celebrated. The queen went to the pond to tell the spirits of all the water witches who had lived there before her, whose magic ran in every drop of its clear water, of her great joy, and to ask their advice on how to manage her child, who would no doubt find it hard to be of two such different peoples. The only answer she received was the ripple of the surface and silence from the spirits. She took that to mean she should not be concerned. She chose to read it that way. She would not allow any concern to spoil her happiness.

The sun shone on the kingdom and, as she bloomed, everything was perfect. The king, remembering the witch's words, sent his men throughout the kingdom and all the spindles in the land were destroyed. He would keep his child safe. Whatever it took.

Finally, the queen's time arrived. The birth was difficult, and a storm raged over the kingdom, heavy rain flooding the streets. For nearly two days and nights she struggled and sweated and bled and finally, in the wreck of her bed, the tiny healthy baby girl was delivered. The best efforts of all the king's physicians, however, could not save the beautiful

queen. She died in her devastated husband's arms.
The magical pond in the forest turned bitter over-
night. In tucked-away corners, the king's advisors
muttered that they could have predicted this. Happy
as they had been, such a union was never meant to
be.

Eventually after a month spent locked away in
his apartments, the heartbroken king took his baby
daughter in his arms, and as she gurgled up at him,
pure white streaks in her soft dark hair, he finally
spoke.

'Beauty,' he said. 'We shall call her Beauty.'

4

'A cursed deep sleep...'

After two hours or more of hacking at the thick branches and vines, the tangle of which made up the thick wall, it was clear to all three of the travellers that there was nothing natural about this occurrence. It was also slow, hard work. As the huntsman cut with his axe, the prince and Petra would hold the space he made open and they would all edge forward and beat at the next section. When the branches behind them were released, they would close up again, the splintered wood and severed vines re-linking and entwining so tightly that no break in the join was visible.

They had started the day bantering lightly – especially the prince and Petra, whose excitement was greater than the huntsman's – but soon the only words any of them spoke were purely related to their task. They were all hot and exhausted and crammed together in a tight space that shuffled forwards very slowly, and the huntsman knew that should they stop, or their axes break, the forest would close in around them and they'd be trapped forever.

They tied handkerchiefs over their faces trying to avoid the heady scents that sprang from several of the flowers and seemed determined to lull them to sleep. Even when Petra's slim, firm body was pressed again his own as they moved, the huntsman's body didn't respond. This forest was dangerous and the trees were clearly against them in their work. The huntsman had always trusted the forest. Nature was honest ... and nature was very keen to keep them away from whatever lay beyond this wall.

Finally, however, the pig-headedness of men prevailed and they tumbled, gasping and free, from the grip of the wood. The spring sunshine was bright and warm, and they sat on the grass for a moment, laughing and sharing some water and regaining their strength. It was a few seconds before the eerie quiet around them became too much to ignore.

'I can't even hear any birds singing,' Petra said softly as their moods and laughter quietened. 'On a beautiful day like this they should be everywhere.'

She frowned up at the empty sky. Ahead of them lay a small city and in the distance, as was the way with all the kingdoms, there sat a castle at its heart.

'It's not just the birds,' the prince said. 'I can't hear anything. No noise at all.'

He was right. Even the trees dotted along the edges of the narrow road didn't rustle as the warm breeze moved through them. The hairs on the back of the huntsman's neck prickled and he kept one hand on the hilt of his hunting knife as they began to walk, once again cursing the king and the prince and the royal necessity for adventures. As if life wasn't adventure enough.

The cart was just over the other side of the slight hill from the forest's edge and Petra gasped when it came into view. The huntsman didn't blame her. It was a strange sight, that was for sure, stopped as it was in the middle of the road with the shire horse laying down in front of it. Around it were a dozen thick-wooled sheep with a dog lying in their midst He wasn't sure what he'd been expecting, but this wasn't it.

As the prince clambered onto the cart, the huntsman crouched and touched the horse. It was warm and blood pumped in a steady rhythm through its body.

43

'Hey,' the prince said. 'I think he's still alive.' Up on the cart, a fat man's head lolled forward, the reins having slipped from his hands. The prince tried to straighten him up, but the man's weight slid sideways and he lay across the seat. The prince shook him. 'Hey!' he said, loudly, the word a stranger in the eerie silence around them. 'Hey, wake up! Wake up!' The fat man didn't move. He didn't even snore or grunt or shuffle as the prince wobbled him.

The huntsman looked at the animals around him; not one of them dead and rotten as he'd been expecting to find in this lost kingdom. The prince had struck on it without thinking.

'They're asleep,' he muttered. 'They're all asleep.'

'That can't be right.' Petra dropped to her knees and stroked the sheepdog. 'They can't have been asleep all this time. Not for a hundred years. It isn't possible.'

But it appeared, as they moved on, that it was entirely possible. Every living creature they passed was lost in slumber, apparently having fallen asleep in the same instant. There was a soldiers' outpost as they walked into the first main streets of the city, and two were asleep face down on a chess board. Others had crumpled in a heap at their sentry posts.

The huntsman counted about fifteen. 'That's a lot of soldiers,' he said.

'Maybe they were at war,' the prince answered. 'The kingdoms are always at war.'

It was an apparently affluent city and there were some beautiful mansions set back in their own grounds, again with sleeping soldiers guarding the high gates, but even the ordinary cottages closer to the castle were well maintained, even though the flower-beds were overgrown with weeds. Here and there long grasses had sprung up everywhere between cobbles and flagstones. Animal life might be slumbering but the plant life still grew, although not to the proportions expected. 'Whatever this is, it's affected every living thing,' Petra said, stooping to examine the flowers.

As they moved closer to the centre of the pretty town the huntsman noticed that some houses had the windows roughly boarded up and when he prised the wood from one they saw that the glass behind was smashed and the contents of the house were either broken or ruined in some way. This had clearly been done before the city fell asleep, and he could find no rhyme or reason to the house that had been wrecked. They were ordinary people's homes. What had happened to the people who had lived in them?

After a while they split up to explore more thoroughly, and everything they found was the same. Men, women and children, all asleep in a variety of strange places. One woman's face was badly burned where she'd been making soup on a stove, now a long time cold, and as she slipped to the floor she'd pulled the pan down over her.

Only in one cottage did the huntsman find anyone in their bed. Whoever it was they must have died before whatever happened to send the city to sleep, and all that remained was a skeleton in a nightdress with wisps of thin hair poking out from beneath a black nightcap. A knife stuck through the thin fabric of her dress and now that her flesh had rotted away, it leaned loose against her ribs where some unknown assailant had stabbed it into her breathing body. It was a strange cottage, with none of the bright colours found in so many of the others, and there was a cold, stale dampness hanging in the air as if none of the outside warmth had crept in during the long years that had passed. He looked in the small cupboards and found jars of herbs and bottle of potions with words he didn't understand on the labels. It was a witch's cottage, he was sure. He shivered and was about to leave when the small stove in the tiny main room caught his eye. The door was open a tiny fraction and something glittered inside. He crouched and pulled the black iron door open.

Inside, sitting on a pile of soot, were a pair of sparkling slippers. He reached in and took them out. They were light and warm in his hands. Diamonds, he thought. They were made of diamonds, not glass at all. Why would someone have been trying to burn them? Was this the work of whoever had killed her? Were the two deeds linked in the strange history of this kingdom? He stared at them for several seconds until he heard Petra and the prince calling for him. The woman upstairs was long gone. She would not miss them, and he and his companions might need something to barter with at some point. He slipped the shoes into his bag and got to his feet. If the city were to somehow wake and the shoes were declared missing he would return them. For now, he'd consider them his fee for this babysitting task the king had set him.

'What do you think they are?' the prince asked, as he and Petra climbed the stone steps and examined the lines on the base of the statue more closely. 'These can't be old, can they?'

'No.' The huntsman frowned. Even though it was clear that the whole city was in some kind of a cursed deep sleep, now they were closer to the castle he couldn't shake the feeling that they were being watched. It was an instinct he was trained not to ignore. 'Look at those ones round the other side. That chalk is fresh.' The lines grew more ragged, but they were definitely some form of counting. Were they charting days? Or months? It was hard to tell. There were a lot of them, whichever it was.

'You mean someone's still awake?' Petra asked.

'That can't be right,' the prince said. 'Even if they hadn't fallen asleep, they'd surely be dead by now.'

'Maybe, maybe not,' Petra said cheerily. 'None of this is normal, after all. And I used to hear howling sometimes. Through the wall. Something's alive in here.'

The huntsman wasn't listening to her. A noise, faint and far to his left had caught his attention. Someone was following them. He was sure of it.

'Hello?' he called. 'Anyone there?' There was no answer but a return to silence. 'Come on,' he muttered. 'Let's get to the castle. If there are any answers, we'll find them there.' The prince nodded, not picking up on the huntsman's point. Trouble, when it came to ordinary people, was normally delivered to them by royalty. Whatever had made this city silent, it had started in the castle.

etra had never seen anything like it. Even as they'd walked through the city she'd felt slightly overwhelmed by the looming building that rose so high above the ordinary houses she wondered if in the right light it would engulf them all with its shadow, but as they walked through the open gates, carefully stepping over the crumpled heap of soldiers, for the first time in her life she felt small and insignificant. The village, the forest and her grandmother's cottage had been her world, and all the time this whole city had been sleeping so close by. How much more was there that she would never see, even if she spent a lifetime exploring?

'Heavily guarded,' the huntsman said.

Petra glanced at him. His dark eyes scanned the heavily armed men at their feet and she could see the sight bothered him.

'Perhaps they had more to worry about than my father does,' the prince said. 'Who knows what lies on the other side of this kingdom?'

The huntsman nodded but said nothing more.

They were a strange pair, this prince and his companion. One so full of charm and courtly grace, the other quiet and hardy. Petra liked them both, but she knew which one she trusted the most. A man of the forest would always win her vote if it came to her own survival. The prince might be good with a sword but she imagined that he'd learned to duel with rules. Killing something living was very different to courtly sword play – the prince had discovered as much in Granny's kitchen when faced by the winter wolf. There were no rules when it came to fighting for your very existence. They were both handsome, though, she'd give them that.

Vines and ivy had crept up the high stone walls, clinging to the mortar between the heavy rocks as if trying to suffocate the life out of the building itself. In the courtyard men and women slept where they'd stood, one still holding a saddle that was no doubt meant for the horse that slept beside him. Another was surrounded by loaves of bread that had tumbled from his basket.

The huntsman pushed a door open and the hinges shrieked, shocked at the movement after so long. The sound echoed as they stepped inside. Dust danced upwards as they moved, suddenly disturbed from its own slumber on the marble floor. Unlike the smaller houses in the city, no passing wind or weather had been able to penetrate the thick wall and Petra felt as if she had truly walked into a forgotten tomb. Her heart thumped as they walked, leaving footprints in the dirt behind them.

'We should split up,' the prince said. His voice was loud and confident. Petra wondered why he didn't find the castle as eerie as she did but then, she supposed, he was used to castles. He was not in awe of the wealth or beauty that lay under the dust of years passed. 'I'll take upstairs. Petra, you stay on this floor.'

'I'll search the lower levels and dungeons,' the huntsman finished. 'But don't touch anyone. If you find anything then shout and wait.'

'Just what I was going to say,' the prince said.

Petra nodded. The idea of searching alone made her shiver but she wasn't going to admit her fear to the two men. If they were happy to do it then she would be too.

'If we can't find the source of this curse by tomorrow,' the huntsman said, 'then we load some riches onto a cart for your father and try and cut our way back out. Agreed?'

The huntsman had barely smiled since they'd found the city. Petra was sure that if it was up to him they'd be leaving it by now. Whatever had brought him here it wasn't thrill-seeking or adventure, but Petra couldn't help feeling a little of those things herself. She couldn't imagine turning her back on this place and not knowing how the story had begun, or how it ended.

'And mark your path on the walls or in the dust,' he said. 'So you can see where you've been and find your way back here.' This time he did give her a small smile and she liked the creases that formed in his cheeks, as if in his normal life he smiled a lot. The instruction was for her alone. The prince might be used to finding his way round castles, but she most definitely wasn't.

The ground floor of a castle, she'd decided within an hour or so, was a very strange affair. There were three ballrooms; two light and airy and with ceilings painted with beautiful dancing couples, and another further back – which could only be accessed through a library and then a small annexed corridor – that was painted red and decorated with ornate gold and heavy black curtains. It was an odd contrast with the other two and she decided she didn't like it very much at all. The air had a metallic tang to it and, although she was technically trespassing wherever she went, this was the only room in which she felt she'd invaded something secret. No one was sleeping in any of the main function rooms, all of which were breath-taking and yet slightly impersonal and as she explored them she decided that royal residences were clearly as much about the visitors as they were about the family that lived there. It was clearly a strange thing to be a royal.

In some kind of meeting room, several grey-haired men in sombre robes were asleep on thick documents and open books and more soldiers slept in the door-ways. A jug of wine had been knocked across the table and where it had soaked into the polished wood and scattered papers, the stains looked like blood on the large table.

She felt happier when she found the smaller, more ordinary rooms where servants were working. In one long corridor boot boys slept over pots of polish, and in the kitchens the tables were full of half-made pies and pastries, the cooks and maids crumpled on the cold stone floor. Despite the huntsman's orders not to touch anyone or anything, Petra dipped her finger in an open apple pie and then tasted it. The filling was sweet and fresh as if the mixture had been placed inside only minutes before. She ate some more. At least they wouldn't starve while they were here. There would be enough food in the city to keep them going for several hundred years.

An echo of a shout carried its way to her and she frowned, abandoning the pie and running back towards the centre of the building, her shoes slapping against the floor and raising dust in her wake. Was that danger? The shout came again. Closer this time.

'I've found something. I need help!'

She almost collided with the huntsman as she rounded a corner into the central hallway and without pausing they both ran up the sweeping staircase, taking the steps two at a time, following the prince's shouts until they found him in a set of luxurious apartments in the middle of the castle.

Petra stood in the bedroom doorway and her mouth dropped open.

'We've got to do something,' the prince said. 'We've got to help.'

Petra cautiously followed the huntsman inside the vast room. At its centre was a large four poster bed, covered in sheets and blankets of pure, soft white. Sheer linen curtains hung around it, tied back to the posts with ribbons like curtains. In a glass by the bed, a single red rose sat in water, all of its petals scattered around the glass save the last one which drooped low but still clung to the stem. A beautiful young woman lay sleeping on the bed. She was fully dressed in a blue silk gown and jewels sparkled at her neck. Her full lips were parted slightly as if something had just surprised her, and her hair, jet black apart from two thick blonde streaks on either side, spread out across the pillow in glossy waves. She was beautiful, but she was also incredibly pale. Given the state of the floor around the bed, that wasn't a surprise to Petra.

Blood. It was everywhere. A pool of it, thick and crimson, had spread beneath her and now almost circled the large bed. The girl's right hand hung over the side of the bed and as Petra stared at it a single tiny drop of blood fell from her forefinger to the floor.

'It's her finger,' she whispered. 'Look. She must have pricked her finger.'

'Have you got any bandages?' the huntsman asked. 'Any salve?'

'Maybe.' Petra yanked the small bag her granny had packed from her shoulder and tipped the contents out over the end of the bed, taking a careful step to avoid the blood. 'Is she still alive? She must have lost nearly all her blood.'

The prince leaned over the bed and placed one hand on the girl's chest. 'Yes!' he exclaimed, smiling. 'She's breathing. Just.' He didn't lift his hand though, but ran it up the sleeping beauty's body. 'I've never seen a girl like her,' he whispered. 'She's perfect.'

'I don't think you should be touching her like that,' Petra said as she handed the huntsman a small jar of her granny's natural antiseptic. 'She's asleep. You can't go around touching girls when they're asleep.'

The prince either wasn't listening or chose to ignore her, because as the huntsman cut a strip of sheet from the bed, the prince stroked the girl's face. 'I should kiss her,' he murmured.

'No you really shouldn't.' Petra glared at him. 'That would be all manner of wrong. If someone kissed me without my permission – handsome travelling prince or not – I'd punch them.'

The huntsman laughed. 'She has a point.'

'She's a princess. I'm a prince. I'm *supposed* to kiss her.'

'We need to talk about the dungeons—' the huntsman started.

Two things happened at once. The huntsman wrapped the strip of cloth tightly around the tiny salved cut and stopped the next tiny droplet from escaping the wound; the prince ignored Petra's warning, lowered his mouth to the sleeping princess's and kissed her.

A sudden tremble ran through every stone in the building, and then, as the prince lifted his lips from hers, the girl on the bed gasped and then coughed, and then her eyes opened.

'She's waking up,' Petra whispered. In the glass by the bed, the rose came into full, beautiful bloom.

A clattering noise came from somewhere close by, followed by a brief exclamation. Outside, a horse whinnied.

'Not only her,' the huntsman said, getting to his feet. 'They're *all* waking up.'

'We've lifted the curse,' the prince said, his hand still holding the princess's.

As the city came alive around them, all three travellers stared at the beautiful girl on the bed who was slowly easing herself into a sitting position. Colour was rushing back into her face as if with the curse lifted her body was restoring itself to perfect health. She looked at them, her eyes bleary.

'Who are you?' her voice was soft and sweet. 'What happened?' She looked down at her bandaged finger and the blood on the floor below and her eyes widened, her confusion gone. 'There was a spindle! Rumplestiltskin!'

57

'I'm a prince from a faraway kingdom,' the prince said. 'My father had heard legends of your city's plight and we came to save you.' Petra could clearly see that the young prince was in the process of falling head over heels in love. 'I woke you with a kiss,' he finished.

The woman on the bed smiled at him and either chose to ignore the fact that the bandage was more likely to have saved her than a stolen kiss, or wasn't awake enough to think it through properly.

'How long have I been asleep?' she asked.

Petra thought of the lines that had been scratched into the statue at the centre of the sleeping city.

'We think nearly a hundred years,' she said softly.

The princess said nothing for a long moment and then, just before the soldiers burst into the room, she muttered that one word again.

'Rumplestiltskin.'

'Tonight is for celebration'

As it turned out the princess wasn't a princess at all but a queen, and her name was Beauty. As the city woke from its slumber she declared the day a holiday and ordered the kitchens to prepare a great feast to celebrate. She was a whirlwind of light and laughter and the huntsman saw that the prince was dazzled by her. She, in turn, seemed quite taken with him, and she kept her arm linked with his as she walked through the castle with her guests.

'My poor father, the king, has only been gone six months,' she said. 'We were a city in mourning but now we must put that behind us and look to the future.' She looked up at the prince and smiled. 'And I can't thank you enough for saving all of us from this terrible curse.'

'We— I –' the prince said, '– am your humble servant. I would have slain a dragon to save you.'

'But why would anyone want to curse you?' Petra asked.

'I don't know,' Beauty answered. She frowned. 'I can't remember. I just know that it was Rumplestilt-skin.' Her voice was soft and her frown deepened into puzzlement. 'Uncle Rumple.'

'Your uncle?' the prince said. 'But that's terrible. He must want the crown for himself.'

'I called him my uncle,' Beauty said, 'but he wasn't a blood relative. He was my father's closest advisor.' Her frown dissolved into sadness. 'I thought he loved me.'

'Everyone loves you, your majesty.' A middle-aged man dressed in heavy, fur-lined robes swept along the corridor towards them. 'You must never forget that.' When he reached them, he bowed deeply. His dark eyes were sharp under his bushy eyebrows. 'Let your faithful advisors worry about such things. He will not get close to you again, that much I person-ally guarantee. For now, you should put it out of your head and be glad that such a dashing prince has restored all to order.'

He smiled at the prince who beamed back, happy to be at the centre of such adulation, but the huntsman caught the sharp edge to the older man's smile and the hint of nervous energy escaping from him.

'Thank you, First Minister.' Beauty said. 'You have always been so very good to me.'

'That's because I know and understand you, your majesty. Let your council worry about such things; you should all be bathing and preparing for the feast,' her advisor continued. 'Tonight is for celebration!'

'You're right.' The queen rose up on tip toes and gave the man a kiss on his bearded cheek. 'You are so often right. I just wish I could remember. There are always so many things I can't remember.' She clapped her hands together, her smile restored. 'But let us retire to our rooms and prepare. Later there shall be music and dancing and everything will be well in the world again.'

The huntsman let the small group walk ahead and hung back with the advisor. 'What does she mean when she says there are things she can't remember?' he asked. 'Is she ill?'

'No, no,' the first minister said smoothly, picking up his pace to return the huntsman to the group. 'She has had occasional small memory blackouts since she was a child. They are nothing unusual. Nothing to concern you.'

The huntsman smiled and followed him, but his skin prickled. He might not be a man of court, but he was pretty sure that whenever someone said there was nothing to concern him, it meant exactly the opposite.

The huntsman did not take much time preparing for the dinner, choosing to keep his own clothes on after washing rather than wear the fancy shirt and trousers left for him in his room. These people were not his people and while he would be polite and respectful, he had no desire or need to impress them. As far as he could tell his job was nearly done. He just needed to get the prince safely home again.

He catnapped for half an hour or so and then wandered the castle and grounds for an hour. After the stillness and silence of their arrival it was strange to see the people suddenly active, like dolls brought back to life. Did they even know how long they had slept, he wondered, as women scrubbed dust from the floors and men polished windows. Most were laughing and talking excitedly, but here and there some cast suspicious looks his way and kept their heads down as they scurried to their next task.

In the central corridors of the castle he passed groups of gentlemen and ministers, each dressed like the first minister but with perhaps less fur and finery on their robes. A few were huddled in deep conversation, only breaking away and pretending mirth and laughter as he went by. Were they plotters, he wondered. The young queen was sweet and kind; were these old men trying to take her kingdom from her? He tried to push the thought from his mind. This was not what he was here for. This kingdom's problems were none of his business.

He climbed high up into one of the turrets, wanting to get a view of what lay to each side of them, but as he reached the summit he was stopped by two soldiers. They were not boys, but men; thick set and gruff. Beyond them, a large black bell hung in a recess.

'You're not allowed up here,' the largest of the two men said. 'Everyone knows that.' His hand was on his sword, and the huntsman raised his hands slightly.

'I'm just a visitor,' he said. 'I wanted to see the view.'

'Then use the windows. This tower is out of bounds. Only the ministers are allowed up here.'

They took a step forward and the huntsman retreated back down the stone stairs. Why would a bell need guarding? Why did he get the feeling that this castle was filled with secrets? There was only one person who could give him the answers: the traitor Rumplestiltskin, wherever he was.

The moon was full that night and the windows were wide open to let the light shine through; the feast was a merry affair. The sumptuous banqueting hall had been decorated with flowers and candles and every table was filled with more food than the guests could possibly eat. The huntsman and Petra sat to either side of Beauty and the prince, who really only had eyes for each other and spent most of the evening holding each other's hands and feeding each other sweetmeats.

Petra, dressed in a beautiful red gown and looking every inch the court lady, was talking to a minister seated on the other side of her while the huntsman, not one for small talk at the best of times, ate and drank while quietly watching the gathered guests. They were mainly older men and women and although they smiled and laughed, he noticed that they did not look often to the main table where their queen sat.

'Some more wine, sir?'

The huntsman looked up to see a pretty serving girl smiling at him. He nodded and she leaned forward to refill his glass, angling her body so that her ample cleavage was clearly on display should he choose to look. Being a hot-blooded man of the forest, he did. 'Tell me,' he said. 'Who are all these guests?'

'Ministers and their wives mainly,' she answered. 'Friends of the old king. Why do you ask, sir?' She continued to lean forward intimately and he could smell her clean warmth and her young skin was clear and bright.

'They just all seem a little old for the queen. Where are all the young men of the court?'

'Oh, they don't come to these dinners, sir. They come to the balls. I don't serve at the balls so I can't tell you about them.'

The flirtation in her voice was replaced with a

slightly defensive edge, but the huntsman squeezed her hand and winked and the blush returned to her face. Suddenly he felt the need for something simple and uncomplicated and this girl was clear about her attraction to him.

'Perhaps, after the feast,' he said, 'we could drink some wine and I could tell you a few things about my homeland.'

'I'd like that.' The girl grinned. 'I'll find my way to your rooms then.' She turned and bustled away and the huntsman smiled after her. Courtly intrigue he could live without.

'Hey.' A finger tapped his shoulder and Petra snuck into the seat beside him. 'The forest hasn't opened up.'

'What?' The huntsman was still wondering how the serving girl would feel beneath him. Petra nudged him again.

'The minister I was talking to. He said that the forest wall is still there. The curse or whatever it is can't have been broken fully.' She paused. 'Is it just me, or does everything seem a bit odd? Bits of this castle just don't make sense.'

'It's not just you,' the huntsman muttered. 'I saw the dungeons—' But before he could say any more the prince got to his feet, tapping the side of his crystal wine glass with a small spoon. His face was flushed and his eyes sparkled.

'Firstly, I would like to thank you all for this wonderful hospitality you have shown me and my travelling companions. We are honoured and humbled at the kindness you have shown us.'

There was a smattering of applause and the huntsman nodded awkwardly at the guests who caught his eye.

'But my biggest thanks must be for the beauty that you have brought into my life.' The prince looked down at the smiling woman beside him and suddenly the huntsman knew where this speech was going. The prince was headstrong and impulsive, he'd already known that, but foolish was about to be added to the list.

'From the moment I saw her asleep on her bed, I knew I would love her forever. I had never seen anyone so perfect,' he said. 'I have asked her if she will marry me,' he smiled at the guests, 'and she has said yes.'

A few gasps ran round the room and then the assembled ministers burst into applause. The huntsman watched as a few of the men exchanged glances as they clapped. Behind their smiles, they weren't entirely happy with the news.

'And so,' the queen got to her feet, 'let there be music and dancing!'

It was when the young couple were on their third dance that the first minister signalled the huntsman and Petra to follow him to an ante-chamber and closed the door behind them. He poured them each a glass of red wine and then sat behind a heavily inlaid desk. The huntsman wondered if the young prince realised who really ran this kingdom. It wasn't the pretty girl he was dancing with, that was for certain.

'I want you to undertake a task for me,' he said. 'Your prince has said I may count on your agreement.'

For the thousandth time since leaving his home, the huntsman once again silently cursed the prince.

'My job,' he said, leaning against the wall and sipping his wine, 'is to protect the prince and ensure his safe return. Nothing more.'

'Then you will do as I ask. For I imagine his safety depends on it: you must find Rumplestiltskin and bring him to me.'

'Don't you have soldiers who can do that?' Petra

asked. 'You do seem to have a lot of soldiers here.'

'The soldiers are looking for him too. But I have my reasons for wanting you to find him rather than them.'

'Why?' the huntsman asked. He thought of the dungeons but didn't mention that he'd seen them. Somehow he thought that might blacken his card and, as Petra had pointed out, there were a *lot* of soldiers in the city. It wouldn't be difficult for the first minister to dispose of a travelling huntsman. And nor did he want to end up on the wrong side of one of those cell doors.

'Just to be certain,' the first minister smiled, hiding an impatient flash of an expression behind it.

'You don't think he was working alone,' Petra said. 'You want names from him.'

'My reasons are none of your concern. Suffice to say that I want him brought to me and the spindle he carries destroyed.' He took a thick piece of parchment from the desk and handed it to the huntsman. 'Those are the addresses of his home and other places he frequents. Perhaps you'll find clues to his whereabouts there.'

The huntsman took it and tucked it into his belt. 'We'll try, but we don't know your city or its people. The soldiers will have more luck.'

'You're a huntsman,' the first minister purred. 'Hunt.'

'We'll wait until the city is asleep,' he said, 'and go then.' He opened the door for Petra and they left the minister behind.

'He thinks there are other conspirators,' Petra said. 'Why would anyone conspire against Beauty? She seems the kindest and gentlest of creatures.'

Without consultation, neither of them headed back to the banqueting room from which music and laughter drifted towards them, but took the central staircase up to their rooms.

'Who knows?' the huntsman said. As they turned onto a vast landing the curtains billowed in the evening breeze coming through the open veranda doorways. Petra paused and her gaze drifted, as if their current conversation was suddenly forgotten. 'Did you hear that?' she asked.

'What?' the huntsman frowned. His hearing, trained by years of tracking, was excellent but aside from the revellers below and the breeze the air was empty.

'Oh nothing,' Petra said softly, heading towards the balcony doors. 'Just something I've heard before. From the other side of the wall.' She pulled the curtains back and stood in the open doorway.

Outside the moon shone full and low in the dark sky. 'I think I'll sit out here for a while. Get some fresh air.'

'You don't have to come with me tonight,' the huntsman said. 'You may be safer in the castle.'

'I want to come,' she answered. 'There's something in this city I need to find too.' She glanced back at him over her delicate shoulder, her eyes dark in the gloom. 'And I'm not at all sure how safe this castle is.'

He couldn't argue with that. His own senses had been humming ever since the queen woke up and the first minister's request made his nerves jangle. He was already a pawn in one royal court's game, and now he was embroiled in another. As Petra wandered out towards the edge of the balcony, he left her and took the stairs two at a time, needing to release some energy.

A figure waited outside his bedroom door. He frowned and then smiled. It was the serving girl. She dropped into a slight curtsey.

'I wondered where you'd gone.' She looked up, her eyes sparkling mischievously. 'I thought p'raps you might like something brought to your room.' She held up a jug of wine. 'I thought I could serve it to you. Personally.'

The huntsman laughed and swung open the door to his room. He bowed. 'Ladies first.'

'Oh,' the girl giggled as she passed him. 'I'm no lady.'

6

'The dark days...'

'Perhaps all this was just fate,' Beauty murmured into his chest as the prince held her close and they danced. 'If Rumplestiltskin hadn't ... done whatever he did, if I hadn't slept, then we'd have never met.' She looked up at him and smiled. It was the sweetest expression he'd ever seen and his heart melted all over again just looking at her exquisite face. Her eyes were the colour of clear water in a summer stream and he wanted to dive into them. To know her completely. 'I would have been long dead before you were born,' she continued. 'You would never have woken me.'

'Then yes, my love.' He kissed her forehead. Her skin was soft and her hair smelled of spring flowers. He was completely enchanted by her. 'It must be fate.'

'You saved me,' she tilted her face up to him, the two blonde streaks in her perfectly black hair hanging loose in styled curls to either side of her pale cheeks. His lips met hers and they kissed again. She was soft in his arms and the feel of her tongue touching his was electric. He *had* saved her. Already, in his mind, he had pushed aside the image of the huntsman bandaging her finger and stemming her dripping blood at the moment she woke. That was simply coincidence.

'True love's kiss is the only way to break a curse,' she said, her mouth only parted from his by a breath. 'Everyone knows that.'

'And I love you truly,' he whispered back, his voice raw. He did love her. It had gripped him from the moment he'd touched her, a wave of wonder and awe and passion that he'd never felt before. It was almost like magic. He pulled her closer to feel the swell of her bosom against his shirt. His mouth dried slightly as he fought the urge to run his hands over her body.

'Let's get married quickly,' he said. His desire for her was so great he wasn't sure he could wait any longer. Everything else had faded away; his father's wishes for an expansion to his kingdom, the desire to return home laden with treasure and be treated like a hero, even his normal lust for drinking and wenching had gone. Home was a distant memory. All that mattered was this girl and possessing her completely.

'Yes,' she said, as breathless as he was. Her eyes sparkled in the light from the glittering chandeliers above. 'I will announce it to the city tomorrow and we shall wed the next day. We'll have a family and live happily ever after. I shall give everyone in the city a gold coin as a wedding gift to show my happiness. And there will be days of feasting. I want my people to be as happy as I am. It's all I ever want.'

The prince was sure his heart would explode. Not only was she beautiful, she was kind and gentle and generous too. 'I can't believe that you weren't betrothed already,' he said. 'What is wrong with the noblemen of this kingdom? Or the princes close by?'

'My father was very protective of me,' she said, quietly, a slight shadow darkening her face and her eyes glancing away. She must have loved him very much, the prince thought. 'Well, now I'll protect you,' he said. 'My huntsman will find the traitor and all will be well.'

'And we'll live happily ever after,' Beauty murmured again, her smile returning. They kissed once more and the music played on. Around them, aware that the young couple had eyes for none but each other, the ministers and their wives quietly slipped away. They were no longer young and neither was the night, and despite having spent a century sleeping their bodies were tired and their feet ached and they wanted to let their smiles drop.

A few paused at the door and glanced back with a mixture of nerves and heart-ache. She was so very beautiful, and so very sweet. And then they shuddered slightly, unable to stop themselves, before heading to their rooms in the castle.

It was a cool spring night, but Petra didn't care. The castle, exquisite as so much of it was, felt claustrophobic, and she couldn't shake the unsettled feeling that had plagued her since Beauty had woken. The prince was blind to it – blind to everything but his sudden love – and even that she found strange. She knew men could be fools where women were concerned, and although the prince was too spoiled and arrogant for her to find him attractive he hadn't struck her as stupid. Her great-grandmother had passed down many tales of handsome princes – stories that were no doubt just flights of fancy – but they had ingrained in her the truth that royals were invariably only true to themselves. This one was suddenly a changed man, if that were the case.

The forest wall was still thick around them. The garish ballroom she'd found while the city slept was now firmly locked. Things were not well in this kingdom. She leaned on the smooth white marble of the balcony and tilted her head back. Above, the moon was full and heavy in the sky, shining its cool light over the darkness of the city below. Music drifted up from the ballroom as the party endlessly continued and she frowned as she tried to listen *beyond* it. It was an irritating distraction from the sound her ears sought. The counterpart to her soulful duet that had drawn her here even before the prince and the huntsman had arrived in her life. She didn't care about castles and sleeping beauties. She didn't even care about curses. These things were best left to run their course. It was the haunting song which had found her through the thick forest wall that held her here.

There it was. She almost gasped as she heard it; a faint low howl. It sang to her, so full of melancholy and yet so strong. Her heart fluttered. Her skin tingled. She stared out into the night. 'Where are you?' she whispered. '*What* are you?' The howl came again. Animal and human rolled into one. Without a thought to anyone who might hear her, she tilted her head back and answered the call. The creature, wherever it was, let its voice join hers, and she was sure she could hear her own excitement in the sound as their cries mingled in the night. Her feet yearned to run down the stairs and out into the strange city night. The huntsman could find this Rumplestiltskin. She would be on a different search.

The sheets were a tangled mess around their legs and the serving girl, whose name it turned out was Nell, lay on her side next to the huntsman, her hair tumbling over one shoulder. She took a sip of wine and then handed him the glass. 'You must be thirsty.'

He laughed a little and drank, enjoying the sweat cooling on his body and then leaned forward and kissed her. She had an earthy beauty and a full voluptuous body that might one day swell into fat but for now was young and firm. She smiled and then settled down against his chest, both of them content in the enjoyment they'd taken from each other. They hadn't done much talking, their needs too urgent, but now they were sated they shared that comfortable space that only exists between two strangers who'd just had good enough sex to be at ease in each other's company. Their bubble of intimacy and affection might not last, but it would at least remain as long as their nudity did.

'How long have you worked at the castle?' the huntsman asked, his fingers trailing through her hair and running down the soft skin of her back. She had been no virgin, her forward behaviour had made that clear before anything she'd done, but she was young – no more than seventeen or eighteen – and a bright enthusiasm shone in her eyes.

'Only two weeks.' Her warm breath tickled the hairs on his chest. 'I used to work at the dairy out on the edge of the city. Been there since I was twelve, when my parents were taken by the flu.'

'I'm sorry,' the huntsman said.

'Don't be. It was years ago and the women at the dairy were good to me. I can't complain. Lots of girls there had no families for one reason or another. I wasn't alone in that and it was a good place. The work wasn't too hard once you knew what you were doing, and they weren't too strict.' She giggled a little and then glanced up at him, her eyes full of remembered mischief. 'I used to sleep in a dorm with six other milkmaids. Some nights there were as many men in our room as maids. Some times *more*.'

'I thought you'd learned a few tricks from somewhere.' The huntsman pulled her closer, enjoying her uncomplicated warmth. Her past sexual encounters didn't bother him – and wouldn't have even if he had loved her. He had no time for bedroom double standards. It didn't fit with his internal logic and just struck him as stupidity. They were all just animals, after all, and why should a woman deny herself pleasure simply because an insecure man might think less of her? If no women gave in to their lusts then his own life would have been much duller – women were by far the more sensuous sex but most men didn't know how to keep those feelings alive in them. Most men made them feel ashamed of their desires rather than delighting in them and then wondered why everything died and dried up between them. It would not be like that for him, should he ever find the girl in his dreams.

'From the dairy to the castle seems a big leap for an orphan girl,' he said. He was probing her but he couldn't help it. Ever since he'd got here his hackles had been up and soon he would have to go and hunt a traitor – a job he didn't relish if he was working in a situation where he felt blinkered. He was no soldier who could simply obey orders. 'How did you manage that?'

'A few of the dairy girls have come to the castle over the years,' she said. 'The first minister visited and he chose me himself. So I packed up my things and here I am. I sometimes miss the dairy though. Even though life is easier, everything's so much stricter here.'

'You still seem to manage to find your fun, it seems,' he said.

'Well when a handsome stranger comes visiting I have to make the most of it.'

'So life in the kingdom is good then?' he asked, sipping wine thoughtfully.

'Yes, why?'

'There are so many soldiers everywhere. The castle is so heavily guarded. I thought you must have recently been attacked by another kingdom. They're always fighting, after all.' He paused. 'When we arrived and you were all sleeping, I saw the dungeons. Some of the equipment in there is . . .' It was hard to find an appropriate word for it. He hunted and killed as a way of life, but he made every death as swift and as painless as possible. The things he'd seen here were designed, as far as he could make out, to cause the maximum agony while keeping someone alive. It was the dungeon of a tyrant king, not of a beautiful, happy queen. 'Barbaric,' he said in the end.

85

'I wouldn't know about that.' She tensed slightly in his arms. 'And there's been no fighting. I think there are so many soldiers because of the dark days. We haven't had one for a month or so. There must be one due.'

'Dark days?' he asked.

'We're not meant to speak of them. No one is. It might upset the queen and no one wants that. She's such a gentle soul.' She sat up, crossing her legs and wrapping the sheet around her for warmth now that their sweat had cooled and heat faded. She took the wine glass from him and sipped. He didn't press her with another question but waited as she drank.

'They say that the queen was one of twins, but her sister was born mad and cruel, and lives locked up in apartments high in the castle. She's been there ever since her father locked her away for the safety of all. Sometimes at the queen's insistence, because she is fair and good and kind and loves her sister despite her wickedness, they change places. The queen locks herself in the apartments and her sister takes control of the castle. A bell rings out over the city and we are all to lock ourselves away until it's over.'

'And what does this other queen do during her time free?' The huntsman was troubled and intrigued in equal measure.

'No one really knows. There are always huge thunderstorms overhead that turn the roads to rivers. They say the other sister has her mother's magic. Sometimes there are parties at the castle.' Her face was animated but not without fear. 'I've heard carriages pass through the streets on those nights. But soon enough the sky clears and the bell sounds again and life carries on as normal.'

'How often do these days happen?' he asked.

'It depends. Although I'm sure they happen more often than they used to.' Nell shrugged. 'Like I said, we don't talk about them. No one would want the queen to know, and she's so kind to everyone. Perhaps there are so many soldiers because the ministers worry that someone might try and hurt her sister?'

It was the same thought the huntsman had. Nell was earthy but she wasn't stupid. A voice cut across the room.

'Well, my dear, now that you've given our visitor a potted history of our city's ridiculous rumours, perhaps you could get back to work?'

The huntsman had reached across the bed for his hunting knife before he realised that the speaker was the first minister. He stood in the corner of the room, his mouth tight with disdain. How long had he been there? It wasn't like the huntsman not to sense a stranger nearby. Maybe they hadn't closed the door to his room properly as they'd tumbled inside.

'I'm sorry, sir.' Nell leapt from the bed, her head down, the sheet wrapped round her as she dropped into a clumsy curtsey.

'She didn't do anything wrong,' the huntsman said, still lounging on the bed, forcing his body to relax so as not to give the statesman any clue how much his sudden interruption without knocking had irritated him. 'I didn't really give her any choice.'

The first minister looked at Nell who, having gathered her clothes, was shuffling to the bathroom door in order to dress with some modicum of modesty. 'Yes. I'm sure,' he said, his tone heavy with irony. 'She looked entirely *coerced* when I came in.'

'I have very strong powers of persuasion.'

'I'm sure you do.' The minister drew himself up tall. 'I hope your hunting skills are as impressive. It's time for you to go and find Rumplestiltskin. Remember, I need him alive.' He paused. 'And remember that your prince is still in the castle.'

The huntsman got up and stretched, enjoying the minister's discomfort at being presented with his nudity, before reaching for his trousers. 'Was that a threat?' he asked. 'When he is so beloved of the queen?'

A sneer crossed the minister's lips. 'Her safety is more important than her happiness. Sweet she might be, but I know her better than she knows herself.'

'But it's still a threat.' The huntsman smiled, his eyes twinkling. He had no time for anything other than plain speaking. The first minister shrugged. 'I prefer to think of it as a reminder of the balance of our relationship.'

'Don't worry,' the huntsman said, pulling his rough shirt over his head. 'I'll do my best.' He tucked his knife into the sheath on his belt and picked up his bag. He wasn't leaving the diamond shoes behind: there was no one here he trusted not to go through his things, not even the prince. He headed towards the door, deliberately brushing past the older man's slight frame. Not enough to nudge him, but just enough to let him know he wasn't intimidated by him. The huntsman might not have been educated in castle politics but he understood that power play amongst men worked in many different ways, and being the stronger of two was a primal strength.

'One more thing,' the first minister called after him. 'The soldiers.'

'What about them?'

'Don't assume they are friendly.'

The huntsman frowned. 'What do you mean?'

'I can't guarantee they are all loyal to the queen.' The minister steepled his fingers together under his chin. 'Let's just say that there may be some amongst my number who are my enemies. The soldiers are ordered to deliver the traitor to the whole council. There are some there who would use him to try and discredit me. That would not be good for the safety of our queen.' His eyes darkened. 'Or, by extension, of your young prince. I think we can both agree that the boy is too blinded by love to see anything other than wonder in the world at the moment.'

'That will be no problem,' the huntsman said. 'I've yet to meet someone here I trust. If I find your Rumplestiltskin alive, I'll bring him back to the castle. You have my word.'

He turned his back and strode through the door. He'd be glad to get back in the fresh air, even if he was to be confined by the city. At least most of the population would be asleep and he and Petra would have some peace from the wily ways of the strangers they had awoken.

Plus, despite the addresses and maps the first minister had so thoughtfully provided for them, the
huntsman had a pretty good idea where to look.

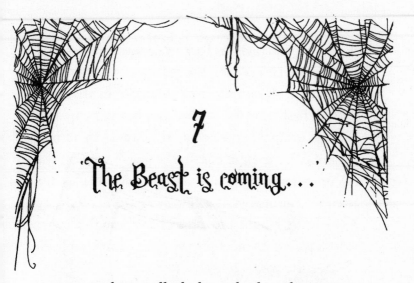

7
'The Beast is coming...'

As they walked through the silent streets Petra could almost convince herself that the city was enchanted again. She wondered how the residents could bear to sleep after their hundred year slumber, but it seemed the whole kingdom had fallen straight back into their daily routine. For them, after all, only a moment had passed.

Night was not that far from day and the sky was shifting to a midnight blue from black above them. Never having been in a city so big before, Petra felt as if she was in a maze. Only the castle dominating the skyline behind them giving her any sense of direction. The huntsman, however, was moving confidently.

'Are we going to this Rumplestiltskin's house?'

she whispered. She was back in her own clothes, and she pulled the hood of her red cape over her head as a sudden sharp breeze cut through an alleyway. For the first time she wished her beloved coat was black or grey or some colour that would blend into the buildings around her. In the dawn, with all the colour stripped from the air, she wouldn't escape attention, no matter if a soldier or the traitor they hunted only caught a glimpse of her from the corner of his eye. Not to mentioned drawing attention from the creature whose howls danced with her soul. Fascinated as she was to discover it, her heart raced with the danger. She knew only too well how wolves could rip weaker animals apart. Perhaps the colour of her coat was prophetic.

'Would you be in your house if you were him?' The huntsman answered quietly. 'I think not.'

His tanned face and dark eyes were lost to her as he kept in the shadows, but his feet moved with purpose. Petra trusted him. They made a strange trio – the prince with his adventure and need for a fairy tale ending, the huntsman who was clearly with him under duress, and then her, the forest girl, drawn by a rare sound that should terrify rather than attract her. Three outsiders with no common aim and only their need to get home uniting them.

'But we might find a clue there. To where he's hiding.'

'Soldiers will have searched it already, and no doubt wrecked anything of any use. They're rarely the most subtle of men.' They turned a corner and suddenly Petra recognised where they were: the large market square that sat at the heart of the common people's part of the city. The huntsman led them towards the monument in the middle. 'And I might not know where he's been hiding, but I have a good idea where we'll find him.' He pointed at the lines scratched into its surface. 'Someone was alive all this time. If it was him then the best hunter in the world won't find him. He's had a hundred years to explore this city. He'll know every nook and cranny and secret space in it. But people can't hide forever and this Rumplestiltskin must know that at some point he will be spotted by someone. What would you do if you were him?'

Petra looked at the lines which grew more unsteady with each marker of time. 'I would want to get away. Before the queen got too organised again.' She pulled her cloak tightly round her. 'But where could he go?'

'We got in. I imagine he saw us. If I was him I'd try that spot in the forest wall first.'

'But the forest closed up again behind us,' she said.

'Which is why we have a chance to catch him. And then maybe the forest wall will be kind enough to let us out again.'

'Good luck getting the prince to leave,' she muttered under her breath as they moved on again, at a faster pace this time. 'He's completely under her spell.'

Petra was out of breath and slightly sweaty by the time they'd followed the road to the city's edge. Here and there they'd ducked out of sight from passing groups of soldiers, but none noticed them, and they made so much noise as they approached that there was plenty of time to find a good corner or shadows to hide in. The huntsman studied the high matted wall of the forest and then smiled. 'Look,' he whispered. Petra followed his gaze. A bronze coin sat in the thick grass. 'A marker. He must have left it here after we came through. Remind him where the place was.' He looked around, scanning the area in the gloom. 'Over there,' he said, nodding towards a cluster of weeds and overhanging branches. 'We'll hide there until he comes.'

She had no real desire to press herself against the forest wall again – the memory of how it had tried to suffocate them on their way in was still fresh in her mind – but she stood behind the huntsman and did as he did. The perfume which enveloped them from behind was almost overwhelming, as if every plant and flower had a place in the wall. There was oak and sandalwood, lilies, lilac and apple blossom mixed with blackberry and the crisp scent of thick green leaves. For a moment, it almost made Petra giddy.

'When will he come?' she whispered.

'Dawn, I think. He'll want more light.'

As it turned out, it was not a long wait. After twenty minutes or so a dark silhouette scurried into view and, peering out between the branches, Petra knew it was the man they sought. He was tall and perhaps fifty years of age, and wore a crimson jacket that had seen better days. He had a heavy-looking knapsack on his back from the top of which the tip of a spindle poked out. Petra held her breath as he came closer to them, muttering under his breath and scanning the ground until he reached down and picked up the coin. In his other hand he carried a small axe and, after slipping the coin into his pocket, he began to hack at the thick greenery in front of him.

Petra barely felt the huntsman move. He dropped

97

to a crouch, below Rumplestiltskin's sightline, and moved silently out from their hiding place, working his way in a circle so he came up behind the man. The trees rustled as the axe beat into them, and with the sky slowly lightening a flurry of leaves danced around Rumplestiltskin while he tore at the wall, focused entirely on his task. Behind him the huntsman came closer, slowly and steadily, no sudden movements to alert his prey, until, with only two or three feet separating them, he lunged forward, fluid and agile.

It happened so quickly that Petra barely had time to gasp before the huntsman had spun Rumplestiltskin around and in his moment of shock, taken the axe from him. The man let out a low moan and slumped against the forest wall. Petra stepped out from her hiding place.

'You,' Rumplestiltskin said, his voice clear in the still dawn as he looked from the huntsman to her and back again. His eyes glistened and shone with despair. 'What did you do? Why did you wake her?'

'We need to take you back to the castle,' the huntsman said. 'This is not our business. You and your peers can resolve it.' Petra was surprised by the kindness of his tone.

'You've made it your business,' Rumplestiltskin

wailed. '*You* woke her. It was so close. After all this time, so long a time, a hundred years of waiting. It was so close. And then you woke her.'

Petra kept her distance. She wasn't sure what she'd been expecting but this complete emotional desolation wasn't it. Not after what she'd seen of the other ministers. But then, this man had been awake for the hundred years they'd all slept. What would that do to a person?

'After everything I lost,' he whispered, his eyes filling with tears. 'Everything I foolishly gave up. And then you *woke* her. And now everything is just as it was before.' He looked up at the huntsman. 'You stupid, stupid strangers.'

And then he broke. His shoulders slumped further and as he wept a low moan erupted from him carrying in it a hundred years of loneliness and despair. It was a terrible sight. She'd thought he would beg them to let him go, plead for his life, ask to be saved from whatever punishment awaited him at the castle, but instead he was resigned to it. Looking at the small axe he'd brought with him, that was now tucked into the huntsman's belt, perhaps he had never truly believed he could cut his way free.

The huntsman, clearly moved by the man's plight, stepped forward to put an arm around his shoulders, and Petra was so focused on the scene in front of her she didn't hear the footsteps rushing up behind her until it was too late.

Suddenly, she was jerked backwards by her red coat, and as strong arms roughly held her she felt cold, sharp steel against her throat. She let out a short yelp and the huntsman turned, Rumplestilt-skin forgotten.

'You'll give him to me now.' The voice was gruff and the breath that hit her cheek was stale. She could feel a metal breastplate against her back and she wriggled slightly to try and break free but his arms were strong. He stank of sweat.

'Why don't you release the girl then, soldier?' the huntsman said. 'We're all on the same side here. We were bringing him back as instructed.'

'He's not going anywhere. I've got my orders. There are more men behind me.' His grip on Petra tightened and she struggled to breathe. 'Kill him now and we might let you both live.'

'Let the girl go. She's done nothing.' The hunts-man took a small step forward and held up his hands. 'You do what you have to. But I'm not killing a man in cold blood.'

'Stay back.' The soldier – Petra guessed from the tension in his body that he was young and nervous under his bluster – pressed the knife harder against her neck. Too hard. A sharp pain upon her skin and she yelped again, knowing the knife had nicked her. Warmth trickled down her neck. Blood.

The huntsman froze. And then, from nowhere, it came, bounding over the huntsman and leaping towards Petra with a terrifying, angry growl.

The wolf.

It filled her vision. Thick blue-grey fur over a vast, muscular frame. This was no ordinary wolf, like those who scavenged her grandmother's goats. This was ethereal and earthy at once. It was twice the size and its fur shone so brightly that even in the dead light of dawn it seemed to glow. It flew through the air before her. Eyes that burned yellow and sharp teeth behind bared black lips. Claws extending from enormous paws. It was rage. It was fury.

Just before it hit her, Petra thought it was the most beautiful creature she had ever seen. And then the air was gone from her lungs and she was on the ground.

The ball had finished an hour or so before, but the prince and Beauty couldn't bear to part company just yet. The prince was sure he should be tired, but the sheer elation of having found love kept him wide awake. Although they had kissed, many times now, there was an innocence about her that stopped him suggesting they go to her rooms despite the throbbing desire he felt for her. He'd wait for their wedding night and then he'd take her gently and sweetly and their love would not be sullied by haste. She was so pure. After all the serving girls and wenches he'd shared his time with he was now almost ashamed of his past earthy encounters. Perhaps he should have kept himself pure for her. But then princes were supposed to be men of the world, and it was right that he should have experience: she was queen, but he would be master of their bedroom.

As night inched towards day they walked arm in arm, pausing here and there as she pointed out paintings she loved, or pieces of ornate sculpture she had commissioned, and slowly she showed him around her vast home; a castle equal to his father's own in wealth and lavishness. They paused in the kitchens where the night bakers had made fresh bread for the morning, and Beauty's kind words to them made the men blush as she praised them in their work.

Nibbling on hot croissants they wandered back into the heart of the castle and through the ballroom that had so recently been full of music and dancing. He pulled her close and they spun, laughing like children, across the floor until they reached the far door and paused to kiss. She was so natural in his arms and he ran his fingers down her face, brushing them across the tops of her breasts and listening to her sigh and shudder slightly with pleasure. She wanted him too, he could see it in the slight parting of her perfect lips and the haze in her eyes.

'I love you,' she said softly and then smiled.

'I love you too.' And he did. She was perfect.

From the ballroom, she led him into the library, all the walls lined with thousands of books which filled polished mahogany and oak shelves. As shafts of sunlight cut through the windows, Beauty ran from one shelf to another pointing out her favourite stories from childhood; princes who slayed dragons on the Far Mountain, pirate tales from the eastern seas and other tales of love, magic and adventure. As she giggled and promised him that they would read these stories together one day, to their own children, the prince spied a small door in the corner, virtually unnoticeable among the beauty and colour of the books around it. It was wooden, mahogany like the shelves, and as he opened it he was sure he heard the tinkling of distant bells. He looked up to see wires running from the hinges and up into the ceiling. A servants' bell? But why here? This was an in-between place, nowhere you would stop and require refreshments or a fire lit. Why would you? It was simply a narrow corridor. Was the door left over from some conversion years ago? Had the corridor once been part of a different room? He stepped forward, curious.

'Beauty,' he called back to her. 'What's down here?' The corridor was unadorned with any portraits and there was only a plain oak door at the other end. He walked towards it, not waiting for her, and lifted the heavy iron ring handle. He turned it and pushed, but nothing happened. The door was locked.

'I never come down here.' Beauty's voice sounded small, all humour gone from it, and he looked back to see her frowning slightly at the other end of the corridor. 'Why don't we go now? I'm tired. We should go to bed.'

The prince crouched slightly and peered through the keyhole. It was dark but he could just about make out the red of the walls and what looked like heavy black curtains. Gold glinted here and there. 'I think it's another ballroom,' he muttered, before straightening up and turning back to her. 'And you've never seen it? How can that be?'

She had started to tremble a little and her mouth tightened. 'I don't want to be here.'

'But aren't you curious? Surely you should know all the parts of your castle. You are the queen, after all.'

'I said I don't want to be here.' The trembling was becoming more visible and as Beauty backed away from him, she tugged at her hair, pulling strands free from the carefully arranged curls piled on her head.

'What's the matter?' What was suddenly upsetting her? Had someone died in this room? One of her parents perhaps? 'I'm sorry,' he said, rushing towards her. 'I didn't mean to upset you.'

He reached for her, but she stepped away from him. Her eyes had glazed slightly and he wondered if she even knew he was there. 'Beauty?' he said.

'I don't like it here,' she muttered, and then, without warning, she slapped herself hard across the face.

The prince was so shocked that for a moment he couldn't react at all. Bright red finger marks stained her smooth skin. Only when she lifted her hand to do it again did he reach forward and grab her wrist to stop her.

'What's the matter with you? What is it?'

She hissed at him and struggled to pull away, the trembling turning to shuddering so strong that the prince thought she might be about to have a fit. Perhaps that was it. Her breathing was coming faster and she hugged herself.

Rapid footsteps came across the library, and the first minister rushed towards them, his robes flowing behind him. 'What are you doing here? Why did you open the door?'

'I didn't ... I just ...' the prince didn't know what to say. The older man pushed him aside and wrapped his arm around Beauty. 'Is she okay?' the prince finished, feeling helpless. She clearly wasn't okay. Not only was she having the strange physical symptoms but something was happening to her hair. The two blonde streaks at the front were darkening and the rest was somehow getting lighter.

'I'll look after her.' The first minister blocked the prince's view. 'Go back to your apartment. Stay there.' He spoke sharply, his words cutting through the prince's shock. The only man who'd ever spoken to him like that was his father. 'Do not come out until I come and say you can. Do you understand me?'

'What's happening?' the prince asked. He felt like a child again.

'The Beast is coming,' the first minister said quietly. 'Now go.'

The prince did as he was told.

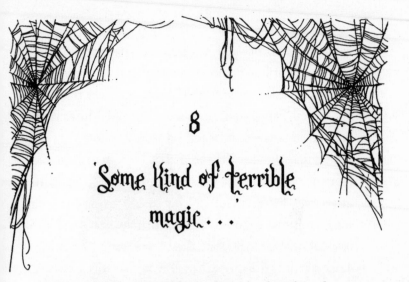

8

Some Kind of Terrible magic...

They left the soldier where he lay, his throat ripped out and his eyes forever staring shocked and surprised at the greying sky, and moved quickly. The man might have been lying that there were others close by but dawn was breaking and soon the city would be alive again. It wouldn't be long before the body was found.

The wolf immediately calmed after its swift attack, standing by the dead man and letting out a long sorrowful howl before padding to Rumplestiltskin's side, its eyes fixed on Petra. The man patted the fierce beast's head and then led the small group away. Petra was staring at the wolf, stunned, and the huntsman grabbed her arm and pulled her along. They had no choice now. He couldn't take the huge wolf on – and nor did he want to. There was something almost noble about its grace and ferocity. Had Rumplestiltskin tamed it? It didn't matter; the wolf had saved Petra, and he trusted animals more than men. Where the wolf went, he would follow.

Rumplestiltskin led them to a large oak tree and crouched to pull up a wooden hatch hidden beneath grass and leaves. 'Get in,' he hissed urgently. The wolf bounded through the dark hole first, and the rest followed. Only once they were sealed up in the dank earth did Rumplestiltskin take a torch from a slot on the rough wall, and light it. Ahead of them was a low tunnel, wooden struts here and there propping up the ceiling. It didn't look overly safe to the huntsman, but he followed anyway, holding Petra's hand in the gloom.

They walked, hunched over so far they might have been better off crawling, for several minutes, until the tunnel opened out into a man-made cave, with a door at the far end and a small hole in the ceiling that let in a shard of natural light from the surface several feet above them.

Rumplestiltskin had clearly tried to make it home and as well as two beds and piles of books there was a table holding a jug of wine, some fresh bread, cheese and a leg of roasted pork.

'If you're hungry, take something,' he muttered, clearing some papers from a chair so Petra, still slightly winded from the weight of the wolf, could sit down. The wolf's arrival and their subsequent flight had calmed him.

'You dug this place out? Yourself?' Petra asked, dabbing a piece of cloth over the cut on her neck to stem the blood.

'We had nearly a hundred years.' Rumplestiltskin put his knapsack down and sat on the bed. 'Relatively, it didn't take very long.'

'We?' the huntsman asked, and then just as the first ray of sunlight pierced through the narrow skylight, the wolf began to change.

His fur glittered a thousand colours and his yellow eyes widened as he whimpered. Myriad lights lifted from his coat and spun in a whirlwind around him until they were so bright the huntsman had to close his eyes. Even then the brightness made him flinch. The beast let out half a howl and then there was silence.

When the huntsman risked looking again the room was back to normal. The light was gone. So was the wolf. In its place, a man lay on the rough ground. He coughed twice and then sat up.

'That never gets any easier,' he groaned, and sat

up, dusting off his white shirt and black jacket. His hair was thick and dirty blond and his eyes were green with yellow flecks.

'You're a man,' Petra said quietly. She stared at him. 'I knew you weren't just a wolf. I knew it. All those times I listened through the wall it was you.' She smiled, and the man smiled back, and the huntsman felt the magic between them. It hummed in the room far greater than the glittering lights had shone.

'You're the girl who howls back.' The two stared at each other with the kind of recognition only people who have never met and yet are destined to be together could share.

'You saved my life,' Petra said.

The man nodded, but his jaw clenched with shame at his deed. 'I'm sorry I killed him,' he said. 'Things are different when I'm the wolf. There are no grey areas. I act on instinct.'

'I'm not sorry you killed him,' Petra said. 'He was going to kill us, after all.' Her elfin face glowed slightly and she trembled.

'Then you're welcome.' Rumplestiltskin had poured the man some water and he drank it and then got to his feet. He bowed to Petra. 'My name is Toby.'

'You've been awake all this time too?' The huntsman asked.

'Yes.' The gregarious grin left Toby's face. 'I was cursed. There was a witch in the city, an older woman, and she fell in love with me. She was a beautiful woman, famed for the diamond slippers that had enchanted many men before me into her bed, and she pursued me relentlessly. But I did not love her and she did not take my rejection well. One night she saw me with a lady of the court and her jealousy overwhelmed her. She cursed me. Every full moon I would spend the nights as a wolf. The first time it happened, my family were terrified. Rumours spread of a wolfman, and I was hunted. I hid in the forest and would only creep back into the city to forage for food and drink. It was on one such trip that the forest formed a wall behind me and the city fell asleep. I can only presume that because I was already cursed, the second curse didn't affect me.'

'Was she sleeping?' Petra asked. 'Will she be awake now?'

'No, I went to her house. She was dead in her bed. Murdered. I wonder if she had picked a man to lure to her bed whose wife's jealousy overwhelmed her fear.' Toby shrugged. 'The city will be better without her. She brought her fate on herself.'

'And I am forever grateful for that, despite your being trapped in this ageless time with me,' Rumplestiltskin squeezed Toby's shoulder. 'I would have gone mad without you.'

'Why didn't you sleep?' Petra asked the old man.

'I caused the curse. The magic doesn't affect he who carries it. Time froze for me, but I did not sleep.' He poured himself some wine and the huntsman noticed his hand was trembling. It had been a long hundred years. But why had he brought it on himself? He seemed a harmless man, unless some natural viciousness had been beaten out of him over the century. It was unlikely. Viciousness grew with bitterness and a hundred years alone would make any man bitter.

'Did you curse the wrong sister?' he asked. 'Surely you didn't mean to attack Beauty.'

'The wrong sister?' the old man smiled, wistfully. 'It was so easy for people to believe that story. The dark days. The second sister. The evil twin. One dark with hints of blonde, one blonde with hints of dark. One so kind and gentle and pure, the other wild and wicked and filled with her mother's magic.'

Somewhere overhead a flash of blue lightning crossed the sky and lit up their cave, and thunder rumbled so hard that the ground around them shook.

Rumplestiltskin looked at the huntsman, his eyes tired. 'There was only one child. They named her Beauty. And beautiful she was. But she was more than that: she was Beauty *and* the Beast.

he young king and his people grieved for their beautiful queen and returned her body to the waters from whence she'd come, but still they stayed bitter, and the king did not blame the spirits of her ancestors for their anger. Being a kind and optimistic man he hoped that one day, when his daughter was grown, they would forgive him for his selfish act of loving the water witch and see that something beautiful could come from the union of earth and magic.

He took great comfort in the infant Beauty for she was a good-natured baby and rarely cried. She smiled and gurgled in her father's arms and soon, although his heart would never truly mend, the cracks began to heal and he poured his love into his little girl, just as his dead wife would have wanted him to.

All the kingdom loved Beauty. It was impossible not to. Even the old and cynical ministers' hearts warmed at the sight of her. Goodness shone brightly from her every pore and she loved them all in return. It was her nature to love. For her fourth birthday there was a feast and the whole city rejoiced. She was showered with gifts, given not for political advantage, which was so often the case with royal children, but from the heart. She received so many that she insisted on sharing them with the poorer children of the city, and that just made the people love her more.

The only present she didn't give away was the one that made her eyes sparkle more than any other: a black and white kitten she called Domino, a present from her father's best friend and closest advisor, Rumplestiltskin. Domino was just like her, she said, his hair was black with some blond bits too. She smiled and cuddled him and all was well.

Beauty loved Domino and the cat loved her back. Unlike most felines he did not crave his independence but, like a puppy, would follow the little girl wherever she went and slept curled up on her pillow. Some said – or whispered – it was because Beauty came from witch's blood and all witches had a way with animals, but even those who found the kitten's behaviour odd couldn't bring themselves to think badly of the little princess who was always so full of kindness and love.

Domino died three years later on the first dark day. They did not call them dark days then, and none had any idea how dark they would become, but it was the first time that Beauty changed. There was no trigger for it. Perhaps if her mother had still been alive, she would have known what to do with her child to make it better. But the water witch was dead, and the half-child princess was alone in the world of men.

It was a perfect day and the princess had finished her music and dance lessons and returned to her rooms to play. Thankfully, her servants were dismissed and she was alone.

It was the king and Rumplestiltskin who found her and for a while it would be their secret to bear. They had planned to take Beauty riding, but the clear summer day had suddenly grown cloudy and rain had burst from the sky. The king, perhaps because of the loss of his beloved wife, was protective of Beauty's health and decided that they would stay inside and play cards instead. The two men were laughing together when they opened the doors to her apartment.

The laughter stopped immediately.

All the king could see was blood.

At first he thought the blood was Beauty's and he ran towards her in panic, ordering Rumplestiltskin to fetch the doctors. But then, as he got closer, he saw the bloody sewing scissors and Domino's glassy eyes staring up from the mess in his daughter's lap.

'His fur wouldn't change,' Beauty snapped, her voice sharp and irritated. 'His fur wouldn't change. And he scratched me.' She was indignant and her normally beautiful face was screwed up so tightly it was ugly. 'He scratched me.'

'What have you done, Beauty?' the king asked in horror, unable to absorb what was so clearly in front of him. He crouched and took the wrecked, lifeless body of the beloved cat from her.

'Look at her hair,' Rumplestiltskin said, having closed the door and locked it to prevent any passing servants from seeing the awful sight within. 'What's happened to her hair?'

'His hair didn't match mine,' Beauty muttered, although she now sounded slightly confused. With bloody fingers she pulled at her own locks. 'He wouldn't change it. Why wouldn't he change it? Why did he scratch me?'

Her hair, which was normally black with two

blonde streaks of her mother's colouring, had re-
versed, leaving her head a cool blonde with mid-
night stripes on each side of her cherubic face.

'This isn't right,' Rumplestiltskin said, grabbing a
towel and wrapping the dead cat up in it. 'This isn't
our Beauty.' For she was more than just the king's
daughter, she was loved by them all. 'Is this some
kind of terrible magic?'

'Daddy?' Beauty was frowning now, looking up.
'Daddy, what are you doing here?'

Her hair began to change again, returning to its
natural state, the two opposing colours bleeding
into each other, and through the window the first
shard of sunlight cut through the rain, the weather
changing with her.

The king swept his daughter up and took her
into the bathroom. 'Get rid of that cat,' he growled.
'Where no one can find it.'

Rumplestiltskin did as he was told. There were
plenty of places he could have thrown the stabbed
and half-skinned animal, but he found a quiet place
in the orchard and buried Domino. He had been a
good cat and he had loved the young princess well,
and Rumplestiltskin, a kind man with a daughter
of his own, felt responsible for the animal's fate. A
little sweat was not too much to give him. That and

a grave where the foxes couldn't scavenge his corpse in the night.

By the time he got back to the princess's apartments, she was washed and changed and sitting on the bed playing cards with the king. She looked up and smiled, all light and laughter again.

'Have you seen Domino?' she asked. 'I don't know where he is.'

From where he stood in the doorway, Rumplestiltskin could see that the king had hastily rolled up the bloody rug and shoved it under the bed.

'He's probably gone to the kitchens,' the king said. His face was a picture of forced normality, his smile stretched across his face as if it were on a rack. 'Maybe he wanted some milk.'

'That's probably it,' Beauty said, but Rumplestiltskin could see the worry on her pretty face for her missing pet. 'I just wish I knew where he was. I don't remember him leaving.'

'He'll be back,' Rumplestiltskin said cheerily as he sat on the bed. 'I'm sure of it.' Inside, he felt a small part of him die with the lie, the first of what he feared would be many, many lies, and life in the castle had changed that day. Of course the change in her had been magic. But it was a magic that she held. This was nothing to do with the witch and her talk of spindles. Beauty was cursed from within.

Beauty was inconsolable for weeks when Domino, rotting in the orchard, failed to return to her. Everyone searched for him, but the little cat was of course not found, and although she missed him terribly Beauty had the resilience of a child and her nature was too full of joy to hold onto her sadness. Eventually she stopped asking after him and life moved on.

The king and Rumplestiltskin remained watchful and stayed close to the princess as best they could to watch for the signs of change. The instances were at first so rare that, for a few years, they did not cause too much consternation, the two men simply sweeping up the child and locking her in her rooms until the skies outside cleared of rain and they'd know that their good girl had returned to them.

They chose her maids carefully but even so, after a while, there were rumours that another child was in the castle, a blonde girl uncannily like Beauty but who huffed and puffed and stamped her foot.

Being a wise man, and knowing in his heart that now that a door had unlocked inside Beauty it would stay that way, Rumplestiltskin didn't try to quell the rumours. Instead, he added one to circulation – that there had been two babies born to the king and queen. Twins. But the second girl was a difficult child who needed special care and the king had chosen, for her own sake, to keep her out of the limelight that came with being part of the royal family. When the rumour was whispered back to him he knew he'd been successful. Should anything untoward be seen then Beauty would not be blamed and that was all that mattered.

The king hoped that as Beauty grew her changes would become less frequent, but it was a false hope. The princess reached puberty late, but as soon as she woke, bloody, just after her fifteenth birthday, things grew worse.

The changes became more frequent. And when the other girl was in charge, she now had all her mother's repressed magic at her fingertips. It was no longer possible to lock her away in a room until the moment passed, and instead of simple thunder-clouds in the sky, blue lightning would crack across the city and rain would flash-flood the streets. She was wild, this blonde girl who ran, laughing and dancing wantonly through the castle corri-dors, tipping trays of food from servants' hands as she went.

She whipped the stable boy to within an inch of his life for not polishing her saddle well enough, and the king caught her half-naked with one of his ministers.

The man went to the dungeons for that.

That was a mistake.

The princess followed. Not to save him, but to watch the punishment.

She liked blood.

Rumplestiltskin caught her once in the butcher's yard at the back of the castle, her hands buried in the hot entrails of a freshly killed deer. Her eyes were glazed, and as he pulled her away she licked her fingers. He didn't tell the king that. His precious Beauty, Rumplestiltskin feared, was also a monster.

The changes did not last long, a day or two at the very most, but they were impossible to hide. Rumplestiltskin amended his rumour to say that Beauty insisted her sister had the run of the castle in her stead for a few days here and there, and although some in the kingdom believed that, the king could not keep the secret from his ministers any longer. But there was no other heir, and for all her wildness and streak of cruelty, the Beast, as she became known on those days, still loved her father, and was always affectionate towards him and Rumplestiltskin as if Beauty, locked inside her, had that much control over both of them.

Beauty

The king had a bell installed high in the castle roof, and proclamations were sent out around the kingdom that when it rang all the people should go to their houses and stay inside until it was rung again. The criers claimed it was to protect them from the terrible blue lightning that spat at the ground during these times, and the dangerous floods, and although it was the nature of the people to do as they were told, rumours were still rumours and there was talk of a monster in the castle and magic at play.

It worked for a while. Several years passed and the kingdom and the castle settled into their new routine. Beauty became a young woman her father could be proud of and everyone continued to love her. She was still kind and thoughtful and full of joy. Young men came to court her. One kissed her and fell so passionately in love that when she told her father she didn't love him the boy hanged himself.

When a second kissed her and also fell completely in love with her – although with less disastrous consequences when she rejected him – Rumplestiltskin and the first minister broached the subject of magic once again to the king. Her mother's magic was not just contained within the Beast. Her kisses put men under a spell, and perhaps, although none could argue that she was not the sweetest of girls, there was a little magic involved in the unconditional love everyone who met her felt.

They decided this was a good thing. It would protect the princess from any who might harm her because of the Beast, and the king took to touring the city with her to ensure that she had all of their subjects' love. There was, he reminded them all, no other heir for the kingdom, and the king refused to even consider marrying again. Things continued in their strange new normality.

But as with all things that we pretend are not so bad as they seem, there comes, for each man or woman, a breaking point.

For Rumplestiltskin it was the poisoning of the king.

He had been growing sicker for a while. At first the changes were not noticeable; just a day or two of feeling off colour, a general tiredness, a reluctance to ride. These times came and went and none of the ministers thought anything of it. He grew thinner. Rumplestiltskin and the first minister noticed that the Beast, when she was in residence, was more affectionate towards her father and this caused them both to be suspicious. They kept her from the kitchens when his food was being prepared and she was followed at all times to ensure she did not go near his wine or water.

They saw nothing suspicious. Perhaps the king was just going through a bout of ill-health.

It was a summer's day when Rumplestiltskin found Beauty in the orchard picking apples from a tree. He did not look down at the flattened piece of earth close by where her forgotten childhood companion lay buried. She smiled at him as he asked her why she needed so many as she carried in her basket, and said she was baking apple cakes for her father and had been doing so for weeks. He liked them and that made her happy. Her eyes were clear and her face shone. She was innocent. She was sweet.

Rumplestiltskin was suspicious. For if Beauty lurked within to protect her father and Rumplestiltskin when the Beast was in charge, logic dictated that the Beast likewise lurked within Beauty.

He watched her from the shadows beyond the kitchen door as she baked. She sang sweetly to herself as she peeled and cored the ripe fruit and prepared the dough. He chided himself for his dark thoughts. There was nothing amiss here – she was still entirely their Beauty. He lingered though, for he was a thorough man, and as he loved Beauty he also loved his best friend, the king.

Just as the cakes were ready to go into the oven, with Beauty's face covered in an endearing dusting of flour and sugar, a dark cloud passed across sky and the room darkened. Beauty frowned, suddenly confused. She had opened the heavy oven doors and had the tray in her hand, but she paused. She turned, returned to the table and put it down. Her eyes were glazed and lost as she reached into her pocket and pulled out a small vial of liquid, tipping a tiny drop of brightness onto each cake. Once the vial was again out of sight, she picked up the tray again.

The cloud passed and life returned to Beauty and she began to hum once more, closing the door and letting the cakes bake. She smiled, content in her work.

Rumplestiltskin slipped silently away, shivering in horror, his worst fears confirmed. He did not blame Beauty. She didn't know what she had done. But still, the danger was there. As she grew, who would win the battle there? Beauty or the Beast? He could not watch her forever. One day he would not be able to foil her efforts.

Separate batches of apple cakes were made that

the king could eat in front of his daughter to keep her happy without being poisoned, and when the bell rang and the Beast came, he would walk a little hunched over and feign some illness.

But the king was troubled. He had grown into a wise king and he knew that above all else his loyalty should lie with his people. There were talks long into the night of what should be done. The Beast grew wilder and less controllable, and her visits more frequent. The king knew that she went to the dungeons and arranged terrible punishments for the prisoners there, then bribed the guards not to speak of it. None would argue with her. It only took one guard to be punished to show the rest that she was not to be disagreed with. She had magic, after all. Worse, there were those among the nobles, Rumplestiltskin could see it, who almost admired her ruthless nature and brought their sons and daughters in to be her companions, and curry her favour. As Beauty herself was divided, she was also dividing those around her. The good and bad in people became more pronounced and factions grew in the court where there had been harmony before.

The king loved Beauty, but he could not love the Beast. He wept for the water witch and for what their love, which should never have been, had created. When his tears were dry he summoned Rumplestiltskin, his most trusted friend, and asked him to go to the witch in the tower and beg her to help Beauty. Perhaps magic could fight the dark magic in his daughter – perhaps the witch would have a power to ensure that the dark days ended. He told Rumplestiltskin to give her whatever she demanded in return, if she could find a way to free his daughter from the curse of her nature.

It was the end of summer when Rumplestiltskin left, taking his own daughter with him. She was uncomfortable in court life and although she had been friends with Beauty when she had been little, after Domino's death Rumplestiltskin had slowly removed her from the princess's company and sent her to a school on the far side of the city. Now she was grown she was out of place amid the stylish confidence of the nobles, and he feared this would mark her as a victim for the Beast while he was away as she took great pleasure in taunting those whom she perceived to be weak.

It was a long journey to the white tower that rose above the trees in the distance, one not without its own adventures, and as they drew closer both Rumplestiltskin and his daughter were in awe of the height of the edifice. There were only two windows they could see, one halfway up and another far away at the very top that would no doubt be lost from sight in the misty days of winter.

There was no visible door and after exploring the perimeter and seeing no way in Rumplestiltskin called up to the window in the hope that the witch would hear him and come down. He shouted himself hoarse, but there was no response. He began to think that perhaps this was a wild goose chase and the witch was long gone or dead within the impenetrable walls. He sat on a rock, ready to give up, and then his daughter shouted for him, begging the witch to show them mercy and hear their plight.

A door, previously invisible, swung open in the smooth curved wall. The witch smiled and invited them in. Rumplestiltskin was not sure what he had been expecting, but she was unchanged – an ordinary middle-aged woman. As they followed her up the winding stairs inside, however, he caught glimpses of artefacts and objects that were hundreds of years old. She noticed his glance and smiled.

'A witch's years are different to a man's. I've stopped counting them.'

She fed them a hearty broth, settled Rumplestiltskin's daughter down on a soft couch to sleep, and then listened to his tale of Beauty and the Beast. The witch was thoughtful after that. She hadn't been out in the world since the king had summoned her, before Beauty's birth, and after hearing his tale she was glad of it.

'A water witch's daughter,' she mused, 'should only be born from a water bed. This trouble is one anyone could have seen coming.'

She sat by the fire for a while and watched Rumplestiltskin's daughter sleep, as if that sight brought her some clarity or peace, and then made her decision.

'Can you help?' Rumplestiltskin asked. 'I fear for our land if the Beast can't be controlled.'

'Come with me,' she told him. They climbed two more flights of stairs until they came to a room with several locks. 'I have something for you.'

It was full of spinning wheels and spindles of different shapes and sizes and Rumplestiltskin's eyes widened. 'Spindles. Beauty's curse.' The witch smiled. 'They are each bewitched or blessed or cursed, depending on how you use them.' She walked between them, her fingers lovingly caressing the wood of each until her hand settled on one. 'I cannot change her nature,' she said, eventually. 'She is who she is, and no magic is strong enough to

131

change that. But I can save your kingdom from her inevitable tyranny.'

Rumplestiltskin stared at her. 'How?' he asked, his mouth drying. He knew the answer before she spoke and his heart was heavy with the decision he would have to make.

'I can give you something which will kill her, should you feel that is your only recourse.' She turned to Rumplestiltskin and in the candlelight he was sure he could see hundreds of years of life in her eyes and a dead heart beating inside her. No good came from magic, his conscience screamed, and he trembled slightly. She looked so very ordinary but in her soul she was a crone. No good could come from a crone. 'This,' she said, and lifted one of her precious spindles.

'How does it work?' he asked, after swallowing hard. Ever since Domino he had known that one day a decision would have to be made about Beauty. And somewhere in his soul, and in his love for the king, he'd known it would be his decision to make. 'And will it be painless?' He paused. 'We all love her, you see.' He wondered if he was justifying his actions to himself or to her. 'Hopefully, I will never have to use it.'

'I will need it returning,' she said. 'Especially if

*you decide some less extreme action is called for.'
She carefully lifted it and handed it to him. 'One
prick of her finger and she will die,' she said, her
voice devoid of emotion. 'And it will be painless.
Like going to sleep.' She smiled at that.*

'It's poison then,' Rumplestiltskin said.

*'She'll bleed to death,' the witch replied. 'But I
assure you she won't feel a thing.'*

*His hands trembled as he took it. 'I must be sure
not to prick myself on the way back then.'*

*'I've given you this magic,' she said, leading him
out of the room and locking it with the keys that
hung from a chain around her neck. 'It can't hurt
you. A curse cannot touch the one who wields it.'*

'And what do you want in return?' he asked.

*'You will leave your daughter with me until you
bring my spindle back,' she said, softly.*

*Rumplestiltskin felt as if all the air had been
sucked from his lungs. His daughter? His only child.*

*The witch squeezed his hand. He was surprised
at the warmth of her fingers. He'd expected them
to feel like the touch of a dead thing. 'She will want
for nothing and I shall teach her many things. She
will be happy here and I am lonely. I have been
lonely for a long, long time.' She smiled again.
Her lips were thin. 'And when you return you may*

reclaim her if you so wish. This I promise you.' She shrugged. 'Perhaps she will also be safer here. Dangerous times lie ahead.'

Rumplestiltskin felt the weight of all his responsibility to the kingdom settle on his shoulders and his heart grew heavy. He had no choice.

'I will come back for her,' he said.

'I'm sure you will,' the witch replied.

He did not wait for his daughter to wake because he knew he would not have the strength to say goodbye, but left her a letter telling her he loved her very much and that he would return soon to take her home. He kissed her forehead and left his darling daughter, Rapunzel, there where she slept.

By the time he got back to the kingdom two months had passed and much had already changed. The king was dead; killed in a riding accident while out with the princess a mere day after Rumplestiltskin had left. While Beauty mourned for her father, the Beast revelled in her new power. She held masked balls for the wild young things of the city and took her vicarious pleasure not only from their bodies, but also from torturing those unfortunate enough to be in the dungeons. If there were no prisoners there, they were brought in, innocents chosen at random to feed her blood lust, their houses wrecked and looted by the soldiers knowing they would not return.

She redecorated the third ballroom to suit her tastes; decadent red and black and gold, and music played long and loud as the young people danced and enjoyed each other, and girls from the dairy came and never left again alive.

The ministers kept these secrets and managed the kingdom around her as best they could until the bell rang once again and they could let out a collective sigh of relief. None challenged her because her mother's magic was at her fingertips, and they had seen the unrecognisable bodies that left the dungeons. They kept their own counsel and shuffled around the castle trying to look invisible as they did exactly as they were told. With the king gone and Rumplestiltskin away, only the first minister had the true affection of their queen and they left the management of the Beast to him.

It could not go on, Rumplestiltskin thought, as he held Beauty's hand beside her father's grave and cried with her for his oldest friend. It just could not go on.

Whispers of murders and torture, wild parties and patricide; that was only two months into the new reign and it would only get worse. Beauty was sweet and kind, but the Beast was stronger, he was sure of that. That Beauty had unknowingly killed the king, he had no doubt. He'd spoken to the terrified stable boy who whispered that the girth on the king's saddle had been nearly cut through and that it had been the princess herself who had prepared his horse for him. Who would be next? Her father's friends?

He sat up late into the night, turning the spindle in his hands. One prick, the witch had said, and that would be that. He wished it could be done while she was the Beast. Somehow that would feel easier. But the Beast rarely slept and her magic would protect her from danger. It had to be Beauty he murdered.

He went to her rooms the next afternoon. It was a beautiful day. The city was full of life. A rose, Beauty's favourite flower, sat in a glass on the window sill. She sat on the edge of her bed and laughed with delight as she reached for the spinning wheel, happy that he'd thought to bring her a gift from his travels, especially a thing she had never seen before in her life, and in that moment where she was joyous he saw her delicate finger touch the spindle.

It was done.

Her eyes widened for the merest moment and

then the spinning wheel slid from her hands to the floor and she fell backwards onto her bed. Rumplestiltskin stood and cried, silently begging her forgiveness, for what seemed like forever, before he laid her out on the bed. He was so absorbed in his grief and guilt he failed to notice the sudden unnatural silence around him.

He did, however, notice that the princess, one arm flopped over the side of the bed, a tiny drop of blood striking the floor from her pricked finger, was still breathing.

It didn't make sense. Not at first. Not until he'd been outside and to the forest's edge and seen the wall that had grown there. And even then it had taken weeks, maybe even months, for the terrible truth to sink in.

'The witch lied,' Petra said, softly.

'Oh no.' Rumplestiltskin shook his head. 'Witches never lie. But they do speak in riddles. The queen *would* die. She would bleed to death and it would be painless. But she would bleed to death one drop at a time.' He shuddered and sipped his wine. 'Before Beauty's birth, the witch told the king that a spindle would send his daughter to sleep for a hundred years. Her prophesy was not destroyed by my deeds. I brought the spindle. I sent her to sleep as I killed her. She would sleep the hundred years it took her blood to drain from her body and then she'd be gone. A hundred years of waiting. And we were so nearly there, when you woke her.'

'Your daughter?' the huntsman said.

'Long dead now. After a life abandoned and locked away in a witch's tower.'

'Locked in a tower,' Petra repeated, her gaze misty as if she was lost in a different story.

'So why is the first minister so keen that we find you and take you to him? You were doing something that surely they all wanted?'

'If I had succeeded, of course. But I failed. The queen is awake, and there's only one other person who knew of my plan and my visit to the witch.'

'Him?' Petra said.

'Exactly. If I'm captured and the Beast tortures me, he knows I'll have no choice but to give up his name. It's better for everyone if she thinks I acted alone.'

'Shhh.' Toby tilted his head and frowned.

'What?'

'The bell,' Toby said. 'The bell is ringing. A dark day has come.'

Rumplestiltskin looked up at the huntsman. 'The Beast is awake.'

'But what about the prince?' Petra asked. 'He's with her!'

'Hopefully the first minister will look after him,' the old man muttered. 'But I fear he's about to have a very rude awakening about his sweet queen.'

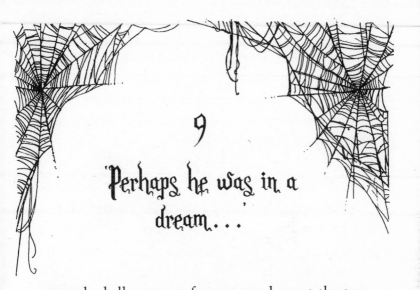

9

'Perhaps he was in a dream...'

The bell rang out from somewhere at the top of the castle, a steady heavy knell, and as the prince stared up at the ceiling of his apartments he shivered slightly while his heart raced. Whatever affliction had struck poor Beauty the first minister had not been surprised by it, but the prince had also seen that he was afraid and that in turn frightened the prince. Much to his own chagrin, he wished the huntsman were here. Surrounded as he was by the kind of luxury he was used to, he still suddenly felt very alone and far from home. He loved Beauty, he knew that to his very core, but he was unimportant here. The way the minister had spoken to him made that abundantly clear.

Blue lightning flashed in jagged lines beyond the

window and a moment later an almighty rumble of thunder shook the sky. He was sure the castle walls trembled. He was about to go to the window to look when the door to his rooms opened and the first minister entered carrying a silver tray.

'I know it is early, but you have had a long night and I thought you might like something to eat,' he said smoothly, placing it on the table against the wall. 'And a hot drink to help you sleep.' His smile was tight. 'I'm very sorry to have rushed you away like that, but our beloved queen has occasional fits.' He nodded towards the window. 'They come with the bad weather.' The minister had regained his usual poise, but the prince remembered all too well the urgency with which he'd spoken earlier, insisting that the prince leave. What was he hiding? 'It's unlikely she will be well again today, so eat now and then sleep as long as you wish. Take time to recover from your long journey.'

'I should be with her while she's sick. I am her husband to be, after all. It's my job to look after her.'

'And when you are married of course you shall. But the queen requires privacy at these times – the fits are quite traumatic for her – and you can understand why she might want to keep them private from you at this early stage. She is young and easily embarrassed. Anyway,' he clasped his hands in front of him and they were lost in the sleeves and folds of his robes, 'once this one has passed, which I'm sure it shall quickly, I shall teach you how best to deal with them. But for now she is well cared for, so eat, drink and sleep. Then you have a wedding to plan.'

His eyes lingered a moment too long on the tray and there was a flash of intensity, almost hidden under the first minister's hooded brows, as he turned his gaze back to the prince.

'Of course,' the prince said, his mouth drying. 'You are right. I was simply worried.' He lifted the goblet and pretended to take a sip. 'I shall see her tomorrow. Perhaps, if she is unwell, we should delay the wedding for a day. We can plan it together so it can be perfect.'

The first minister smiled. 'Perhaps that is wise.'

The prince felt the red wine touch his lips but refused to let it pass. Why would the first minister bring him his food and not send a servant? He was a proud man – the prince had known enough counsellors and politicians to know they did nothing to diminish their status in the eyes of others. The minister must have wanted to ensure the prince received it and was going to consume it, and that meant he had probably added an extra ingredient between the kitchen and his rooms. The prince was spoiled and could be selfish but he wasn't stupid. All castles housed ruthless men with their own personal agendas – what if the first minister had decided that Beauty marrying a royal was not in his best interest? She was sweet and gentle – her husband might not be. Who would wield the power then?

He looked down at the silver plate containing half a roast chicken covered in gravy and surrounded by potatoes and vegetables. 'That looks delicious. Thank you once again. I think I'll read while I eat it and then sleep if you think that's for the best. But please,' he knew he had to keep some of his urgency. 'Tell Beauty I love her and am thinking of her.'

'I will.' The first minister's eyes twinkled and he bowed before he backed away. 'Remember to stay in these rooms. We like to keep the castle peaceful for the queen while she's unwell.'

'Thank you,' the prince said, and sat at the table, picking up his knife and fork and cutting a piece of the succulent chicken. The first minister paused in the doorway and watched as the prince put the food into his mouth and then quietly closed the door behind him.

As soon as he was gone, the prince spat the meat out and ran to the water jug to rinse his mouth out.

He picked up the plate and wine glass and went to the window. Outside it was dark as night and the storm was raging. As soon as he lifted the catch the glass flew back, propelled by the wind that sent the curtains billowing up around him as if they were suddenly enchanted. He flinched against the torrential icy rain that blasted into his face, and tipped away the food and wine. It fell into the gloomy grey street below as more streaks of blue cracked the sky and stabbed at the city. He pulled the window shut and put the empty plate and goblet back, before closing the curtains and turning out all but one lamp.

There were several old books on a shelf in the corner and he took one and opened it somewhere near the beginning and then lay on the bed, placing the book at an angle across his chest as if he had dropped it there. He closed his eyes. Now all he had to do was wait.

His heart thumped in his chest as the minutes ticked by and the fire in the grate slowly burned down. After a while he thought he might have drifted to the edge of sleep, but was woken by the sound of carriages arriving below. He opened his eyes and where daylight should have been creeping through the gaps in the curtains, instead there was a strange darkness, as if the raging storm had created an artificial night. There was something unnatural about it, and he shivered. Shrieks of laughter carried on the wind as carriage doors closed and people ran inside and away from the rain. The prince was suddenly alert again. Who were these people and why were they arriving? There had been a formal ball the night before and if the queen was ill, and the first minister insistent on peace and quiet, surely none would disobey him? So what was really going on? Did he take advantage of the queen's fits to stage entertainments of his own? Maybe that was it.

He was just about losing patience with lying still when he heard the quiet click of the door opening. He forced his body to relax and dropped his mouth open slightly, taking long, deep breaths. Feet padded softly across the carpet. The prince's eyelids twitched, but he remained motionless. After a moment the feet moved away, and the door clicked shut.

The room once again in silence, the prince kept his eyes shut for several seconds longer, afraid that perhaps it was a trick and the minister was still watching him, but eventually he opened them and let out a sigh of relief that he was once again alone.

Back at the window he looked out at the storm. In the courtyard below sat several carriages made of gold and silver and sparkling with jewels. Noblemen's carriages, he was certain of it. Perhaps the first minister was trying to claim the throne for himself and had called some kind of meeting while Beauty was ill? The question was, what could he do about it? What did he really know about this kingdom?

He turned away and glanced at himself in the mirror. He was tall, and blond and handsome; everything a prince should be. Princes should also be brave and honourable. Princes, he reminded himself, did not sit back politely if they thought the security of the one they loved was threatened. And if there was one thing which was beyond doubt, it was that he loved Beauty with every inch of his body. Being apart from her was a physical ache that he almost couldn't bear. He pulled back his broad shoulders. If nothing else, he was going to explore and see what was going on, and he would talk to her about it when she was better. It wasn't as if the first minister could do anything to him. He was betrothed to their queen. Soon he would be their king and he would not be manipulated by old men, even if his sweet-natured beloved was.

He waited another thirty minutes before creeping out into the silent hallway. He stayed close to the walls and followed the wide corridor until he reached the central staircase. He paused and strained his ears to hear. At first there was nothing, but then he was sure he caught the faintest tinkling of music. Two kitchen hands crossed the central atrium below, their heads huddled together and whispering, and then they disappeared from sight. In their wake, the air carried the hint of roasted meat. They'd delivered food somewhere, but where?

When he was certain there was no one else about, he went quickly down the stairs and headed towards the main ballroom where he and Beauty had danced before. He opened the door a fraction but the space beyond was quiet and empty. He stepped inside. The music was definitely louder here. He jogged across the vast space, his footsteps echoing eerily around him.

The second ballroom was empty too, and he frowned for a moment, before the thought struck him. There was the third ballroom. The locked-up room beyond the library that Beauty had known nothing about. Was that where the first minister was entertaining his guests?

He'd passed through the library and reached the door to the small corridor. He opened it a fraction and slid his hand up to keep the bellwire steady before squeezing the rest of his body in. He was in the right place. The music, slightly discordant and darker than any of the jolly tunes that he and Beauty had danced to, was much louder, and above the notes he heard the occasional laugh.

With sweaty palms and a racing heart, he crept forward and lowered his eye to the keyhole but couldn't get a clear view of what was happening inside. The chandeliers were giving off a muted light rather than glittering brightness, and he saw flashes of the red walls and movement of clothes and bodies. From the other side of the thick wood, a woman laughed, a tinkling sound like breaking ice.

His curiosity overwhelmed his fear, and he carefully twisted the handle and quietly pulled the heavy door open an inch to see inside. As his eyes widened, so did the door. All sensible thought tumbled from his mind, and he stared, for a moment completely astonished, at the tableaux that faced him.

The room was smaller than the other ballrooms and with the heavy red and gold decoration and the thick black drapes that covered the windows it seemed to shrink further. A fire blazed in the vast ornamental grate and large candles flickered in sconces decorated with gargoyles that cast strange shadows across the floor. Along one side was a table laden with food; roasted chickens and hares, piles of fruit, and all manner of exotic dishes, but instead of using plates and knives the food had been torn apart by hand and gnawed bones littered the floor around it. Silver jugs of wine were scattered everywhere and the thick rug that covered most of the central area was splashed with red where glasses had been carelessly knocked over. Even without the people, it was a decadent sight. With them, the scene was one of flagrantly wild abandon. Men and women in beautiful expensive gowns laughed and talked in groups, some dancing together, some eating or drinking, but all with a lack of formality unlike any royal ball he'd ever attended. All the guests wore elegant masks across their eyes; some black, some ornate bird feathers, some with beaks and all fitting closely to their young features. None were over thirty, he was sure of that, and whereas they were all handsome and beautiful people, the dark shadows they cut in the candlelight across the floor and on the red walls were strange and gothic, the women flirtatiously and confidently moving among the men; no standing on ceremony or waiting to be approached.

There was more though, and from his place in the doorway the prince felt both aroused and revolted as his eyes moved to the others who were lost in their actions, oblivious to the party around them.

On the low stage angled from a corner, three men

dressed in black screeched out the strange fiddle music. Two women danced in front of them; but this was no courtly waltz. They swayed slightly, their slim hips gyrating against each other's as they kissed, their eyes half-closed and lost in the pleasures of their soft mouths. The taller of the two, a brunette whose hair had fallen free and hung down her back, ran one hand down her partner's body stroking the bodice of her dress, freeing her breast and teasing the nipple between her fingers before lowering her head and flicking her tongue across it. The other girl tipped her head back and gasped.

A little further away, a full-figured woman was bent over a chaise-longue by the wall. The skirt of her ballgown had been pushed up over her hips and the pale skin of her thighs was visible above the tops of her stockings. She moaned as a man behind her gripped her buttocks and thrust into her, panting loudly with each of his movements and lifting herself up to meet him. After a moment another man, a gold mask across his face, joined them and slid his hard cock into her mouth as he leant backwards and drained his wine. The woman sucked greedily, matching her movements with those of the man behind her.

On the thick fur rug two women straddled a naked

man and faced each other, one spreading her thighs across his face, the other his pelvis, and as they ground themselves into him for their pleasure, they leaned forward and kissed between their moans.

Other pairings and groups were dotted here and there, all in some stage of undress as they pleasured each other with wanton abandon. As well as their lust, they were feeling love for each other, these people hidden behind their masks. It was strange and unnatural, but despite his revulsion the prince was throbbing.

One woman was alone in midst of the party, and she moved among the people smiling, pausing to laugh with those still dressed, and trailing one hand gently across the skin of the naked as she passed and when she did so the whole group would shudder with pleasure. She wore a dress so sheer the firm curves of her body were clearly visible beneath it, but none of the revellers made her part of their depravity.

When her tour was complete she stood in the centre of the room and turned slowly, her arms outstretched, sparks of gold flying from the tips of her fingers. The air instantly grew heavier and a wave of something warm and sweet hit the prince where he stood. His head spun as if he'd drunk too much wine too quickly. Suddenly he wanted to be in the room, to be part of this madness that was taking place before him. Unable to stop himself, he pushed the door further open, and the woman at the centre of it all looked up. She smiled.

The prince's heart stopped. How hadn't he recognised her before? It was Beauty. *His* Beauty. Except for her hair – her hair was the wrong colour. What was this? How could his sweet fiancée be part of this? Was it really her? Was it a different girl? The last sober shred of his mind knew he should turn and run, but the strange intoxication that tingled in his blood refused to let him move. He remembered her in the corridor behind him. Her confusion. Her trembling. *Her hair had been changing colour.*

She walked towards him, lithe and supple, her movements like a cat, and her eyes sparkled. His eyes drank in the outline of her breasts, the dark circles of her nipples visible through the sheer cream fabric that floated around her as she moved.

'My darling,' she purred as she reached him. 'I knew you'd find me.' She took his hand and his arm shuddered with sharp sparks of something between pain and pleasure. As he crossed the threshold she closed the door behind him and any resistance he might have had was gone. The air was heavy and filled with a musky scent of sex and magic and he longed to tear himself free of his clothes and tumble to the floor with Beauty, not caring who might see their act of love. He pulled her towards him and kissed her. The surge of passion he felt was greater than any that had come before. What was this? Was she enchanting him? She pressed her body confidently against his, teasing him, and then drew back, wriggling free of his grasp.

'Not until our wedding night.' Her voice was slightly deeper than normal, and although he was sure that this was his Beauty, she was, at the same time, a completely different woman. 'Not for me.' She ran her fingers down his shirt, teasing some of the buttons free as she went. 'I have different lusts to fulfil tonight.'

'What is this?' he whispered, as she led him over to the two dancing women who were now writhing with each other on the floor. 'What are you doing?' Warm hands reached up and tugged him down. He didn't resist. The women made space for him between them and, as Beauty smiled at him, they slid their fingers and tongues under his clothes and his head whirled and he gasped.

'Sometimes,' Beauty said softly, sipping from her silver goblet, 'everyone needs to let the beast inside them out for a while.' She laughed, a sound like a waterfall meeting the sea and more glitter escaped from her fingertips. 'I like to see it. We all have our dark lusts. We should enjoy them.' Somewhere inside him a voice screamed witchcraft and then he was lost in sensation as his hands found firm breasts, and a soft mouth touched his as another explored a far more intimate part of him. And for a while, even his love for Beauty was forgotten.

Time meant nothing as the groups of bodies moved and merged and created new formations, but by the time the first minister brought the serving girl into the room, the prince was covered in sweat and his body ached from both desire and the desire to be free of it. The world was a bleary haze and he felt as if perhaps he was in a dream.

The minister walked, his back stiff, without looking at any of the decadence that surrounded him, until he reached Beauty, who was sitting on a throne from which she could survey all around her. She clapped her hands together in delight as she saw the blindfolded girl he'd led inside.

'A special night!' she cried. 'I shall drink!' From his place on the floor, the prince watched as she leapt to her feet and embraced the man before her. He flinched. 'Her name is Nell,' he said. 'She was talking to the huntsman.'

'Why do you tell me the names?' Beauty frowned, cross. 'I don't care for the names. My guests have had their pleasure and now I shall have mine!'

The first minister nodded. His face was tight, as if he dare not show any emotion he might have. 'I shall wait outside,' he said. 'Your guest's carriages are prepared. I suggest you dismiss them before ...'

'Yes, yes,' she snapped, and the first minister took his leave. She clapped her hands together again, louder this time, gathering the attention of the revellers.

'Ladies and gentlemen,' she said, addressing them as if this were any normal ball. 'It has been wonderful to see you all again. A *pleasure*.' The guests laughed at that as they re-clothed themselves where necessary, and smiled while seeking out their original partners and preparing to leave. 'We shall have another such evening soon. But for now it's time for you to return home and continue your delights at your leisure.'

The room cleared relatively quickly, as if they were used to the parties ending abruptly, and while many came to say their goodbyes to Beauty and thank her for her hospitality, none paid any attention to the blindfolded girl who was swaying slightly in the middle of the room. Beauty held the prince back with her and when the musicians scurried out, the doors clicked shut and the three of them were alone.

'And now for my pleasure,' Beauty said, smiling at him, her eyes dancing with excitement. Her face was flushed and the prince thought, in that moment, he'd never seen her so aptly named.

She circled the girl, an earthy-looking buxom wench, one hand trailing around her waist and the servant gasped but didn't speak. Was she drugged? What did Beauty want with her? The expression on the first minister's face when he'd brought her in flashed before the prince's mind's eye. He'd looked like a tortured man.

'Pretty Nell,' Beauty said softly. 'They're always so pretty.' She reached down to the silver jug on the table and refilled her goblet and then poured a second for the prince. The red wine looked thick and dark and he stared into it as she drank hers.

'Drink,' she said. Her eyes had hardened and the prince suddenly felt unsettled. He lifted the cup and sipped. The taste was metallic and the substance too thick to swallow easily without gagging, as if his body recognised it before his brain had time to.

'Is this ... blood?' he asked, as the awful truth dawned on him.

She smiled at him and he could see where the

crimson liquid clung to her teeth. 'This is cold, but soon we'll have warm. Fresh and warm and so full of life.' She clung to him and pulled him close and kissed him, seeking him out with her tongue. The prince's stomach churned. *Blood*. His princess, his Beauty, was drinking blood. *He'd* drunk blood.

Beauty broke away, breathless, and laughed, tipping her head back and then pouring the glass of blood over her, coating herself in it, the sheer material of her dress clinging to her every curve with the weight of the liquid. She dropped the empty goblet and the sound of the metal hitting the ground echoed loudly in the empty room and the serving girl – Nell, the prince reminded himself; she had a name – flinched.

Beauty stroked her face and hushed her, kissing her cheek and leaving bloody marks on her pale skin. She looked at the prince. 'Are you ready?' she whispered, and pulled something from a hidey hole in the side of her throne. The prince nodded, despite his need to run far from this place and vomit. He shivered as she nodded at him to drink more from his cup. Cursing his own weakness, he did. He thought it couldn't get much worse than this. He thought she would want him to have blood-drenched sex with the poor girl before him.

It was only when he saw the knife in Beauty's hand and she folded his own over it and they both held the cold blade to the girl's warm neck, that he realise it was all going to get much, much worse before it got better.

Too late he remembered what the first minister had said before sending him to his room.

The Beast is coming.

The prince's mind had cracked a little by the time it was done and the first minister was leaning over him, his eyes wide with anger and hissing, 'I told you to stay in your room! I tried to ensure you would, you stupid, stupid boy.' The prince cried after that, rocking backwards and forwards as the old man put his arm awkwardly round him and tried to pull him to his feet. His feet slipped under him on the blood and he fell back down.

He couldn't get rid of the taste. He didn't think he'd ever be able to get rid of the taste, or of the images that were burned into his mind. The things the Beast had done to the poor, dead girl.

'Why?' he whispered. 'Why would she do that?'

Beauty and the knife. Watching as she ... as *they*

... and then her terrible dancing in the warm blood, smearing it over herself and him, filling wine glasses with it. Forcing him to drink. Being too weak and afraid to stop her doing any of the terrible things she did.

He groaned and, trying to preserve his sanity, he curled up in a small ball in the corner of his mind. He needed to forget. He *had* to forget.

'Get up,' the first minister hissed again. 'Get back to your room. The bell will ring soon and then the castle will be busy again. You can't be seen like this.'

'The bell?' the prince croaked.

'The Beast will leave now.' The minister forced him to his feet. 'The blood precipitates the change. Our queen will return to herself and she can't see you like this.' He glanced at the blood-soaked woman who was starting to tremble. 'She can't see herself like this. Now go. Burn your clothes. Wash and sleep. Forget this ever happened.'

The prince didn't know whether to laugh or cry at the ridiculousness of the suggestion that this could ever be forgotten. That he could ever be normal again. As if he'd heard the prince's thoughts spoken aloud, the first minister gripped his wrist tightly, his thin fingers digging into his skin. 'You will forget it.

Or change it in your mind. It's all you can do.' He glared at the prince. 'Now go.'

This time the broken prince did not hesitate.

'A deal like that is worse than a witch's curse...'

It was early evening when the skies cleared and the bell rang out again over the city. The group hidden in the hideaway beneath the tree had slept for a while and then eaten. Petra and Toby escaped to the surface to walk in the fresh air, leaving the huntsman and Rumplestiltskin to talk.

After the fierceness of the storm damp lingered on every surface and the trees glistened green as water dripped from their branches, but although there was a light breeze it was not cold.

'Do you think Rumplestiltskin's story of his daughter and the witch is true?' Petra asked as they walked. 'Or in his fragile state of mind did he just make it up?'

'It's the story he's always told,' Toby slid his arm

around her waist as if it was the most natural thing in the world, and Petra believed that it might be. 'I think it's true. Why do you ask?'

'Oh, no reason. No reason that matters right now, anyway. Will you change again tonight?' Petra asked, as Toby glanced up at the sinking sun.

'Yes,' he said. 'There's two more nights of the full moon.' He smiled at her. 'But I've got an hour or so before it'll come on me.'

The city sparkled ahead of them, clean and bright, and Petra stared at it, still fascinated by a sight so different from any she'd experienced before. 'It's very beautiful,' she said quietly. 'But it must have been so very lonely for you with only Rumplestiltskin for company.'

'Yes, it was lonely,' Toby said. 'But it was good to be free. To not have to hide for several days a month and to not have to lie to people. They would have killed me, I'm sure of it, had the curse not come.'

'I don't understand how anyone who heard your howl could hunt you. I found it beautiful.' Petra blushed slightly.

'I'll never forget the first time I heard you howl back to me. It was like seeing a light in the darkness.' Toby said. 'When you called to me from the castle, I knew I had to find you. And I knew when I saw the soldier with his knife at your throat that I had to save you.' He stopped walking and looked at her. 'I'd happily die to save you.'

She smiled at him, warmth rushing through her body. The howl beyond the forest wall had drawn her to it, and this was why. Toby leaned forward and kissed her and for a moment after his lips left hers she was breathless with the rightness of it all.

'I thought the prince was a fool with his love for Beauty,' she whispered. 'Do you think this is what he feels?' She slid her arms around Toby's waist and rested her head on his chest as he held her. His laughter vibrated through his shirt.

'No, you can't blame the prince for his stupidity. He kissed her and that was his downfall. The water witches are famous for their allure. Their sisters, who live in the Eastern Seas, are called Sirens. They lure men to their deaths on the rocks because the sailors can't resist getting closer to them. Your prince may be a fool in many ways – I can't judge him on that – but where our queen is involved, it is hard to not love her. Her blood dictates that we do.'

He kissed her forehead and she liked the feel of his stubble against her skin. 'This, however,' he said. 'This is a different kind of magic altogether.'

She didn't need to ask what he meant. She felt it

inside her. They were made for each other and were destined to be together. Was that why the wolves had come to her grandmother's house so often? Had her longing for him been what had drawn them?

'You should go back,' Toby said softly. 'I can feel it coming and I would rather change alone.'

In his last sentence she could feel the weight of shame he felt about his curse, the loneliness and dread it brought with it, and as she headed back to the oak tree she vowed that, whatever it took, she would break *that* part of the curse – he would never be lonely again.

He joined them ten minutes later, padded over to Petra, curled up beside her on the floor and rested his heavy head in her lap, one ear cocked as the huntsman and Rumplestiltskin continued to talk.

'I won't do it again,' the old man said. 'Everyone I love is dead. My child is dead. Let the city live with the Beast until we're all dead and rotting behind the forest wall.'

'I don't care about your curses or your Beast,' the huntsman countered. 'My responsibility is towards the prince. We cut our way in through the forest, and we can get out again the same way. We don't belong here, it will let us pass. But I need to get to the castle and force him to come with me, and do it without the first minister seeing me. Once we've gone you can do what you like. Hide and die in here, or destroy the spindle and free the city.'

'I will never release them while she lives.'

'Then you should do what you promised your friend the king you would do,' Petra said softly. 'Prick her finger again.'

'And wait another hundred years alone?' Rumplestiltskin's voice trembled with horror at the thought. 'A hundred years, only for someone like you to come along and ruin it again?' He shook his head. 'I could not. I could not. No good comes from curses.'

Petra stroked the wolf's head and thought that Toby should have been dead for decades before she was born. 'Sometimes it can,' she said.

'Just tell me how I can get to the prince without being seen,' the huntsman said. 'I have no loyalty to your first minister and I have no desire to see you dead. But I do have to see the prince and if you can't give me another way in then I'll have no choice but to walk through the castle doors, and then he'll want to know whether I found you. If what you say about the dungeons is true then I will have no choice but to tell him.'

'This isn't my only hiding place,' Rumplestiltskin said roughly, but the huntsman's words had clearly caused him alarm. 'But I will give you a way in. Our tunnels go everywhere.' His untrusting eyes flashed darkly. 'But I will go with you, to be sure you don't betray me. And I will not bring the spindle.'

The network of tunnels that Rumplestiltskin had built was extraordinary, and even with his natural sense of direction and eye for remembering details of a path, the huntsman knew that he would never find his way back without the old man. They'd left Petra sleeping and the wolf had slunk out, no doubt to feed on nearby chickens or other domestic animals. He pitied the cursed man, wondering how terrible a thing it must be to spend part of your life trapped in an animal's body with all the cravings that came with it. He made a quiet vow to himself never to cross a witch if he could avoid it.

They eventually came up into the dark castle through a fireplace in what appeared to be an empty set of apartments. Rumplestiltskin lowered the hatch back down and stretched as he straightened up.

'How did you know it would be empty?' the huntsman asked, his hand on the hilt of his knife.

'These are my apartments. I doubt anyone is keen

to take a traitor's rooms just yet.' It was the dead of night and the castle, the tension eased now that the Beast had left them for a while, slept soundly. They crept through it undisturbed. Under the prince's door, however, a strip of light shone out.

He almost shrieked when he saw them, leaping from his bed and grabbing at an ornament to use it as a weapon. The huntsman rushed over to quieten him as Rumplestiltskin secured the door.

'What did we do?' the prince said, trembling. 'We should never have woken her. We should never have touched her.' He gripped the huntsman's arm. 'I can't get rid of the *taste* of it.'

'You've met the Beast then,' Rumplestiltskin said and the prince shuddered again.

'We need to put everything back as it was,' he said quietly. 'We need to put them all back to sleep.'

'Forget about that,' the huntsman said. 'That's not our business. We need to escape. Cut through the forest as we did before and return to your father.'

'I can't forget it. You didn't see. You didn't see what she did to that serving girl.' The prince frowned slightly and his pale face turned to the huntsman. 'I'll never be able to forget. Not while she's awake.' He paused in his mutterings. 'You *knew* her. That's what he said. He brought her because she'd been

169

talking to you. And then she ... and then she ...'

'Nell?' the huntsman's blood cooled. 'What did she do to Nell?'

The prince's mouth opened as he worked to force out some words, and then he simply burst into tears.

'Blood,' Rumplestiltskin said, quietly. 'She'd have taken her blood. The Beast has a blood lust and the orphaned servants feed it. When the lust is satisfied, the Beast often leaves. It's a price the kingdom must pay.'

'Beauty killed her?' The huntsman was stunned. Even after hearing Rumplestiltskin's tale he found it hard to equate the pretty, kind queen with cruelty. And Nell? She killed Nell?

'She danced in her blood,' the prince moaned. 'She made me ... she made me drink it with her. I couldn't stop her. I couldn't ...' He looked from one man to the other. 'I was too scared. Can't you see? Can't you understand? I couldn't do anything.' He stared into space. 'She was so beautiful when she was sleeping. How could we have known?'

The horror of his words hung in the air.

'And you want to let her live?' the huntsman rounded on Rumplestiltskin as he thought of poor Nell. The feel of her soft skin and the sound of her easy warm laugh were fresh to him. She had been a sweet girl who'd done nothing wrong and he loathed himself for falling prey to his nature and taking his pleasure with her – especially when he had inadvertently drawn her towards her death. His anger raged. 'Then you let her live. But give me the spindle. You go with the others and cut through the forest. I'll stay behind and curse her again.' He gritted his teeth knowing what he was subjecting himself to. A hundred long years alone. But if it wasn't for him Nell would still be alive. If they hadn't woken Beauty then she would have been sleeping peacefully, her whole life waiting for her when the Beast was dead. He would do it. He had to do it.

'No,' Rumplestiltskin said. 'Why should I? No one cares that my daughter spent her life trapped in that witch's tower. No one cares that I will never look on her face again. So what do I care of the fate of the city?'

'What if you could have another child?' the prince blurted out. There was a mania in his eyes and the huntsman knew that if Beauty wasn't returned to her long dying sleep then the prince would never feel free of her. His terror would drive him mad; if it hadn't a little already. The young man had endured far more adventure than he'd bargained for.

'My wife is dead,' Rumplestiltskin spat bitterly. 'I will not take another.'

'I will give you my child. My first born.' He grabbed the man's arm, his whole body trembling.

'What?' The huntsman turned, his anger over Nell's death sideswiped by shock. 'You can't make a deal like that!'

'I can.' The prince didn't take his eyes from Rumplestiltskin. 'My first child. I promise you. You shall have the first child from my marriage bed to raise as your own.'

'A child?' Rumplestiltskin sat on the edge of the bed and stared at the fireplace. 'A child to raise as my own. Away from court. Away from the games of others. A child to love and never leave.'

'Yes!' the prince nodded, enthusiastically. 'Yes! You have my word.'

'Don't do this,' the huntsman growled. 'This kind of deal is worse than a witch's curse.'

'I have your word?' Rumplestiltskin reached out his hand to the fevered prince.

'You do.'

The two men shook and the deal was done. Watching them, aghast, the huntsman wondered how much madness could be held in one kingdom. Suddenly a hundred years alone did not seem too terrible a fate to be waiting for him.

'Let's go,' the prince said. 'The huntsman can come

back with the spindle while we're cutting through the forest. We could be gone by morning.'

'No,' the huntsman gritted his teeth and tried his best to ignore the prince's indifference to his sacrifice of a hundred years. 'The castle will be waking soon and there won't be enough time. If you're not here then the first minister will know we're escaping and the forest wall will have soldiers along every inch. You have to stay here and act normally. Plan the wedding. Lull them into thinking all is well. Tell them you want another party to celebrate your bride. Make sure all the ministers – and Beauty – drink heavily. Tell her she must sleep well before the wedding and make sure she's in bed by midnight. We will meet you back here and you will leave. I'll give you four hours from then. If you haven't cut through the forest wall, then you will be trapped in slumber with the rest of the city until she is dead.'

'But I can't!' The prince looked horrified. 'How can I pretend everything is fine? With her? How? Surely the ministers will be suspicious?'

'The mind is capable of many things,' Rumplestiltskin said, 'when exposed to true horror. It will protect itself. You should put the day's events down to a dream. A nightmare. They will think you have chosen to forget.'

'I don't know—'

'You have to,' the huntsman snapped. He was tired of the prince's weakness. He was tired of these royals who wrecked ordinary people's lives. 'It's the only way.'

Finally, the prince nodded and straightened up. 'I'll do it.'

He made it sound like a noble sacrifice in the way that only a prince could when surrounded by the sacrifices of others on his behalf.

'Good,' the huntsman said, and nodded to Rumplestiltskin. 'Let's go.'

'I will hold you to your promise, young prince,' the old man said. 'First, I will go to the witch, and then I will come to you. Do not forget me.'

'You have my word,' the prince repeated.

When Petra woke, a small streak of light was cutting through the earthy ceiling. Rumplestiltskin was asleep in the chair and the huntsman had made a place for himself on the floor. There was no sign of the prince. Of Toby. Not wanting to wake them, she crept quietly along the narrow tunnel and up the ladder into the fresh air.

Toby was sitting under a tree in the morning

sunshine and he smiled at her. 'They still asleep?'

'Like babies.'

'What a beautiful day.' She sat beside him, the grass dry even though it was only just past dawn. 'Warm too.' He was staring out at the slowly-waking city and Petra thought she'd never seen anyone more handsome in her whole life, and nor was she likely to. She reached up and turned his face to hers and slowly kissed him. Despite the stubble on his face his lips were soft as they met hers, his tongue and hers entwining until the heat inside her was too much and she fell backwards, pulling him with her. She slid her hands under his shirt and felt him quiver as she traced her fingers over his flat stomach, teasing the line of hair that ran down from his chest to beyond his belly button.

He groaned and wrapped one hand firmly in her hair as her own moved lower, her breath coming harder as he pushed up her dress. She reached for him through his trousers and he paused and gripped her wrist. His face was flushed and the yellow flecks in his green eyes had brightened with his lust.

'Are you sure?'

She answered by smiling and wrapping her legs around his hips, pulling him towards her.

'I'll take that as a yes,' he managed, before their

passion overwhelmed them and any words were lost in mouths and hands and movement and love.

When they were done, they lay together and looked at the sky and laughed and smiled in the way new lovers do, and then kissed some more. Soldiers could have stood over them and Petra wouldn't have noticed. This was true love. She'd realised it the first time she'd seen him, and her heart had known it the first time she'd heard his distant howl through the forest wall. He was for her, and she was for him. Petra and Toby. Petra and the wolf.

'Are you hungry?' he said eventually, gently pushing loose strands of hair out of her face. 'There's a bakery just down there. We could get some bread.'

'What about the first minister's men?' she asked.

'They're not looking for us, they're looking for Rumplestiltskin.' He grinned and got up before pulling her to her feet. 'And if he's not carrying a spindle I doubt very much they'd recognise him. Soldiers, as a rule, aren't the brightest boys. Not in this kingdom at any rate.'

'Then let's get some bread.' She linked her arm through his and they strolled down the path in the sunshine as if they had no cares in the world.

As soon as the waft of baking hit the light breeze, Petra realised just how hungry she was, and they joined the small crowd of early risers waiting for their turn at the baker's hatch. She was lost in her own thoughts of love and laughter, leaning her body into him, needing as much contact as possible, until she felt Toby's grip tighten slightly on her arm, and then the words of those around them became more than just background hubbub and her appetite vanished.

'I just saw the blacksmith's wife. It came into their house through the back door last night. The blacksmith came down to catch it ripping a haunch of venison they'd been saving apart. He said he'd never seen such a beast. Its eyes glowed, that's what the blacksmith said.'

'It's not natural, everyone knows that. All that blue fur. And twice the size of a normal wolf.'

'Should be hunted down. Maybe then the forest will open up.'

'Maybe the wolf's what's cursed us.'

Toby mumbled at the baker who presented him with four large freshly baked rolls, and then he tugged Petra away.

'We'll go to the queen and she'll send soldiers to find it. Nowhere to hide with the forest closed round us. They'll hack it to death. Before it starts coming for the children.'

She kept her arm in his and kept their pace slow

as they walked back up the path and the voices faded behind them. Their sentiment echoed loudly in the silence though, Toby's jaw stayed tight and all smiles were gone.

'Don't listen to them,' Petra said. 'They're just stupid gossips.'

'I would never attack children,' he said, through gritted teeth.

'I know,' Petra said. 'Forget about them.' It was easier said than done, and she knew it. 'Come on, let's see if the others are awake. Find out where the prince has gone.'

Beautiful as the day was, she couldn't help but feel a wave of relief when they were underground again. Whatever she'd said to try and make him feel better, Toby was right to worry. Petra might know very little about court life, but she understood village gossips. It didn't take much for a few exaggerated words to become blazing torches and pitchforks, and the idea of a mob coming for Toby made her stomach lurch up to her heart and vice versa.

'No,' Toby said, when they'd heard the huntsman's plan. 'You don't have to do that.'

'Yes, I do.' The huntsman glowered up back from beneath his dark hair. 'That girl's dead because I bandaged Beauty's finger and woke her. I have to put it right.'

'It has to be put right, yes. But not by you.'

Most of the bread lay half-eaten on their plates, any hunger forgotten after hearing of what the Beast had done, and of the prince's deal with Rumplestiltskin. Petra felt quite sick. But nothing could prepare her for what came next.

'I'll do it.' Toby said simply. 'You can all go back to the forest and I'll stay.'

'No,' Petra gasped. 'That's stupid. You have to come too.'

'Why?' He looked at her, his eyes flashing bitterly. 'You've heard what they said. Why would it be different anywhere else? Wherever I go, I'll be hunted. At least here I'll be free.'

'You can't!' Tears sprung to Petra's eyes. 'We can't be apart. I won't leave you!'

'You're better off without me,' he said. 'Safer too. When the mob comes, which they eventually will, they won't take kindly to anyone who's protected me.'

'You can't do it anyway,' the huntsman sighed. 'It must happen tonight. You'll be a wolf.'

'Wait until the morning,' Toby said. 'I can do it then.'

Petra stared at him. The idea of living without him – of knowing that he was just the other side of the wall, living on, young and healthy, as she grew old and died with only the sound of his distant howling drifting through the wood to haunt her – was too much to bear. For a moment she couldn't breathe.

'We can't wait until morning,' Rumplestiltskin said. 'It will be too dangerous; the Beast will be too alert. The plan is set for tonight.'

Petra's head spun. She could see Toby's distress. He didn't want to leave her, but neither did he want to spend his life as an outcast. Always lying to people. Always hiding.

'Wait,' she said, suddenly. 'Wait.' As the perfect thought struck her, she smiled. 'The curse doesn't affect the one who wields it?'

Rumplestiltskin nodded.

'Then I'll do it,' she said. 'Toby can guard the room and I'll prick her finger.'

11

'I give you this magic . . .'

The prince was surprised that after the huntsman and Rumplestiltskin had left he did manage to fall asleep for a fitful few hours although he had left all the lamps burning. He met Beauty on the terrace for breakfast and she rose from her chair and dashed towards him, a sweet smile making her face glow.

'I missed you,' she whispered, reaching up on her tiptoes to kiss him. She tasted of the sweet apple she'd been eating, but still his stomach flipped and churned as their lips touched. He focused on the darkness of her hair, so different to the blood-streaked blonde of the Beast who'd tormented him the previous day. He forced the memory away, doing his best to lock it in a far corner of his mind.

'I missed you too,' he answered weakly. 'I barely slept.' The last part wasn't a lie. He wondered if she had realised an entire day was missing from her memory. She took his hand and they sat in the sunshine and she talked merrily about their wedding plans as he forced a pastry and some juice inside him. In the bright daylight, and in the presence of her gentleness, it was almost possible to think that all that had happened had been with someone else completely. The girl was good-natured and lovely. She didn't even sound the same as the other.

'And how are you both this morning?'

The prince turned to see the first minister standing in the shadow of the awning.

'Wonderful, thank you,' Beauty answered, gracing him with an affectionate smile. 'And what a glorious day.'

'Just the man,' the prince said, happy to hear how confident his voice sounded. He may have had a moment of weakness when he failed to defend the servant girl – he knew from the huntsman's expression that he thought him a coward – but he was brave. How could the huntsman know what it had been like in there? Would he have behaved any differently? Probably not. The prince could be brave. And he would play his part well today. 'I wanted to have a private dinner tonight. Just Beauty and all her ministers. I'd like to get to know them better – and for them to get to know me – before we have our wedding.' He smiled at Beauty. 'I don't want them to worry that perhaps she's made a bad choice.'

'What a lovely idea,' Beauty exclaimed. 'But how could they think that?'

The prince stood up and went to kiss her. 'I would like to make sure. I want you to be proud of me.'

She wrapped her arms round his neck and laughed and then he spun her off the ground and kissed her. More passionately this time. It was strange this allure she had. He ached for her beauty even as he was re-volted by the knowledge of the dormant woman who shared her body.

'This shirt is too hot,' he said. 'I need to change. Shall I meet you by the maze?' he asked her. 'We could walk and make our plans together.'

She nodded, her face shining with love, and he turned away. The first minister followed him back into the castle, his face thoughtful.

'How are you feeling this morning, your highness?'

'Oh, I'm fine.' The prince smiled. 'Tired but fine. I had some terrible dreams. I think I might have had a fever. Or too much wine. And that terrible storm raged all night.' He shuddered as memories of blood and the Beast and the knife rose up unwelcome. 'But now the sun is shining and all is well.'

He knew he wasn't looking entirely normal. He could feel himself trembling and there was an entirely surreal quality to the day, as if perhaps this was the dream and all the horrors he'd experienced were the reality that was waiting for him to wake. But perhaps that would help the first minister to believe him.

'Dreams can be strange things,' the first minister said reassuringly. 'I find it best to keep busy and then they fade quickly.'

'Exactly,' the prince flashed him a smile. 'So will you organise the dinner?'

'Certainly,' he said. 'Hopefully your friends will have returned to us by then.'

'My huntsman is thorough,' the prince said, balling his hands into fists to stop them trembling. 'He will return when he has your traitor and not before. Unless your soldiers find him first, of course.'

'Of course,' the first minister agreed.

'And then we can all live happily ever after.'

The prince had never been so happy to close a door behind him. This was going to be a long day.

He did, in part, take the first minister's advice and kept busy. His stomach was in a knot that somehow the huntsman's and Rumplestiltskin's plan would be found out, and then the full wrath of both queen and ministers would land on him. He wasn't afraid of the dungeons, although he was sure that were he dragged there that would change, but he was afraid of anything that might bring the Beast back. As he walked through the maze with Beauty, pretending to be enthused about finding the right path through it and laughing loudly when they found themselves in yet another dead end, he fought back images of the writhing couples and the extraordinary pleasure he'd felt before the horrors of the serving girl's death. How could Beauty have wrought it all?

Finally, they found the centre of the maze, a circular space with a waterfall and a stone bench decorated with woodland creatures, and Beauty pulled him towards her and kissed him again, and despite his inner torment he felt himself responding to her. He remembered the full curves of her firm body under the sheer dress the Beast had worn and he felt a sudden urge to rip her clothes from her and take her rough and fast over the bench.

'I can't wait until our wedding night,' she said, softly, her own eyes glazed with longing. 'When at last we can love each other properly.'

A part of his heart broke then. He couldn't help it. He had thought she was so perfect – and, here in the maze, she *was* so perfect – that he wondered if he was still, after everything, a little in love with her. That thought revolted him and instantly all he could see behind his eyes was blood, and the heat of the sun was the feel of it on his skin, and the rush of the waterfall was the sound of her mad laughter as she revelled in death, but still he wanted her. Was that her magic at work, he wondered? How could he tell? If he ever loved a princess again, he decided as they finally strolled back out and towards the castle, he would make sure she was as beautiful on the inside as out before he kissed her. Whatever spell Beauty held over him would soon be over, he comforted himself with that. And when he was gone from here, he would think of her and the Beast no more.

Dinner finally came around and the prince was the perfect host, ensuring everyone's glasses were constantly full and regaling them with tales of his life back at his father's castle. He took time to question all the ministers about their families and their roles in the queen's cabinet and they in turn, as the wine flowed, told him tales of their city that clearly filled them with pride. In the main, he was surprised to realise, they were good men. How much did they love Beauty that they could cope with the Beast? Or were they simply too afraid of her to act? Once again, he felt proud of his own bravery and vital role in the plan to return them to the safety of their slumber. He sipped his wine, careful not to drink too much, and reflected on the huntsman. It was good that he would stay behind and put her back to sleep; that would ensure that when the prince returned home he could tell the story as he wished, with whatever small adjustments were required. This was his adventure; it would be told his way.

'Goodnight, my love,' the prince said, about to leave a swaying and giggly Beauty at her bedroom door. 'Until tomorrow. Until our wedding day.'

Even though his sane mind was desperate to get away from both her and the castle, his heart ached with the knowledge that if all went well, he would never see her face again.

'I love you so much,' she said, squeezing him tightly. 'Tonight, I will go to sleep the happiest girl in the world knowing that you are to be my husband.

I'll be dreaming of you and our happiness until I wake, of how perfect our life will be together.'

He was glad her face was pressed against his chest, because although the prince could be weak and self-ish and part of his mind and heart had been more damaged than he could yet imagine by his experiences with the Beast, he did not consider himself a cruel man. The knowledge that he was sending her to her death ached inside him in the echo of her happiness. He did care for her – for this sweet girl – how could anyone not? He felt every one of his flaws like knives in his skin, and for a moment she was only Beauty; there was no Beast.

'Dream of us forever,' he whispered. 'And may your dreams be wonderful.'

'Oh, they will be,' she said, squeezing him tighter. 'My sleep will be wonderful because tomorrow we wed.'

When the prince finally walked away, he did not look back. He couldn't bring himself to, and then there was the click of a handle turning and she was gone.

'So, you're not staying?' he said, slightly dismayed, when he heard the new plan. They'd arrived together an hour or so after the prince had returned to his room, the wolf – a part of the story that the prince felt he could wait until later to hear about – guarding the room outside while they fetched him. He'd changed back into the clothes he'd arrived in, his royal cloak freshly cleaned, and bundled towels arranged under his sheets to look like someone was sleeping there. With the arrangements made and his things gathered and ready to go, a little of his confidence had returned.

'It's better this way,' Petra said. 'And he knows the forest and the forest knows him. If anyone has a chance of cutting you out, it's the huntsman.'

'Yes,' the prince said. 'Yes, I suppose it is.' He smiled at the huntsman. 'It will be good to return together.' In many ways, on reflection, it would be. The prince wasn't entirely sure he could find his way through the forest on his own, and he'd had enough adventures for a lifetime. As for how the story was relayed to the king, he doubted the huntsman would care. He was a rough sort, but he wasn't stupid. He'd know not to contradict the prince. 'And I shall make sure you are rewarded for your noble offer anyway,' he finished.

The huntsman simply nodded, but the prince shook the slight away. They were leaving and that was all that mattered.

'Do you want to stand here all night talking about it, or shall we get on?' Petra asked. The huntsman grabbed her arm, as she turned towards the door.

'I'm still not happy about this,' he said.

'Well, I am.' She smiled and her elfin face was transformed into something beautiful. 'We'll have a hundred years together, and then after that we'll get to grow old. What other lovers have had that opportunity?'

Rumplestiltskin was carefully pulling the spindle from his knapsack and the girl looked at him with a strange affection as she opened the bedroom door and led them back out into the corridor, the wolf immediately rubbing itself against her leg. She stepped closer to the huntsman so the old man was out of earshot. 'When you get back to the forest, tell him he must go to my grandmother's house and tell her his story. '

'Why?'

'Just make sure he does. It's important. Also, have him tell her to listen for me at the forest wall.' She reached up and kissed the huntsman on the cheek, and then did the same to the prince before taking the spindle from Rumplestiltskin. 'Now go.'

'I give you this magic,' Rumplestiltskin said. 'I hope it brings you better luck than it did me.'

Petra smiled at the old man. 'It will. And we'll make sure it works this time.'

'Good luck.' The prince said, his feet itching to be gone. Every second they loitered was another moment they could be caught.

'Three hours, remember,' Petra said. She smiled once more, and then with her red cloak flowing behind her and the blue wolf leading her, she turned and ran down the corridor towards the queen's apartments.

12
'See to the queen!'

The forest wall was battling them every inch of the way as the three men hacked and squeezed their way through the branches and vines, repeating the method the huntsman, Petra and the prince had used, holding a small space open while they cut through to the next. None spoke as they worked, all three aware that they weren't going fast enough. The forest had been tough before but this time the branches seemed aggressive. Even before they'd travelled the first foot, the prince's shirt had been torn, leaving a small piece of cloth flapping on a thorn behind them.

The enchanted kingdom was still visible through the gaps and they must have been working at it for more than an hour. Even in the dead of night it was hot, sweaty work and they gasped and cursed quietly with every tiny step forward.

'Will we make it?' the prince asked, breathless.

'Maybe,' the huntsman grunted, hacking at a thick branch with his small axe. 'Maybe not. 'If we wake up in a hundred years with trees growing out of our arses, then I'd say we didn't make it.'

'*Hey!*'

Light from a flaming torch swept over them, and a horse whinnied as the patrol came to a halt.

'*Sir, look! There's someone cutting through the wall!*' The light pressed against the branches and for a second the three men froze, but it didn't help. They'd been seen.

'*It's him! Rumplestiltskin! Get after him!*'

'*You! Get back to the castle! Quickly! Tell the ministers!*'

Suddenly, the greenery behind them was being vigorously attacked by swords and a group of soldiers was following them into the wall.

The huntsman beat at the wood faster, painfully aware that there was only three or four feet between them and that the soldiers would be stronger.

'Come on, come on,' the prince muttered, pressing his weight against the resistant hedge so the huntsman could move further.

'I'm doing my best,' the huntsman growled.

'I can see them. The bastards! I can see them!'

There was a flash of steel as the men behind them lunged forwards, thrusting their blades through the gaps.

The prince cried out as the tip of a sword slashed into his side.

The huntsman found he could work quicker after that.

Petra had pulled a chair close to the queen's bed, and with the wolf beside her, occasionally licking her hand, she'd held the spindle on her lap and watched Beauty sleep as the quiet minutes passed. The prince had done his job well and she was dead to the world. The phrase hurt Petra's heart with the truth in it. If everything went according to plan, she'd never wake again.

She couldn't help but feel sorry for her. Despite the Beast who resided inside her she was the sweetest of girls and, water witch magic or not, Petra felt a pull towards her. The terrible things that were her nature were also not her fault. Petra imagined that if Beauty knew the suffering she'd inflicted on her subjects, or what she'd done to her poor father, she would prick her finger herself. Still, lying there so still, she looked perfect.

Petra wondered how many more hours in the decades to come she would sit in this chair and wonder about the girl who would sleep until her last drop of blood had fallen. She ran her fingers through the wolf's rough fur, taking comfort from the heat of his head.

Suddenly, the wolf's ears pricked up and he let out a low growl. All thoughts of the queen's tragic life vanished as Petra sat up straight, her nerves jangling.

'What is it, Toby?' she whispered, but within a second she had her answer. There was movement in the corridors. From outside, the sound of people urgently calling to each other drifted up to them. Despite the urge to get up and look, Petra stayed by the bed, her hand hovering over Beauty's delicate, pale fingers. Her heart raced as the noise in the corridors grew louder, footsteps dashing this way and that, and men barking commands.

Her heart raced, and the wolf's hackles rose, his fur puffing out so much that he truly looked like a magnificent unnatural beast. She needed to give the huntsman and Rumplestiltskin the longest time possible to get away. They did not deserve a hundred years sleep, or to wake to find everyone they loved lost. And her grandmother did not deserve to die without knowing Petra's choice or meeting Rumplestiltskin. She gritted her teeth. She was ready to do it, but not until the very last minute.

As the noise grew around them, Beauty stirred but she did not wake. The wolf was ready to pounce and pin her down should she try and run, but Petra hoped beyond hope it wouldn't come to that. What if the Beast woke when she was terrified? What would happen to them all then?

'The prince is gone!' a voice shouted. 'He's tricked us!'

'See to the queen! Check her majesty is safe!'

Petra was staring so fixedly at the main doors to the queen's bedroom that the secret side entrance, hidden in a panel in the wall next to the wardrobe, slid open and the first minister was inside before she could react. She almost dropped the spindle in surprise and with a growl, the wolf prepared to spring.

For a moment, amidst all the commotion outside, the old man said nothing. He stared at Petra and the spindle and then at the girl in the bed.

'Stay quiet,' he said and then strode to the doors.

Petra's mind was racing and she kept one hand firmly on the wolf who she could feel was ready to spring and rip the minister's throat out to protect her. She still had time to do it. Even if he screamed blue murder into the corridor. There was no need for more bloodshed than necessary but the wolf, although still Toby, thought in more black and white terms than that.

The first minister opened the door a fraction. 'Her majesty is sleeping. She's fine,' he said quietly. 'Now find that prince!'

He closed the door again and leant against it. For a long moment he stared at Petra and she saw the conflict in his face, and then the tired sadness that he carried for his own complicity with the Beast.

'They will come back,' he said quietly. 'And she will wake. The Beast will sense the trouble.' He walked over to the window and stared out at the peaceful kingdom for a moment, before sitting down on the window seat with a heavy sigh.

'If you're going to do it,' he stretched his legs out and leant his head back on the soft cushions, 'then do it now.'

Petra looked out at the sky that was streaking with purple dawn and hoped that she'd given them enough time, and then, with a deep breath, she carefully lifted the girl's slim forefinger and jabbed the sharp spindle into it.

The huntsman and Rumplestiltskin pulled the bleeding prince through the last of the branches just as the air around them trembled and a wave of heat rushed through the tightening branches, filling the air with the scent of a thousand types of bark and leaf and flower. The wall shimmered momentarily and sparkled in the breaking dawn.

The three men stared as they panted, the prince hunched over slightly as his side bled. If they had thought the wall was dense before, it was now completely impenetrable.

'Well, that answers that then,' the huntsman said, nodding at the men who had been so close behind them. The soldiers had fallen instantly asleep and, held up by the branches, vines were now curling up around their limbs. After a few seconds they were no longer visible.

They all stared at the wall as the relief of their freedom sank in, along with the exhaustion in their limbs.

'I want to go home,' the prince said, weakly.

Rumplestiltskin looked around him, scanning the horizon for something familiar.

'What now for you?' the huntsman asked.

'The tower.' There was no hesitation. 'I will have my revenge on that witch, and I will see my daughter's grave.' His freedom from the city and the return of Beauty to her sleeping death had not eased his bitterness. He looked at the pale prince, who was examining his flesh wound with more than a touch of horror. 'And then I shall be back to hold you to your word.'

The prince nodded but said nothing.

'There was something else,' the huntsman added, as he slung his bag back over his shoulder and prepared to move on. 'Something Petra made me promise to tell you. She said it was important. About visiting her grandmother ...'

Dawn claimed the silent city as the first drop of blood hit the floor beside the sleeping Beauty's bed. In the glass by her bed, the rose drooped ever so slightly. Petra gave Beauty one last look and then went out into the corridor to join Toby who smiled at her and her heart sang.

'No more wolf for a month,' he said.

'Shame,' she said, taking his arm. 'He's a good

looking creature. I guess I'll have to make do with you at night until then.' They stepped carefully over the sleeping bodies and their shoes tapped out against the marble, the only feet that would walk these corridors for a long, long time. 'Let's get some breakfast. I'm starving.'

'Do you think they made it?' Toby asked as they turned onto the sweeping staircase.

'I think so,' she answered. 'This adventure deserves a happy ending.' She rested her head on his arm. 'Other than ours.'

'What was all that about your grandmother?' he asked. 'And Rumplestiltskin.'

Her smile stretched wider as she thought of how happy those two would be when they met. 'I couldn't tell him. I don't think he'd have let me stay here if I had. My great-grandmother made me this cloak, you know. Well, she made it for my grandmother. She said it was her favourite colour because it reminded her of her father.'

'I'm not following,' Toby said. 'What's that got to do with Rumplestiltskin?'

'She was a strange woman,' Petra said. 'She arrived in the village out of nowhere when she was twenty-two. When my grandmother was little she told her stories of her childhood, of being trapped in a tower by a witch until one day a handsome prince rescued her.' She paused. 'It clearly didn't work out, but she left my grandmother and then my mother and then me, with a healthy cynicism about Prince Charmings that stuck, even though we never really believed her stories.'

Toby turned and stared at her. 'You think your great-grandmother was Rumplestiltskin's daughter?'

Sunlight burst through the castle windows and Petra knew it was going to be a beautiful day.

'Her name was Rapunzel,' she said. 'So yes, I think she was.'

Epilogue

'You stay here,' the huntsman said, after carefully bandaging the prince's wound and setting a fire. 'We'll make camp for the night and then tomorrow we'll figure out where we are.'

Somehow, and he wondered if it was the forest's wiles at work, they had lost their bearings and even the huntsman thought they might have strayed into a separate kingdom rather than the prince's own. Still, what more could happen to them? They'd have a good rest and then they'd be on their way. The prince's wound would not kill him and a few extra days in the forest would do neither of them any harm.

'Don't be too long,' the prince said, a sorry sight

with his royal cape wrapped round him and his face pale and sweating. 'I don't want to be alone. I keep thinking about her. About Beauty.' The huntsman slapped him gently on his shoulder.

'These woods are rich. There'll be food a plenty and I'll be back soon enough.' He picked up his bag and carried it with him, even though he only needed his knife. He'd earned the diamond shoes, but if the prince found them he would have to give them up, and something raw and animal in his soul told him that he could not let that happen.

He left the prince staring into the fire torn between grief and celebration – Beauty and the Beast – and headed out of the clearing.

It was a warm day in the forest and even though it made the hair on his chest tickle with sweat as he moved through the trees, that pleased the huntsman. Heat slowed animals as much as men and although his skills were such he had no doubt meat would roast over the fire tonight, the task was going to be easier than expected. He could counter the laziness that came with the sun and force himself to be alert. It was unlikely to be the same for the animals in this dense woodland. So far, apart from an old crone scurrying between the trees just before he'd spied the stag, he'd seen little sign of human habitation and he'd heard no horn blowing for a Royal hunt. It was wild here. He liked that ...

THE END

The end ...
or is it just the beginning?

High in her tower the clever witch smiled,
the spindles around her so many beguiled.

How easy it was to riddle with men,
and now Beauty was deep in her death-sleep again.

The princess was cursed, both without and within,
Yet one thing could save her: a love free from sin.

The Kingdoms would change; there would be war
and fear,
And Beauty would sleep for a full hundred years,

What happened then was a mystery, she knew,
But she had great faith in kisses that were true ...

Acknowledgements

First off, I have to thank my editor Gillian Redfearn who started this fairy tale with me, and without whose input they would not be so magical. Secondly – or in fact, on a par, as I'm sure Gillian would agree – I owe a massive debt to Les Edwards whose beautiful illustrations really bring the stories to life and also to those in the cover department at Gollancz who make the books a joy to hold and look at. Also thanks to Jon and Genn for their hard work promoting these, and to my agent Veronique for always being there when I need her.

On a more personal note, thanks to Lou Abercombie and Muriel Gray for their kind words on the books, and to my flatmate Lee Thompson for putting up with boxes of books arriving, paper everywhere and my general writer stresses. And for buying me wine when required.

THE OTHER SIDE OF SILENCE

A Psychiatrist's Memoir
of Depression

Linda Gask

THE OTHER SIDE OF SILENCE

Vie Books is an imprint of Summersdale Publishers Ltd

Summersdale Publishers Ltd
46 West Street
Chichester
West Sussex
PO19 1RP
UK

www.summersdale.com

Printed and bound by CPI Group (UK) Ltd, Croydon, CR0 4YY

ISBN: 978-1-84953-754-4

Substantial discounts on bulk quantities of Summersdale books are available to corporations, professional associations and other organisations. For details contact Nicky Douglas by telephone: +44 (0) 1243 756902, fax: +44 (0) 1243 786300 or email: nicky@summersdale.com.

For John

Acknowledgements

Thanks are due to everyone who has taken care of me over the last four decades through some difficult times. I've not used real names in this book, but would like to say a particular 'thank you' to Sarah Davenport. For help with writing, many thanks are due to Judith Barrington, and her legendary memoir-writing workshops at the Almàserra Vella, and to Ben Evans from Cornerstones, who critically read and commented on two earlier drafts. An earlier version of the chapter 'Taking the Tablets' was originally published in *Open Mind*. Jane Graham Maw at Graham Maw Christie believed there was something here worth saying; Claire Plimmer and Madeleine Stevens at Summersdale brought it to fruition, and John Manton has kept me going – the most difficult task of all.

Contents

'If we had a keen vision and feeling of all ordinary human life, it would be like hearing the grass grow and the squirrel's heart beat, and we should die of that roar which lies on the other side of silence.'

George Eliot, *Middlemarch*

Introduction

This is a story about overcoming depression and also about coming to terms with loss. The two are closely related to each other. I know about this not just from my personal experience, but because I am a psychiatrist. I have specialised in treating those who suffer from the same problems which have afflicted me throughout my adult life. I've survived and come through it, and I know others can too.

There are moments of sadness and even of frank despair described here, but this is not intended to be a depressing tale. My aim is to provide hope to other people who have lived as I have lived. I want them to know that it is always possible to feel better: about yourself, your life and the future. The problem is that when you are caught deep in the jaws of depression, recapturing a sense of hope seems almost unimaginable. Low mood colours the way we see our lives and clouds our judgement, not only about others but most particularly about ourselves. It is hard to think *positively*, as others often insist, when you consider yourself to be completely worthless. What I want to show in this book is that, whether you feel like this or are the one caring for someone who is depressed, there is always a way forwards.

Depression is often triggered by loss, not only of relationships but also of other things which are important to us – our role in life, our health or our self-esteem – and the fact of being depressed can then result in further losses, because we become difficult to live with and unable to play our part in life. Human beings grieve when they experience a loss of something or someone special to them. Grief is normal, and usually resolves over time, but if it doesn't then it can become indistinguishable from depression. Both leave us vulnerable to the impact of further losses.

Very few people know my entire story but my current doctor is familiar with most of it. She is the custodian, at least for the time being. The first time I saw her, about seven years ago, seems as good a place to start this tale as any.

I was in a bleak new consulting room at Wythenshawe Hospital in South Manchester, in the Laureate unit, a modern building where every ward is incongruously named after a writer or poet. Outpatient clinics take place in bare, impersonal offices where doctors camp for one or two 'sessions' every week. There wasn't even a filing cabinet in the room, which I could illicitly try to open and explore. Although it wasn't quite new enough then that I started to get high from inhaling the solvent in the carpet adhesive, I could still detect a faint whiff of Evo-Stik in the air. The only distraction was the previous month's dog-eared hospital newsletter on the corner of the desk. I read about fun runs for breast cancer to distract myself while I waited for my new doctor, who had rushed back to reception to collect my notes from the desk. I felt alone once more and more than a little afraid.

Of course it wasn't my first time in the psychiatrist's chair as a patient. But it was a strange occasion because the person sitting opposite me, whom I shall call Dr V, was a colleague I had known for several years, who had agreed to see me and take over my care. She was polite and business-like, and looked at me in the way I know I look at people sometimes – over her glasses, which I have been told can be intimidating – but I could see that she wasn't entirely at ease with the situation either. She fiddled with her pen while I spoke. And it was almost as though I could read her thoughts, because this process of finding out about the patient's problem was so very familiar to me. My palms were sweating in anticipation and my heart jumped a beat. My tongue seemed inexplicably glued to the roof of my mouth and I had to take a deep breath to reassure my mind that I was still in control of my body. I knew these were physical symptoms of anxiety, but I worried: what would she make of me? How much should I tell her? When you are on the receiving end of a psychiatrist's questions, you find yourself subtly judging how much to give and what to leave out.

'On a scale of one to ten, where ten is as good as you have ever felt, where would you put yourself at the moment?' She paused, waiting for my reply.

'About six or seven.'

This is a very hard question to answer. I tell people not to think about it and instead answer instinctively, but did I really feel like a 'seven' or did I simply want to justify taking up this time, this 'slot' that someone else could have used? I had most of the answers prepared, rehearsed even, in my head, because I knew exactly what was coming.

'I know quite a lot already, from the letter,' she continued, indicating the notes that she had received from my previous consultant. 'But can you tell me more about your past? When did this all begin?'

'When I was a teenager, I used to get very anxious, especially before exams,' I explained, omitting to add that I still had nightmares in which the main fear was not yet having passed my finals.

'There was something about the death of...' she began, rustling through the letter.

'Yes,' I replied. I didn't feel ready to talk about it; I didn't know her well enough yet. I wasn't sure whether I wanted to begin again, getting to know another doctor – or rather, allowing them to get to know me – because allowing that bond of trust to be forged makes it much harder when they disappear.

Unaware of my doubts, Dr V carried on with her questioning: 'You had difficulty getting over it?'

I have often asked the same thing to others. But is a death something you really 'get over'? I wonder how you can ever know the answer but I simply replied 'yes' because that seemed to be the right answer. I also know that it was many years before I really began to grieve, and successive losses, such as the retirement of my doctor, could resurrect the ghosts of the past once more.

'And what treatment are you on at present?'

'I'm taking sixty milligrams a day of duloxetine and two hundred micrograms of thyroxine,' I replied, considering how many different tablets I had tried.

I had to stop a combination of lithium, which is a 'mood stabiliser', and venlafaxine, an antidepressant, because my electrocardiograph was abnormal (I had a 'prolonged QT interval', which increased the risk of my heart just forgetting to beat one day). I wasn't sad to see the end of the lithium, as taking this had resulted in my thyroid gland becoming underactive. And then, as now, if I don't take the thyroxine tablets, I get tired and put on weight, which makes me feel even worse.

'... And I've tried psychotherapy, too; it was helpful, at least some of the time,' I added.

'What type of therapy?'

'Psychodynamic... I've never had CBT.' That was true at the time although I did try it later on.

I've spent a lot of time trying to make sense of why I get depressed and understand why some things can tip me into utter despair in a matter of days. Psychodynamic therapy is about trying to understand the impact that past relationships have on the present. CBT (cognitive behavioural therapy) is different and more concerned with learning how to address unhelpful ways of thinking about the world in the present which can lead you to become depressed in the here and now.

'And when was your last episode?' came the next question.

'A couple of years ago I had to have time off because of problems at work... six months... but I am OK now.'

Wasn't it always work? Or at least this was what I found most stressful. It was never the patients who kept me awake at night but my interactions with the system. My skin was too thin; I was too easily affected by what people said and did around me.

'... But I do seem to get a bit lower in the winter months too.'

We continued talking for about three quarters of an hour and then came to an agreement about what should be done next and when to meet again.

As I got up to leave, Dr V said, 'You don't have to wait out there next time you come; we can find somewhere quieter...' I knew she was trying to spare me the embarrassment of being recognised by colleagues, but this was something I spent hours telling my patients not to be ashamed about.

'That's OK, I'm fine out there.'

I was quite happy to watch daytime television with the sound turned down, along with everyone else in the waiting room.

Perhaps my depression coincided with the start of every academic year and the subsequent increase in my workload. Or maybe there was a more biological explanation linked to the fact that I, like many people with depressed mood, find the absence of light at these latitudes intolerable in the winter months. I didn't know the answer – I still don't. This is who I am. I cope most of the time; I am well for months, sometimes even for more than a year, but there are recurring periods in my life when the world seems a darker, more hostile and unforgiving place. I am a person who gets depressed.

In the last 30 years I have listened to many stories of depression and despair, and learned a great deal from the people who have shared their lives with me. Although their experiences have resonated with my own, I generally haven't revealed my own history of depression. Whenever I haven't been well enough to treat others, I have sought help and worked at achieving my own recovery first. It wouldn't have been ethically correct to try to treat someone when I wasn't well myself. Yet, I believe that my experience of depression has helped me to be a more humane and understanding therapist. Psychiatrists get depressed too, more often than other doctors. Being an expert in depression doesn't confer any immunity from it and I am aware that I don't have all the answers.

What I do know is that when a person is first asked to explain what is wrong, they may find it almost impossible to articulate exactly what the problem is. They may not yet have matched words to the feelings they can sense in the hidden rooms of their mind. They may still have no clear ideas about the 'what', 'why' or 'how' relating to the origins of their difficulties. Instead of words, their angst may be expressed in behaviour which may be hard for them, or anyone else, to make sense of and can manifest itself as irritability, anger or withdrawal. Sometimes they will delay seeking help until they are in a state of crisis. It's not easy to ask; I struggled at first, too.

History is not static but organic and changes over time as it is shared and retold. At any one time I only *really* know how I feel *now*. I sometimes struggle to remember how I felt a year ago, and what my worries were then, or perhaps I actively forget. What follows is an account of what I understand about myself today and what I believe will help others similarly afflicted. I have learned that when I talk with a patient, I should not simply 'find out about the history' of their problems but instead try to listen to their story.

This book was initially meant to be just about me, but in the process it changed from a straightforward memoir to something more: my attempt to make some sense of how depression is experienced. The patients in each chapter are based upon a number of people from whom I have learned a great deal in my career. There is a mixture of original names that have been changed (as some people may not want to be a character in someone else's story) and events that are largely fictionalised but based on truths. I should also add that the alleged events described in Chapter 10 did not take place in that hospital during the time I worked there.

My own personal journey through depression is real, though. Importantly, this is not only my story – it is also about what I have learned from all those who have shared their experiences with me. My aim is to help others in the same situation to have a better understanding of what they are going through and to cope with it more effectively – both essential tools in overcoming depression.

CHAPTER 1

Vulnerability

The easiest way to understand why a person becomes depressed is to think in terms of the concepts of vulnerability and stress. The former determines our personal risk of depression and is affected by family history, the genes we inherit from our parents and early life experiences. The stresses, on the other hand, are the many different life events that we experience along the way. So the more vulnerability factors we have, the more likely it is that when something stressful happens, it will trigger depression. Each of us seems to have a particular threshold level for depression, beyond which, if life throws up enough difficult experiences, we will begin to suffer. Some people seem to be very resilient, while others much less so in the face of similar levels of stress. Moreover, our vulnerability increases as we grow older and if we have long-term physical health problems, such as arthritis or heart disease.

I am in a dimly lit office in a clinic in the centre of Salford, where I sometimes see patients. The watery afternoon sunshine is struggling to penetrate the security grating bolted on to the outside of the window, and the air filtering in from outside is stale and heavy with tobacco smoke from the nicotine addicts' mustering point. A sallow-faced young man called Richard is attempting to tell me about his family history of depression. It isn't easy for him and he is struggling to concentrate on the task. His thinking processes are slowed up – severe depression can do this.

'My mother... Well, she used to go very... odd, strange,' he begins to say.

'What do you mean?'

Richard looks down at his hands before continuing, 'Well, frightened like. She used to stop speaking to us sometimes. She would tell us she could hear... voices... She was in Prestwich a couple of times when I was a kid... I think.'

Prestwich was at one time the asylum for people from this part of the world.

'Anyone else?'

'Well my dad had... a drink problem, and he used to pick on me and my younger brother...'

'Did he hurt you?'

Richard's mouth moves but no sound emerges. A tear rolls down his cheek. He tries to speak again, his voice choking with emotion. Then his words come in a rush, as though they have been expelled from him.

'He used to beat up my mother... I tried to stop him once, and he broke my arm.'

Yes, it had hurt, but not only physically. I can begin to understand why Richard started to suffer from depression as a teenager and why now, in his mid-twenties, his mood is quite severely low. He managed to rise above a difficult start in life and get a good job in an office, only to feel that he had lost everything he had worked hard to achieve because of complications caused by diabetes, which he has had since childhood. His mother had diabetes too. Richard is now beginning to have problems with his eyesight and, given his early life, he is also particularly vulnerable to getting depressed. And although we can *understand* why that *might* happen and how it might feel to develop a serious illness like diabetes, most people really don't get significantly down; they manage to find ways of coping and carrying on. Richard has not.

Doctors sometimes make the mistake of assuming that feeling low is simply *understandable* given the circumstances in someone's life – a case of: 'Well, you'd be down if that had happened to you, wouldn't you? I would!'

They don't recognise that there is sometimes more to it than this: a person might actually be depressed, and depression is not the same as unhappiness. It is a much deeper and more powerful sense of despair which colours how you see the world and interferes with your ability to go on with your life.

My own past reveals the reasons for my particular vulnerability. My maternal grandfather, who was a coal miner in the west of Scotland, died of tuberculosis when my mother was only 17 years old. My grandmother had already died suddenly from a brain haemorrhage, when Mum was 12; they were out together in the street when she collapsed. I cannot begin to imagine what impact this had on Mum and she never talked much about it. I do know that she had a difficult childhood, in a place which is still, like Salford, one of the poorest corners of Britain. This is where an important part of *me* comes from and explains something about the person I am today and perhaps why my mother and I had such different expectations of what our lives would be like. Even though on the surface of things my mother and I have so little in common, I know that the deprivation of the west of Scotland is recorded both in my genes and in the impact that my mother's personality and beliefs had on me during my early childhood years.

My mother moved down to England in the early 1950s to look for work and met my father at the seaside in Skegness where he was working on the Figure Eight, a huge wooden 'switchback' ride built at the turn of the twentieth century.

Some of the most vivid images I carry around in my head of my dad are of him climbing up the steep track of the Figure Eight, repairing the chain which pulled the cars up to the top of the ride. When the cars reached the top, gravity eventually pulled them down but when the chain broke, which it did frequently, everything came to a standstill, which meant no fares. Dad was never afraid to walk the tracks, high up above the beach, checking for problems. Yet I can only remember once going on the Figure Eight with him. My heart pounded as we clanked along in the red wooden car with only a thin metal bar to cling on to, and my sweaty legs stuck to the scratchy leatherette seat. Each time we reached a bend, I was certain we were going to launch off the track into the sky.

'Calm down! Don't cry, we are nearly there!' he had tried to reassure me.

'I can't! It's awful. I just want it to stop.'

'We can't stop. Just try to enjoy it!'

I was crying as we came back down to the entrance. Dad jumped out of the little car and looked like he wanted to pretend we were not together; this tearful girl was not his daughter. Even then I understood something fundamental about my father: although in many ways we were very alike, we were also different. He was at least as physically strong and brave in the face of outward danger as I was anxious and fearful.

My earliest memories of my dad are of his coming into my little bedroom over the front door to help me get to sleep by stroking my head and whispering gently to me, 'Just relax, drift away... go to sleep.'

The feared bogeyman would retreat behind the worn green baize screen by the window, as his huge gnarled hands, the fingernails bitten away to the flesh, caught the tender skin of my temples. They smelled of engine oil from the amusement park and the greasy white Brylcreem he combed through his hair each morning as he stood in front of the bathroom mirror. Mum would always be outside the room somewhere, and from an early age I think I sensed she was unhappy – really quite deeply unhappy at times – but I did not understand why. I wonder now how much the chronic shortage of money, unvoiced disappointment at my father's lack of career success and my brother Alan's mental illness all contributed to the constant and growing sense of unease in our home.

'What's wrong?' I would ask as Alan put his T-shirt on and took it off again several times each morning before school. I was responsible for getting both my brothers out in the morning, as my parents started work at 7.30 a.m. Ian, the youngest and 11 years my junior, was no problem and cheerfully munched on his cereals. Alan, seven years younger than me, was tortured by something to which no one could put a name. 'Go away and leave me alone,' he shouted.

'Tell me,' I pleaded in an effort to understand.

'Too many creases.' His replies would usually be muttered or spat out between tears.

I tried to insist, 'We're going to be late.'

'I don't care! Leave me alone.'

He would rip up his clothes in fits of frustration as he tried to get dressed. Then once more, in the evening, he would stand by his bed in the dark for hours before getting into it, because something was wrong in his execution of the complex bedtime ritual that he was unable to explain in words.

This drove my father to despair. 'Alan, please try to put it on won't you, son?'

'No, I can't.'

'Ray... it's nearly midnight,' my mother would implore as she stood at the bedroom door.

'Leave him. Let him stand there and put the light off,' she pleaded.

I would see his silhouette, poised next to the bed but unable to get in, petrified into immobility. Then the door would bang shut, and all we could hear was quiet weeping. Eventually, my father too would retreat, to his bedroom and his bed, crippled with disappointment and anger. It would be many years before my brother was finally given the diagnosis of obsessive compulsive disorder (OCD).

'Mum said a while ago that she sometimes thought of leaving, running away and going back to Scotland; it was all so awful,' Alan told me during one of our long telephone conversations many years later.

But she didn't. She stayed.

I do wonder whether I would have stayed rather than tried to escape, if I had found myself in the difficult place where she had been.

My father became increasingly affected by what I now recognise to be social phobia, which for him manifested itself as a fear of talking to people in public places so that, for example, my mother had to persuade local shopkeepers to let her bring home shoes and clothes for him to try on. This anxiety extended even as far as going into the library to collect books. Although a little alcohol eased the difficulty, he rarely drank, preferring instead to smoke up to 40 cigarettes a day.

My mother always seemed more confident, at least on the surface. As a young person she had always loved singing and dancing, and would say, only half-jokingly, 'How did I come to marry a man who won't dance?' But she became increasingly anxious too, beset by physical symptoms of tension, such as headaches, acid reflux and stomach pains. As time passed, she began to take tranquillisers – Valium and Ativan – which were willingly provided by the doctor.

A sense of anxiety and unease gradually became the usual emotion in our house. Dad argued with us all at every opportunity and after a particular vicious row with my mother, he went to bed for several days, barely eating anything.

'Just bring us a cup of tea, Linda,' he said, 'then leave me alone.' He turned his head away from me to face the corner of the darkened room.

'Aren't you going to get up?'

'There's nothing worth getting up for, is there?'

Mum and Dad went to family therapy sessions with Alan. Dad hated the way the consultant psychiatrist peered at him and didn't explain anything. 'I honestly don't know what they are trying to achieve,' he said. 'They just make me feel guilty.'

The doctor had asked for me to go along too, but I refused, telling myself that this was nothing to do with me. I was too busy with my schoolwork.

Biological explanations for mental illness were largely unknown then. Parenting was more likely to be blamed than faulty wiring of the brain, whereas the real reason, as I know now, is likely to be a complex combination of nature and nurture, rather than simply one or the other. My brother had, I suspect, inherited a tendency to suffer from anxiety from both my parents. He had a difficult birth, with a few crucially important minutes when his heartbeat could not be detected and which may have caused some minimal hypoxic damage (this is an injury caused by insufficient flow of oxygen) to his brain. Subsequently, the tension that his problems caused between my parents served only to make him more anxious, leading to a vicious cycle of bizarre behaviour, anger, recriminations, and more difficulties with dressing and going to bed.

My brother was not their only child to show signs of mental health problems.

In my early teens I, too, started to experience the physical and emotional symptoms of anxiety which would later become so familiar to me: a fear that something terrible was going to happen, severe headaches, a churning stomach and sweaty palms whenever I was stressed.

I now realise that growing up in such an environment, where getting through the day required the full use of my emotional antennae in order to assess what mood everybody was in at home, prepared me well for empathising with my patients in my everyday work as a psychiatrist. Yet it also resulted in the development of a sometimes crippling oversensitiveness to the actions of others, such that I have learned that I cannot always trust my own instincts in relationships. It also predisposed me to becoming, from my early twenties, quite severely depressed. As well as inheriting the neurotic genes, I also struggled with the fact that my family never really provided a safe, emotionally secure base for me to grow up and learn how to explore the world with confidence. Though my mother had a naturally confident way of approaching life despite her anxieties, I think I inherited more of my father's quiet reserve, and in my early years I was much closer to him. But the quality of my attachment grew increasingly more anxious and fearful throughout my teenage years, and this change contributed further to my own particular (fairly low, it sometimes seems) threshold for coping in the face of what life throws up for me.

So, as I listen to Richard, I can understand why he has been vulnerable to depression. His early life was far more deprived and detrimental to his health, both emotionally and physically, than mine ever was, but in our own way we each carry within us the seeds that could germinate into future problems with our mood, given the right (or perhaps wrong) circumstances.

'I know it's been awful, and the way life seems at the moment you probably think it can never get any better at all...' I offer to Richard.

He looks up but says nothing. I can sense his scepticism, but also his growing desperation.

'But I'd like to see if there are ways we can help you to feel better. I feel sure there are. Would you like us to try to work on it?' We need to approach this collaboratively if the treatment is to be effective. The silence lasts for seconds, but seems much longer. Then Richard makes eye contact with me and there is the merest hint of a nod.

'Yes I would,' he eventually says.

'That's great,' I reply, 'and I guess we need to think about what problems you would like to try to work on. There is quite a lot you've told me about the past, and what happened to you growing up, but there are also some things to do with how you are coping in the present.'

'Do I have to talk about the past?'

'No, we can start with the present to try to help you get going again and managing life better.'

Richard begins to work with one of the psychological therapists, setting simple goals to try to move forwards. This is called 'behavioural activation' and is based on the theory that when we get depressed, we stop doing all sorts of things: those which are pleasurable, those which are routine like getting up and getting dressed, and also important ones like opening bills and paying them. In order to recover, we gradually need to start becoming active again, as our level of activity and involvement in life is closely related to our mood. It isn't a case of waiting to feel better to get on with life, but rather of acting better to feel better. There is good evidence that this really works.

Richard embraces this, and over time his mood begins to improve.

'I've started to check my blood sugar again regularly,' he says during a later appointment. He makes eye contact, and his face cracks open into an uncertain smile. 'I'm feeling much better... but...'

'But?'

'I can't help being afraid. I mean, I am worried that one day I will still end up like my mother. I mean, it's in my genes, isn't it? Madness... It's hereditary.'

I understand what he is saying because I know that fear too, but I can also tell him quite honestly, 'Just because it's in your genes it doesn't mean it cannot be overcome. Lots of people are vulnerable to getting depressed, as you are, but there are things we can do to prevent it and to treat it early if it returns. It doesn't mean you are going to go mad.'

'Really?' He sounds surprised.

'Yes.'

There is a long silence and then he says, 'I don't think I want to talk about the past now. I want to forget it.'

It is his choice and I think it is probably the right one for him, at least for the moment.

People brood about the past when they are depressed but can more easily dismiss those thoughts when they are well. It isn't always necessary to work through past memories in order to feel better in the present. What is more important is being aware that our vulnerability to depression does not mean that we are weak or lesser human beings in any way. This is sometimes difficult to remember but it is crucial to our survival.

CHAPTER 2

Fear

At times of stress I become increasingly fearful and anxious, and when I feel as though I am losing control over my life, despair soon sets in. That sense of being in charge is important to me. Yet I also know that this need to retain control can prevent a person from seeking assistance when they really need it, as accepting help can also be seen as relinquishing power over one's own life, of giving in and losing personal freedom, which can feel very frightening indeed.

Jess was frail and thin but did not understand what people were concerned about. 'Look, there is nothing wrong with me. I'm fine. I don't want to be here. I just want to go home,' she told me. 'My mum will be worried about where I am.'

'I think the ward sister has let her know that you've come in. Your mum is very concerned about you. She wants you to stay here.'

'No, you've got it wrong. I know I told the professor I'd stay but I've changed my mind; I need to be there to look after her, don't you see?'

She rubbed a tear away from her eye with a bony finger. Her hands were beginning to look quite blue, but it wasn't particularly cold. Her nose was turning a dusky shade of purple. She seemed fragile, but her will was still strong and determined.

Jess was one of the patients I saw when I began studying psychiatry as an undergraduate medical student at the University of Edinburgh. She was 17 years old and desperately unwell.

I hadn't always wanted to be a doctor. The idea came to me quite suddenly around the age of 15, when I realised that I didn't want to be a biology teacher, which was the direction in which I thought things were heading. I was, quite simply, good at science, the first member of my family to go to university and, when I wasn't feeling anxious, determined to make the most of the opportunity. The problem was that I did feel anxious about it, quite a lot of the time. Anxiety became my default state of being.

Some consider anxiety and fear to be interchangeable concepts, and the distinction isn't always very clear. I find it easier to think of fear as a negative emotion evoked by a specific stimulus; quite simply, we can identify what it is that's generating the feelings and emotions within us. In contrast, we experience anxiety when our personal safety is threatened in some way and we can't identify a cause. We just feel unpleasant sensations in our body and begin to worry about everyday things without understanding why. What we fear may be something in our lives that we haven't yet acknowledged or something we are brooding about but have still to put a name to.

During most of the five years of my medical training in Edinburgh I had never considered focusing my career on the problems of the mind. My friend Jane was going to be the psychiatrist and I would be the physician, concerned with the diseases of the body.

Jane had become my best friend, although I never really felt I was hers. She was a diminutive, fiercely bright southerner with long, untidy dark blonde hair and a raucous laugh. Dressed in our brown overalls sodden with the formaldehyde used to preserve the cadaver in anatomy, Jane and I had worked on the same 'body' throughout our first year. The oily smell of partially dismembered torsos and limbs, with carefully dissected nerves and blood vessels hanging like loosened latticework, penetrated our clothes and hair, and followed us home at night. We all lived in collective fear of oral examinations from one of the anatomy teachers, an elderly woman with a tight grey bun who indicated the muscles and nerves in a dissection with a pointer fixed into a hook where her hand should have been. She barked questions at a girl a couple of tables away from us.

'What happened to her?' I asked, transfixed by the dexterity with which she manipulated the cadaver with the hooked limb.

'She broke her arm,' Jane whispered to me, 'and the casualty officer made a mess of it. The blood supply was cut off and it had to be amputated.' Jane turned and fixed me closely, adding 'And she likes to make female students cry.'

'Because...' I knew what was coming.

'The casualty officer was a woman.'

The five years of medical training were essentially about learning how to talk with confidence about something you had precious little knowledge of. The problem for me was that confidence was something I had in short supply. I felt out of place in Edinburgh. I didn't share the same background as most of my fellow students, including Jane: my mother worked in a factory, assembling transistor radios, and my father in an amusement park.

'You are not happy,' my friend Stephen announced one evening. Stephen was Irish and *very* bright. The week before, we had spent an evening drinking together and fortunately I had remained sober enough to turn him on to his side into the recovery position after he had consumed half a bottle of Glenmorangie.

'I should thank you because you saved my life,' Stephen mumbled, changing the subject.

'What do you mean "I'm not happy"?' I retorted, changing it back.

'Separation anxiety – that's what I think.' We had just started 'behavioural science'. He looked a little nervous as he raised the possibility and couldn't look me in the eye.

'Why would I feel that?' I enquired.

I didn't know what it meant but it sounded uncomfortably accurate. I was missing something about home but I could not work out what it was. There was nothing I felt I needed to rush back to. Dad and I had become distant and angry with each other during my rebellious teenage years, and I didn't really understand why. I applied to go to university in Edinburgh to get so far away that I could not go home during term time.

'Separation anxiety,' repeated Stephen. 'I know I'm right.'

At the end of my first year, my father had a heart attack. I didn't find out about it until six weeks afterwards. I had spent my first summer vacation in Scotland, working in a hotel in the West Highlands. I called home regularly while I was away and there was never any hint that anything was wrong. On my return to Edinburgh, I called again from the phone box across the street from my friends' flat.

'Your dad's been in hospital,' said my mother in a matter-of-fact voice. 'He had pain in his chest after he had been out swimming. We were all in the car, and he collapsed on to the grass verge when we got home.'

'Why didn't you tell me? I can't believe it.'

'He didn't want to spoil your holiday for you.'

Had we really grown so much apart that he couldn't let me know he was seriously ill?

I remember an evening during my A level exams before university. It had been warm, with a gentle breeze blowing off the sea.

'Pack up your books! Let's go down to the beach,' Dad said.

'Ray, you said you were going to sort out these insurance papers tonight,' countered Mum, but her pleas had been ignored.

'I have to carry on revising,' I tried to refuse. I could not stop thinking about the upcoming examinations and my fear of failing them.

'Ray!' My mother tried once again to change his mind.

'I'll sort them out tomorrow, don't worry. You can't even concentrate,' my dad continued, looking at me. 'We're going to get some relaxation time.'

'Have it your way then,' shouted Mum, as she slammed the back door.

When we arrived at the beach, I luxuriated in the sensation of the warm sand between my toes, pulled off my clothes and waded into the cool water in my swimsuit, watching Dad confidently crawling out to the sandbank that ran parallel with the shore. I couldn't swim – I had never learned. The North Sea was usually grey, but in the evening sun it looked almost blue as the waves ebbed away, leaving frilly lace edges of foam behind on the smooth shoreline. I squatted down in the waves and let the cold saltiness refresh me. Dad swam back and held my hands as I began to float just for a moment. Then, suddenly fearful, I struggled to get my feet back again on to the muddy seabed and the clear water turned cloudy with sand.

'Trust me. I won't let go of you.'

But I couldn't. I couldn't trust him enough to take my feet off the seabed and I sensed his acute disappointment in me.

I finally realised one morning in my last year at Edinburgh that I would never be a successful physician. I was standing next to a bed in the Royal Infirmary, the curtains drawn around it, holding a syringe in the air above a terrified woman lying on her back.

The senior house officer stood at the end of the bed and instructed, 'Push now!'

The expression on the face of the woman must have mirrored mine almost exactly as I bore down on her chest to obtain a sample of bone marrow from her sternum. I could sense the sweat on my forehead pooling, running down my nose and dripping on to her neck.

'That's it. Did you feel it give slightly just as it went in?' asked my teacher.

'Of course I did,' responded the woman lying on the bed. 'I thought you were going to bloody well kill me.' I hoped no one would tell her that a medical student had indeed killed a patient the previous year by going right into the chest cavity and rupturing a major blood vessel while learning how to take a sample of bone marrow.

I nodded, but I wasn't sure what I had felt. My hands were so wet with fear that I had difficulty pulling off the sterile gloves.

I understand now how getting married as a fourth-year medical student was one way in which I tried to control my gradually increasing anxiety. Somehow it made me feel safer and more secure about the future. I had met my boyfriend Jim, who was writing up his PhD in physics, in a Rag Week computer dating game in my first year (Jane had entered me for it). We married against the wishes of our parents after scandalising them by living together in the same room of a shared flat for two years.

Well, it was the 1970s and morals were still quite different then, particularly in Scotland.

My life began to revolve around this room on the first floor of a tenement block in the New Town that served as our bedroom, living room and study. Here I would fall into the single armchair and stare at the gas fire in the marble fireplace criminally painted white by a previous tenant, listening to the flames in the cracked and discoloured element hissing through the damp darkness of an Edinburgh afternoon. We continued to live as students, eking out our finances, drinking and partying with everyone else. But at the same time, as the months passed, we were settling into married life: shopping on a Saturday and making plans for where we would live in the future.

I drew up a complex timetable of revision for my final examinations. I was halfway through my fifth year and my training was almost at an end, for the time being anyway. For a while that year, I carried on trying to pretend to myself that things were completely normal and that I was coping with the pressure of work. I was as fearful of failing exams as I had been before, but there was also a terrible sense of unease about what was happening to me, to which I couldn't put a name. I convinced myself that the best way to stay in control of my world was to design a kind of map for my mind and contain everything within it by the time the exams arrived. I ruled out lines on paper to create a chart governing every waking hour for the next few months. I did not want to acknowledge the obvious parallels with the way my brother used his obsessions to try to control his anxiety. I told myself that this behaviour was perfectly rational.

The weeks passed in a blur of endless work and no play. One spring afternoon in early 1979, a couple of months before the finals, Dave, the psychiatric registrar, found me sitting in the corner of the treatment room on the psychiatric ward. I hadn't slept the night before. My heart was thumping away in my ears and I was willing it, without success, to slow down.

'Are you OK?' he asked.

I turned my gaze away from him, unwilling to give anything away. 'Yes, I'm fine, just a bit tired and tense.'

'Presenting to the boss, eh? Exhausting, isn't it?'

Professor L was a great psychiatrist but a scary audience for a medical student eager to impress. He was able to maintain an extraordinarily expressionless face as his dispassionate grey-blue eyes scanned the room where the entire team were seated in a circle for his ward round. I had just talked to him about Jess, who I had seen the previous day.

'So what is your favoured diagnosis?' Professor L had asked.

'Anorexia nervosa,' I replied, 'but I think Jess is also very depressed; she talked about feeling quite hopeless at times.'

'Depression is common in anorexia,' he commented, pausing for a moment before asking, 'What concerns you about her?'

I took a deep breath and thought back to Jess's anguished face. 'I think she feels trapped in something she doesn't understand; she is really afraid of gaining weight if she begins to eat.' Indeed, her words to me about trying to eat normally were: 'I can't risk it because once I start, I will never stop.'

'So,' I said, looking up from my notes, 'she can't see a way out and considers being here as something somehow threatening her control over the situation. She is terrified of losing that.'

I paused for a moment and looked over to Dave, who was seated at the far side of the room, for reassurance, as I had tested out my ideas with him earlier before the ward round began. He nodded and smiled.

I went on, 'At the moment, I think Jess feels that she can control what she eats, but nothing else.' There were deeper fears and concerns about herself, her family and the future that as yet she was unable to acknowledge.

The professor nodded. 'I agree. I saw her myself. You did very well.'

There was an almost imperceptible emphasis on 'very'. I experienced a brief twinge of satisfaction, but it did not linger. I was able to imagine myself without too much difficulty into the mental world of the people on the psychiatric unit: the anxious, the depressed and even the paranoid. I felt like I had finally reached my destination, not only because I seemed to have some kind of aptitude for psychiatry but because life on the ward resonated with something inside of me. However, it also worried me, as I could relate to some of the experiences described by the patients only too well – not as an observer from the outside, but from inside.

So, when Dave had found me alone in the treatment room after the ward round, I could see he was concerned. 'Are you sure you don't want to talk?' Dave persisted, reaching out as though to touch me.

'No, honestly, I'm OK,' I said, pulling away from him. 'Just a bit worried about finals... that's all.'

But I knew this was not the truth. My heart felt as though it was going to stop beating from exhaustion. It's a feeling now familiar to me.

Sandra was another patient I had come to know well during my time as a student in the psychiatric ward in the months before my final examinations. She had a strong family history of bipolar disorder, meaning that a person experiences not only episodes of depression but periods of being 'high', overactive and elated. Sandra had started electroconvulsive therapy (ECT), which is used today very much as a last-resort treatment for severe depression when a person stops eating and drinking. It involves passing an electric current though the brain to induce an epileptic seizure as a life-saving measure. This treatment sounds barbaric, and indeed in the past it was, and many are aware of it from watching *One Flew Over the Cuckoo's Nest*. Nowadays it is given under general anaesthetic and with drugs which paralyse the muscles so that the fit is almost imperceptible, but ECT is still controversial and sometimes problematic.

Sandra was gradually improving, as she had done before, but I knew she suffered from the memory problems that ECT can cause. I sat down next to her in her room, and after a few moments she slowly, almost mechanically, turned her face to look at me. Her eyes were full of an unspeakable anguish, which seemed beyond tears. There was such a depth of pain there that I could somehow understand how she would not be able to speak about it. It was a world of bleak silence, so I stayed with her, saying nothing, and from time to time we made eye contact, but no more.

A couple of weeks later, Sandra was to tell me how, when she had been very low, she had not believed she deserved to exist. She told me: 'I didn't want to talk to you. I wanted you to go away and leave me alone, but I couldn't bear for you to leave me either; I was so afraid of what was going to happen. I was terrified of having the ECT again, but it wasn't just that. I wanted to die... I was very afraid of dying too at the same time. Can you understand?'

This was the awful dilemma – the terrible ambivalence about accepting help or retaining control over her life, even if it eventually meant no life at all – I had both read and recognised in Sandra's eyes.

As the weeks drifted by, I woke early each morning, listening to the milk float clattering along the Edinburgh cobbles and the swell of the rush-hour traffic beginning in the distance, dreading the start of another day. My life was charted out in blocks of time, each specifying a goal I must achieve. If I failed to attain the daily objective, I might lose even more time by obsessing over how to rewrite the timetable. I became enslaved by white sheets of paper spreading out over the floor. It began to take longer and longer to get out of bed in the morning. Sometimes I forgot to wash or dress if I didn't have to leave the house, which was often the case as the days went by. I crawled into the revision lectures but avoided having conversations with anyone. From a distance I observed the ebb and flow of my classmates in and out of their conspiratorial circles. I was sure they knew all of the things about me that I didn't want them to know. And I was convinced that they knew I was going to fail. A few of us, of course, were going to. I paced around the flat at night, fearful that the mental problems my younger brother had suffered throughout his childhood were beginning to catch up with me.

Jim, in contrast, operated in a scientific world of reason and logic. My increasingly erratic behaviour puzzled my husband in the way I imagined one of his experiments failing to go as predicted perplexed him.

'What the hell are you doing?' he asked one night, as I sat rocking backwards and forwards in the chair by the fire.

'I'm trying to get rid of the pain,' I muttered. The tension in my gut made eating difficult and I woke in the night wracked with colicky pain that I could only relieve by rocking, just as I remembered my little brother doing as a child when he was upset.

'Don't you think you ought to go and see the doctor?' he asked.

'There's nothing bloody wrong with me,' I screamed back across the room. But he could see I was afraid. I know now what it was, although I would have struggled to name it then: fear of failure was stalking me in the shadows.

There came a point when I couldn't go on. My head was splitting open and I struggled to hold the pieces of my brain together. I can't remember exactly what happened. I was sitting in the flat, obsessing over the timetable and my failure to comply with it, while at the same time listening intently to the noise of the people in the tenement stairwell. They were walking up and down and chatting to each other about the weather and whose turn it was to clean the stairs, as though everything was quite normal. I was acutely aware of the sounds of the main door on to the street clanging shut as our neighbours came and went, the traffic below in the Crescent, the birds outside the window and the hum of life passing me by. I wasn't sleeping or working – just sobbing.

Finally, I gave in and made an appointment to see the doctor. I went to my GP and he referred me to a psychiatrist (whom I shall call Dr P) who did sessions at the University Health Centre. It was even more embarrassing, because Dr P recognised me straight away.

'You've just been...'

'Yes,' I said, 'I did my psychiatry attachment on your firm.'

He asked me to see his colleague, another professor, later the same week. Professor M, as I shall call him, was elegantly dressed in a grey suit, with a pink handkerchief sticking up out of his breast pocket. It was very distracting. I found myself trying to decide how many times it had been folded, and whether he would ever take it out and offer it to someone if they started to cry. I decided he probably wouldn't.

'What's worrying you? What are you afraid of?' he asked in a way which demanded a reply. Here was someone who wanted to enter into my world, and my instinct was to resist and protect myself from him – to retain control. It felt as though, underneath the outer cracked shell of my ego, he was trying to pierce the last thin, fragile membrane. Maybe his will was stronger than mine, because I told him not just about the exams, but also about my brother and his mental illness, the strange behaviour that had started when he was only seven years old.

'And you are worried this is what is happening to you?' he asked.

'Yes,' I said. I knew this was my deepest, darkest fear, the one I still face even now: that I will lose control of my mind.

'I'd like you to come into hospital.'

I gazed through the window to the eighteenth-century buildings of Edinburgh Medical School where I had spent much of the last five years. And I knew then that I didn't want to become a psychiatric inpatient in the seductively safe but very public goldfish bowl – visible to all of my classmates – of the professorial psychiatric unit, upstairs from where I had so recently been a student. A couple of students from our year had been inpatients there already.

'I want to get through these exams,' I said. 'I can't go in there now.'

He scribbled something in my notes and I immediately sensed his annoyance with me for not being a good, compliant patient. I knew I had to maintain some semblance of normality, even if I did not feel it.

'Take these,' he said, handing me a prescription and ushering me to the door.

'Should I come and see you again?'

'No, there's no need to see me, but you should see Dr P.'

'What's the matter with me?'

'You are very unhappy, very distressed, but you don't have the same kind of problems that your brother has, and I think you are going to get better.'

Looking back, I think I might have benefited more from having antidepressants rather than tranquillisers but they were the only thing on offer. Unlike now, intensive psychological therapy wasn't available unless I had been prepared to be admitted to hospital for group therapy. I had tried the student counselling service but not found it particularly helpful, just oddly frustrating having someone listen to you and then repeat the last few words you said back. I do now think that counselling is appropriate when it's quite clear what the focus of the problem is and you have something to work on together, but back then I could not easily articulate my fears and put into words what my problem was. I just had a sense of wanting constant reassurance, but I couldn't say exactly what about other than being told that I wouldn't fail my exams. I had become chronically and severely anxious, and then this turned into something else. I had almost certainly slipped into a depressed state of mind, which can occur when anxiety is unremitting, and it really felt as though there was no way out of it. Nevertheless, there was enough of a survivor in me to look over the edge of the abyss and turn back – I was still able to make a choice. I managed to pass the finals with support from Dr P.

Months later, when I started my first junior doctor post as a house officer on a medical ward in the Infirmary, one lunchtime I bumped into Dave, the psychiatric registrar I knew from my attachment on the psychiatric unit. He was working in the self-poisoning unit up the corridor.

'What happened to Jess, the young girl with anorexia?' I asked him.

'She put on some weight and went home, but she has started psychotherapy. There's a long way to go yet; she still hasn't really acknowledged how bad things are.'

'And Sandra?'

When I had finished my attachment, Sandra had been away from the ward and I hadn't had the opportunity to say goodbye to her.

'She's really well. I'm just a bit concerned that she might get *too well*. Last time I saw her in the clinic, her mood seemed to be going up, but she insisted she was fine.'

Like many people with bipolar disorder, Sandra enjoyed the period when her mood was elevated or hypomanic (a less severe form of mania), as she was able to be much more productive because she had more energy and needed less sleep. Kay Redfield Jamison, an expert on the topic, who also has bipolar disorder, has described how she managed to write so many more papers when her mood was high. However, she also depicts in her writing the terrible paranoid fears that she experienced when she spiralled into psychosis and lost touch with reality, suffering both frightening delusions and hallucinations. When severe anxiety complicates depression and causes agitation, it is more difficult to treat, and in bipolar disorder the presence of anxiety can also increase the risk of suicide.

'Is she taking her lithium?' I asked. Lithium stabilises the mood, but it has some unpleasant side effects.

'No, she stopped it. She says it prevents her from feeling how she really is, from being her real self.'

Later I would understand exactly what Sandra meant. When I took it, I felt as though the volume had been turned down on my personality. I felt flat, dampened-down – but at least I did not feel depressed.

Dave glanced up at me from his plate of fish and chips. 'You look exhausted.'

I had spent a considerable part of the night trying to get a cannula into the foot of a severely dehydrated teenage girl in diabetic ketoacidosis – a life-threatening state caused by a high blood glucose level – in order to give her some intravenous fluids. My consultant was convinced that her hormones caused her lack of control of her blood glucose but I was much less sure. I began to tell Dave about her. 'She loves being in the ward; she doesn't get on with her parents. I just think it might be psychological factors which push her out of control. I mean, is she taking the insulin properly?' Dave looked at me and laughed. I was embarrassed, thinking I had said the wrong thing.

'You know, you really should do psychiatry.'

I summoned up the courage to telephone Dr P. I wanted to know what he thought about the idea – whether he believed that I could ever cope with the stress of it and if I was a fit person to even attempt to do it.

'How are you?' he asked.

'I'm OK, working, really much better.' I paused for a moment. 'I wanted to thank you,' I said, 'and ask if you thought it would be out of the question, after what happened to me this year, for me to train as a psychiatrist?' There was a barely perceptible pause at the end of the line. 'No,' he said, 'I don't think it would be out of the question at all.'

I was excited by the possibility, but I recognised that this was tempered by anxiety and a very real fear of what impact such a decision would have on the rest of my life.

CHAPTER 3

Loss

The life events which trigger an episode of depression usually have one important thing in common: they are concerned with loss. In a person who is vulnerable, perhaps because of their early life experiences or family history, this is often the case. Losing someone important, or something which means a great deal to us, causes us to grieve for that loss. But grieving is a normal human experience and it is not the same as depression. We can grieve for the loss of a person we love, a job which means a lot to us and our health when we become chronically ill. We grieve the loss of our dreams for the future and the lost opportunities we will never have. Sometimes it is too painful to begin to address and manage the thoughts and feelings connected to what we have lost and we simply get stuck; we ruminate about the past, going around in circles, unable to let go and move on. We might feel that life is no longer worth living without what we have lost or even become unable to talk about our feelings at all. This 'complicated grief' is what is indistinguishable from depression.

It was about 1.30 p.m. on a cold January day in 1980 when one of the nursing staff came into the ward to tell me there was a personal call for me. I had been working as a medical house officer in a small hospital, in one of the more genteel suburbs of Edinburgh, which specialised in rehabilitating people who suffered from heart disease. I was almost halfway through the year I had to work before I could choose my speciality and hopefully begin to train in psychiatry. In retrospect, it was ironic that at the time I was working with people who suffered from heart disease. I was also planning to become a member of a profession for which my father had total disdain, with good reason given its inability to do anything to help with my brother's mental illness. I had telephoned at Christmas but I hadn't been home. I didn't speak to Dad on the phone; in fact, I couldn't remember the last time I did talk to him.

'He's got a pain in his back. He thinks he's pulled a muscle, but he can't move and it isn't going away,' my mother had said back in December.

'What do they think it is?'

'They don't seem to know. He's seen the GP, and he's just told him to stay in bed. All the strength seems to have gone out of him. You know, it's not like him.'

It was almost as though he had given up the fight, as though he knew.

As a doctor, I've often had to tell people things that they really did not want to hear, but this in no way prepares you for the chilling experience of being told by another person that your own life will never be the same again.

The sky was grey, the steely pall that covers Edinburgh for most of the winter. The ward smelled, like it always did, of a potent mixture of institutional dinners and disinfectant. Out in the main thoroughfare, from the sounds of rattling pill bottles and a key scraping in a lock, I knew that the staff nurse was setting up the trolley to do the medication round. I took the call in the doctor's office, a large bare room where I usually perched on the desk rather than sitting down. I picked up the phone.

'Hello? Dr Gask here.' The novelty of the title had not yet worn off.

There was no preparation. No statement of warning, no 'I've got something upsetting to tell you' to portend the bad news, like I teach the junior doctors to say now. Just the hard cruel facts: 'Linda, it's your Uncle John. Your dad's dead.'

A cold numbness shot through me. My chest tightened up and I retched. I wanted to vomit.

Of course, I went home for the funeral. My husband Jim had by then started to work in England as a research scientist and planned to drive straight there, so I travelled alone. The morning after Dad's death I took the mainline train down to Grantham and then changed as always to the dark green, smoky diesel train which chugged its way across the Lincolnshire Marsh, between fields of cabbage and telegraph poles, down an arrow-straight track to the vanishing point at the coast, somewhere on the horizon. No one met me at the station – nobody ever did. I walked out across the cobbles with my rucksack on my back. With each step taking me nearer home, the tears began to flow down my cheeks.

Three weeks after the funeral, I started my second compulsory six-month job required for me to be registered as a doctor, as a surgical house officer at Falkirk and District Royal Infirmary. I had already started to wall up the grief inside me, although I didn't realise that was the case back then. I did not allow myself to feel it. My anxiety about starting a new job and the knowledge of the hours I would have to work served to help me push away the grief I should have been experiencing. Instead, I felt only increasing numbness and a strange kind of reprieve from having to try to finally resolve my differences with my father. The tears dried up. I carried on.

In a hospital, death is a commonplace event. What was the significance, in the grand order of things, of the death of one man who had stubbornly refused to stop smoking and thus try to prolong his life? A hospital is a place where normal people have to make dispassionate decisions every day about who can be helped and who cannot be saved, where awful things just happen for no reason, and where events can seem carelessly sanctioned by a remorseless and relentless fate.

Mr Evans was about the same age as my father had been when he died. He had come in with a probable large bowel obstruction and a history of colon cancer. I was assisting the day he was opened up in the operating theatre. As I held back the abdominal wall with the large metal retractor, my arms aching for a change of position as the theatre lamps burned down on us like tropical sunlight, Steve the surgical registrar and Mr Thomas the consultant surgeon (or Tommy, as we called him) explored whether the cancer had returned and, if so, the extent of its spread.

'Look there,' said Tommy. I peered over the end of the retractor to where he was indicating something like a fleshy fungus growing along the outside of the gut wall. 'Definite local recurrence involving the abdominal cavity and probably the liver. Let's do what we can for him and close him up.'

A few days later, I walked down the corridor past the door of Mr Evans's room. His complexion was still a sallow yellow colour, although he had stopped vomiting and was taking fluids again. His hair was plastered down against his skull, giving him a strange, unearthly appearance. He called me into the room. We had chatted a little before his operation, when he was first admitted. His son was at university and he wanted to see him graduate, although I knew it was unlikely that he would survive until then. I sat down on the chair next to the bed and looked out of the window, towards the smoking chimney stack of the boiler house across the way. Then I turned my head towards him, very conscious that I wanted to continue looking at the spiralling metal, to count the number of times the thinner outer pipe twisted around the inner one, as though I had never seen it before.

'I know,' he started, 'that you know.' He looked straight at me.

'What?' I replied. My mouth went dry.

'I know I am going to die.' He paused for a moment. 'And do you know why?'

'Why?' I croaked.

'Because of the way you look in at me every time you pass this room. I can see my death reflected in your eyes.'

'No...'

'Oh yes,' he said. 'It's all there written in your face, lassie. You give yourself away.'

And then he turned his head away from me and faced the wall, our conversation over. He never spoke to me again.

I was so ashamed and I simply did not know how to try to get him to talk to me, or even whether I should. How could I talk about the son he would never see grow up and leave university? Or about the grandchild his daughter was expecting, who would never know him?

He began to refuse his food. A couple of weeks later he was dead.

There were 13 of us living in the hospital residency in Falkirk: five medical house officers and eight surgical house officers. I knew three of the group already from my final-year class. The rest of them came from the other Scottish medical schools: Glasgow, Dundee and Aberdeen.

We were the people who did all the tedious jobs that needed to be done and which technically required a doctor. In reality, most of them could be carried out by nurses, and they were the ones who taught us how to do them. Here the men in our group had the advantage, as nurses were usually female and wanted to go out with a doctor. Some of them would do anything for a baby-faced young houseman, even cook him breakfast, if his request was accompanied by the right mixture of charm and the offer of a night on the town – as much as it was feasible to have a 'night on the town' in Falkirk. The really heroic things which actually saved people's lives were done by our seniors.

They relied on us implicitly to have all the blood results and X-ray films available for the consultants' ward rounds and to help with the tasks they were unwilling to do. I soon realised that this meant anything which involved talking to patients, which was something that, in my experience anyway, surgeons avoided.

Mike was my immediate colleague, a wiry Aberdonian with an accent I could barely understand at first. (At medical school I had spent a term thinking that a pathology lecturer was Scandinavian, only to find out later that this was simply how they spoke English in the north-east of Scotland.) Mike and I understood each other well enough and developed an easy working relationship. He was going out with the ward sister, a fact which filled me with an unwelcome sense of jealousy. I was a married woman, even though I rarely saw Jim since he had started working down in England. The marriage I had made less than three years before, at 22, had already begun to feel restrictive in ways I could not yet put into words.

As we were sitting in the ward office after an exhausting day, Mike and I shared a conversation as usual about the messy way in which painful issues of life and death were discussed on the ward. I told him about Mr Evans and how what had happened had deeply affected me.

'I felt very guilty, cowardly, like I should have talked to him. But nobody knew whether he wanted to talk about it.'

'Nobody asked him, you mean. Surgeons are playing God, deciding who wants and who doesn't want to know.' He had the practical unblinkered approach of someone who was destined to be a GP.

'And perhaps a person needs to be able to prepare for their death,' I insisted.

'Don't feel guilty about it,' Mike said, looking up at me and giving me a reassuring smile which made me want to hug him. But I didn't.

What I didn't know then is that learning you are going to die can also trigger a kind of grieving for the life you will never have. Indeed, the five stages of grief described by Elisabeth Kübler-Ross in her classic book *On Death and Dying* – denial, anger, bargaining, depression and acceptance – are actually observed not in the bereaved, but in the dying. In my time as a junior doctor in hospital, I saw many people trying to come to terms with what was happening to them, often with very little help from those who were caring for them. Some of those were what is now often described as 'demoralised' by their illness. Others were fearful of what was to come or angry about it. And some, like I suspect now had been the case for Mr Evans, were frankly depressed: unable to communicate and facing death alone because nobody had managed to reach out and penetrate their silence.

We have liaison mental health workers nowadays in general hospitals that can help in situations like this, but we didn't back then. We all just muddled on. Yet it wasn't difficult to spot the degrees of distress, from fear and demoralisation to despair, experienced by people all around you in a general hospital, and not only among the patients. It still isn't if you are willing to open your eyes to it.

I wonder now if my father had an opportunity to talk about his fears and worries when he was lying in bed in those last few days of his life. Perhaps, knowing him, he would not have wanted to. I will never know. All I could think at the time, and still do, was that he would have hated to have survived and been unable to live his usual active life. I could not imagine my father crippled with angina – that, for a man who had climbed up the Figure Eight in all weathers and swum in the North Sea, would have been a loss he would have been unable to come to terms with.

Almost half of the time during the six-month period, we worked two out of every three nights and two out of every three weekends on call, as well as all day Monday to Friday. One night I would be first on call and then the next night second on call, backing up my colleague – not working but unable to leave the hospital, watching TV or leafing through the *Daily Record* to pass the time. The third night I was off duty, yet we often just went to the pub next door, as it felt like nowhere else in the world existed except for the hospital. Also, there were often parties, as there was usually something to celebrate: a birthday, passing an exam or a successful job interview. At first I tried to avoid these gatherings. I felt guilty because it didn't feel right that I was enjoying myself when Dad had died so recently, but at the same time I told myself that my life would be easier now without him judging me from a distance, never knowing what he was wanting or thinking.

Gradually, as the weeks passed, my confidence began to increase and I was able to sleep again, something I had not been able to do since Dad's death. I began to regain the outward persona of an organised, competent and efficient house officer. I had found fitting into the routine of my first house job much more straightforward. The atmosphere in general medicine was less macho, and there seemed to be more time to talk to the patients. Surgery was about doing, not talking. The surgical approach to life and death was simple: either you could cut it out or you couldn't. It was a seductively clear view of illness and disease, and I could see its attractions.

In casualty, I learned how to remove sewing-machine needles from the fingers of women who worked at the Wrangler jeans factory down the road (usually two at a time, as Wrangler's jeans were indeed 'double-stitched' as advertised), pieces of metal from sore, red eyes and glass beads from infants' noses. I also administered the antidote to noxious chemical injuries sustained at the petrochemical plant on the Forth Estuary nearby. I could cure people or at least make them instantly feel very much better – something that I realised I would never be able to do as a psychiatrist.

One Sunday morning, I was awakened from my bed at 8.30 by the sound of the emergency bleep. I had only been in bed for 3 hours and it felt like considerably less. Saturday night was always busy in the hospital and I had to hide my English accent for my own safety when confronted with the alcohol-fuelled nationalism of central Scotland as I attempted to examine yet another foul-mouthed drunk who had fallen over and injured himself.

Faced with an emergency about to arrive, I ran the couple of hundred yards down to casualty in the blue theatre scrubs which doubled up as my pyjamas. The casualty sister briefed me as we waited in the cool morning air outside the front door of the A&E department for the ambulance to reach us.

'Wall fell on a kid is all we know. Out playing in a building site. Crash team is on its way.'

'How old?' I asked.

'Nine,' she replied, pursing her lips.

We fidgeted and slapped our arms against our bodies to keep warm as the siren approached, changing its tone as it grew closer. My heart was pounding; it still pounds when I hear that noise.

As the van drew up, two ambulance men jumped out of the back and whisked the stretcher on to the waiting trolley. By then the crash team had arrived and they rushed the trolley into the resuscitation room, where they all huddled around. The doors flopped shut behind them and I knew that I was no longer needed now they were there. As the youngest medic, I felt the least useful. I backed away to watch and wait.

Then sister caught my arm as she rushed past me into the resuscitation room.

'They are the parents; you go and talk to them.'

A couple in their early thirties were hovering in the waiting room outside. As I approached, the man stood up hopefully and started to walk towards me.

Talk to them… What could I say?

'What happened?' I asked.

'Is there any news?' he enquired eagerly, ignoring my question.

'Not yet.'

The man sagged. The woman burst into tears. She made a terrible keening sound, like a wild animal in pain. He put his arm round her shoulder, hiding her face from me with the palm of his big hand, and turned to face me.

'We thought she was still in bed; we didn't even know they'd gone out to play. It's Sunday for God's sake! We were having a lie-in. We told them to stay away from the place next door but they couldn't. I knew the old wall wasn't safe… I told them.'

'What are they doing? What's happening?' asked the woman. 'I want to see her.' She tried to pull away but the man, her husband and I assumed the child's father, held her fast.

'There's nothing you can do. Let them get on with it. They'll do something; I know they will.' The quiver in his voice belied his expression of hope.

Around 20 minutes passed. I brought us all some tea and sat down. Their drinks stayed on the table getting cold while I drank mine to try to revive my brain. The A&E department was otherwise completely empty and the cleaner had arrived to do the floor. The sweet smell of the floor polish began to spread up the corridor towards us. The Saturday night drunks, who had fallen over but were as yet unable to feel their injuries due to the anaesthetic effects of alcohol, usually came rolling in by 11 a.m., whereas the gardening injuries and kids falling off bikes would start arriving in reception by mid-afternoon. But now it was quiet.

Eventually, the orthopaedic registrar came out of the resuscitation room and walked towards us.

'Mr and Mrs Banks...' he began.

But the woman, with the sixth sense that all mothers possess when it comes to the well-being of their children, knew what he was going say before he needed to utter another word.

'She's dead, isn't she?' She was strangely calm; her husband seemed more shocked.

'I am so sorry. We did our best to revive her, but she had stopped breathing by the time she arrived and the extent of her injuries made it impossible for us to save her.'

He thrust a sheaf of notes into my hand and pulled me to one side.

'Put it down as a dead on arrival. I've scrawled a few notes. There were multiple chest and head injuries, and it wasn't possible to resuscitate. Better call the procurator fiscal's office tomorrow to inform them.' In Scotland, sudden, suspicious or accidental deaths were reported to the fiscal's office rather than a coroner.

'But what shall I say to... What shall I do with...' I gestured at the couple standing speechless by the door.

'You deal with them. Find out what exactly happened. The police will want to interview them. I need some breakfast.'

And with this parting statement, he sauntered up the corridor, hands in pockets, as though he had just been out for a gentle morning stroll.

I wondered later if he had felt anything at all – or had he just become completely impervious to human suffering? Perhaps he had never had his own experience of receiving bad news. I knew I did not want to become the kind of doctor for whom pain and despair are commonplace, but this knowledge would ultimately bring its own risk – the risk of sometimes caring too much.

I never found out what happened to the parents of the girl who died. I hope they were able to talk to each other about their daughter, and to shed their tears for the child they had lost and the adult they would never know. Later in my career I would see many people who were unable to come to terms with their losses and, as a result, sank into despair and depression. I would learn how medication can help with the physical symptoms: with the loss of appetite and weight, with boosting energy levels, and diminishing the power of suicidal ideas. However, in order to begin to resolve the pain of loss, you have to do something that I failed to do when I lost my own father: talk about it.

CHAPTER 4

Wounds

Most of us need to feel close to some people, with whom we can be intimate; but it is within those very relationships that we can be most at risk of being harmed: emotionally, physically or sexually. Indeed, the worst emotional wounds are often those inflicted by the ones who are closest to us and in whom we have dared to trust. Experiencing such emotional trauma early in our lives increases our vulnerability to depression because it makes us less emotionally resilient as adults, and likely to have more difficulty achieving successful relationships and coping with stress. It may also manifest itself later in the form of self-harm because of the negative impact of emotional trauma on how we feel about ourselves.

At the end of July in 1980 I said goodbye to my colleagues in the surgical unit in Falkirk and began my training as a psychiatrist in Manchester. Part of me didn't want to leave. I had grown close to my fellow workers and particularly to Mike, whose company I knew I would miss. At our final party, with the usual excuse of intoxication, we ended up hugging, kissing and whispering to each other in the corner of the darkened residency lounge, amidst a sea of half-conscious bodies and empty cans of lager.

'You've changed a lot, from when you first came here,' he told me. 'You were very stand-offish.'

'My father had just died,' I said, realising I had never told him about it, 'and now I'm afraid. I don't know if I'll be able to cope.'

'Oh you will. You'll be a good psychiatrist,' he laughed, leaning his head back against the wall.

We stayed there in the darkness, without speaking for a moment. He didn't quite understand what I had been trying to say. I wasn't sure how I would cope with my new life, with all the changes – and not only in my job. I felt very alone.

'You'll be a good psychiatrist because you're the most sensitive person I've ever met.'

Sensitive or too thin-skinned? I was able to give the appearance of steel and ice but this was, and still is, just a performance; inside, beneath the surface, I was just jelly and water. I was too easily wounded and my interactions with others, especially my family, had left their emotional scars. I knew I had always tended to dwell more than I should on the significance of what others said or did; I would mull over difficult conversations in my mind long after they had finished, hurt by things said without any cruel intention. I was acutely aware of mood changes in the people around me, yet would sometimes fail to notice other more obvious details about a friend's appearance, such as a new pair of glasses or hairstyle, because I was lost in my own thoughts, dissecting my interactions with the world moment by moment. I often found myself wanting to please other people in order to be liked but then resenting how this prevented me from doing the things I wanted to do. I would say something hastily in irritation, only to regret it later, and then begin the cycle of ruminative thought all over again. People with sensitive traits in their personality worry about what others think of them and are often told that they 'take things too seriously'. If they become severely depressed, these concerns about others can change into paranoid thoughts. They begin to believe that people really do not like them and actually *are* talking about them behind their back, especially if their self-esteem is already low.

I knew the loss of my friends in Falkirk, particularly Mike, would hurt and I didn't want to feel any more pain. I had to get on with life; I had a career to begin and a marriage to return to. So I took the train down to the north-west of England and moved into our temporary accommodation: a flat in Runcorn, Cheshire, near the laboratory where Jim had already started work. As I couldn't drive, he dropped me off each morning at Warrington Central station, 20 minutes away, from where I caught the train into the city. I had stepped on to the lowest rung of professional medical training in a teaching hospital.

Fine Manchester rain fell one evening in September 1980, leaving a crystalline sheen of tiny droplets on my hair and woollen cardigan as I walked over to the Royal Infirmary situated 5 minutes away, across the congested artery of Upper Brook Street. It was getting dark, and the car headlights dazzled me as I crossed to the other side of the road, trying to avoid puddles and bus drivers' repeated attempts to soak me as they cruised along the gutters. I turned into Nelson Street and dodged between the ambulances as they arrived at and departed A&E.

The doctor in the Accident and Emergency department at Manchester Royal asked me to talk to Janice after they had given her the antidote for the paracetamol she had taken the previous evening. She had sliced herself, once deeply on each wrist, with a Stanley knife and lain down on her bed to die. When she arrived in casualty, her wounds had long stopped bleeding, as she had wrapped them in ice to reduce the swelling before calling a cab to bring her to the hospital. I was the duty psychiatrist then, with the job title but only two months' experience to my name.

As I entered, I was directed to a young woman of about 25, lying on an old examination couch in a dingy ward. It was hardly private. In the next cubicle, behind a faded curtain, we could hear a breathless man being interrogated about his chest pain by the medical registrar and all around us the relentless rhythm of the casualty department: the tap of urgent footsteps, the clatter of metal trays and the tuneless monotone of merciless bleeps summoning junior doctors to the next challenge. Janice lay quite still and oblivious to the noise, staring wordlessly up at the ceiling. Her face was pale and waxen. Bleached blonde feather-cut hair stuck up at all angles, revealing dark brown roots. There was about her the sickly smell of rancid alcohol that would soon become familiar to me as the usual accompaniment to self-poisoning. But this wasn't just an overdose of tablets. This had been a serious, cold-blooded attempt at ending her life. Janice was lucky to be alive, having neither bled to death nor slept long enough for the paracetamol to damage her liver irreparably.

'I suppose you want to know why?' she asked, twisting her head towards me.

Our eyes met, and for a moment I was so transfixed by the surprisingly pale blue irises framing ink-black pupils, which seemed to bore directly into my soul, that I could not speak.

'Why I did it?' she repeated, and then carried on, 'I didn't want to live any more. I couldn't see the point. I've thought about it for quite a long time. Everything in my life has gone wrong.'

Her voice was surprisingly strong, not quite a Cockney accent but certainly from the south of England, indicating that she was a long way from home. It was almost a growl and had no hint of self-pity. She told me that she lived alone and had not expected anyone to find her.

I picked up the notes from the metal bedside cabinet and started to flick through them, trying to hide from her how much she intimidated me. Attempted suicides weren't supposed to be so self-possessed. I took a deep breath and set about doing my job, taking a psychiatric history, establishing exactly what had happened to her: when, how, why and in what order.

'What I'd really like to know,' I asked a little time later, putting my notes to one side, 'is why you changed your mind? Why did you call a taxi and come here?'

A smile flickered across her face, as though she was enjoying the challenge of jousting verbally with me. I wondered if she had seen a psychiatrist before – although she had denied it, she seemed to know what I was going to ask.

'Well, it didn't work, did it? I woke up. So I guess I don't want to try again.' She looked me straight in the eye before adding, 'At least, definitely not at the moment.'

'What if I suggest you come into hospital for a while?'

It took some persuasion on my part but eventually she agreed. She screwed up her face in an exaggerated mime of 'thinking' and then laughed for the first time, and her appearance changed from one of a morbid waif to a punkish pixie.

'OK, I like you,' she grinned at me. 'I tell you what... I'll stay until tomorrow, for you. Then I'm going back home.'

There were many differences between my new job and my previous one as a house officer in a surgical unit. Firstly, I didn't wear a white coat, and the nurses didn't have uniforms either, which sometimes made it difficult to distinguish them from the patients. Secondly, most of the time my patients came to my office to see me rather than me going to see them in the ward. Occasionally, someone would take to their bed because they didn't feel that life was worth getting up for, as my father had once done. But most of the residents in the small inpatient unit were up and about all day.

And thirdly, the ward round was a completely different experience from a round in a general hospital. We would all assemble in the conference room at the end of the corridor above the outpatient clinic on a Wednesday at 2 p.m. to meet with Dr James, the consultant. He would always arrive exactly on time and sit in the winged chair at the end of the room, while the rest of us perched on high-back chairs in a circle facing him.

When I accompanied Dr James to interview Janice – their conversation was relayed on CCTV to the rest of the team – I watched and listened in awe as she verbally fenced with him, deftly parrying his attempts to get past her robust defences. Janice was an art student. We learned that she had decided she wanted to die because she hated the shape of her nose so much that she didn't want to go on living. She was painfully sensitive about her appearance, which disgusted her, yet she looked entirely normal to me, if not quite attractive. She had become so depressed about it that she considered suicide as the only solution. The way she explained it, it all seemed so logical to her. This was a way of thinking and being that I struggled to understand, but I tried very hard to. Appearance should never matter so much that it affects an individual's desire to live but I began to understand that her real wounds lay beneath the surface of her skin.

Excessive concern about the appearance of one's body to the extent that it gets in the way of functioning in life is given the name body dysmorphic disorder. In Janice's case, this seemed to have developed as a result of her relationships with her parents. Her mother had been intensely critical of her and, beneath the tough exterior, Janice had a very low opinion of herself, which had become focused on dissatisfaction with her appearance. Her relationship with her mother in the past had damaged not only her view of herself, but also her ability to forge successful relationships in the present. There were painful memories, deep psychological wounds which remained unhealed.

'She told me once... I would be very lucky to find anyone who would love me... I was ugly inside as well as outside,' she confided to me.

'That must have hurt very much...'

She looked at me and smiled almost apologetically. 'It still does.'

A few days after that conversation with Janice, I was in Dr James's office. The secretaries had all gone and the streetlights lit up the railings around the park on the opposite side of the street. It was after 6 p.m. and suspicious-looking shadows lurked in the children's playground in the centre. Something in the quiet, calm tone of his voice and in the way his head was tilted made me suddenly want to talk, to confide in him.

'It's been a difficult year,' I began. 'My father died in January and then my father-in-law died too… Sometimes it's seemed as though I would never get through it.'

I blurted it all out in a rush, and then felt embarrassed because I was sure he would not want to hear about my problems; the moment of connection was gone as soon as it had come. I muttered a hasty 'goodbye', rushed out of the office and set off for the station, making sure I stayed in the safe glow of the streetlamps. Once again, I felt terribly alone with my thoughts but during the six months I spent working for Dr James, I never felt able to share any more. I continued to hide my feelings, worries and fears behind my cloak of competence.

A few weeks later, in my next post, on a ward in the psychiatric unit at Withington Hospital, I met Frances for the first time. The consultant said that Frances was depressed but didn't *feel* depressed; she just hated the world and everyone in it. She was angry, hostile, fearful of the motives of others and, in the opinion of most of the staff, deeply ungrateful. In retrospect, she was not the most suitable candidate to be someone's first patient with which to learn about psychotherapy, because her problems were quite complex, but there was something about her that I liked. In a place full of well-behaved middle-aged women with depression, who showed far too much deference to the doctors, and others who had been there so many times they treated all the nursing assistants like old friends, Frances just didn't fit.

'Personality disorder,' the nurses muttered every time she had an argument with one of them.

Sigmund Freud would have called it identification: an unconscious way of reducing one's own anxiety about life by allying one's own psyche with that of another. It was a strategy which was later identified and exposed gently to critical examination by my supervision group, with whom I met every week to discuss my progress. However, I didn't so much feel that I had found a psychotherapy patient, as Frances had found me. I could sometimes guess what she was trying to tell me as though I had a sixth sense.

The early events in a person's life shape their personality: the particular combination of emotional, attitudinal and behavioural responses that an individual displays to others in relationships. How our personality develops has an important impact on how successful we are at relating to other people and it plays a significant part in whether or not we get depressed. The experiences that some people have leave them feeling persistently low from quite an early age. I've often asked the question: 'When did you last feel like your old self?' only to receive the reply, 'Not since I was about twelve.' This kind of persistent depressed mood is sometimes called 'dysthymia' but older texts sometimes call it 'depressive personality'. Personally, I dislike this term because it's so commonly used in a pejorative way. People with depressed personalities can become more severely depressed from time to time and when this happens, their inability to forge successful relationships often means that they lack the support which is needed to make them feel valued in the world and which is necessary to help them recover.

Frances was sitting in the chair opposite me.

'What is it like, at home?' I asked.

'Difficult... No, forget I said it,' she replied.

'What's hard about it?'

She picked silently at a scab on her left arm. I could see blood beginning to ooze from beneath the hard carapace as she worried away at it with what remained of her fingernails. On both of her forearms were marks where she had scratched herself repeatedly with a razor blade. The newer injuries were still an angry shade of red. The older ones looked like the silvery trails that a snail leaves on paving stones. She had told me how she felt a strange sense of relief when she cut herself. She didn't want to kill herself, but there were times when she needed to have some relief from her inner pain, and this was something which seemed to help, albeit for a short while. Other people have conversely told me that they cut themselves in order to experience pain, to punish themselves for whatever they feel guilty about.

'Can you tell me a little bit about home?' I tried again.

'I can't say I hate it, can I? I mean, they care about me, I suppose. But I can't be what they want me to be,' she sobbed.

'Do you have to be what they want?'

'I don't want to be... different.'

'Maybe you are?'

Silence, but a shrug. A response.

'Maybe that's OK... to be different?'

'Why? Why should it be OK?'

'Maybe it's a beginning. A place to start from.'

She looked up. I detected an uncertain, conspiratorial glance and the first flicker of a smile.

Some days after this breakthrough with Frances at the hospital, my widowed mother arrived at our newly acquired terraced house for a visit. She had begun dating within a few months of my father's death, but none of these relationships had seemed particularly serious. This time, though, she came to visit with a new boyfriend, Joe, with whom she had been going out for about six months. He was a balding haulage contractor who didn't mince his words. We were all sitting around in the lounge – Mum, Jim, Joe and me – drinking tea and pretending to feel relaxed, when he suddenly asked me, 'So you're a head-shrinker then, are you?'

'I'm a psychiatrist, yes,' was my terse reply.

'So what do you think of this ECT business then?'

'What do you mean?'

His reply surprised me: 'Well, they gave it to me in hospital, but it was a waste of time…'

I didn't know he had been in hospital. I looked up at Mum but she avoided my gaze and seemed reluctant to enter the conversation. She was leafing through a magazine that she had brought with her.

'Well, we do still use electroconvulsive therapy, yes. Sometimes it's necessary when a person is depressed, in order to save their life.' This was true; I had seen ECT work for people like Sandra, but it was also often given in certain cases when I wasn't so convinced it was needed: for people with less severe depression or where their recovery was clearly being hampered by feelings and thoughts which they could not resolve. In these instances, other types of treatment, such as psychological therapy and/or medication, might have been not only more acceptable, but also safer and more effective. I wondered if this had been the case with Joe but I didn't say so.

'Can't see the point of it all myself, psychiatry,' he carried on.

I didn't attempt to reply.

Instead, I decided to change the subject and ask them what they wanted to do during their visit and Mum replied, 'We'll do whatever you like. We're fine with anything, aren't we, Joe?'

I didn't entirely believe her, as her answer sounded forced. We took them shopping, to the pub and out to dinner. It was a relief when they set off on their drive home two days later. We had done our best to find out what they might enjoy, but it was rather like trying to guess someone else's hand in a card game.

Mum rang up later in the evening and her comment was: 'You could have made an effort... tried to entertain us today.'

'What do you mean?'

'Took us out, shown us a good time.'

We had spent Sunday morning eating breakfast and reading the newspapers. I thought this would be relaxing, but it seemed that it was not what my mother had wanted to do.

'Why didn't you say?' I asked her.

'Well, I thought you would have realised. Sometimes I just don't think—'

'But I thought we had done what you wanted to do! You said...'

I could feel the tears coming. With my mother it felt as if the goalposts were being constantly moved further away, out of my reach. I could never get it right – or rather, I was usually quite wrong. I would never be able, however hard I tried, to please her.

'I thought you wanted to see the house... I'm sorry, I'm on call. I have to get off the phone now,' I told her, even though it wasn't true.

'That's you! Always working, putting your job before your family. And you've not got much to show for it, have you, for all this university education?'

'What do you mean?'

'Well, just a lot of old books and a second-hand car.'

And a husband you never liked, I stopped myself saying aloud.

'What were you going to say? Sometimes you don't think... what?' I pushed her to go on with what she had started to tell me. It was an urge, rather like that of picking at an old scab to make it bleed again. I knew what she would say was going to hurt, but I wanted her to say it anyway so that I could reopen the wounds from the past and experience once again the pain they would cause.

'Sometimes I can hardly believe we're related,' Mum continued.

We certainly had very little in common. Maybe I was a changeling, a child who had accidentally been swapped with another at birth, but the mirror told me every morning that this couldn't be true. In the reflection I could see clearly my father's thick wavy hair and large nose, and my mother's pale white skin, with the Scottish freckles, and the same long neck and stubborn jaw. There was no mistaking my heritage.

Not long after Mum and Joe visited, my brother Alan called.

'Can I come and stay with you? I can't stand it at home.'

'Why?' I asked.

'Mum's new boyfriend says there's nothing wrong with me that a good day's work wouldn't sort out.'

Joe didn't believe that Alan might have a mental illness.

'And something else happened... He lost his temper with me... I was...'

'What happened? Tell me.'

'He forced me down the stairs. He told me to get out of the house and leave Mum alone and stop upsetting her.'

As I listened to Alan on the phone, I realised how I missed Dad; why did he have to die so soon and so young? He was the one person who had shown, at least early on, some sympathy with my desire to be in control of my own fate and who had wanted me to succeed. He was also the only person who had ever had the patience to cope with Alan's problems. Dad had been a difficult, sometimes impossible, person to be with towards the end, but whenever I tried to think about him, there was just a deep and awful sense of emptiness.

An acquaintance once asked me why I didn't see more of my mother. It was very difficult to tell her that Mum and I could not tolerate each other's company. Although the general belief is that 'all mothers love their children', I wonder why people make such assumptions when there is so much evidence in the world to the contrary. So many battered unwanted children, so many unhappy souls, so much damage done in the name of parental love. In moments of generosity I could believe that my mother probably loved someone who looked and sounded exactly like me. The problem was that I could never be that person and retain my sanity. Instead, my mother and I engaged in a kind of prolonged warfare, each of us not receiving from the other what we really wanted and inflicting more punishment in return.

I no longer belonged with my family; it felt as if there was no room for me there. I realise now how it never provided the kind of warm, secure and loving home that many of my friends seemed to have had. I didn't feel there was a real place for me anywhere, except at work, on the ward.

There I had an identity and a purpose, and my history was unknown. No one knew I was my mother's 'ungrateful child'. I could continue to create the new persona that I had been constructing since medical school. I was efficient, caring and, outwardly at least, quite tough. I was succeeding in my new career and I had something crucial in common with my patients: we had all been wounded by life. Unlike Frances, I did not cut myself and I did not physically bleed, but I understood her drive to regularly relive pain by picking at the wounds, to comfort oneself with familiar pain. If you feel guilty just for being alive, it can feel perversely reassuring to be reminded of the hurt that you know well, as each telephone conversation with my mother invariably re-established. However, if you keep picking away at the scab, the wound never heals.

It sometimes felt that, like some of my patients, I looked at the real world as though through a window, uncertain as to whether I wanted to be outside the walls of the hospital. I tried to help my patients as much as I could by connecting with them. It seemed that I had found something – a career, a vocation – which enabled me to feel that my life was indeed worth living. It was easier to deal with other people's problems than my own doubts, uncertainties and growing sense of pain at being alienated from home. I did not realise the vital importance of addressing my own problems first.

Frances and I began to work together, meeting every week to try to trace the origin of her wounds in the mental, physical and sexual abuse she had suffered at the hands of her family during childhood. She began to recognise her inner strength and the power of her own determination to survive. However, she still found it difficult to stop cutting herself during periods of stress. The emotional wounds inflicted in the past by her truly vile mother and father were still driving her need to harm herself in the present. This had become her way of coping with life and it was not for me to insist that she stopped doing this.

I know now that if she had wanted to do so, a cognitive behavioural approach – helping her to mentally capture and record in a diary the thoughts and feelings she experienced in the moments before her decision to cut – might have been the best way of helping her to learn how to pause and consider other ways of coping with her distress. This therapy wasn't available then, but it is today. It is important to remember that although a person who self-injures may not be immediately at risk of dying, they have a hundredfold greater risk of suicide. Self-injury and self-harm are never just 'attention-seeking'. There has been a three-fold increase in self-injury in young people over the last decade in England, almost certainly related to the more pressurised lives experienced by teenagers in our society.

Several years after I last saw Janice, the young woman I met shortly after starting psychiatry and who had tried to kill herself, I recognised her name on the poster for an exhibition. I visited the gallery to see some of her work. The pictures were vivid abstracts with panels of black and scarlet. They made me think of blood seeping through the canvasses, as though from somewhere beneath, but they were very beautiful. I wondered if painting was a way Janice had discovered of turning her wounds into some kind of metaphorical representation of the pain she still experienced. Whatever her motive, I was so pleased to discover that the artist was still very much alive and creating such powerful images. I have learned that however bleak the world may seem, we are able to find reasons to carry on living in it.

CHAPTER 5

Losing the Plot

The most toxic kind of life event that can trigger depression is one that resonates with a particular aspect of the person's underlying vulnerability. Life almost seems to conspire to match the event to the person, like a key finding the lock for which it was originally cut.

~~~

One day in late 1983, I was sitting in a room in Rubery Hill Hospital, a former asylum in Birmingham, just up the road from the old British Leyland car plant. I was undergoing the clinical examination for membership of the Royal College of Psychiatrists. The man seated opposite me had just told me how he'd been arrested for 'stealing body shells'. Of course, I didn't know what a body shell was and it took me a while to realise that it was something to do with manufacturing a car rather than connected to science fiction.

'I can't help you any more, doctor,' he said through his nose in a thick Brummie accent.

One part of me felt inclined to tell him that he could not have been of any less help even if he had tried, but I didn't want to appear churlish. He had volunteered to take part in the clinical examination, and perhaps he really didn't have a clue why he had been admitted to this desolate and dreary place.

Then there was a knock on the door and somebody shouted, 'Time's up.'

I followed the young man up the corridor to a dusty room lit obliquely from a high window, and furnished only with a table and two hardback chairs, like those rooms used for prison visits that you see in films. Outside, the sun was struggling to escape from the clouds. The light illuminated a shard of dust suspended in the air above us. I tried to convince myself that my companion had a sympathetic expression on his face, but all I could see in his eyes was pity as he took in my bright, red wool crepe suit. I had bought it on impulse in the sale at Kendal's department store in Manchester two years before, in one of those rare moments when red seems like a good idea. It was the only suit I owned and it felt completely wrong. I knew I should have really worn black; not only did I always feel more comfortable in black, but it would have been better suited to my funereal mood.

'You have fifteen minutes to prepare yourself and then we'll call you in.' He stepped out then put his head back around the door. 'They *are* running on time.'

Just 15 minutes to summarise my notes and put together my formulation of the case. Differential diagnosis (a discussion of all the possible conditions this might be), musings on 'aetiology' (causes of the condition), any investigations I thought were required, a comprehensive management plan (immediate, short-term and long-term; psychological, physical and social aspects of treatment) and not forgetting the likely prognosis.

After what seemed like a very short time later, I entered the examiners' room. Two square-shouldered and suited middle-aged men, seated behind a table, were chatting to each other but fell into silence as I slumped into the chair opposite. I did not recognise either of them and they did not introduce themselves. They wore the universal uniform of British male hospital consultants: pin-striped suits and sensible ties. Not a hint of red. I presented the case to them, going through my formulation, and they both looked at me with quizzical expressions which suggested that they thought I was really making it all up as I went along. This was strange, as I proposed to them that the patient I had interviewed might have been fabricating too. I muttered something about the Ganser syndrome, a state in which people give 'approximate' or nonsensical answers to questions in order to appear to be mad.

Ganser, a German psychiatrist, first described it while working at a prison where he came across three men apparently pretending to be psychotic, probably in order to avoid taking responsibility for their crimes. Classically, the patient replies with answers which indicate that they have indeed understood the question and wilfully misunderstood it in giving their answer. The example I always remember goes something like:

Question: 'How many legs does a sheep have?'

Answer: 'Three, doctor.'

Meanwhile, I was providing my own version of approximate answers.

'Are you quite certain this *is* your preferred diagnosis?' the examiners asked.

'Yes,' I replied.

They exchanged knowing glances.

Whatever I was doing or saying was clearly not what they wanted to hear. There was a pregnant pause, after which they both turned to face me and one of them opened his mouth to speak – and my heart stopped beating.

'Well, thank you very much, doctor. You can go now.'

And then it was over. I knew I had failed the Membership Examination of the Royal College of Psychiatrists as clearly as if I had walked out of a written exam after handing in a blank sheet of paper.

We drove back up to Manchester in the fading daylight along the M6. Winter was approaching fast. It was rush hour and the traffic dragged around Spaghetti Junction like red blood cells congealing in a hardened artery. Catherine, my colleague who had also taken the examination, chattered away while she was driving, as though she really believed I was listening. And I was, in a manner of speaking, but the negative voices in my own head were far more compelling than usual.

This is it. You've done it now.

What? What have I done?

You've proved yourself.

How have I proved myself when I know I've failed?

Who said you had to succeed! No, you've proved you really don't have what it takes to do it. You've been found out. It's only a matter of time now.

Perhaps this was really as far as I was going to go in my career in psychiatry. I had only achieved what I had so far under false pretences, by pretending to be competent.

I had been feeling increasingly anxious for some time. Three months before I took the examination in Birmingham, in the autumn of 1983, I had been promoted to senior registrar on the Professorial Unit at Withington Hospital. I was given a new job after employment as a junior doctor for three years without yet passing the required test, although I was expected to do so very soon and psychiatry isn't a subject which fits well into the simplicity of modern examination methods. I could write an erudite essay discussing the possible causes of depression, detailing the conflicting evidence from different sources, but I found it much harder to deal with multiple-choice questions that demanded I understood the received wisdom about subtle differences in frequency implied by imprecise terms such as 'commonly', 'often' and 'seldom'.

I had a history with examinations. My colleagues and seniors didn't know about this. They didn't know how my hands used to sweat and shake before my piano examinations as a child. How I could be so paralysed by the fear of knowing I could destroy my chances of passing in the next moment that it would actually seem easier just to accept I had failed, turn in a rushed and careless performance, and get out of the room as quickly as possible.

The new job was tough. I was expected to oversee the inpatient care of a diverse and complex group of people, including a few 'celebrity' patients and relatives of important doctors who had developed their mental illness while at university in Manchester.

Daniel was an inpatient in the Professorial Unit. His father was a professor of medicine at a university in the south of England. He too had been studying medicine in Manchester, but had realised it was not his chosen career. Shortly before his finals he had dropped out and continued the heavy drinking that he had started as a student. He was now in his late twenties and, I began to suspect, was going to die young. We had admitted him after another serious suicide attempt.

'This isn't what I want to do. It's what my bloody father wants... It's always what he wants...' His speech was slightly slurred.

'Daniel, have you been out for a drink?' I asked.

'What the fuck does it matter if I have? S'no point in anything anyway now, is there? I've lost the fucking plot...'

'What do you mean, lost the plot?'

'That's what my father always says to me: "You've lost the plot, Daniel",' he laughed as he mimicked his father's arrogant tone of voice. I recognised it from his telephone calls to the ward, demanding information about his son that I was unwilling to provide. Daniel was an adult and details about his care were confidential. I can understand how this often antagonises family members and carers, but Daniel's father did not need to know the information he was asking for, and his son denied permission for us to meet as a family. Unless there was an imminent risk of Daniel leaving hospital again, there was no reason to share information, and Daniel's father had refused to discuss his concerns with our social worker, insisting that he wanted me to answer his questions. Professional people who should know better are sometimes poor at respecting such boundaries where their own family are concerned.

Daniel started to weep, collapsed against the wall and slithered to the floor. I could smell strong spirits on his breath. His skin was sallow and the whites of his eyes looked even yellower than usual. I knew our ward sister would want to discharge him for returning to the ward under the influence of alcohol, which was against the rules, but I also suspected there was something more going on that I needed to find out about. Eventually, he told me.

'I saw the consultant in the liver clinic today. He says I've got advanced cirrhosis. So that's it then. I've had it. My life's completely shit and I've had it. My father was right, the bastard.'

I called in one of the nurses and we got him on to the bed. He wasn't fit to go anywhere for the moment, if at all. I could see that Daniel thought his life was over. The problem was that he felt he had never been allowed to decide what to do with his life because the script had been written for him by his parents. Although that was how it seemed to him, he had still tried to please them – and failed. The challenge was to try to help him to discover how *he* wanted to spend his life, however long was left of it. My fear was that he would avoid this challenge by continuing to poison himself with alcohol simply to hasten the end.

Sandy, the ward sister, arrived a few minutes later. 'If he has been drinking he'll... My God! What has he been taking?'

'I don't know,' I replied. 'Probably alcohol, but possibly something else too. I think we had better get him down to casualty.'

Later that night Daniel was admitted to a medical ward. I called his father to let him know and he seemed to me to be rather more disappointed for himself than concerned about his son's health.

It was not, however, only the patients that I needed to worry about. In this new job I also supervised junior staff for the first time: young doctors who were eager to please and reluctant to ask for help when they had strayed beyond their capabilities.

'You'll have to speak to her. She can't talk to my staff like that,' Jennifer said. She was a nurse for whom I had a good deal of respect and she had taken a dislike to Judith, our new registrar.

'What's the matter?'

'Who does she think she is, coming in here and telling me what she wants doing?'

Judith was outwardly confident but when I sat next to her in the Admissions and Discharges meeting every Thursday morning at 8.30 sharp, I could almost smell her fear of failure. Professor Davies liked to play complicated mind games with the young female doctors he selected for his unit. I had been one once, and knew all the verbal garden paths and logical cul-de-sacs along which his searching questions could misdirect you. The task was to defend, word by word, what you had written in the brief summaries produced each week for all the cases that had been either admitted or discharged.

'So tell me, doctor, what does it mean... the patient's insight was "good"? How did you assess it? Perhaps you can enlighten me? So what if I'm willing to take the treatment, does it follow my insight is "good"? Might it still be possible I don't believe myself to be ill? What do you say? Would my insight still be "good" then? Come on tell me! If my insight was "good" then why did I come to the hospital seeking help when I believed I was being pursued by the KGB? Why didn't I go to the police station and ask for protection? Why on earth did I come to see you? Explain to me what you have written.'

In psychiatry, like any other branch of medicine, the junior doctors survived the working week on a combustible fuel of fear, caffeine, alcohol and occasional tears.

If anxiety is the manifestation of the fear that something will happen, depression occurs when fear becomes reality.

'What's up?' asked Lee, my colleague at the weekly psychotherapy supervision group that by then I struggled to attend.

Lee was older than most of us, having come to psychiatry as a second medical career after starting out in obstetrics and gynaecology. There was something very grown-up and wise about her.

'What do you do when you think you probably feel worse than some of your patients?'

'Get some help.'

'Where from?'

'Leave it to me,' she said. 'I'll organise something.'

The letter from the College arrived two months after I took the examination, in mid-December. I finished on the ward early, as it was the staff Christmas dinner. I usually didn't get away until after 7 p.m., but I knew the envelope was waiting for me. The others who took the examination with me had found out their results already.

Catherine had called me, announcing, 'I've passed! I can't believe it! You know I really thought I had failed.'

'That's great.' It didn't feel great but what can you say when you know, *really know*, you will not be celebrating?

'I'm really pleased for you.' I tried to say it with conviction, but it was very difficult. As I rapidly scanned the piece of paper and extracted the information, my heart seemed to stop beating. *We are sorry to inform you that you have failed to reach the required standard... to satisfy the examiners... failed the multiple-choice paper and the clinical examination.*

Professor Davies collected me from home to take me to the restaurant where we were to meet up with the rest of the clinical team for our Christmas party that very evening. As we drove there, a painful and frightening idea kept intruding. I could hear a voice speaking in my head. It sounded like my own.

Open the car door and jump out. Wait until it picks up speed on the motorway and then do it. Go on... It will be easy. Go on... now!

But I didn't. I resisted. I tried to distract myself by watching the headlights of oncoming cars as they flashed by and pretending that this moment, of being lulled into an oddly comforting trance by the rhythm of the city, would go on for ever and we would never arrive.

But the desire to escape from my life – perhaps even to end it, if I allowed myself to listen to that inner voice – was stronger than I had ever felt before. I had not told anyone how bad I was feeling, particularly not Professor Davies; I had a feeling that he disapproved of people who chose suicide. I had seen evidence of this when Catherine and I had been with him one day in the staff common room, where he held court every lunchtime. He expressed his anger at the poet Sylvia Plath for having killed herself and left her children without a mother. He knew Plath's GP in London who had been trying, in vain, to treat her depression before she died.

'It's a very selfish act,' he said.

'But if it seems like the only way out…' I argued. I couldn't blame someone for feeling like this. When you are so depressed, you cannot think of the consequences for others. You think only of yourself and you cannot believe it is ever possible to feel differently. 'She might have thought the children were better off without her.'

'But could you forgive someone for killing themselves? That's the question.'

'Could you?' I retorted.

He didn't reply, but instead smiled enigmatically. He didn't have to provide us with answers.

The car pulled up at the restaurant and I realised the professor was talking to me.

'How can we make things easier for you?' he asked.

'I need time to study.'

He looked at me with knowing eyes. I didn't need to say more. 'You feel ashamed about failing?'

I nodded.

'You needn't, you know. There are a lot more important and terrible things a human being can feel ashamed of than failing an examination.'

He was right, of course. Not about there being many worse things than failure, or so it seemed to me at that moment, but about the terrible sense of shame and humiliation which made it painful to sit and eat with my colleagues, aware as I was that they knew but would not be talking about it.

'And are you getting some help?' he enquired.

By then, I had started seeing a psychotherapist who I shall call simply E, arranged through the referral that Lee had made for me.

'I am.' I smiled through the tears.

'We won't stay long, and I'll look after you.'

I struggled through the next few weeks in a state of unreality, managing the ward from day to day, still working but not seeing my own psychotherapy patients. There was nothing of myself left to give them, and I could not work with them without giving something of me. The vital energy I drew on in those intense moments in therapy, when it felt like I could connect with another person in order to help them to change or grow, seemed to have all drained away from me.

Then I fell acutely ill with a salmonella infection. It took a physical disease to get me away from work because a part of me did not accept that my mental ill health was a reason to stop working. Work had almost become my only reason for living and my relationship with psychiatry had become the single most important dimension of my life, far more important to me than my marriage or my friendships. This was why, I realise now, failure in the examination shook my sense of identity so profoundly. It had resonated with my own particular vulnerability: a style of coping with the stresses and demands of the world through immersion in my work that I had learned in childhood. If all of this bothered Jim, he didn't say, but I knew he cared for me and tolerated my moods. However, it was as though I was there in our relationship in body only and even then, hardly at all.

Soon after I returned to work, a stone-and-a-half lighter, one of my patients with a diagnosis of schizophrenia (in which a person usually not only experiences hallucinations and delusions, but also difficulty in thinking and changes in behaviour) told me that she had recently met an old friend of mine who had encouraged her to try to manage without her medication. I was intrigued and asked her if she would tell this person how to get in touch with me.

It turned out to be Jane, my best friend from medical school. She was in Manchester and living in a basement flat in Didsbury, not far from the hospital where I was working. Jane and I had often talked about dropping out of our medical training. In some ways she seemed less comfortable a student than I did, as though she had simply drifted into medicine with her straight As, unlike me who hadn't quite made the grades demanded but had been accepted anyway. It was only when we had started our psychiatry attachments that she really began to show enthusiasm for a medical career, or more specifically, a psychiatric one. So we were all amazed when, in our fourth year, Jane suddenly announced that she was going to give it all up and leave medicine.

'I can't tell you what's going on. It's too difficult to explain,' was all she had said to justify her reasons for changing to Philosophy and then, a few months later, dropping out altogether.

'It's just... Well, everything's changed. I just see things really *differently*.'

Her down-to-earth room-mate had a pretty clear idea: 'She told me she was hearing voices.'

I understood why Jane was not inclined to share these experiences with me, realising, as we both did, the potential significance of such an admission.

If you tell a doctor, and particularly a psychiatrist, that you are hearing voices, chances are they will suspect you may be suffering from some kind of psychotic illness and are really experiencing hallucinations, although many illicit drugs can also cause this to happen. Nowadays we also know that many people hear 'voices' at some point during their lives, particularly when they are under stress, and it does not necessarily mean that they are 'going mad'. Sometimes people hear their own thoughts, as I had done, apparently spoken aloud but inside their heads. Other times they hear people speaking to them – and they hear these voices as clearly as they hear other people talking – from outside their head. All of these experiences can occur in severe depression, but Jane had not seemed depressed – quite the opposite, as she had been almost euphoric at times.

Jane was working in a bookshop and when we met, she told me that she had been to India and was now a devotee of Raja yoga, which demanded not only a strict regime of meditation, but dietary restrictions too.

'How are you?' I asked her.

'Oh I'm fine. You have to believe me; I'm *really, really* well!' She laughed, the same old raucous laugh, at my apparent disbelief that she could be happy with her lot. She looked physically well but I could detect the same troubling sense of total self-absorption with her inner world and the same inexplicable quiet euphoria about her that had been evident at the time she dropped out of medicine. It was as though she had discovered the meaning of life and was bursting to tell me about it but couldn't, because I would not have believed her. And yet, in a strange way, I found myself envying her. She was living the life of her own choosing. Perhaps she had discovered a secret worth having? Or was this, as the professional part of my psyche whispered to me, quite simply a terrible tragedy and a wasted life, which might have resulted in so much more? Had she, in losing one set of hopes for life, stumbled upon something more meaningful to sustain her?

But she had a curious, almost transcendent detachment from the world; she was familiar, yet no longer the same. I could not work out if she was possessed or simply and truly self-possessed. I missed her habits and mannerisms so much, yet the part of her who had been my friend was no longer to be found. There was no connection between us, and I felt the sharp sense of loss all over again for the person who had been my closest friend and confidante during those strange, rich times we had shared as students in Edinburgh.

Daniel died a few weeks after he was moved from our unit. His liver function had deteriorated, and at that time, unlike today, it was not usual for people with alcoholic liver disease to be offered liver transplants. I wish he had been given another chance at life, but there would still have been a great deal of work to do together in disentangling his depressed mood from his dependence on alcohol. Some people drink because they are depressed; sometimes drink can make you depressed. It can be difficult to work out what came first, and it's very hard to treat depression with either drugs or therapy if a person is still drinking.

The news Daniel received about his liver was the final straw, the confirmation that his father had been right about him all along. Unfortunately, however, there had been an awful self-fulfilling inevitably about this, given the amount of alcohol he had consumed.

'I started to drink because I couldn't bear life,' Daniel had told me when I visited him the last time in the general hospital, 'and for a while it made it more tolerable. I could bear the pain, I could sleep and I could block it all out.'

'What happened then?' I asked.

'It stopped working; I felt worse. Mornings were lethal. But if I tried to stop, I felt suicidal. So I just carried on. There was no way out, was there?'

He looked up at me and smiled. He did not expect a reply.

'Thank you for coming to see me, I'm sorry I can't entertain you better, Doc, but there's no booze allowed here, you know.'

After a few months working in therapy with E, my mood had gradually improved, and I regained enough confidence to try the examination again, although I was still very apprehensive. I re-sat it at Northwick Park Hospital, in Harrow, just north of London, six months after my first attempt. I did not wear the red suit. My patient provided me with a clear and concise history. This time I passed. I was relieved I seemed to be back on track and settling back into the apparent safety of the narrative I had mapped out for my life a few years before: marriage, medicine and becoming a consultant.

I have seen many people in my career who almost believe it is really possible to magically plan out how your life will turn out, and they try to plan their children's lives too. Sometimes it seems as though they can, because nothing terrible has ever happened to them in their lives thus far; everything has gone as expected. Then they experience a loss, and the closer this loss relates to their sense of who they are, and where they see their lives going, the greater the difficulty will be in coming to terms with it. In failing the exam I had temporarily lost the plot I thought I had safely sketched out for the story of the rest of my life. No one else created this plan. I was quite sure it was mine alone. I disregarded any thought that I, too, like Daniel, might have been still trying to please my father in some way, even though my father was dead and gone. I realise now that I was effectively papering over the cracks which had threatened to appear after my father's death. At the time it merely seemed as though I had temporarily lost my way and then found it again, but I failed to understand that coming off the pre-ordained track of my life might have been what I really needed. I have learned that sometimes those moments of chaos, when life careers off the rails, hold important messages about things we need to change in our existence – and the rigid expectations that we, and others, have of us that we need to challenge – before it is too late. If we address these, we can start to move forward once more, towards achieving our own goals. If we choose the goals ourselves, we have a better chance of success.

CHAPTER 6

Love

Feeling loved is a basic human need, yet 'love' is hard to define. There are many different kinds of love: the powerful unconditional love of a parent for their child, the erotically charged drive of a couple in the first passionate throes of romance and the mature commitment of partners who have spent many years together. Love can be reciprocated, unrequited, abusive or healing. A loving family can protect us against depression later in life, just as a supportive, loving relationship in adulthood can counteract the harmful effects of emotional adversity in childhood. However, disappointment in love or the breakdown of important relationships are life events that often trigger depression and can reignite the pain of earlier losses in our lives.

My patient Theresa was absolutely certain that a man who lived down the street was in love with her.

'How do you know this?' I asked. She had agreed to come into hospital after being seen urgently at the outpatient clinic.

'Well, there are lots of things...'

'OK but can you explain a bit more? What things?' I needed to try to understand on what exactly she based this belief. My consultant had thought her reasoning was far from lucid.

'Well, I know he is thinking about me when I go past his house.'

Theresa was Spanish and in her late forties. She had come to England, she told me, to marry an Englishman, but after a few years they divorced and she was living alone, working as a cleaner. As she spoke, she passionately waved her hands around, enacting her words for me. Almost every day for the last six months or so, when she was not at work, she had been spending time hanging about on the pavement outside her neighbour's house, leaning against a lamppost and catching glimpses of him as he moved past the windows in his flat. He had already complained to the police about her behaviour several times but this did not deter her.

'So tell me, how do you know he is thinking about you?'

'Well... Well, you see,' she looked up and framed the shape of a window with her fingers and thumbs. She was smiling broadly, as she was about to reveal to me how it was all very simple and straightforward. 'When the venetian blinds are open, *that* means he is thinking about how much he loves me and how he can't wait to see me.'

'And when they are closed?'

'He is doing something else, something he has to get done and out of the way,' she shrugged. 'But they always open again and then I know he wants me. Really wants me but he just can't say.'

'Are you sure? I mean he has just applied to the court for an injunction against you, hasn't he?'

'This isn't really what he wants to do. I mean, his wife... She made him do it. I know...' she whispered. Then she banged her fist down on the desktop beside her. 'I know it isn't how he really feels about me. I know it here.' She jabbed the middle finger of her left hand at her head. 'And here, I know it here.' Her fist slammed against her chest with ferocious certainty. 'I love him very much too, very much!'

There are curious parallels between being 'in love' and being 'deluded'. The accepted medical definition of a delusion is a false unshakeable belief out of keeping with a person's social, cultural or religious background. It sounds almost straightforward but in practice it's much harder, for example, to judge what is 'in keeping' with that background if you don't know the mores of a particular culture, religion or society. Those who are in love and the deluded both inhabit worlds fraught with misunderstanding and apparently irrational behaviour. However, being in love isn't defined as a delusion by psychiatrists, except in the case of 'erotomania', where the affected person firmly believes that somebody – usually a stranger, as in the case of Theresa's neighbour, and sometimes a celebrity – is in love with them.

But how do we know if someone really loves us? Doesn't that also, just like being deluded, require an act of faith to read those signs and interpret them the way we want to? Not signs as clear-cut as the opening and closing of venetian blinds – much subtler signs. We learn how to read the socially sanctioned cues, which don't generally include signalling with the window cords, but it's a process fraught with misperceptions at the best of times.

I was a latecomer to the experience of falling in love. It caught me completely unawares and flipped my life upside-down so that it would never be the same again.

By the beginning of 1985 I was working in the suburbs of Manchester in one of the first community mental health centres in England. It was an ordinary-looking stone and red-brick building on the corner of a terrace where people who needed help could drop in and ask to see a mental health worker. There was no sign outside saying 'mental health service', just a simple house name. The atmosphere was very different from the one in the psychiatric unit where I had worked before. We worked in the community, as a multidisciplinary team, and Dr Lyle, my new consultant, had blue twinkly eyes and a Geordie accent. He wore a shirt and sweater, rather than a pin-striped suit, and I thought he didn't look at all like a consultant psychiatrist.

I was, or so I believed, finally starting to get to where I wanted in life. I dressed conservatively, in tweed skirts and buttoned shirts, and was about to move into a semi-detached house in one of the better neighbourhoods of South Manchester. I would soon be a consultant too. My life script was written. Jim was moving on in his job as a research scientist and seemed to have a vision of where he wanted our lives to be, modelled on his senior colleague, whose wife was an obstetrician.

'Julia's just become a consultant, and they've moved into a much larger house. Don't you think it's time we thought about moving upmarket a bit?' he would say.

James and Julia regularly ate at restaurants recommended by the *Good Food Guide*. Sometimes they even sent in their own views for acknowledgement in future editions; I always looked for their names at the back of the book where they listed all the correspondents. We too seemed to be working our way through the establishments listed in the North Cheshire section. James and Julia didn't have children. Jim and I had not discussed this particular topic but I felt sure it would be brought up sooner or later. It was something in which I thought Jim would want to differ from his role models. However, I could never imagine myself in the role of mother.

I told myself I was happy in my marriage, but somewhere deep inside I was still struggling with my personal demons and trying to achieve a sense of contentment with a life where my role was becoming that of dinner party hostess first and professional woman second. The problem was that at dinner parties I usually drank too much to cope with both the anxiety about my culinary performance and the boredom with the interminable conversation about nursery schools and soft furnishings. I was occasionally known to slip sideways off my chair with 'fatigue'.

All this changed when I met my grand passion.

I remember the first time he smiled at me. I wondered what he was thinking, but he remained, for the moment, something of a mystery. He was a community psychiatric nurse and I hadn't known him long so I wasn't sure what to make of him. He drove an old sports car which was always breaking down, hinting at vulnerability. I thought it would be a good experience to be one of his patients. No, not patients – he, like everyone else in the multidisciplinary team, had clients. I was still holding out against the political correctness police. For me, the term patient didn't mean so much that I had power over a person, but an obligation to them greater than if they were merely my client.

'How are you?' E asked, after a long silence in the therapy session. I visited him every week in a dingy outpatient clinic in an old former workhouse, an hour's drive north of Manchester.

'I'm lonely.' My eyes pricked but I didn't cry.

'What do you want?'

'I don't know.'

I really would have wanted you, I thought to myself, but I couldn't say it. My therapist was out of bounds. My colleagues, well, they should have been too, but...

'I think, maybe you do...' he gently insisted.

'I want someone to love me,' I finally admitted.

He said nothing, just waited for me to go on.

'You know what I mean,' I added, irritability in my voice.

'No, tell me.'

He looked straight at me and I noticed that his eyes were bloodshot. He looked very tired and sad. This observation filled me with anxiety rather than simple concern. I knew I did not want to lose him. I had developed a close bond with him. He had helped me to learn how to relax and even to feel confident enough to pass the examination. But now that this hurdle was crossed, I did not understand what else I needed to work on.

I did not know then what I know now. To put it simply, the human psyche is, in one way at least, rather like an onion. You can peel away one layer of problems, but you may simply uncover another layer underneath, which then also demands to be addressed sooner or later.

Let's say, just to clarify what I mean, that a person – let's say she is a woman – becomes very depressed and anxious about what she thinks is the problem in her life. She cannot decide whether to give up a high-pressure job in which she appears to be, on the surface at least, very unhappy and stressed. For some reason she can't quite make the move, which is causing even more difficulties with her boss, who is in turn concerned about her 'commitment'. In trying to do some simple 'problem-solving' with her – getting her to brainstorm the different solutions open to her and to consider the reasons for and against each of these options – it becomes clear to her therapist that the job isn't the biggest problem. It's something else: her husband, who is putting pressure on her to have a child, and how this would relate to how she views her place in the world – her loss of independence and her own professional role outside the home. The job *does* stress her, but not because it is inherently wrong for her; it is because there is a serious failure of fit between the roles she plays at work and at home. She begins to see that she needs to address the tensions at home before she can make any meaningful decisions about her job. The situation at home, in her marriage, has emerged as the real problem. The whole thing becomes even more complicated if she then embarks on a love affair with one of her colleagues rather than addressing the difficulties at home *or* at work.

But it isn't always easy to acknowledge problems in relationships we have invested so much of our lives in building, and repairing them takes time and a willingness to try from both parties.

A few months after we had started working together, the community psychiatric nurse and I were seeing a couple together, Mr and Mrs Brown, for marital therapy. Mr Brown had been referred for depression, and it had become clear that there were underlying problems in his relationship with his wife. They found it increasingly difficult to talk through the issues they disagreed about in their family life. The male nurse and I were trying to demonstrate, in the way we interacted with each other, how it was possible to have good communication between the sexes. We looked at each other as we spoke and checked out our ideas with each other.

'We can see that you still really do have some deep affection and care for each other,' my colleague began. I caught his eye, trying not to show my doubts.

'The problem is in the way you show those feelings to each other. It isn't easy for each of you to see how much the other still cares about you. I can see how you, Anne,' he looked at Mrs Brown and gestured towards her, palm upwards, the sunlight glinting off his wedding ring, 'show how strongly you feel about Steve staying out late by getting angry. Steve copes with his feelings of rejection and hurt by refusing to talk, going drinking and staying out even later, because he still cares so much.' He sounded so reasonable. 'Positive connotation' is what they call it, making the negative sound positive: hurting each other because their relationship still mattered, failing to provide each other with those vital signals of affection and love. The Browns exchanged cautious glances. My colleague smiled at me. I smiled back.

By the end of the session not only were they eating out of his hand, but they were also touching hands, for a second or two anyway.

They both acknowledged that they did still have strong feelings for each other. I watched my colleague as he spoke. I noticed his mouth, the fullness of his lips, his slightly hooked nose. I can still smell the lingering scent of the aftershave he used. Once or twice, as he glanced in my direction, I noticed how blue his eyes were.

After the Browns left the room, we sat together in silence in the twilight. Then he took my hand, lifted it to his lips and kissed it. I was overwhelmed by a rush of emotion of a kind I had never before felt with such immediacy and intensity. It was exciting yet also very frightening. I was beginning to fall in love.

'I think we communicate very well, don't you?' he said.

I could rarely work out what E was thinking. He steepled his fingers together and looked at me. I looked at the fish in his aquarium; there were five of them.

'Have you been to bed with him yet?' he asked me.

By now I was accustomed to E's directness.

'Not yet.'

'But you will?'

'Yes, I think it's inevitable now. I didn't think so before.'

'What would you say if I told you that I thought you were trying to make me jealous?'

I didn't reply.

'You know you are acting out, don't you?' E said. 'Maybe this new relationship has something to do with what is happening here in these sessions, something you don't want to deal with or face up to.'

'You mean it isn't real?'

'I didn't say that.'

'But you implied it. Look, you've really helped me. I don't think I would still be able to do this job – hell, I wouldn't be here at all! – if I hadn't been seeing you but I need, I want, more than this.' I gestured to the dusty office with its piles of books and dog-eared case notes.

'I know you do.'

'I want to take a risk, fall in love for *real.*'

And be loved.

'This is real too, you know.'

And I believed him. I looked at him and smiled as the tears pricked my eyes. I saw myself reflected in the windowpane against the night sky. Another lamp, another me, beyond the glass, just within reach.

'Maybe it's real for him too,' said E. 'I hope for your sake that he doesn't just have a thing for women doctors.'

There were times when E could be very cruel – we shared the same twisted sense of humour – but it turned out that he had been right to warn me.

And he could see that I was not only failing to address the problems at home, but also the powerful feelings that therapy was stirring up within me.

A few weeks passed. Within a brief period of time almost everything in my life changed. Midsummer 1985 found me sitting alone in my newly rented apartment in Manchester. The sun was fading and the evening light was reflected diagonally across the windowpane. On the new stereo system – the only piece of furniture apart from the TV which belonged to me – a saxophonist improvised in a minor key. The music touched something raw inside me and I thought about how I had come to be here alone. There were times when I replayed everything in my head, trying to work out what I had failed to recognise or see in all the conversations and liaisons. How could things have turned out differently? This wasn't how I planned it. When I had first viewed this apartment, it had seemed perfect. He liked it too, my colleague – the man for whom I had finally ended my seven years of marriage. But he never moved in. On the Saturday night after I collected the keys, we went out to celebrate. When we got back to the flat, we were weeping tears of happiness as we collapsed into bed.

But next morning the mood changed. He sat up and swung his legs around to the floor, rubbing his eyes and looking down at the varnished pine because I somehow guessed he couldn't look at me.

'I can't do it. I've got to go back. I cannot leave my child.'

I simply couldn't believe what he was saying. It was a few moments before I could speak. 'But you wanted to be with me... You said so!'

'I know, but I didn't think it would feel this painful.' He turned and looked at me as though for the first time with honest eyes. 'I am so, so terribly sorry.'

'But I believed you. I am here now. I believed you so much.' I began to cry and tried to grasp his hand. He squeezed it firmly, but then a few minutes later he had dressed and was gone. The door clanged shut. I was alone.

I had been so sure when he said he loved me.

The first few days and nights after he left were the worst.

My brother Alan called. 'Have you spoken to Mum?'

'No.' I hadn't. I wasn't entirely sure why.

'Well, she knows.' I could hear the caution in his voice. He wasn't sure about telling me.

'What did she say?' I asked him.

'She says she doesn't know how you will ever cope on your own.'

I didn't call her. I felt low enough already.

Jim wrote to me and asked if we could start again, but I knew, despite the desire to return to the comfort of the familiar, that it would be wrong for both of us if I went back. I had to come to terms not only with the fact that my marriage was over, and all the guilt associated with this decision, but also with the knowledge that I missed my lover of three months more than I regretted the loss of my husband. But I did call E at those times when I felt I could no longer go on. He was there for me when I needed him.

Some of my friends were surprised by what had happened, wondering, 'How could you leave a man who is such a good cook?'

Others were not at all puzzled by my actions. 'It always seemed to me you had almost more of a business partnership than a marriage,' said Catherine.

'What do you mean?'

'Well, there was no *passion*.'

And now at last I understood what passion was about: the excitement of stolen kisses on a secret lunchtime tryst; the exquisite pain of saying goodbye and 'this has to end' in the middle of an empty Manchester street at midnight; the declaration of 'I'm going to leave him!' on a windswept hillside one Sunday afternoon; the final consummation of the affair on a joyous weekend by the sea. And, finally, the sense of utter, painful despair and rejection when he left me – where had I gone wrong?

I drove north towards Scotland. I needed to return to a place where I had been *before* – before I had made those fateful decisions about marriage and love, before my father had been ill, before I even went to university. Somewhere I had taken a wrong turning on the road, and I thought that if I could simply go back, maybe I could find a route back through the years.

The experience of therapy with E was allowing me, in some way, to start again, to move forward in time from a reference point. I have seen this in my own patients: there may be past issues which have to be dealt with so they can begin to be able to move forwards in their lives, and this might mean retracing their lives back to the point where key decisions were made. Lives cannot be lived over but, with insights gained from the past, more emotionally satisfying and truthful choices can be made about the future.

I knew what my reference point would be. When I was 18, the summer before going up to Edinburgh, I spent two weeks travelling around Scotland alone. There was a magical moment I always remembered, when I was en route by bus to the youth hostel on the east side of the Isle of Harris. It had been a day of almost white sunlight and as the bus came down the hill towards the west side of the island, across the rather lunar landscape of rock – unbroken apart from the ribbon of road – the horizon shone with woven strands of silver and azure. As the mirage began to focus and form into shimmering shapes, I could see this was a beach – a vast, white sandy beach fringed with purple mountains.

'Let's all get out for a walk for five minutes,' the driver had said, parking his red bus by the sands.

As far as I was concerned, 5 minutes was not enough and infinity would have been too short. This was a place I connected with.

Returning to the white sands of Harris more than a decade later, feeling older but no wiser than when I was 18, little had changed from what I remembered, apart from the weather. For the first couple of days sheets of horizontal rain wrapped the whitewashed hotel in a grey impenetrable fog. I sat in my bedroom and stared at myself critically in the mirror: once again a little thinner and paler, with large, sad green eyes that seemed only to judge the source of their reflection.

Then, on the third day, the sun shone out clear and bright in the sky. As I walked across the meadows encrusted with wild flowers, called *machair*, and through the weathered gate on to the beach, rabbits scurried in all directions in front of me, eager to reach their burrows before I could glimpse them. I pulled off my shoes, luxuriated in the feel of the cool, wet sand between my toes, and tiptoed in the fringes of the surf. The water was ice-cold, clear and sparkling like a thousand many-faceted diamonds. I knew that no matter what happened in my relationships with people, I would always love this place. This was a place and a moment to which I could always return, a link to the person I had been before experiencing marriage, death and disappointment in love.

I can see now that this was the moment when I began to sense the importance of accepting myself as I was, with all my flaws and failings, before I could move forwards in life again. Psychotherapists talk about self-love, and some people misinterpret it as selfishness, but it isn't. However clichéd this may sound, in order to really be able to care for others, you do need to be able to love yourself first: to acknowledge your own strengths, admit and accept your weaknesses, and begin to make peace with them. I had begun to recognise the need to take some responsibility for the life choices I had made thus far, in order to avoid repeating the same mistakes again. This awareness didn't mean that I no longer made the wrong choices, of course, particularly where rushing rapidly into relationships was concerned, but it was a beginning.

Sometimes when a person has been convinced of a delusional idea, they gradually begin to realise that what they believed to be true was never really the case. They accept that they did indeed misinterpret or misunderstand what was happening to them. Other times, though, as was the case with Theresa, the delusion remains encapsulated in a moment in time.

'He did love me,' she told me. 'I know he did; he's just changed his mind now. His wife has made him change it, I bet. I think she controls everything; he had no choice. He didn't want to lose his home and his children – otherwise he would have come to me.'

'So you won't go back to the house again?' I asked.

'No, there's no point at the moment. I really think he has changed his mind, but...' Theresa paused.

'And the police would be called and you would be charged this time.'

'Well you never know. He might change it back again.' Theresa looked at me and laughed. 'Yes, I know I have to take the medication.'

I didn't believe her.

I know why it is important to hold on to those beliefs, even in the face of so much evidence to the contrary: it is a way human beings cope with disappointment and loss, and it is sometimes necessary for survival. I had to convince myself that the love I had experienced had been real but not sustainable. Like everything else in my life, ultimately it was transitory; at the end of their treatment my patients eventually said goodbye to me and I would at some point in the future have to stop seeing E. I could not bear the thought of ending my therapy with him. I knew the difficult conversations I had had with E helped me to move on in my life and in many ways he had been right about my actions.

So, on my return from Scotland, as I sat in the new apartment at sunset, with music playing, I reflected on what I had lost. I began to weep, but after a short while I realised that it wasn't my lover or even my husband I was crying about, even though both of them were gone. These were very different tears from those I had shed since the end of the affair. It was someone else whom I had loved, whom I was missing more than anyone else. A new loss had reopened an unhealed wound and after five long years I was finally starting to grieve for my father.

Losing someone we love causes pain, yet out of that pain opportunities may emerge to reconsider past decisions and change the future direction of our lives.

CHAPTER 7

Loneliness

By the time I reached my thirties, I was beginning to understand that if I wanted to overcome some of the problems I faced in my life, and be more successful in my relationships, I was going to have to learn how to manage my fear of loneliness and tolerate my own company.

If I spent an evening at home on my own, I would feel very alone, wishing that I was instead in the company of friends and wondering what everyone else was doing. I imagined their lives as much more exciting than my own. Yet when I did spend time with them, I felt irritated, as I was unable to get on with things that I wanted to do at home. It sometimes felt as though there was so much I could learn, do or achieve in life, if only I had enough time on my own to be able to do it. However, for me, being alone also meant having to tolerate all the old uncertainties and fears that invariably dominated my thoughts. In order to learn to cope with being on my own, I realised that I had to go away to a place where I would be forced to spend time getting to know myself a little better, well away from distractions.

So one autumn evening I found myself once again in Scotland, which had become, and still is, my place of refuge from the world. From the lime-washed attic bedroom of an old mill cottage on an island off the west coast of Kintyre, I watched the pale September moon slide behind the clouds. In the bay, the lamp on the mast of the fishermen's boat, which was my nearest neighbour that night, swayed in the late evening breeze. All was silent except for the faint sound of the waves lapping on the rocks a few feet away from my window. This was the only house for half a mile occupied by the living. Down by the water's edge I had found the ruins of a once thriving community of blackhouse dwellers, people who had inhabited simple stone houses and grown potatoes in raised lazy beds fertilised with seaweed harvested from the shore. Although they were long gone from this place, where they had eked out a harsh existence on the land, the evidence of their labours in the furrowed slopes of the hillside was all around me, and I felt a strong and not unpleasant sense of their company.

'It's very basic so we don't usually let it out,' the owner had told me. 'My mother lived there and we were all brought up in the house. You have to go outside to the shower and toilet we installed in the byre – the cowshed.'

As soon as I crested the track in the afternoon sunlight and saw the ruined watermill by the shore, I knew this was the place where I needed to be. In this remote, quaintly furnished cottage I did not feel the gnawing physical pain of loneliness in my heart quite so acutely. I wrapped a plaid blanket around my shoulders to keep warm, sat up in bed, opened my notebook and began to write, to record on paper my thoughts and feelings about being in this place, and the events of the preceding months.

Since leaving Jim, I had acquired my own home – a three-bedroom Mancunian red-brick terrace with a vertiginous staircase – a 5-minute walk away from my office at the hospital. At night if I left my bedroom window open, I would hear the creaking of the exit barrier as it lifted to let the ambulances coming from the Accident and Emergency department drive out of the hospital grounds. There was a small, walled back garden, with a large honeysuckle bush in the corner, which laced the evening air with its pungent scent. In this house, for the first time in my life, I was truly devoid of human company, something which I had never really managed to be for any length of time previously.

By that point I was doing research and working towards a PhD. My objective was to find out if teaching doctors how to be better communicators had any impact on the lives of their patients with mental health problems.

One of the women I interviewed over the summer for my project had stuck in my mind. I found myself thinking about her as I wandered across the boggy meadows by the Scottish shore. Her face still haunted me. Jennifer lived in an area in the midst of ancient beauty, too, but she was deeply unhappy. She was not alone and yet she was unutterably lonely.

Her home was in a remote village in Derbyshire and as I was driving there from Manchester, I fantasised about what it might be like to settle down among all this wonderful tranquillity and isolation, such a long way from anywhere. I nudged my Mini through ancient stone villages, where the houses seemed to be watching for urban intruders through mullioned windows, and finally down to the bottom of a peaceful valley, where a large farmhouse squatted by a river.

I was confronted by a slight young woman who was struggling not to weep as she opened the door, while a baby screamed in the next room.

As she answered my questions, Jennifer rubbed her chest with her knuckles, so hard that I was sure she would bruise the skin beneath the pale pink sweater, which was marked with a small patch of dried vomit at the shoulder. I was fascinated by this small imperfection because it was so out of keeping with the rest of her appearance. Jennifer didn't look anything like a farmer's wife. She wore tight black trousers and large hoop earrings, but what was missing was the make-up. With such an outfit she should have been wearing foundation, lipstick, eyeshadow, mascara and blusher, yet her face was pallid, almost grey. Her hair was swept back from her face with a pink Alice band and the whole ensemble, suited more to a chic urban setting, was topped with a frilly apron on which a toddler with a dripping chin pulled with one hand. The little girl's other thumb was firmly fixed in her mouth and she turned her big, brown eyes on me. I smiled at her. Almost immediately her mother disentangled her from the apron and she burst into tears, showing off four newly minted front teeth.

Jennifer didn't try to comfort her daughter, but instead pushed her away. She looked tired, as she surveyed the washing-up waiting to be put away on the draining board. It was the only thing out of place; all the work surfaces were clean and shiny, as though they had been polished. It was a kitchen my mother would have aspired to, right out of the pages of *Homes and Gardens*.

'It's not as if I don't love my husband. I do, really; he's a wonderful man. It's just I can't stand it *here*.' She seemed to be talking to the walls like a rural version of Shirley Valentine, the Liverpudlian housewife who found herself talking to the wall while preparing her husband's food.

'Would you excuse me for a moment? I have to go and do something with the other one,' she said, referring to her other child.

'Shall we take a short break?' I asked.

'Would you like a cup of tea?' she replied.

'Yes, that would be great. How long have you lived here?'

'Four years and three months – since we got married. I know I don't look like a farmer's wife.' She paused while she filled the kettle from the tap and then carried on as she stared out of the window, turning her head to one side as though she could see a different view from the one I did – a barn, an old tractor and a haystack. 'I used to work in public relations.' She turned to me and smiled but the smile didn't reach her eyes.

'It sounds quite busy,' I commented.

'Yes, I really loved it. I miss it.'

'How did you meet your husband?'

Her eyes softened. 'It was at an agricultural show. He was organising it and I was working for a sponsor. He bought me some flowers to thank me for my help. White roses they were... my favourite.'

As she went away to see to her children, I pondered on the vicissitudes of fate. Two people meet by chance as their pathways through life cross at the same intersection, they take a risk on getting to know each other better and they decide to stay together, even to get married. But do they really believe that they will manage to communicate effectively enough with each other to be able to solve all the problems that life will throw at them over the next three or four decades?

'It's so quiet out here,' she continued when she returned to speak to me. 'Mark doesn't understand because this is all he's ever known. His family have been here for generations, but...'

She got up to make the tea and then brought two china cups to the table. We carried on with the questions, which were mostly concerned with her mood: whether she was experiencing symptoms of depression or anxiety, her energy level, how she was sleeping and whether she was able to enjoy life.

'There is something else I have to ask; in fact, I ask everybody this,' I said, which was indeed true. 'Have you ever had any thoughts that life isn't worth living?'

The clock ticked away in the kitchen.

'Do you have to write this down?' she asked.

'No, I don't have to.'

We exchanged glances.

'But as I said at the beginning, I do have to let your doctor know if there is anything which might give cause for concern about your safety.' *And*, I thought, *the safety of these children who are driving you to despair*. Or at least, that was my guess.

'What if I tell you that I feel like killing myself?'

'And do you?'

'I don't know. Maybe.'

'So how often have you had this thought in the last couple of weeks?'

'Umm... Most days.'

'And have you told your doctor?'

'No, I can't really speak to him.'

'Have you told anybody?'

'No.'

'So how close have you come to doing something?'

'I don't know. I suppose... not very.'

'Have you made any plans?'

'No, not really.'

'What has stopped you from doing it?'

This is an important question. It lets you know whether you can take a deep breath and judge, for the moment at least, if the person is safe.

She inclined her head towards the bedroom with the crying child and turned her face away from me so that I could not see her expression. Her next words were spoken with a sob.

'I want to... God I really want to love her, but I just can't feel anything for her. Do you know what I mean?' She gathered the apron in her fingers so tightly that I thought she would rip it into pieces.

I nodded.

'I just wouldn't care if she were gone. Don't get me wrong, I wouldn't do anything to hurt her but everyone keeps saying how lucky I am. I've got a good husband and a beautiful baby, and this one,' she gestured to the toddler looking up at us from the carpet, 'she's teething and keeps us awake all the time. I can't feel any of it. I don't see it means anything. I just feel numb inside, but... I wouldn't do anything, no.'

I wanted to tell her that I understood how it felt, that I knew what it was like to feel numb and dead inside. I had experienced those feelings after my father's death. I thought I knew what she was describing to me but I didn't say anything. We simply looked at each other in silence, which seemed to express something neither of us could express in words.

Then the spell was broken as the door burst open and in walked a tall, fair-haired man bringing with him the smell of the farmyard. And as I watched them, I began to understand, in my own mind, her story.

He walked over to her and hugged her roughly around the shoulder with his giant arm.

'So who is this then?' he gestured towards me.

His eyes were very brown in his long, clean-shaven face – his daughter's eyes. I could see the attraction and I could tell he loved his wife.

'This is the doctor. I told you she was coming, don't you remember? She's doing some research at the surgery.' As she pushed him away, I saw how his face clouded over briefly.

'I told you not to come in here with those boots on! I can't keep this floor clean and the little one could pick up all sorts from it,' she berated him.

'Sorry, love.'

He looked shamefaced at me and smiled. 'So can you help her to cheer up then? She's been a right pain in the a— lately, haven't you, love?'

'Shut up and go and change your shoes, *please*!'

'OK, OK.' He sat down in a chair next to the kitchen range and pulled off his boots.

'I'm here doing research—' I began.

'It's about the baby. I went to the surgery with the baby...' She looked at me and I could tell from her gestures and the rising tone of her voice that she did not want me to give anything away to her

117

husband about our conversation, which I had no intention of doing anyway. He looked at me and frowned. I thought he understood, that he had guessed, but I couldn't be sure.

'Did you tell the doctor how you were feeling?' he asked her.

'No, there wasn't time.'

He looked helpless.

She sat down at the table and it seemed as though she was about to burst into tears once more. My instinct told me it was time to leave these people alone.

'I'd better be going. So I'll write to you in three months, send you another form to fill in and then it's done. Is that OK?'

She waved me away. 'Fine, fine.' It was clear that she wanted me to leave.

The mood had already changed in the room. I could feel the growing tension between them. Her husband's puppyish charm and simple affection were being frozen out by her silent resentment.

Jennifer's depression had started after the birth of her first child. Postnatal depression may have hormonal triggers, particularly if it occurs in the first few hours or days after birth, but most commonly when I see it, it is related to social factors: a stressful delivery, lack of support from husband and family, disappointment with the role of motherhood and the enormous changes it brings. People approach having children with many expectations, some of which can never be met. A child will not solve the problems within a marriage, and may just postpone the point when they have to be confronted. Having a child is a major life event. Jennifer had not fully recovered from depression when she became pregnant again, compounding the severity of the issue. But her real problem, the factor preventing her recovery, was her sense of complete isolation from the world that she had known before. When she completed the questionnaire I sent her three months later, she was no brighter in her spirits. I suspect this was because nothing had changed for her, but I will never know for sure. Like many women with small children under the age of five, with no work outside the home and no confidant with whom to share her feelings, Jennifer had an increased chance (as George Brown, the sociologist, has shown in extensive research) of becoming depressed. She needed to talk but seemed unable to share her distress.

The last image I have in my mind's eye of the farmer and his wife is of her standing at the sink and him putting on his clean inside shoes as he sat by the Aga. I wondered what happened to them. Did they ever manage to recapture the spark of a connection which had brought them together or did they both carry on with their lives, together yet apart?

So many people do not share a confiding relationship with the person with whom they share their bed. They fear being lonely, and yet being in such close proximity to someone with whom you cannot talk about your everyday hopes and fears can only result in an acute sense of loneliness. Too often they cannot make the break, commonly for financial reasons, or are unable to persuade their partner to join them in seeking help for their relationship. Instead they live in a kind of limbo, an emotional stalemate.

Perhaps the conversation with Jennifer stayed with me because there were echoes in her farmhouse kitchen of the suppressed unhappiness and unfulfilled expectations that, I was starting to realise, had been lurking at the heart of my parents' marriage throughout most of my childhood. I had also begun to recognise how fear of loneliness had prevented me from addressing the shortcomings of my own marriage after the death of my father. My life too had been emotionally 'on hold' – a future postponed.

I thought about Jennifer as I sat down on a large stone by the mill cottage and contemplated the view: the wind whipping the spray off the waves, the purple hills rising from the sea across the water and the sheer overwhelming beauty of the place. I understood the pain of loneliness – the terrible fear that I would be on my own for the rest of my life, that there would come a time when I would never again experience the physical warmth of a sleeping lover by my side in the morning. The fear that there would be no one there to irritate by complaining about the impact politicians were having on the National Health Service as we ate supper together in the evening or to hug me, and tell me to shut up about my work and eat my meal before it got cold. I was scared that I would be one of those old women who die alone and are found in their kitchen having not been seen for several weeks, ostensibly dead from 'natural causes' but gnawed away by their hungry cats so that the actual cause of death could not be determined.

Like many of my patients, I was afraid of feeling isolated and cut off from the rest of the world. Isolation, loneliness and depression are closely related to each other. Being apart from others can contribute to us becoming depressed and also prolong our recovery. The problem is that when we become depressed, we often begin to actively isolate ourselves from others, because it's difficult to talk, enjoy company or trust anyone. This leads to a vicious cycle whereby we become more isolated and, thus, even lower in mood. The solution isn't always as straightforward as simply being with people again. Those who are naturally gregarious miss the company of others more than the introverted, who may need time alone to recover from the stress of too much interaction – something I can certainly identify with. When we are depressed, we may feel particularly ambivalent about being out there in the world with other people.

As I sat outside the cottage, contemplating the view, I knew that I was beginning to find ways of facing my fear of being alone; I was learning how to be with it, tolerate it and get the measure of it. Many of us need time alone to achieve things that we simply wouldn't be able to do otherwise: to read, write and create. In his book, *Solitude*, Anthony Storr suggested that the capacity to be alone, even for those who are not creative, is a sign of personal maturity and that we do not all have to be successful in relationships to achieve some happiness in life.

Buddhist philosophy and practice have contributed to the concept of 'mindfulness', which teaches about opening up your mind and getting to know your inner self – observing rather than trying to repress those painful thoughts and learning how to pay close attention to the present. I didn't know anything about it back then, but in the process of focusing on achieving the detailed tasks of my everyday life in the cottage – preparing and cooking my food, walking the 2 miles to the shop and back, reading, writing at the table by the window and sketching the views across the water – I began to practice some of the techniques of mindfulness and, in doing so, discovered that being alone was really not such a terrible state after all.

Many of us fear loneliness. All of us need to be with others – to a greater or lesser degree – to share our feelings, worries and concerns. If we cannot do this, we will, like Jennifer, become and remain depressed. However, I also believe that we can learn to embrace our solitude, and even enjoy it, by learning to 'be' with ourselves. By doing so, we can cultivate a greater sense of who we are in the world and better understand what we can give to others. Each of us has to find our ideal balance of intimacy and aloneness.

CHAPTER 8

Trust

Whether or not you pay for therapy, it's essential to experience a degree of trust for the conversation to be truly therapeutic and facilitate change. In order to do this, the therapist may need to work to engage you, addressing the fears you may have about therapy. Some people, particularly those who are depressed because they have experienced traumatic losses, need to learn how to trust all over again; they will fear taking a risk because they do not want to go through the pain of loss once more. Others, who have had very difficult early lives due to unreliable parenting or loss of parents in childhood, may have never experienced a trusting relationship at any point in their lives. For them the process will be much slower, and fraught with uncertainty and fear of getting close to anyone.

Anne was waiting for me in reception in the department of psychotherapy, where I still went every week to continue my therapy training. She was a university student in her early twenties. I knew she had already seen my supervisor and had agreed to see me, but she seemed quite indifferent to the enterprise, at least on the surface. I introduced myself and we sat down in a small room at the back of the building overlooking the garden, not facing each other but with our chairs at an angle.

I tried to begin the conversation, to get her to talk. 'I know something about why you wanted to come here, but it would be really good if you could tell me a bit more about it...'

'OK. Whatever...' I hadn't expected quite such an immediate brush off, as though our first meeting was of no great significance to her, but I wasn't going to be deterred.

'So...'

I allowed the silence to continue and she gradually, as time passed, began to fill it. She talked for a while in a monotone about things going on in her everyday life – problems with housing and money – yet what she was saying felt disengaged from how she might be feeling inside, as though we were not quite touching what the real problems were. Most of the time she stared down at her handbag strap, which she twisted around her fingers in her lap, as though ready to seize it and run out.

Then she suddenly said, 'But *I* need to know something first. Who are you going to tell about all this? What is going to go down on my GP records? Who has to know?'

She looked directly at me. I knew on one level that she was quite understandably asking me about confidentiality of information, not wanting really personal things – which I knew, from what I had been told, would relate to her difficult and sometimes painful relationship with her father – spelt out in unnecessary detail in letters to her doctor. But I also suspected there was something else.

'Well, you're right to ask about it. I will write to your GP, but only with minimal information that he really needs to know. But...' I swallowed and made a guess based on my instinct for what was happening at that precise moment between us, 'I wonder if... Are you perhaps saying that you are not sure if I am someone who can really be trusted?'

I was still seeing E for my own therapy, and I had grown to trust him completely.

'So,' said E, 'are you going to take the risk then? Get involved?' We were discussing the possibility of a new relationship.

'No, I don't want to go through it all again, not yet. I've told him we'll take it as it comes.'

E smiled and looked down at his hands. He seemed to be teasing me and I didn't like it.

'Are you sure?' he asked.

'I don't think I'm quite ready to take a risk again just yet.'

Not very long after I had returned home from Scotland, a man in the street had called out to me, offering to help as I struggled to unscrew the headlights from my Mini. I had seen him before, as he only lived a few doors away. He had recently moved in with an attractive woman who I thought at first must be his girlfriend or perhaps even his wife.

'Are these your cats?' he had asked me, smiling. My large black and white tom, Samuel, had been sitting on the bonnet of his car, soaking up the heat from the engine, while his sister Suzy prowled nearby in the gateway. Sam, I could tell, was attempting to ingratiate himself with our new neighbour.

'Yes, they are. Do you like cats?' I didn't need to ask the question, just like I knew he did not need to ask me if the cats belonged to me, as he already knew. It was simply a way of starting a conversation.

After several months of getting to know each other as neighbours and then friends, I had finally started to see him regularly: John, the man who liked cats or, to be precise, the man whom cats loved. I discovered that the person he was living with was not his wife or his girlfriend, but his sister.

'So it's nothing special then.' E raised an eyebrow and gave me one of his quizzical looks. He didn't believe me.

'No!'

Even as I said it, I knew it was a lie. The man whom cats loved became my companion and my lover too.

E remained a kind of safety net in my life and I thought he would be there for as long as I needed him to be. However, I was also aware that there would come a time when I would have to move on to another phase of my life, to try to 'leave home' and separate from my parents – not only physically but emotionally too. Then one day everything changed. I had seen E for an hour a week over the previous three years, apart from a few months when he had been ill, but suddenly he was no longer there.

His secretary called me to cancel the session but provided no explanation for his absence. 'You'll be getting another appointment through the post,' she said. 'Someone will be covering for him.'

But nothing arrived. Anyway, I didn't want to see anybody else.

'E's off work with depression,' someone said at a meeting. 'Did you know?'

They weren't aware that I had been seeing him. I was only A. N. Other.

I called his secretary again. 'E no longer works here,' she said in a rather cold and dismissive tone of voice. 'I can't discuss it.'

I was shocked, but there seemed to be nothing I could do other than what I had done before when I lost someone very dear. I put the feelings away in a cupboard inside me and hid the key.

I didn't consider seeking another therapist – I thought no one could replace E and, in some ways, my life settled down into a routine I had not experienced before. A couple of years passed, during which I spent more and more time with John, and I began to realise that he was indeed very important to me. I made quiet progress with my career. For the first time in a long while my existence seemed to lack those long periods of raw, excoriating emotion I had almost grown accustomed to. But as time went by, I started to experience again a sense of increasing despair inside me that was deeper than my usual downswings in mood: a feeling of unfinished business in both the past and the present, and the prickling sensation of a spider weaving the two together in an invisible web.

I found the name of a reputable therapist by contacting a fellow consultant I knew in the department of psychotherapy in a nearby city for a recommendation. I didn't need a referral from my doctor; I could call the therapist and arrange a private consultation.

There is a scene in Alan Parker's original film, *Fame*, where one of the lead characters goes to see a therapist. After she has summoned up immense courage to go in and ask for help, the receptionist enquires if her payment will be by Visa or Mastercard. This has always disturbed me, as it reduces the therapist–patient relationship to an entry on your credit card statement. However, there are many therapists who believe that the financial transaction is an important part of the therapeutic process. You are more likely to value and work at something in which you personally have to invest.

Money was a topic that Anne had raised as she gradually seemed to become more emotionally engaged in our conversations.

'You don't really care what has happened to me; you're only here because you get paid for it,' she shouted at me one afternoon, suddenly becoming quite angry. This statement seemed very important and, although it was directed at me, I suspected it wasn't entirely to do with me but rather with feelings relating to other important people in her life, which were being projected on to me.

'So the fact that I get paid means I could not possibly care what happens to you?'

She stared at me. We seemed to have finally hit some kind of 'pay dirt', as one of my North American teachers used to call reaching the things that really mattered, since pay dirt is the earth in which valuable metals can be found.

'I don't know... maybe... I'm not sure.' She looked away through the window, into the garden, at the newly mown lawn. The scent of grass cuttings had permeated the office. A gardener was emptying them into a bin by the gate. She watched him intently and said no more.

'It seems hard to talk about it,' I offered and she nodded but still didn't look at me.

Five minutes later I told her that our time was up, and she muttered 'Goodbye' and left the room.

'See you next week,' I called after her.

I visited my new therapist for the first time one spring afternoon. I arrived 15 minutes early so I sat outside for a few anxious moments before summoning up the courage to lift the great iron door knocker exactly at the time appointed.

The first thing I noticed was the smell of the place, the faint scent of what I thought was probably rising damp mingled with sickly beeswax polish. This was the therapist's own home and it was furnished as though he was in a kind of 1920s time warp which matched the rather dapper three-piece tweed suit he wore. He consulted in a room at the back of a terraced stone townhouse overlooking the moors. Curious exotic plants – some easily recognisable as varieties of palm, others with dark, velvety leaves in shades of green and chocolate-brown – sprouted here and there from richly coloured Victorian pots. In the fireplace there was a tarnished brass fire screen bearing a fading embroidered flower picture. An ancient, two-bar electric fire struggled to heat the space around it, and the couch felt hard and lumpy under my thighs. The therapist sat diagonally across from me, in a winged armchair, with his elbows bent and the fingers of his well-manicured hands joined together as though in silent prayer.

'I started off as a psychologist in the NHS but moved into private work three years ago,' he explained.

This was fine with me. E was a psychologist too and I did not feel the need to consult a psychiatrist like me. Anyway, I already knew that, because he had told me when I had rung to make the appointment.

'And I now also lecture at the university.'

I looked up at the carriage clock on the dark, elaborately carved mahogany mantlepiece. Five minutes had gone already. I still had 45 left if he was working to a '50-minute hour'.

'This first assessment session costs forty pounds,' he carried on.

The raw skin around my fingernails was bleeding where I had been biting it while sitting in the car outside. I could feel it smarting.

'Afterwards, if we mutually agree to continue, the terms are: four weeks, in advance, at thirty-five pounds an hour.'

There was no sound except for the ticking clock.

'So, if there is anything else you want to know, ask me now.'

The chiming of another clock in the hallway interrupted the long silence. The fire made a strange humming sound. I shuffled from side to side, sitting on my hands to keep them warm. I couldn't stand the silence. Why didn't he speak? Ask me something? I didn't know how to begin this.

'Are you cold? I'll turn the heating up.'

He left the room and a few moments later a pump started chugging away somewhere below. There was a low, answering rumble from the radiator behind me.

'I don't know where to start,' I offered.

There was so much I could tell him but I didn't know if he would understand so I found it difficult to say anything. He sat perfectly still, like a judge in a courtroom about to give a verdict.

'I guess I'm wondering why you've come?' I could sense a hint of impatience in his voice, even though I could see that he was trying very hard to mask any show of emotion.

'I've been feeling much better again,' I heard myself saying defensively, although it wasn't true. 'So I don't really know if I need to come.'

'You must have wanted to talk about something when you telephoned me...'

'There are a lot of things that have happened in my life.' I let out a deep breath.

'Things?'

'When I was younger. In my family... and lately too.' I decided to risk sharing some of it with him – the well-rehearsed parts anyway.

'My father died, suddenly. I was working through a lot of things to do with his death with my last therapist, but he disappeared from work unexpectedly.'

He had indicated on the telephone that he knew of E, by reputation only. I could have concluded quite easily without expert help that I was developing a history of rather unreliable father figures. No wonder I had difficulty in trusting men. However, the therapist did not seem to sense – or if he did, he didn't indicate it – that I was having some difficulty in trusting *him*. I wanted him to say, 'It must have been difficult coming here, talking to someone new after all that has happened,' but he didn't. It is something I teach my students: when the patient finds it difficult to talk, comment on the process. But this therapist just sat and looked at me. I said nothing, as I did not want to share my fear and uncertainty with him.

From another room came the sound of chiming once more. Three quarters past the hour.

'I think these are issues we could work on, but it would take time.'

'How long?'

'A few months, or it might take a little longer.'

'So...' I hesitated for a moment, feeling embarrassed to talk about money, but not wanting to do something 'wrong' which might be interpreted back to me later in the way that psychoanalysts share their understanding of the hidden meanings in what their clients do or say. 'Shall I pay you now?'

'Yes, a cheque for four weeks will be fine please.'

But did I really want to continue? I wasn't sure.

One afternoon when Anne arrived, after we had been meeting for three months, she suddenly announced, 'I don't want to come here again.'

We had been making some progress. She had begun to tell me about the difficult and distant relationship she had with her father. I suspected there was something very painful she had yet to talk about, but I didn't want to push her in any way.

I began, 'I'm just wondering why. I guess...'

She suddenly burst into tears. Great sobs racked her small frame and tears began to soak her blouse.

'I can't... I don't want...'

She was so distressed that instinctively I leant forwards and stretched out my hand.

'Don't *touch* me! Don't come near me!'

Her response was so sudden and violent that it seemed to shock both of us. We sat in silence for a few moments.

Then she spoke. 'Everyone who has ever said they cared about me has hurt me.'

'Hurt you... in what way?'

'You know what I mean.'

It took some time, but eventually she told me. It wasn't only her father, but her mother too, which explained some of her fear when I reached out to comfort her. It wasn't only physical and emotional abuse, but sexual abuse too. The people she should have been able to trust the most had betrayed her in the most horrific way.

'What are you going to do?' she had asked me at the end of the session. 'Do you think I should be locked up? Am I crazy for saying this about them?'

'No, I don't think you are crazy,' I replied. Many people who have told me such things about their lives fear not only that they will not be believed, but also that their confidences will have consequences.

'What you have told me stays here.' Even as I said it, I knew there were some exceptions, particularly if anyone – and most particularly a child – was still at risk from Anne's parents. I took a deep breath and continued, 'But, there are some things I need to check out.'

I saw the new therapist for four months. I was never sure whether to pay at the beginning or at the end of the session. The handing over of the cheque assumed a significance I could not explain. The decision to stop seeing him was quite spontaneous. I parked the car, too early as usual, and sat for a moment, examining the recent damage I had done to my fingers. I felt fearful of going through the door.

He opened it on the first knock. For a moment I thought I saw a hint that he was pleased to see me but then he assumed once again his analytic persona – the cipher or person without any obvious identity – on to which, at least according to psychoanalytic theory,

I was supposed to project my fears and fantasies. He would then interpret them for me, and with this interpretation, insight would come... Well, I didn't really know what would come. I pretty much knew what my fears and fantasies were. Why hadn't I shared them with him during the sessions? I was paying him – not an insignificant sum – for his expertise.

'I don't think I shall come again,' I said suddenly, as I watched the sun go down over the hills beyond the wall.

'You have paid me for another two sessions for this month. Perhaps we could fix a proper ending date if that's how you feel...'

'It is.' I felt a sense of relief.

'Can I ask why?'

He seemed hurt. The pitch of his voice had moved up a key from the usual measured tone.

'I don't think it's working. Maybe I'm not ready to start this again. I think you have to be ready, don't you?'

He visibly relaxed, and I saw that it wasn't him I had hurt, the real person inside, but the therapist. Just like I had been playing at being the patient, he too had been playing the part of the private practitioner who I could see was quite satisfied with his particular life script and performance. I had no more idea of who he really was after three months than when I had first seen him. I had offended his ego: he had thought I might not think him skilled enough. I provided him with a soft landing by saying that it wasn't him; it was me.

Only this wasn't entirely true, because his qualifications and curriculum vitae weren't what I wanted to purchase from him. First and foremost I wanted to feel that he cared about whether I lived or died. In the absence of this basic humanity, my visits to him had begun to feel like a kind of chore at best, and at the very least rather poor value for money. The emotion he had mostly evoked in me was anger at a wasted opportunity. We had never really reached a level any deeper than this but then I experienced a certain strange and paradoxical kind of pity for him so I let him off lightly. He carried out what he was trained to do but with an automatic detachment: he was doing his job but without any real sense of commitment to, or passion for, the enterprise. You cannot fake genuine trust and care, either in therapy or in life, and you cannot buy it.

I saw Anne for her therapy every week for almost a year. During this time she was gradually able to share with me the awful details of what had happened to her. We discussed whether she wanted to go to the police, but she insisted that she didn't want to. There were no other children in the household, so I had no reason to inform social services about others at risk – this was the potential exception to the rule about confidentiality that I had to check out with her.

'Sometimes it feels like you really do care what happens to me,' she felt able to say a few weeks after her outburst. A window of hope had opened.

'Yes, I do,' I replied, and I meant it.

We knew there was going to be a point when we would have to say goodbye; our meetings were unlikely to go on beyond 12 months. If I had not really cared then perhaps it would not really have mattered when the end finally came and it would have been a relief to both of us. But if Anne never experienced someone caring about what happened to her, she might never have higher expectations of her future relationships, and might never risk caring for someone who genuinely cherished her. Anne needed to try believing that she could trust someone not to hurt her, rather than confirming her low expectations by repeatedly choosing people who would undoubtedly let her down.

'I will miss you,' she said.

'And I will miss you too,' I replied

'Honestly?' She looked up at me. She was smiling, but in her eyes were unshed tears.

'Yes, honestly. Do you believe me?'

There was a pause and then she said, 'Yes. You know, I think I do.'

I, too, needed to feel that someone would care enough to help me contain the terrible feelings which sometimes still made me want to push everybody away and inflict pain on both myself and those who ever got close to me. I had felt safe enough to reveal those darker parts of my psyche to E and I was beginning to allow John to truly get to know me too. I was starting to trust John not to run away, to believe that he was indeed a person who might be able to appreciate the lighter sides – and to tolerate or even value the darker sides – of my personality and the different aspects of the whole that constituted 'me'. This felt both like a relief and a terrible risk to take, in case he disappeared too.

Whatever the form of therapy, whether free or paid-for, it will be ineffective unless therapist and client can establish a positive and mutually respectful working relationship. Without this you will never be able to even begin to develop trust in your therapist to dig around in the emotional pay dirt of your life.

CHAPTER 9

Compulsion

Sometimes it's quite difficult to make sense of the relationship between addiction, compulsion and dependence. They are all linked to depression, but in different ways, which can become blurred with one another as problems become more severe. What I certainly understand well from my own clinical experience is that many people rely on alcohol or other drugs to anaesthetise their emotional pain. They may then end up compulsively seeking intoxication in order to prevent the onset of the physical symptoms of withdrawal, which are the hallmarks of dependence.

It was a dank night in the autumn of 1992 when the detective arrived to interview me. I suggested he come to my home, a small stone-built terraced cottage in the Pennines, which I shared with John.

Despite his ponytail, faded jeans and long camel overcoat, Detective Constable Miller's way with the English language marked him out as an officer of the law.

'We want to ask you some questions about an individual you treated some time ago,' he began to say as he consulted his notebook. 'Two years to be precise, name of Paul David Anderson.' He produced a large brown manila envelope from his coat pocket. 'I thought it would assist you if I brought you photocopies of the records you made at the time in the Substance Misuse Service.'

I sat down in front of the fire and scanned the pages, recognising my slightly faded black scrawl and remembering the couple I had seen only on one occasion.

My first consultant post, at the age of 34, had been at a District General Hospital, a 1970s-built concrete palace of ill health situated on top of a hill in South Yorkshire. It was possible, as one of my patients once wryly commented, to see it from miles away. By 1990 there were only a few coal mines remaining after the bitter confrontations surrounding the pit closures of the previous decade, but many of the people I treated in the Substance Misuse Service were, like Paul Anderson, ex-miners who had rapidly drunk away their redundancy pay.

I remembered Paul without any difficulty. He had come to my Wednesday morning clinic with his girlfriend Julie. I asked her to wait outside; I like to see a new patient alone first, regardless of whoever has accompanied them, but Paul insisted on Julie coming into my room with him and she nodded silently at me, as though to say, 'Please placate him otherwise he'll blame me.' He was quite intoxicated at 10 a.m., even by the standards of our clientele, and the receptionist had told me, as I passed her on my way to the waiting room, that he had been abusive towards her on arrival. Paul must have started drinking as soon as he had woken up to try to stop his hands shaking – he told me he had been doing this for a few months by then, on most days.

'Just an eye-opener,' he said as we sat down to face each other.

The morning drinking to prevent the onset of withdrawal symptoms was just one of the characteristic symptoms of Paul's physical addiction to alcohol. His eyes were bloodshot, his hair was greasy and there was a sickly sweet odour about him – the smell of someone who cared more about alcohol than food. You might have found it difficult at first to see how he could even be somebody's boyfriend, but then he smiled his sad, little-waif smile and you would have understood.

'Do you mind if I smoke, Doc?'

He didn't give me a chance to reply but pulled a tin of tobacco out of his pocket and started assembling a roll-up. Sometimes when I went home, I smelled like I had been in a bar, as the tentacles of cigarette smoke clung to my clothes and hair.

Paul licked the paper strip and carried on fiddling with his cigarette, struggling to light it with still-trembling fingers.

'You see, it's like this...' He pointed at me unsteadily with a nicotine-stained finger and then at Julie sitting next to him. 'I love this lass and I treat her well...'

His mood switched suddenly and it took me by surprise. For a moment I thought he was on the edge of tears but then he leaned back and took a drag on his cigarette.

'She just has to realise she can't keep fucking me around.' His speech was slurred but there was a new edge of steel to it that I hadn't noticed before. Something twisted in the pit of my stomach.

'What's been happening?'

'She's always eyeing up other blokes, like.' There was an uncomfortable silence.

Julie laughed and broke the tension. 'No, I'm not y'daft idiot! I don't know where you get these ideas from.' She squeezed his arm and looked ill at ease, unsure of whether she had spoken out of turn. She was a prematurely aged girl-woman, with lanky hair and a thin polyester miniskirt unsuited to the cold weather outside.

At the sound of her voice, Paul turned back into the little boy again, put his arm around her affectionately and squeezed her, just a little too tightly.

She flushed with embarrassment and almost a hint of pride, and then tried to push him away.

I asked her to leave us for a while and, judging he had settled into conversation mode with me, she left the room. His probation officer had written a referral letter requesting that I help him with his drink problem. I was reserving judgement about whether or not it would be possible. I took a deep breath and regretted it – the air in my office was rapidly turning stale.

'You sound worried about Julie. Why do you think she might be seeing someone else?' I asked him.

'It's the way she dresses when she goes out with her mates, like. She puts on lipstick.'

'What's so strange about that? She has lipstick on today.'

'I just know she's doing it... for a bloke, like.'

'Who?'

He paused for a moment then blurted out, 'The bloke she's seeing.'

'How can you be sure she is seeing someone else? Has she told you?' We seemed to be going round in circles, but something about the way he replied to me didn't quite fit.

Another round of 'how do you know?' got me no further than a suspicion that a myriad of everyday things had taken on a new and more sinister meaning in Paul's brain. I could hear something I couldn't even describe in words. Call it experience, but I began to feel nervous.

'No, she keeps saying she isn't but I know she must be. She is.'

'I don't follow, why must she be?'

'It's the *new clothes* and things.' His voice had taken on a pleading tone. He was desperate to be understood.

'New clothes?' I thought Julie definitely looked like she needed some new clothes — warmer ones.

'Is that the only reason?' I decided to go a little further.

He was avoiding looking me in the eye. He didn't answer.

Sensing I was going too far, I backed off. 'OK, I won't push. I just wondered if I could help, but you don't have to say.'

He looked at me with exasperation, as though I was a complete fool. There were visible unshed tears in his eyes this time. 'I can't! I'm embarrassed.'

'I'm hard to shock.'

After a few moments, he sighed deeply and his shoulders dropped. 'Oh fuck it! I can't get it up any more, can I? So she's getting it somewhere else. I know she is; I can see it right there in her eyes. She's getting it.' He gestured straight at my eyes with two fingers. I pushed my chair backwards.

'Maybe we can help.' Or maybe we couldn't, unless he cut down his drinking.

'No one can fucking help, and now I've lost her.' He looked at me, his voice rasping with emotion, before adding, 'She won't want me now but he isn't going to have her either.'

Anyone passing in the corridor could have heard what Paul was saying, as he was speaking so loudly. The walls of my office were thin. Someone was laughing in the next consulting room.

Paul looked around suspiciously, as though wondering who was listening, but he carried on. 'There's times she makes me so angry I've hit her. I don't like doing it mind you, but what else can I do? She won't take any notice of me and I can't bloody bear it. She can see what it's doing to me.'

I thought I had noticed a trace of an old bruise around her left eye. She had tried to disguise it with a smear of blue eyeshadow.

'What does she say when you ask her what she's been doing and where she's been?'

'Out with her bloody bitch pals! They're all the same. They hunt in packs, they do, women... They're all the fucking same.' He leaned towards me conspiratorially, seeming to forget for a moment that I was one of them. 'I bloody love her but she belongs to me. She's got to realise it.'

'You care about her very much,' I commented. I could see that in his own way he did – not in a way I would want to be cared for, but these were strong, powerful feelings.

'I'm telling you, if she left me, if she went off with him, I'd have nothing. She's all I've got, the only person I ever wanted. I'd fucking kill her and myself. I'd do it.' He broke down and wept on to the carpet. Salt, ash and spirit mingled together.

After I had spoken to Paul I asked to see Julie.

'It's helpful sometimes to get the other person's perspective on things', I told him. 'It might be easier for Julie if I saw her on her own.' I don't usually see patient's partners on their own, but there are exceptions and this was one of them.

He eyed us suspiciously and then he laughed. 'Mind what you tell her,' he said, catching my eye with what seemed to be a warning.

I held my breath.

But Julie was not surprised. I had underestimated her. 'He says he loves me but he won't let me bloody go anywhere. I can't breathe; he says I'm seeing someone but I'm not. I keep trying to tell him but he won't listen – it's in his imagination.'

I believed her. 'How do you feel about him now?'

'I used to think I loved him. I mean, I still do. I'm crazy about him, really; when he's sober, he can be such a lovely guy. He used to make me feel so good...' She hesitated for a moment, perhaps thinking she hadn't convinced me of this, but then she confirmed my growing anxiety. 'But he frightens me too. My friends say I'm a fool to stay with him, but I've got no one else, nowhere to go.'

She told me there was always a can of beer or a bottle of cheap vodka next to the bed. If Paul got drunk and forgot where he had put it, he knocked it over and the carpet stank even more. Then he shouted at her, even though it wasn't her fault. He had hit her hard across the face, kicked her and grabbed hold of her to shake her violently. Twice she had been to casualty but he had insisted on accompanying her and told them she had fallen over and injured herself. Despite her growing fear, she didn't know how she would manage without him or how he would manage without her.

'He is always so sorry and says he'll never do it again.'

'They always do.'

She looked at me with a sad, knowing half-smile. 'You don't know the half of it.'

Julie showed some of the characteristics of 'co-dependency': over-involvement with the needs of others as a way of perhaps coping with her own underlying emotional problems, possibly to assuage her own desire to be needed. A 'compulsion' is an irresistible impulse to do something, usually accompanied by – at first, anyway – a desire to resist. I could see that Julie recognised the consequences that staying with Paul would have on her life, but she was torn between her fear and her compulsion to love and be loved, regardless of the consequences.

Generally, when people are ambivalent about a life situation – unsure whether they want to do something about it or whether to leave an unhappy relationship – advice isn't the best option. What they really need is your help to find their own solutions to problems. If they own the solution, they are more likely to put it into action. I do not have the answers to all the problems that people come to me with, but I can help a person to find them. I have learned ways of motivating a person to change, by getting them to explore for themselves the potential advantages and disadvantages of their particular lifestyle. They have to hear themselves say that they want to lead a different kind of life, as it doesn't work if I just tell them this.

But this was not – and never is, in the context of abuse – a time for subtlety. I gave Julie the only recommendation I ever give in these circumstances, and this is one of the few instances in which I do give clear advice.

'I think you might need to get away from him for your own safety.'

'But he loves me.'

'It's a kind of love,' I said, 'but it could kill you.'

Two years later, I looked up from re-reading my notes at the detective who was sitting by the fire, waiting for me to finish. 'What do you want me to do?'

I knew Paul Anderson had attacked his girlfriend; this much I had gleaned from the brief telephone conversation with DC Miller when he requested the interview.

'It's a good while ago,' I said. 'Surely very little of what I found on examination of him then will be relevant now?'

DC Miller looked up at me and frowned. 'Things have changed since I spoke to you on the phone,' he said. 'It isn't a case of assault any more. The young lady died from her injuries yesterday and Paul David Anderson has been charged with her murder.'

Later, after the detective had gone, I sat in the chair remembering Paul Anderson's boyish smile. DC Miller told me that Paul had not killed Julie. Fortunately for her, she had heeded my advice and left him a few weeks after I saw them. She had scraped together enough self-esteem to escape. No, he had not killed Julie but her successor, the next person who had tried to rescue him – or perhaps hoped he might rescue her. I hesitated for a moment, and then poured a glass of red wine and settled down in front of the crackling fire.

I had realised by then that if I did not actively limit what I drank, I too had the potential to develop a dependence on alcohol; it could change from a pleasurable way of controlling my anxiety to a compulsive need to seek out the next drink. I've seen many who started to drink as a way to manage their mood, and there is an excess of people with alcohol problems in the families of those with depression.

I thought of Julie and how it must have been for her to end the relationship. How did it happen? Had she found it hard to let go, to imagine life without him? Did she keep forgiving him, believing his promises that he would change? Did he let her go without a fight? I had never seen either of them again after the first meeting. Paul didn't come back for his follow-up appointment and she did not get in touch.

Compulsive behaviour was something only too familiar to me. I had grown up with a brother with obsessive compulsive disorder. But there were other compulsions, more in tune with Julie's co-dependent behaviour, that I recognised only too well. Glancing at the telephone across the room, I recalled how a particularly painful relationship had finally come to an end some years before. I remembered how nothing had seemed more important than just trying once more to speak to him; how I had hoped that he, my lover, would change his mind and come back to me after all; how I had hoped that he was thinking about me, missing me as much as I missed him. I was convinced all of my friends were wrong – I knew he really cared about me and that I just had to try once more.

I had dialled his home telephone number, not daring to breathe until the call was answered, in case his wife picked it up. What would I say to her? How much did she know? How could she have taken him back after how he had behaved? Did she have no self-esteem? I struggled to comprehend this, even though I was still quite prepared to have him back in my life at any cost to my own self-worth because, just like Julie, I believed I could not manage in life without a man. But not just any man – this man. Only I was more pathetic in some ways than Julie, because she had at least managed to instigate the end of her painful liaison with Paul. I was prepared to beg this person, who had rejected me so painfully, to come back to me.

The call was picked up on the third ring. I held my breath for a second.

'Hello?' he answered.

'I'm so pleased you answered. I had to speak to you.'

There was a silence at the other end. I could hear his breathing. I sensed his impatience with me but I couldn't help myself.

'Why are you doing this to me? We know it's over and now you ring me here.'

It was a kind of love but it was far from kind. This tortuous pattern had repeated itself in my life more than once before I finally, by extraordinary chance, happened upon John. I had a series of relationships with unsuitable men who, rather like Paul had drawn in Julie, seduced me with their charm but rejected me when they discovered that beneath my veneer of independence and apparent self-possession there was another – much less confident and sometimes needy – individual who was often anxious and uncertain of herself. The desperation I so often felt was a compulsive need to try to touch the soul of another, in order to patch up my own wounds and deaden my inner sense of despair.

I recognised the vicious cycle just in time to pull myself back from the brink but I knew it well enough to narrate each step. You start to hope again. You watch him all the time, and try to please him. You cannot afford to be yourself in case he doesn't like you – until the day arrives when he doesn't seem to like the 'other you' either, the person you are trying so hard to be. Your other self, needy and voracious for both love and tenderness, seems to have revealed herself despite your best efforts to suppress her. He is distracted. He says he is working late. You call him and the line is engaged. You go around and he isn't at home. His friends cast strange, pitying glances. You know it's over but you can't bear it. You love him. You hate him and you hate all men. You think about him all the time.

You can't sleep. If this is love, you don't want it and yet you still really do. But he doesn't want you. He says he has finally fallen out of love with you because you are 'no fun any more'. He walks away but you beg him to hurt you one last time.

Unlike so many of my female patients, I had never allowed myself to fall prey to someone like Paul. Perhaps I had always possessed, even at the lowest point in my life, enough self-love to avoid falling under the spell of a sociopath. Yet I could see what the fatal attraction was: the seductive smile, the belief it is possible to change a person, the determination to use the power of your love to heal both of you.

I need to state that I am not condoning adultery, but – both as a therapist and as someone who has been in relationships with married men – it is not my place to stand in judgement over others. Like many people who have difficulty trusting in the fact that they can be genuinely loved, I had chosen men who were not available. These were married men who could not give me what I needed and with whom I simply repeated the experience of rejection, which just confirmed my negative self-perception. I finally began to see that only I had the power to heal myself. Moreover, I knew it was even more important that I prevented myself from driving a decent and loving man away with my sometimes difficult and unpredictable moods just so that I could give myself the perverse yet familiar comfort of making history repeat itself once more. This recurring compulsion to feel the pain of rejection had its origins somewhere in the complicated relationship I had with my parents, in particular with my father.

I remember how I could feel the tears welling up in the corners of my eyes when I spoke to my former lover that last time on the telephone. My throat was tightening. I hadn't wanted him to hear me disintegrating. I wanted him to love me, to find me desirable. Instead I knew I was becoming pathetic, but I couldn't help myself. I couldn't feel any worse. I was repeatedly compelled to seek out destructive and hopeless emotion just as powerfully as if it were drugs or alcohol.

'I just need to hear your voice; my life seems so empty without you,' I said to him.

There was a pause at the end of the line and then he replied, 'Don't call here again.'

Withdrawal from such relationships is painful and sometimes slow. There is a constant sense of compulsion to hold on. But, like recovery from an addiction, withdrawal is possible – with time, support and complete abstinence from the object of desire.

CHAPTER 10

Asylum

An asylum should be a place of sanctuary. Sometimes when a person cannot cope with the pressures of everyday life, they need a period of asylum, in order to be away from the world and fully recover. A person who is in crisis and at risk should be offered asylum in the original sense of the word: shelter, compassion and protection from danger. All these are basic human rights. But the word 'asylum' has become synonymous with the enormous mental hospitals of the nineteenth century, described in such clear and brutal terms by Erving Goffman in his classic book *Asylums* – places in which the staff became as institutionalised as the patients.

In the early 1990s I found myself working in a hospital where I first admitted patients to beds in my own ward. The hospital was due to close down soon and was therefore entirely bereft of any investment from the managers of the local health service, yet people were still being admitted here for *care*. I hated the idea of 'the mental hospital', and deplored the increasingly primitive conditions in which we found ourselves.

One day I was struggling to get a needle into a young man's arm to take a blood sample. Kevin lay inert on the top of the bed, still dressed in his pyjamas.

'I saw a mouse. It ran across the floor over there,' he shouted.

'Don't be silly! There's no bloody mouse in here.' Mary, the domestic in the pink polyester overall, pushed her grimy mop into the bucket and splashed the cracked linoleum floor, futilely rubbing at a fresh cigarette burn.

On the bed next to Kevin's lay Mick, a middle-aged man dressed unseasonably in a thick, grey tweed jacket. He held a roll-up awkwardly between nicotine-stained thumb and forefinger. 'You'll be seeing pink elephants next,' he shouted at Kevin. 'Won't he, Doc? Eh? Eh? Ha ha! Maybe that's what he's looking at now.'

I thought it was actually a positive sign that Kevin had noticed something – anything – beyond whatever was projected on to the private screen to which he had once again retreated, somewhere behind his wide-open eyes. This place had plenty of mice and a couple of cats too, but at that moment I was more concerned with finding a vein. Kevin's tongue was dry and his skin showed no elasticity. When I gently pinched it, it retained the imprint of my thumb and forefinger: he was dehydrated. Next to my elbow, on the bedside table, was a full glass of water. I could not persuade him to drink more than a few sips, but even this was encouraging. I wasn't entirely sure what was wrong. Kevin hadn't wanted to tell any of us about what he could see or hear, which we clearly couldn't, but that until now had been all-engrossing to him. He had not spoken for three or four days before mentioning the mouse. Maybe we were making progress at last.

Mary shouted, 'Oh shut up Mick, and put your cigarette out! You know you're not supposed to bloody well smoke in here!'

'Why? You do it.' He grinned and swung his legs over the side of the bed, ready to bait Mary, a regular sport of his.

'No I bloody well don't, and you know that. I smoke outside, in my break.'

'Doc, did you hear her? She swore at me—'

'Mary, I saw a mouse too. Can we possibly get another mouse trap up here, please?' I pleaded.

'You'll need to talk to Ron.'

Ron was the charge nurse.

When I went into the ward office, Ron was holding court. A circle of impossibly young faces turned around to stare at me: student nurses, accompanied by two qualified members of the staff. 'We're having the handover,' said Ron. 'Can it wait?'

I sensed I was intruding but pushed on, 'I'm worried about Kevin. He doesn't seem to be drinking and he's dehydrated. Didn't we have him on a fluid balance chart? Wasn't there supposed to be someone specialing him?' 'Specialing' is where one nurse constantly stays with one patient to protect them from harming themselves.

Ron shrugged and pulled a face at the older of the two staff nurses sitting next to him. His hand was trembling slightly as he gestured to the younger woman sitting opposite. Not for the first time, I caught a whiff of alcohol beneath the sickly scent of Brut aftershave. 'Pass us the chart Janice, there's a girl,' he said.

Janice, the new staff nurse, pouted with just a hint of seduction. I looked away, feeling slightly embarrassed. I knew

Ron had a reputation, but frankly I couldn't see the attraction of a potentially alcoholic divorcee with a sizeable paunch. He handed me the card which was used to record Kevin's fluid intake and output.

I scanned it rapidly. 'Nothing has been filled in since yesterday morning.' Before the words were out of my mouth, I sensed rising hostility.

'Well, we've had a rough time here. You should know. You agreed to admit Lucy Brown again and we've had a lot of problems with her. We can't manage patients like her on this ward; we don't have the staff or the facilities.'

'I am very concerned about her. She is very low and needs to be here for her own safety,' I replied. 'She's made two serious attempts on her life in the last month.'

But Ron looked unconvinced.

'Who is with Lucy now?'

Ron looked at me with tired, bloodshot eyes. 'Bill. He says he knows how to handle her.'

I hesitated to ask again who should have been with Kevin.

In the female ward, which occupied the upstairs floor of the building, Lucy was sitting hunched over, with her face buried in her lap. Her fingers, blood-red with peeling nail polish, scratched at the roots of peroxide hair. She raised her head as I walked in and peered at me, her eyes bleary with medication and smudged mascara.

At the opposite side of the room sat Bill – one of the staff nurses – long legs splayed apart, reading a magazine. He exuded boredom and something else I couldn't quite put a name to.

'How are you today, Lucy?' I asked, sitting down next to her.

'I don't fucking want to be here.'

I looked up at Bill.

'Doc Aziz had to put her on a five-two last night. You have to decide what to do this morning.' Dr Aziz, my registrar, had been up most of the night and hadn't arrived on the ward yet.

'So you came in voluntarily?' I asked Lucy. A 'five-two' was a short-term holding power, which could only be used to detain a person against their will when they had already been admitted to hospital voluntarily, so Lucy must have initially agreed to come into hospital. She had been admitted several times.

'Yeah, but then she didn't want to stay. Wanted to go and throw yourself in the lake you said, didn't you, Lucy?' said Bill, as though he was talking to a badly behaved child.

There was no reply.

'She smashed a couple of windows downstairs. Doc Aziz persuaded her to have some medication, but we need to get her on to a section two so we can medicate her if we need to.' This was a longer-term period of detention, lasting for up to a month, under which a patient could be treated with medication against their will.

Lucy recoiled violently, as though an invisible hand had reached out to grasp her. She wound both arms tightly around her chest and spat out her response to Bill between her teeth. 'You're not touching me, you fucking bastard! Never.'

Beyond the window, the sun suddenly surprised us all by catching the waxy leaves of the rhododendrons through the windowpanes.

Our chief executive never came to the ward but, occasionally, his deputy honoured us with his presence. He was a burly ex-nurse who had completed all of his training in the hospital and been promoted well beyond the limits of his capability. His smart suit and tie looked out of place in the dingy surroundings of the ward. Like many managers, he only ever wanted to hear the good news.

'So how are you settling in here?' he asked me, a couple of days after we had detained Lucy.

'Fine.' I had rapidly learned that a long list of complaints resulted in fewer changes than if I tackled one thing at a time. 'But can you let the boss know I'm a bit concerned about the quality of care on the ward?'

'Anything specific?' he frowned. This sounded like work – he might have to do something.

'Well, we are having problems with quite a few things,' I paused as he grimaced. 'I'm worried about the safety of the building. Yesterday evening all the telephones were completely dead for a couple of hours. If there had been a serious incident, we wouldn't have been able to reach anyone.'

'Anything else?'

I hesitated, about to say something regarding the problems with Kevin's care, but I stopped myself. I would have to try to deal with it once more by gently reminding Ron that a patient, in a hospital not far from here, had recently died of lithium toxicity when he had stopped eating and drinking, and the coroner had been unable to find evidence that the fluid balance chart had been adequately completed.

'And we have mice again,' I said instead.

Kevin took a drink from the glass by his bed.

'Can I talk to you, Doc?' he said. He was drinking a little more and speaking again but I was still worried about his intake.

'Of course,' I said, hoping he would tell me a little bit more about what tormented him.

He looked over at the student nurse who sat staring out of the window.

'Maggie, can you leave us alone for a minute, please?' I asked.

'I'm specialing him,' she replied, jutting her chin towards Kevin. 'Ron said I had to stay here.' Her speech was flat but with a hint of defensiveness.

'Well, tell Ron I told you it was alright to go.'

Kevin looked at me. This was the first time in two weeks he had made anything like normal eye contact with me. 'You know Lucy?' he asked.

'Yes.'

'Bill touched her.'

'He was probably stopping her from leaving. They had to stop her from jumping into the pond the other night; it was for her own safety.'

'That's not what I mean. It happened last time she was here. You ask her.' He lay down, turning his head to stare at the glass of water as though to test its power of magnification, before closing his eyes again.

Lucy turned her head away from me when I tried to speak to her. This didn't surprise me, as we were being watched from the other side of the lounge.

Ron wasn't happy. He was in the doorway of the nursing office, nonchalantly leaning against the frame with his arms folded. 'It's not a good idea for you to be on your own with her, Doc,' he shouted towards me, apparently not caring that Lucy could hear him too.

'Why? I don't understand. The nurses are.'

'Because you can't hold her when she runs. You just stand and watch but we have to pick up the pieces afterwards. It's us who take the rap when she gets out and hurts herself.' His voice was bitter but for the first time I sensed a hint of humanity behind the regular macho exterior.

Ron hates it here too then, I thought, as I walked into the office. I pushed the door shut and gestured to him to speak quietly. 'According to Kevin, Bill, our staff nurse, has done something to Lucy.'

'What?' Ron asked.

'Kevin says Bill has touched Lucy. I don't know when, what or how – or what he means – but that is what he said. I had to tell you.'

He swallowed hard, and looked up at me. I could see he was worried. 'You'd better try to talk to her then, hadn't you?' said Ron.

Lucy and I sat in silence, in the doctor's office. It didn't belong to any single doctor and we all used it as a place for interviewing the patients. The room was spartan, with a battered table, two uncomfortable wooden chairs and a filing cabinet which wouldn't open. The light shade had long disappeared and a bare light bulb dangled from the ceiling, which was stained nicotine-brown from years of people using this as a smoking room. Someone had left behind a dirty coffee mug which said 'Lustral' on one side with a happy face on the other – a free gift from a drug company.

Lucy was slumped in one chair, sitting opposite me.

A nurse hovered outside the door.

'Lucy, I have to know what has been happening to you,' I started.

'I don't want to talk about it. Nothing fucking well happened. Go away! I just want to die! I can't stand it all any longer. I can't bear feeling like this. I hate you all!'

'I'm here to help.'

'Help!' She looked at me with amusement. 'Look, I've just been through all the stuff with my ex-boyfriend. He raped me,' her voice lowered to a whisper as she leaned forward conspiratorially, 'but they didn't believe me in court. They got some doctor to go through my records, drag up all my history. He didn't even ask me what happened!'

'So you don't think anyone here would believe you?'

'Course you all fucking wouldn't, would you? You're all the same. Nothing happened. Go away!' She turned away from me and refused any further attempt on my part to engage her in conversation.

Like many of the young women I saw in my clinic, Lucy had suffered neglect from absent parents and emotional abuse in her early life. These had left her vulnerable to depression, but also made it difficult for her to build trusting relationships with others. Some people have great difficulty in maintaining a stable mood from day to day, and experience rapid shifts into depression and suicidal thoughts in response to stressful events. A lifelong difficulty in relating to others is called a 'personality disorder', but I am always unhappy about using this label, particularly in the case of a young person, as it can be very 'sticky' and serve as a convenient excuse to blame the patient for the problems they are experiencing. I also know how common it is for people with 'difficult' personality traits, who may be angry, depressed or confrontational, to be labelled as having a personality disorder when their normal methods of coping are disrupted by severe depression. I have come across so many situations where the mental health team blame the patient for failing to recover, rather than looking at how they can work at engaging the person in a therapeutic alliance. I know I am not always an easy person to help when I am low, so I can speak from some personal experience.

Nevertheless, the combination of depressed mood and personality disorder, where a person does have major problems in relating to others, is not easy to treat. Lucy needed to build up trust with a therapist who would gradually be able to help her to control her tendency to self-harm when she experienced sudden changes in her mood. As this may be hard in an outpatient setting, when the risk becomes too great, admission can seem like the only option. My concern was that for Lucy, the institution had become yet another abusive experience, and ultimately very unhelpful.

I could empathise in some ways with the powerful and frightening emotions that Lucy was facing. In the early days of my relationship with John, it had sometimes felt like I was driven to experiencing extreme and dramatic highs and lows, as though my life somehow failed to have any real meaning without them. One evening, when John had been out with a friend – an ex-girlfriend – I had not been able to prevent myself from going around to his house at midnight, after she had driven off down the street.

'Why are you here? I wasn't expecting you,' he asked as he opened the door and I pushed in.

'I just needed to see you... Why did she stay so late?'

'She just came in for a coffee.'

I refused to believe his innocent explanation. 'How could you do this to me?' I screamed at him at the top of my voice.

'I'm not...'

I could feel the tears coming but I didn't want to cry. We stood in his narrow hallway. I thought I could hear his sister moving around upstairs and I suddenly felt very embarrassed. Somewhere, on one level of my disordered brain, I knew that I did believe him, and I wanted to let things go and just return home – but I couldn't. I was out of control. I did not believe I could trust him. Instead, I burst into tears.

'I'm sorry, really I am.' I wiped my face with my hands and tried to take some deep breaths as I leaned against the wall, quietly cursing myself. And yet I wasn't sorry. Part of me wanted to prolong the agony, accuse him of trying to hurt me. I wanted to wound him and thus hurt myself once more in the process: to feel the familiar pain once again.

'Go home.' He was very calm now, almost detached. 'I'll see you tomorrow.'

I paused to argue, 'But…'

'Go!' He pressed me out of the door. 'Go home!'

Whenever I pushed him to the limits of his considerable patience and I began to lose control of my emotions, John provided me with feedback, which was realistic but tough and uncompromising.

'I can't cope with you when you are like this,' he would tell me. 'You just seem to lose touch with reality. The best thing is to let you calm down and reflect on things later. Your moods really are all over the place at times. You know how I feel about you – at least, I think you do – but you can be very hard work and you know that too, really, don't you?'

I reluctantly conceded that he was right, but unfortunately I didn't know how to begin to contain these frightening feelings when they took hold of me. There were times when I felt low in mood and physically exhausted, as though there was a weight bearing down on my chest, which prevented me from moving. On other occasions, it seemed as though anything and everything was possible. John was right; at those times I did seem to lose control and retreat from reality. It was then that the suicidal thoughts would return, although by then usually only fleetingly. Nevertheless, I recognised only too well the persistent state of emotional chaos that Elizabeth Wurtzel described in her book, *Prozac Nation*. I particularly empathised with her when she talked about wanting a therapist who could help her to learn to be a grown-up and to show her how to live in a world where the phone company didn't care that you were too depressed to pay the phone bill.

Later on the same day when I had the conversation with Lucy about Bill, I saw my other boss – a professor who I was now reporting to at the university – on his weekly trip out into the sticks. As the senior lecturer in his department, I answered both to him and the National Health Service. Our aim was to replace the asylum with a shiny new community-based service. However, I could see that there was a serious fault in this plan. The same people who currently worked in the old institution were going to be transferred to the 'new' service and expected to relinquish the familiarity of the hospital where they had worked for so long. With the benefit of hindsight, it's obvious why my fears that things would not really change were not entirely misplaced, as news reports continue to emerge, showing how the care provided to the mentally ill and vulnerable in our 'community' institutions is not only lacking in compassion but sometimes shocking and cruel.

'Can I tell you what I really think about this place?'

He looked at me, and I could see that he didn't really want me to tell him, but he said, 'Go on,' all the same.

I hesitated for a moment, aware that I was crossing an invisible line by revealing thoughts and feelings that perhaps would have been best kept to myself.

'I think there is real evil here,' I said.

He looked shocked, then slightly embarrassed, but I carried on.

'There's an atmosphere. I've never experienced it anywhere else, but I feel it here. I'll be really glad when this place has gone. It's not just what is going on here in this ward. There are at least two members of staff currently suspended for allegations made by patients elsewhere in the hospital and I think this is probably just the tip of the iceberg.' I didn't add that it seemed to me the problems which I knew had been there in the past had never really gone away. I didn't believe in ghosts and yet I had been increasingly aware of the building's walls exuding a terrible, indescribable aura of dread, about which everyone around me was strangely complacent. Was I the only one who felt it?

He looked at me then as though I was deluded and I thought, *No, I am not going mad; this is real. I really feel this.* But I didn't say anything more about it to him. I could see from his expression that he was perhaps beginning to question my judgement. I needed to learn when to keep my own counsel, like the quietly insane.

Ron was on the late shift and it was 5 p.m. when I found him sitting in the ward office, writing up the nursing process notes. He didn't give me a chance to speak and immediately blurted out, 'I've seen Bill this afternoon, and he says Lucy's talking rubbish.'

'I guess he would, wouldn't he?' I replied.

'Not if—' he started.

I interrupted him. 'She says nothing has happened, although I'm not entirely sure I believe her.'

I had caught Ron off guard. His face changed, as the tension began to drain away. For a moment I thought he intended to say something profoundly personal but then he seemed to think better of it. 'Well that's it then, isn't it?' he shrugged. 'But I'll make sure he isn't anywhere near her all the same.'

I took a few days of annual leave; I only realised how exhausted I had become after being away from the hospital and back in my own home for a few days. I noticed that I was becoming afraid of being trapped by that place, as though I too was being committed to the asylum forever. For me, as for Lucy, it was definitely not a place of safety.

When I returned to work the following week, I discovered that Lucy had absconded during the previous night.

'Climbed out of the bathroom window. The police have her description – no word yet,' said Ron while writing his notes, without looking up at me. 'The good news, though,' he continued, still looking at the desk, 'is that Kevin is drinking much more. He says he was trying to starve out the worm he thinks is inside him but I persuaded him that the tablets will kill it off, poison it like they usually do, so there is nothing to worry about.'

Kevin had been diagnosed with schizophrenia, but it was not something he accepted. He hated taking his medication because of the side effects.

'And Bill?'

'On a late shift today.'

He didn't say it but he might as well have added, 'So there's nothing to concern you at all, is there now, doctor?'

There *was* something to concern me, though: the immediate welfare of Lucy above all, but also the situation on the ward. It was just very difficult to find someone who wanted to listen to me and help in dealing with it.

Lucy was found the day after she went missing. This time she had succeeded in ending her life. She had hung herself from a banister rail in a disused part of the hospital using a leather belt. I wondered if she had at last found the peace she craved, but I was sad and angry that I had been unable to save her, because I knew it could have been possible.

Even now I sometimes dream of driving down the lane to the asylum for the last time, through the lengthening shadows of the trees. The street lamps are no longer lit, but forgotten faces still peer out of the cracked windowpanes, between the rotting plywood boards that they tacked over the doors after we left. The deserted asylum which once echoed to a century of sorrows now hears only the call of feral cats chasing the mice through deserted buildings. It was a terrible place. I would never have wanted anyone I personally cared for to pass through the gates, never mind be admitted, but there I was, working within it and feeling powerless to change it.

Like my patients and the other staff members, I felt as though I was just being sucked further down into a *total* institution, a place where, as Goffman had described, we were all forced together for a long period of time, patients and staff alike, leading a controlled existence quite cut-off from the outside world. In this place I was losing my individuality, my sense of purpose and any sense of free will. The asylums have long gone, but the attitudes and methods that pervaded them remain in the psychiatric inpatient units that we have today. I know some people might disagree with my view that there is sometimes a need to detain a person in hospital, for their own safety or for the safety of others, but there have been occasions when I have seen no alternative to this. However, for the overwhelming majority of people with depression, a period on a psychiatric inpatient unit is neither necessary nor will it aid in their recovery. There are alternatives now, including better psychotherapeutic services (particularly important when depression is complicated by personality difficulties) and other places in the community, such as women's crisis houses, which could have provided a short period of true asylum to Lucy. We still do not have enough true asylums – it's still something we have to fight for.

CHAPTER 11

Taking the Tablets

I can understand why people are very suspicious of antidepressants. Many fear that they are addictive and others tell me how they believe that they should be able to recover from depression without them. There is even a respected body of opinion that they do not work at all.

When he first came to see me in the clinic, Alan had lost all hope to the point of feeling that his life was not worth living. He was a middle-aged heavy-goods driver, who travelled the country most of the week. He appeared slightly dishevelled, as though he wasn't taking particularly good care of himself. His fingernails were ragged and dirty, and he was unshaven.

'It says in the letter from your doctor that he has prescribed some fluoxetine...' I began, as I scanned the referral. Fluoxetine was an antidepressant. His GP didn't generally send people to me, unless he had already tried to treat them or was really worried. He was very skilled at helping most people who were depressed.

'I haven't taken them, though. I'll be honest. I mean, I told the doctor flat-out that I wouldn't. He's been trying to get me to for weeks.' He looked up at me, a little shamefaced perhaps, waiting for what I would say next.

'And now you are here... How does it feel?'

'A bit scary, I guess. But I told him I'd come.' He shrugged as though there really was little else to say.

A little while later, after Alan had told me his story, I asked him, 'So can you tell me why you didn't want to take the medication? What are you worried about?'

'Well, I'm not worried... as such. It's just that I know what the problems are: I hate my job, my wife hates me, my kids hate me and I don't see how taking a tablet every day can change all that!'

'And how are you feeling at the moment, today?'

'To be honest, Doc, I can't sleep, I can't eat, I can't think. I wouldn't care if I was run over by a bus tomorrow. Do you know what I mean? And I don't think anyone would miss me. There's just no point to life any more.'

'Have you considered taking any steps to end your life? Sometimes people do when they feel as bad as you do at the moment.'

'Well, I've thought of driving the load off a bridge. I wouldn't be telling the truth if I said it hadn't crossed my mind...'

'More than once?'

'Well,' he looked at the wall of the office and then at me, and I could see tears welling up in his eyes. He blinked and one trickled down his cheek. He wiped it away with his fist. 'Pretty often to be honest.'

'And what has stopped you from doing it?'

'My kids,' he admitted, before bursting into tears and burying his face in his hands. 'I couldn't do it to my kids.'

When I once again reached a moment when there seemed little point to living my own life, it was still strangely unexpected, despite what had happened in the past. If I had recognised, in the midst of my constant mental replaying of events at the hospital, the echoes of the awful winter in Edinburgh, when the future could no longer be glimpsed as a shimmering promise on the horizon, I might have done something sooner. Instead I ignored the warning signs: the early-morning wakening, the sapping of energy from my limbs, the increasing irritability and anger. And then there had been a series of losses, each of which undermined the tenuous hold I still had on my sanity.

Sam was a GP I had known for several years, and he worked in a village near the mental hospital in which I was now working. He had been a source of much needed support during the previous year. The last time I saw him, we shared a glass of wine in his kitchen. He told me about the eccentric behaviour of my predecessor at the hospital, whose approach to managing one of Sam's patients with an alcohol problem had been to empty the entire contents of the patient's cocktail cabinet into the boot of his car and drive away with it.

'So did the patient make a complaint? Did you?' I asked.

'What do *you* think?' he smiled.

Eventually, this consultant, who had on occasions been reportedly too intoxicated to take the ward round, accepted retirement, with a generous pay-off. But not before he tried to intimidate me with a letter from his solicitor. I realised an indiscreet comment I had made about previous standards of care must have been conveyed back to him, possibly by one of his regular drinking companions.

'We're very lucky to have you here – to hell with them all!' Sam had said as he gave me a farewell hug on the doorstep of his cottage, and I wished him a good holiday. He was going climbing in the Cairngorms with his brother and son for a couple of weeks.

One Saturday afternoon, as John and I were driving home, we heard the shocking news on the Radio 4 bulletin at 3 o'clock. Sam's climbing group was, I learned later, painfully ill-kitted-out for the unpredictable conditions of Scotland in spring and was caught in a blizzard with only one pair of crampons between the three of them. All of them, including my dear friend, were found dead.

And then, another loss.

'Have you heard about E?' a psychotherapist colleague rang to ask me. She knew I had seen E as a patient in the past, but she did not know for how long I had depended on him or how important he had been to me. 'I thought about you. I didn't know if you knew.'

'Knew what?'

Once again, as had been the case when I had heard of the death of my father, there was little or no warning to prepare me for the bad news to come.

'E drowned himself in the river last week. He's gone. He's dead. I can't believe it.'

I could hear the tears in her voice, but I could not speak. 'I'm sorry, I have to go.' I made an excuse and added, 'I'll call you back later.' Then I slumped into a chair and simply tried to keep breathing.

The fact that he had been my therapist was a secret known only to one or two people. And E was in disgrace; I had discovered a couple of years after he disappeared from my life how he had been suspended from his post and then dismissed for reasons unknown. He had become a *persona non grata* in the circles in which he had once been local aristocracy as a senior therapist. I knew very little about what happened to him. Now I would never see him again.

My response to these events, as in the past, was to work even harder, with ever-decreasing efficiency. This time I did not draw up plans on paper to master my problems but ruminated ceaselessly instead about the mounting difficulties on the ward.

One Sunday evening, as I contemplated the long early Monday morning drive back to work in the winter fog, my mind seemed at last to disintegrate into small sharp-edged monochrome pieces. I was unable to think with any clarity. I sank down into the sofa in front of the fire and wept. John found me there, in a room lit only by the ghostly glow of the coals in the stove, watching the flames and listening to the fire crackle as the air was sucked in through it, yet strangely unable to feel any warmth. I was just cold and lifeless. He sat down next to me and cradled me in his arms, stroking my head gently as I sobbed and shook. I was forced to admit at last that there was something seriously wrong with me.

'So, do you want to try an antidepressant?' my GP had asked me the first time I told him the story of my recurring symptoms, after the abortive attempt at restarting my psychotherapy with the private therapist with whom I had failed to connect in any meaningful way.

What I know now, but was only beginning to learn then, is that a consultation with your general practitioner is like a dance. Both of you in turn 'hold the floor', as social psychologists call it, and enter into a negotiation which has a clear beginning, middle and end. If you want your doctor to know more about you, you have to give him the right kind of cues: the words that hint at just how crap you are feeling. The doctor then has to pick up these cues. He might not necessarily feel obliged to explore your problem unless he is interested enough, but you may not want him to anyway. You may want to get out of there as fast as possible and just resent any attempts on his part to 'analyse' you. I knew that GPs varied a great deal in their interest and expertise in helping people with depression. Some were comfortable in talking about it, whereas others asked the right questions but didn't necessarily understand what it really felt like. Then there were a small number with whom you would feel very cautious in talking about feelings at all.

I knew exactly what I wanted. I had tried talking therapy and it had worked for a while. My life had been turned upside-down by the work I had done in my sessions with E and the decisions that it enabled me to make. I still believed those changes were only for the best. For a few years I had allowed myself to hope that I would never feel so unbearably anxious and fearful again, but then the bleak, hollow feeling returned. This time I also felt exhausted, weak and dead inside.

I liked my doctor. He was a giant of a man about the same age as me, with the look of someone who, like Sam, spent his spare time climbing mountains and vaulting streams. He clambered up real peaks, wet rock faces and crags with treacherous slopes – there were photographs of them all around the walls of his consulting room. He probably took risks but, I suspected, always with due regard to safety. There was something immensely reassuring about him.

However, I wasn't sure whether he really got what it was all about for me. What I scaled were the obstacles in my mind. I felt then, and still do now, that I was living on the edge of the abyss and sometimes, I suspected, I wilfully threw away the rope. I had begun to see that others thought I did this. I didn't think my doctor quite understood, but I watched him trying hard to do so.

'How have you been sleeping?' he asked.

'Not good. I wake up early in the morning, and I lie there thinking about everything and getting anxious.'

'What do you think about?'

'Work, all the problems I've told you about before.'

'What do you do then?'

'I get up and make a cup of tea.'

'What's your energy level like?'

'Terrible. I just want to sleep.' I helped him out: 'But I can't sleep and I've lost interest in most things. I think I'm losing weight too.'

He paused for a moment and considered what he had written. Then he looked up at me. 'So do you want to try an antidepressant?'

'Yes, I think I do.'

He knew he didn't have to tell me what they were. I knew only too well. I was a psychiatrist after all – I gave them to my patients, too. I was also desperate enough to try anything in order to feel better.

There were things I did not tell him: how I cried myself to sleep on a pillow, damp with sweat and tears; how I believed I was hopeless at my work and could never make a success of anything; how I felt isolated from the world and cut off from everyone around me. I did not tell him about the recurring dream in which there was a task I had to do – an examination to pass, a piece of work I had to finish – which required me to depend on others: colleagues at the hospital usually, but sometimes my mother appeared, or my father, and I found myself back in the home of my childhood, in my bedroom. Whoever I had to confront did not want to do what I wanted them to do and so we began to argue, because of my certainty that they must do it. I stated my case in clear and precise English, or at least this was what John would tell me in the morning ('You've been talking in your sleep in paragraphs again'), and I spoke the words aloud to the waking world, sometimes bringing myself into consciousness in the process. This dream world seemed all the more real to me because of the power of inchoate emotion with which it was imbued. I was thwarted at each turn, as though I were trying to move through glue – viscous, sticky, sealing me off from the world – and the final steps I needed to complete in order to achieve my goal were getting harder and further away.

I also did not tell my doctor about the terrible weight pressing down on my chest, which became lighter when I cried or talked to John, but only for a while. When it returned, it was as if an invisible demon had loaded ten more pounds on each side of a bar that I was unable to push off my chest. Maybe this is where the expression 'getting it off your chest' comes from, only I couldn't. The talking didn't work any more.

I started to recover after two or three weeks on the tablets, that first time I took them, and from then on I stayed on and off medication for about three years, while I coped with more examinations, and changes in my job and my home. As I had experienced the effectiveness of taking the pills, I was well aware that the cause for the return of my depression this time was not just linked to everything else that had happened over the preceding year. Three months before the severity of my decline had become apparent, I had stopped taking antidepressants once again, despite the serious difficulties that I was facing at work. And as a result the depression was back again, with all the same symptoms, but with greater intensity than ever. The weight on my chest was too heavy and I no longer had the strength to shift it at all. My body felt as though lead had seeped into my blood vessels and bones, slowing down my whole being.

This time, I didn't go to see my GP immediately, but instead I called a colleague and friend, Susan, who was one of the few people I trusted to give me an honest and forthright opinion of my mental state. She asked me to come and see her that same afternoon, at Prestwich Hospital just north of Manchester. I didn't contact her because of the job she did then, but because I knew she had trained as a psychotherapist. Even if I suspected, though with some ambivalence, that I needed first and foremost more medication, it was important for me to talk to someone who would be able to appreciate my story as well as my symptoms.

We met in a small room off the main hallway of the old administrative building at Prestwich Hospital, and its similarity to the other mental hospital where I had been working caused me at first to hold my breath. Inside, the place had the same aura of neglect and drabness: dark woodwork, worn linoleum and unpolished brass in a room only barely lit by windows stained black by decades of Manchester soot and rain. But despite the physical similarity between the institutions, there was a different atmosphere here: a sense that this might possibly be a place of real asylum for me, a feeling that I was near a potential source of help. A person I believed I could trust greeted me, smiled and took me into a room just off the main corridor, while John waited for me outside.

Susan set about taking my history, with the sensitivity and care I had hoped for. As I feared, however, it was not long into our conversation before she approached the death question.

'I have to ask this,' Susan looked directly at me with her clear and calm grey-blue eyes, 'have there been times when you have felt so bad that you have thought life isn't worth living?'

'Yes,' I replied. There was a sense of relief to be able to talk about it but it wasn't easy to find the words to describe such a painful feeling, and I could not stop sobbing as I replied, 'Sometimes when I'm on the motorway... driving... I just can't get the thought out of my head that I could simply put the handbrake on when I am speeding. I know it would spin the car and turn it over, and I don't think I really want to do it... but I can't... I can't get it out of my head. I can't stop thinking it.'

'So you know what you are describing,' she said, looking up at me again as she stopped writing for a moment. 'Do you think these might sometimes be obsessional thoughts?'

I had talked about my brother's illness, and the delay in beginning to grieve for my father. The past I had tried so hard to leave behind was catching up with me once again. I told her about the problems I had been having at work. 'So do you think I'm paranoid?'

'I don't know,' she replied. Then, after asking me a lot more questions about the feelings and thoughts I had been having about the hospital, she said, 'OK, possibly you have been a bit paranoid in your thinking, but this is understandable given your mood at the moment. It doesn't mean there haven't been some very unpleasant things going on, but do you think you might have just got them a bit out of proportion?'

I nodded. I knew what she meant. I might be paranoid, but it didn't mean the buggers weren't really out to get me.

'I think,' Susan paused for a moment, 'that you are really very ill, and I'm so pleased you got in touch and came to see me. I know how difficult it must have been for you.'

'Thanks for seeing me so quickly.'

She looked directly at me. 'I can tell you what *I* think. I think you have a severe depressive illness. But what do *you* think?'

Susan's words did not come as a complete surprise. Yet, despite taking antidepressants intermittently, and considering all my knowledge and training, it was still difficult to accept this diagnosis.

One of the problems for me was the growing belief among many members of my profession that depression was primarily caused by biological factors: changes in the level of chemicals or 'neurotransmitters' in the brain. This message was reinforced by the drug companies that were energetically promoting the latest type of antidepressants, 'selective serotonin reuptake inhibitors' (SSRIs), such as Prozac. As Tim Lott says in his memoir, *The Scent of Dried Roses*, it is really hard to believe that the complexities of human thought can be explained by a simple chemical imbalance. I did not believe then, and still do not think, that the nature and essence of mental illness – the most subjective and personal of human afflictions – can be distilled down to something quite so simple. Nor did I think that treatment was quite as straightforward as just the replacement of a substance depleted from the brain. I was trained to consider biological, social and psychological determinants of mental illness, and had always leaned towards the latter two in my approach to therapy, although I did prescribe medication too. Yet, at the same time, I could appreciate the positive aspects of the biological explanation for depression; it did legitimise my absence from the hospital – I was unwell and needed help – and it did begin to absolve me of a sense of responsibility for my own condition, although guilt is difficult to banish from your world when you are depressed.

What is even more difficult to understand sometimes is the dilemma that my patient Alan posed. How can tablets help when it's perfectly clear that the cause of the problem lies in external events? It isn't always easy to answer this question. Life events trigger depression, but then it sometimes seems to take on a life of its own. This follows a particular trajectory, which may be brief, especially if a positive life event – known by researchers as a 'fresh start event' – happens to boost recovery. Alternatively, it may be much more prolonged, particularly if the problems that triggered it are not resolved. 'I can see why you might wonder how taking a tablet each day would solve your problems,' I began, looking at Alan.

He nodded. 'Absolutely.'

'And you're right; the tablets won't make your problems disappear, of course. But what they will do, after a couple of weeks, is begin to boost your energy and help you to sleep a bit better. They will help you to think more clearly again and to feel more up to beginning to sort out some of these problems.'

He looked at me quizzically. I had a strong feeling that pushing him was not going to be the right thing to do, even though I was convinced he would benefit from medication. I was seriously worried about his safety.

'I still don't think it's what I want to do at the moment,' Alan declared, looking away.

It was very important that he didn't feel I was determined to make him take the tablets, and I was worried that we would lose the connection we had started to make. So I said, 'Well you have a choice. It's up to you. We could look at the different options, and then you can tell me what you want to do.'

'So I don't have to...'

'As I said, it's up to you. I cannot force you to take them. I wouldn't want to. I can tell you what I think would help, and I think this medication would really help you feel better. You wouldn't have to be on it for a very long time.'

'I wouldn't?' He sounded a little happier with this suggestion.

'But let's just consider all the options first...'

I had succeeded in engaging Alan in a conversation by giving him a choice. He decided to give the tablets a try and began the slow but eventually successful process of recovery, which also included a period of problem-solving therapy to help him tackle difficult decisions about his life.

In a similar way, my psychiatrist went through the different options with me. She was also sure that I would benefit from antidepressants. The problem was that I had hated taking them previously.

'You have been on dothiepin in the past. What did you think of it?'

I pondered the question. I couldn't stand the side effects: the dry mouth and weight gain. When I got out of bed in the morning, I would regularly feel faint due to a drop in blood pressure when I stood up; that was a problem because my bed was at the top of a steep flight of stairs and there was a danger I would fall down them just after rising. The side effects explained, at least partially, my keenness to stay off the tablets.

However, I considered what I knew about them: they had worked for me in the past and my personality had not been changed in any way by taking them. Some people have withdrawal symptoms when they stop taking antidepressants (as I would later experience myself), but they are not addictive in the sense of craving them or having to take an ever-increasing dose. I had seen them work for my own patients, particularly those with more severe depression.

I replied honestly, 'I don't want to go back on a tricyclic. Can I try an SSRI?'

Susan agreed. 'Given the obsessional nature of your thinking, it's the recommended treatment.'

I also suspected that she didn't want to give me something which was as lethal in overdosage as I knew dothiepin (now called dosulepin) to be, but she didn't say it. We agreed that I would try the antidepressant paroxetine, but it wasn't the only treatment she advised. Susan was also quite sure, although I had doubts, that I should embark on another period of formal psychotherapy, but in the state I was in, unable to string my thoughts together coherently, there was no hurry. I could wait until a suitable slot arose with the consultant to whom she decided to refer me.

I was nervous about taking new medication, and over the first few days I felt quite nauseous, especially in the morning. I learned to take the tablet with food, which helped me to tolerate it. I also noticed I was getting even more headaches than usual. Apart from giving me side effects, which gradually disappeared, 20 milligrams of paroxetine did not seem to do very much at all. I felt less agitated, but the morbid bleakness did not leave me. I began to wonder if I would ever feel any better, as I still found it difficult to get out of bed before the late morning and – most distressing of all for a person who had always surrounded herself with books – I felt unable to even open one of them, never mind concentrate for long periods of time in order to read. An increase to 40 milligrams didn't make much difference and in retrospect, given what I know now about the comparative efficacy of the SSRIs in more severe depression, this isn't surprising. So, after three months or so of treatment, I started on lithium. It is well known as a treatment for bipolar disorder but, in about half of the people who are not responding to an antidepressant, can also be an additional therapy for depression, as it improves mood fairly rapidly. The problem is that – amongst other more unpleasant things such as kidney disease – it requires regular blood tests and can, as I would discover, cause underactivity of the thyroid gland.

One morning, a couple of weeks after starting the lithium, something happened. I turned over to bury my face in the pillow, which was damp from another night of dreaming, chasing after a resolution to a problem that I could never quite define. I realised that the bed was empty and cold beside me. John was up. What time was it? How long had I slept? I checked for the awful weight on my chest, as it usually caught me unawares in the moment between waking and full consciousness. But this time it didn't. I opened my eyes and looked around: a hint of sunshine through the curtains, the scent of grass wafting in the breeze and the sound of birds singing. When had the birds returned? I hadn't noticed them for a long time.

Something had changed; it was a subtle alteration. Looking back, this was when I began to recover. It was a lightening of my heart, a new ability to notice the world around me again. Could these improvements really be connected to the tablets I had been swallowing every night? I found it hard to believe. Although I knew that tablets could change your perception of the world, I didn't want to believe that the solution to *my* problems could be so simple – and yet it was true. The terrible weight seemed considerably lighter and, while I could still sense its presence in the wings of my mind, something else was preventing it from taking centre stage: the sound of the birds, the smell of the grass and the brightness of the daylight. The world was singing to me. Life had returned.

The tablets worked for me then and they have continued to work for me on most occasions whenever the terrible burden returns. Without them I don't think I would have survived to wonder again at the sharp, fresh beauty of a spring morning. I know they do not work for everyone, but even the sceptics agree that they do seem useful to some degree when your mood is very low.

I remembered a patient I had seen many years ago in my first year as a psychiatrist telling me how when she was elated, she could actually hear the grass growing in the lawn. I knew then just what she had meant. Ever since my childhood, I had always been hypersensitive to the moods of others: able to pick up and then worry about the significance of minute changes in their words and behaviour. This is the downside of sensitive awareness. But as I began to recover, I recognised other moments when I started to feel totally at one with the world again and back in tune with what seemed to me like the rhythm of nature itself; *oceanic* moments I would not denigrate with a pathological label.

At those times I wondered whether the weight really had been as heavy as I had thought. Maybe it had not so much melted away as never been there in the first place? Perhaps I had been exaggerating, pretending, trying to escape my responsibilities at work, in life? Wasn't this what everyone else was thinking? It is hard to remember how heavy the burden of depression can feel when all you want is to forget about it.

But I realised once more, just as I had as a medical student, that I found it all too easy to understand how other people, clambering up their own personal mountains of the mind, managed to find themselves at the bottom of a crevasse with no obvious way back up. This time I had found someone who was willing to throw me a rope.

Antidepressants can only ever be *part* of the treatment for depression, but I think that when you are severely depressed and find talking treatment just too difficult to engage with, they are definitely worth a try.

CHAPTER 12

Revisiting the Past

There are times when the past still seems alive in the present. We relive the difficulties and problems from our early relationships with those who are important to us now. Sometimes if a person is failing to recover, or having repeated episodes of depression, it becomes clear that he or she needs to revisit their past to understand and challenge its continuing impact.

'So this is your third experience of psychotherapy?' Jenny, who was sitting opposite me, enquired. She looked up and smiled at me. It was a greeting which helped me to feel less pessimistic for arriving at this point once more.

'Yes, third time lucky I hope.' I tried to make a joke of it and she didn't wince. We had met before professionally but not personally. She was quietly spoken, with very sharp eyes which missed nothing. I had waited six months for this 'slot' with her. 'I've decided I have to make space to try to make some sense of the last few years.'

We were seated in a large and rather bare upstairs room in a big terraced house, in another city in the north of England. The walls had at one time perhaps been painted white but now appeared grey. There were dirty smudges near the door, where it looked as though the troubled spirits cast out of people who had sat in this chair before me had jostled and rubbed past each other to escape from their exorcist. Two armchairs were placed facing each other at an oblique angle, and against one wall – the first time I had ever seen one in an NHS psychotherapist's office – was a couch covered in a faded red paisley throw. The air was still and warm, with a barely perceptible scent of old flowery perfume.

'And so you are still on medication now?' Jenny turned over the letter from my consultant, Susan.

'Yes, and I'm back at work too, after six months off, and I've just got married.' John and I had our wedding just after I went back to work at the hospital again.

'Hmm... congratulations!' she smiled at me. 'So,' Susan said, 'there were problems at work. What happened?'

'I had a terrible time with the management at the hospital. I got very low... and a bit paranoid. I thought there was some kind of conspiracy going on. There wasn't, but... There are still some problems between me and them.'

I was back at work with the tolerance rather than the welcome of the management team, having been told that there had been undisclosed complaints about me.

Jenny continued, 'And Susan also mentioned that something happened to your previous therapist, E...'

'Yes, did you know him?' I asked tentatively, unsure whether I wanted to talk very much about him to a person I had only recently met.

'I knew of him, but I don't think we ever came into contact.'

There was nothing in her tone of voice to suggest she was not telling me the truth, but I wondered how much she knew about what had happened to E. Psychodynamic psychotherapy is a small and incestuous world.

'I thought he helped me the most,' I said swiftly, and I could tell from her expression as I looked up from staring at my fingers that she had noted my ambivalence about dwelling on this topic. Nevertheless, she captured my gaze, inviting me to go on.

'The second therapist I just didn't like at all – and I didn't think he liked me either.' I knew I was rushing to change the topic.

'And that is important to you...'

'Yes, very.'

'So how do you feel about therapy now?' she asked in a quiet voice.

It was a good question. 'Still positive, I guess. Otherwise I wouldn't be here.'

'And what was most helpful about talking to E?'

'The work we did in helping me to begin to grieve for my father.'

I began to tell her about the events that took place in the winter when my father died, about the end of my marriage and the lessons I had learned from therapy with E in beginning to understand the difficult relationships I had with powerful men, starting with Dad. Jenny listened for a long time. When I paused, I noticed the concern and kindness in her eyes.

'You haven't mentioned your mother.'

'No,' I replied, 'I don't think I have.'

'Would you like to tell me about *her*?'

'I don't think my mother and I were ever really close,' I began.

'What makes you say that?' she asked.

'She was always criticising me. It always began in the same way: there would be an argument over me not helping enough with the housework because I had homework to do or because I wanted to go out with friends. Whatever I did was never, ever enough.'

Painful memories stay fresh, ready to take advantage of the moment when they see an opportunity to regain the centre stage of our conscious minds.

Whenever I thought about my relationship with my mother, I remembered the summer long ago when I first really acknowledged feeling alone in the world.

'Here we are, working all hours God sends, and all you can be worried about is yourself, as usual,' said Mum. 'I never thought I'd say it of my own flesh and blood but you are a selfish piece of work.'

'That's not fair. I've been working too,' I replied. That summer I was studying hard for my mock A levels.

'Work! You don't know the meaning of the word. I was out working for a living when I was fifteen. Well, that's it; I've had it with you. I was looking after myself when I was your age. It's time you did the same, madam,' she said, storming out of the room.

I followed her. 'I just can't win in this house. You want me to do my homework and I need time to do it. You never ask the boys to do anything!'

I had a Saturday job working a full day in Marks & Spencer; dressed in a hot and sticky blue-and-white-checked nylon overall, I sat on the food checkout till or stacked the shelves with bread and cakes. I bought all my own clothes out of the money I earned and I studied hard, well into the night sometimes. After Mum told me it was 'time I looked after myself', I took care of my own laundry, washing and ironing. I managed to do all of this, but still I would displease her. The mistake I always made was answering back – in our home, this was considered to be one of the worst sins that a child could inflict on a parent. I now know that these conflicts are a normal part of growing up. However, the parental reaction that my behaviour provoked was not the love and understanding – tempered with firm limit-setting – which would have helped me to mature and grow, but instead an outpouring of anger and a harsh sense of rejection which stunted my emotional development and probably delayed it for quite some time. There are occasions when I feel, even in my fifties, that I will always be an angry, rebellious teenager.

'Things in the family were pretty awful anyway, during my teenage years.'

'How?' asked Jenny.

'Well it was partly the stress caused by my brother's obsessive compulsive disorder. We didn't know what the illness was back then and it was just sapping everyone's strength. Dad tried to get Alan to see reason about his behaviour but...'

'But?'

'It's difficult to argue with someone who thinks they have to do something when you know it doesn't make sense. It was just terrible... awful. It affected all of us.'

It was impossible to imagine the torment inside Alan's head as he struggled with the demons that only he could understand. Yet, despite the awfulness of it all, our family life had settled over the years into a strange kind of routine in which tears, temper tantrums and disappointment were perfectly normal. It was almost like living through a prolonged natural disaster; you believe you have become immune to further trauma. My brother's mental illness was in no way comparable to a monumental event of death and destruction, but it was an everyday domestic tragedy that quietly stole away all our hopes and dreams – not least those of my brother.

'Anyway, that summer, when I was fifteen, Mum said she'd been tidying up my room, which was strange because she never did it, and she'd found my diary.'

I had usually kept the diary under my dressing table shelf, behind the green-and-blue-patterned curtain that I had made from a remnant of cloth. The diary was an A4-sized notebook which I covered in a sheet of leftover wrapping paper decorated with autumn leaves. In this book I wrote about films I had seen, places I had been to (only a few) and places I dreamt of visiting (many), and boys I fancied in my class – all of a typical teenager's feelings, thoughts and desires.

'Where was it?' asked Jenny.

'It was always kept out of sight, so I knew it meant she had been going through my belongings, my private things.'

'What did she say?'

I looked up at Jenny to gauge her reaction.

'Mum said, "How could you say such awful, horrible things?" I can't even remember what I wrote, and it's so long gone now.'

There had probably been a lot of childish anger splashed across the diary's pages, in capital letters and double underlined with coloured pens – such was my style. I was always dramatic when I got annoyed, and I still am.

'You see, I was somehow always in the wrong at home.'

'Your dad wants to talk to you,' my mother would say.

'You've really upset your mother,' he would admonish me. 'Apologise to her.'

I always knew when he was angry with me, and I always seemed to know how to make him even angrier, by criticising her.

I would mumble an apology. 'I'm sorry.'

She would look at me with a satisfied smile playing over her Max Factor-stained ruby-red lips, managing to appear and sound hurt (for my father's benefit) yet emotionally cold (to me). 'You might at least behave like you mean it,' she would comment. She was never conciliatory.

After the diary incident, there was no opportunity to even fake a solemn regret.

Mum was sitting in the lounge next to Dad like they were magistrates at the bench ready to deliver a jointly agreed verdict.

'You can't imagine how much your mother's feelings have been hurt.'

'This has really upset your dad. He just couldn't believe it when I showed your diary to him.'

And what about me? I wanted to say. *She hurts my feelings all the time.* I have never felt loved, wanted or comforted by my mother. At best, she tolerated my presence in the world. No, I didn't say those things then because I was unable to express them clearly. Now that I am older, I can frame the bitter resentment into phrases and sentences.

'But it all still hurts you,' Jenny suggested.

'Yes. I suppose it always will.' I paused for a moment, catching up with another memory. 'I had a seventeenth birthday party at home. It was going fine, no trouble, no complaints about the noise, and then my boyfriend vomited in the front garden after his younger brother put washing-up liquid in his pint of beer. Mum and Dad were just passing at the time to check that "everything was going smoothly" and met him rushing out to throw up over the bedding plants behind the privet hedge.' I pulled a face and then started to laugh as I savoured the memory. With hindsight I really could see the funny side of it, even if I hadn't been able to at the time; my parents certainly didn't.

'What else?'

'I had my purse stolen at my eighteenth birthday party, downtown in a restaurant, and had to wake up the house at two a.m. to be let in.'

'Doesn't sound so wild to me,' commented Jenny. I wondered if she had teenaged children.

'No, me neither.' I smiled. 'I had so many books on my bedroom floor I'd worked out this way of leaping straight from the doorway to the bed. I thought it was really clever!' I started to giggle with a strange forgotten pride at my ingenuity. 'I didn't get pregnant, have an abortion, get cautioned by the police, use drugs or run away from home. I knew people who did – well, one or two of those things.'

My misdemeanours were just minor teenage sins in the grand order of things, but in our household they somehow, when catalogued and scrutinised in detail, became evidence for my ever increasing 'unacceptable behaviour'.

'When my parents told me off, I always answered back.'

Jenny picked up something in my voice. 'What did they do?'

I could feel the tears forming behind my eyelids. 'Dad slapped me really hard. On one occasion I remember, the imprint of his fingers on my arms and legs lasted for hours and it really stung. I just sat in my room all night and cried.'

'How did you feel afterwards?'

'Terribly, terribly ashamed... and guilty for making him so angry.'

'Why did you feel that way?'

'I didn't want him to hate me! But I... I was beginning to believe those things Mum said about me too.' I started to sob uncontrollably at the memory of that awful day. No one had come up to my room to see how I was. I felt completely alone.

I am aware now that in that period the terrible sense of guilt I bear for being the person I am – the unacceptable, ungrateful daughter – had been given succour. It would grow and flourish as I struggled and failed to rebuild my relationship with my family before my father died.

'It still hurts very much,' Jenny said. She took off her glasses and put them on the table beside her.

'I don't have any contact with Mum...'

I looked up at Jenny and saw the question in her eyes, so I continued, 'But she phoned me last week and left a message on the answering machine. I haven't got back to her.'

'And will you?'

'No. It's easier this way. It's a form of survival, I suppose.'

'Survival?'

'I can keep myself together if I don't have to deal with the way she screws up my head.'

'Strong words.'

'Strong feelings.'

'You sound very angry with her.'

'Yes I am. I think I'm quite an angry person really.'

A few days after my slot with Jenny, I was sitting in my office at the hospital, listening to my own patient called Mary.

I had recently treated her for severe depression and there had been times when I had been very seriously concerned for her safety. Considerable progress had been made, but then something had happened which risked plunging her back down again. Her parents had been injured in a coach crash while on holiday and, as a result, both needed a great deal of care. They were in their seventies and recovery was slow. Mary's father was more emotionally traumatised than physically disabled by the accident.

'I've been going in every day since they came home,' Mary said.

'How does it affect you?'

'Well, I've just got to do it, haven't I? She's my mum...' Her voice trailed off and she looked down at the floor.

'Yes she is.'

'Not that she's ever behaved like a mother, I know. But my brother's got his family to look after and his job, so it's down to me to do for her and I like to see my dad.' Mary's voice softened as she spoke his name.

'Doing for her' involved getting her mother out of bed, dressed, fed and toileted, staying at their house most of the day, and then returning to get her settled for the night. 'My brother comes over sometimes in the evening.'

'Does he help?'

'Not a lot but Mum's always really pleased to see him. He brought a new cup for her last night because I broke her favourite one.'

'You broke it?'

'I didn't mean to; it just slipped out of my hands when I was drying up. She cried out for me to come quickly and it gave me a shock. Then it turned out she just wanted the TV switching over.'

I thought to myself that I probably would have smashed the cup long ago if I had experienced the cruelty Mary had suffered from this woman since childhood, but I didn't say anything.

'What did she say about it?' I asked.

'She said I was a useless, lazy good-for-nothing and a complete disappointment to the whole family.'

'Is this how it has always been, Mary?'

'Yes.' She looked down at her hands. 'You know I hadn't realised until recently, when you asked me, just how angry it makes me feel. Mum's always said these things to me but not to Jason – he's always been the perfect one. He is the youngest,' she continued after a moment, 'but I think I have always felt very angry with him too. I used to hide his toys when we were kids. I smashed them up once. I think I wanted to make him cry.' She looked up at me. I could sense she was recalling something important that happened a long time ago. We sat in silence for a few moments.

'Mum used to say, when we were young, that I was just thick and he was the clever one.'

'So you wanted to get back at him?'

'And her. I wanted to *really* hurt her too. She didn't like my first boyfriend and neither did Dad... so I ran off with him.' She looked at me as if recognising for the first time how she had come to make such an important decision, one that had a profound impact on her life: pregnancy and a hasty marriage to a man who had abused her even more. 'I think I did that to annoy her more than anything else, you know. I can see that now... I still feel like I want to run. And now I can't.'

People have a way of living up to what is expected of them.

My father had expected me to work hard and do well at school, and I did fulfil his expectations, although by the time I was ready to leave home, I was no longer sure whether this was what he wanted or expected from me. He seemed to have difficulty in relating to me as an adult who might make life choices he disapproved of, such as going out with boyfriends he didn't particularly like when I should be studying.

I don't think my mother hoped for the same things from me at all – on the contrary, I realise now that she had much lower expectations. I think she assumed I would get married, live somewhere nearby, provide her with grandchildren and go shopping with her on a Saturday afternoon. In many ways I suspect that she was quite disappointed I didn't fulfil her hopes for me, but most of all I suppose she cherished the belief that I would not seriously compete with her or challenge her – in looks, in life experiences, and for the affection and attention of my father. I let her down, even though I didn't understand what I was doing at the time to make her so unhappy. It's difficult to cope with a mother who is jealous of her own daughter. Instead of fulfilling her hopes, I nourished her disappointment in me.

It was particularly difficult for me not to think about my own mother when Mary was talking about hers during our consultations.

'What's it like for your father?' I asked her.

'How has it ever been for my dad?' she sighed. 'He just puts up with her. Whatever she says to him, he goes along with things; he always has, for a quiet life.'

'So when you were a kid, and you were always the scapegoat if something went wrong, did he ever say anything?'

She studied me for a moment, with large grey eyes, and then glanced away at the window with its view out to the front of the hospital. 'I love my dad.' Her voice had sunk to a whisper. The noise of the wind and rain hitting the windowpane was in danger of drowning out the sound of her voice. 'It's terrible weather outside. I'll get wet walking to the bus.'

'You said you love your dad,' I repeated, 'and I know you do.'

'And he's had such a hard time in his life.'

'So have you.'

'He's just soft with Mum.'

'Maybe he loves her.'

'Somebody has to.'

'Perhaps he's a little like you?'

'Yes, my dad and I always had more in common.'

'And Dan? What does Dan say?' Dan, Mary's elder brother, had got away as soon as possible.

'I haven't heard from him lately.'

'No? But what did he say last time you spoke to him?'

'He said I was a bloody fool for looking after them and I should leave it to His Majesty – that's what he calls Jason – but he isn't here. He doesn't have to face them, does he?'

I thought to myself that I didn't have to face my mother either. It was easy for me to identify with Mary's older brother, and to want her to tell her mother and younger brother to 'go to hell'. But I could not do it. If Mary did not want to change the situation, my responsibility lay in trying to help her cope with it. Mary was still fragile from other recent events in her life. Although I could understand how her relationships – both in earlier life and at the present time – were contributing to her problems, I wasn't sure she would necessarily benefit from a therapy that would seek to challenge her shaky defences and potentially leave her even more vulnerable. She needed understanding, acceptance and support through the current crisis. Afterwards we could review how much she wanted to revisit the past and potentially relive some of the awful incidents in her childhood, such as when she had been physically punished by her mother to the point of injury.

'What do you feel for your mother now, Mary?' I asked.

'She's my mother, so of course I love her...' She pondered for a moment. 'And I hate her too. I really, really hate her.' She looked up at me and reddened slightly. 'It's a terrible thing I just said, isn't it? I'll have to go and ask the priest for absolution.'

'No,' I replied, 'I don't think it's terrible at all. It's how you see it. Now we have to help you to live with it.'

Jenny had not been shocked either when I talked about the hate I still bore for my mother. 'This is a different kind of emotion than what you feel for your father, isn't it?'

'I was angry with Dad for dying before we got to know each other again. I wanted him to be proud of me.'

'I am sure he would have been.'

'But I don't know that, do I?'

'Don't you?' she replied.

I believe that a woman's success in the wider world owes a great deal to the quality of the relationship she has with her father. Mine encouraged me and pushed me. However, he could not cope with the reality of my maturing into a young woman who was just as moody, intense and bad-tempered – and perhaps as creative and warm, or at least I like to think so – as he was.

It was my mother who, instead of trying to heal the rift between us, drove a great wedge into the gap and successfully managed to lever the two of us terminally apart. Yet I am quite sure that if my mother were sitting here now, she would either fail to remember or completely deny many of the things which I can recall so clearly. She has her own way of coping with the world, her own truth which sustains her. She has friends and family members who support her viewpoint and who have never seen the person I know her to have been.

With Jenny's help, I was beginning to see the positive as well as the negative aspects of being a 'difficult' and sometimes angry person.

In my arguments with the hospital management I had been standing up for something I believed to be right.

'That's just how I am,' I tried to explain to Jenny. 'I just can't stop myself.'

'You shouldn't feel ashamed for being this way but maybe you will need to learn how to stop yourself sometimes,' she replied. 'It isn't always helpful to say exactly what you think.'

I knew Jenny was right, but this was something I didn't feel able to deal with just yet. There were some things I wasn't ready to challenge or change about myself, even though I could make the link between my strong sense of injustice and quickness to anger in the present, and how I had felt long ago towards my mother.

There is no single truth in this world, but a variety of different perspectives filtered through the several lenses through which we view our lives. We do not have to adopt as our own the memories, values and perceptions of others. We negotiate the truth that sustains our belief in ourselves, in our personal narrative – for good or bad – through our conversations with friends, on the written page in our diaries and journals or in psychotherapy. In these ways we can begin to revisit the past and start to understand how it helped to make us who we are, and then finally challenge and dissipate the power it still holds over us.

CHAPTER 13

Exorcising Ghosts

Some of the most difficult relationships are those in which there is no apparent possibility of resolving conflicts because one of the parties is no longer living. Many people who are depressed remain haunted by the persistent power of ghosts from their past.

By the end of my therapy with Jenny, 18 months after we first met, I no longer felt as much guilt about my failings as a daughter. However, I knew that some particular ghosts still troubled me; I had tried to lock them away in the dusty cellars of my mind, but spirits have the power to move anywhere they wish. Every now and then they would seep through the barrier into my awareness and trouble me intensely with unexpected bleak moments.

Once again, something had happened to upset the delicate balance of my mind.

I had telephoned Susan and asked for an earlier appointment.

'I don't know where to begin,' I said. 'It's about E.'

'Oh.' Susan inhaled deeply.

Throughout therapy, and afterwards, I had kept in contact with Susan, my psychiatrist, who not only supervised my medication but also provided me with the sense that someone was continuing to care for me. This was very important to me, more so than the relationship I had experienced with Jenny.

In Susan's office I focused on the pictures on the shelf behind her. There was a photo of someone who looked like her daughter, dressed in riding clothes, standing next to a pony and another of a rider jumping over a fence. There was a family resemblance; the same thin, aristocratic features and light-coloured hair. I wondered what it would be like to be her daughter.

'Go on,' she gently nudged me to continue.

'I found out something awful about E, about why he was dismissed from work.'

I suspected she knew what was coming – but if she did, she didn't say. She just asked, 'Shall we talk about it?'

I realised that I had not allowed myself to grieve for E, and the unexplained and abrupt manner of his exit from my life, followed by his suicide, had left me in a kind of anxious emotional limbo I had not mentioned to Jenny. I had also found myself, as a result of E's departure, unable to continue with the gradual uncovering of the truth about my relationship with Dad, intimately connected as it had been to the progress I had made in my conversations with E.

'Did you know him?' I asked Susan.

She nodded but didn't say anything or reveal any expression. *It's the training: never show how you feel*, I thought to myself.

Except sometimes Susan did, which was why she was able to reach out and help me. Like E had done. He had been human too – only too human.

'I can't exactly remember what he looked like,' I went on, 'which is weird, because I saw him every week for three whole years.'

What I recalled most clearly about E was his office: a small, cluttered room, piled high with his books, in a whitewashed first-floor corridor of a hospital listed for demolition. In the waiting room there were half a dozen bent wooden chairs and, on the wall, a faded print of a picture by Heath Robinson entitled *The Psychic's Ball*. I knew every character in the drawing after three years of sitting there, listening, waiting for E to walk down the corridor and put his head around the door. Depicted in it were a man in tails dancing with an imaginary partner, a waiter serving a drink on a tray to an empty chair and a couple deep in conversation with someone who was quite invisible to anyone else. There was something wryly amusing about the picture being in a psychotherapy waiting room, because this was a place people came to have their unseen demons driven out, to make the past visible and to lessen the power it still held over them.

'Three years is a long time,' said Susan. 'What comes into your mind when you think about him?'

He wasn't a physically attractive man. He wasn't particularly tall, and he had a beard and a developing paunch. But there was something about him that captured your attention: a spark of vitality – a sense of unpredictability, of mischievous fun, of not always doing what was expected. E was not afraid of me.

And in an instant, despite everything that had happened, all I could tell Susan about E was: 'I loved him.'

I loved the sound of his voice, the smell of his armchair, the carelessness of his appearance, the peel of his laughter and the firmness of his grip on the single occasion he gave me a brotherly hug – not that I wanted it to be brotherly.

On every journey to visit him I would pass a red-brick ivy-clad hotel near the slip road from the motorway, and I would find myself thinking: *What if we could meet there after our session? What if we could have a drink at the bar? What if the hug could have been more than a comforting gesture and turned out to be the prelude to an hour or so of sensual pleasure?* The hour we spent together was filled with recriminations, tears and sometimes a memorable coming together of minds, but never bodies.

However, I know that if E had weakened and given me what I desired, he would have lost his power to help me. I would have lost the respect I had for him, and the belief that he could contain and tolerate all the rage I had within me.

'What are you thinking about?' E would ask.

And I would sit there in silence, picking at my fingernails, determined not to say. There were times, of course, when I felt sure he could read my mind. There were occasions when I arrived and burst into tears, cursing the world, and, in particular, the men in it.

'I'm a man, so what do you think about me? The same?' E would challenge, and then persist: 'Anyway, you haven't even bothered to ask how I feel; all you ever do when you come here is to complain about your life. There are two people in this room... as if you would ever notice.'

Sometimes I was so furious with him that I drove far too fast all the way home. One evening I recklessly tried to overtake a lorry on the crowded Barton Bridge viaduct over the Manchester Ship Canal, having failed to see another car pull out from behind me at the same time. There was a loud exchange of horns and I pulled back just in time. My chest tightened as my sweating palms gripped the thin steering wheel of the Mini. I opened the window to inhale the cool evening air, and then choked on the mixture of exhaust and effluent from the sewage works 30 feet below the bridge, next to the deserted waterway.

E provoked me and berated me in turn, but I think this was what he intended to do. He knew anger was better than nothingness. Now I think he understood it all too well.

By not fulfilling my fantasies, he retained his power to help me understand how and why such powerful emotions arose in response not only to him, but also to other key people in my life with whom I had struggled and still continued to do so. 'Transference' is the phenomenon whereby we unconsciously transfer feelings and attitudes from a person in the past on to a person in the present. My conflicted feelings towards men in particular, especially my father, were transferred to E.

Looking back, as I grew stronger, I can see that E began to grow weaker, both physically and emotionally. Was it first the smell of alcohol on his breath that alerted me to it? No, that was later. It was the dark rings around his eyes, the change in his posture, as he no longer seemed to stride down the corridor in front of me from the waiting room to his office, and the clues that he hadn't been home the night before and had probably slept there: the rumpled and discarded clothes on his chair. He didn't try to hide it. It was almost as though E wanted me to see his vulnerability, yet he could not and should not admit it.

'So,' said Susan, 'you eventually came to think there was something wrong with E?'

'Yes, I did. I did. It wasn't such a surprise, really. I had just pushed it all to the back of my mind. I didn't want to recognise it, but the signs were all there.'

E was suddenly taken ill and had a life-saving operation on his bowel. He recovered and came back to work, but something was never quite the same again. A few months later he disappeared.

'I've told you this part before,' I said. 'He left his post. I heard he was depressed.'

'Did you see him again?' asked Susan.

I didn't need to tell her all the details. I sensed she knew more of this story than I had ever told her but I did not ask her how she might have found out. I knew: her partner was a consultant psychotherapist, and a colleague of E's.

The shadows in the room were growing, and the appointment was coming to an end. I had talked, but I also knew, Susan had listened. She had teased the words out of me with care and skill, and I trusted her.

'I saw him only once more,' I replied eventually, picturing the scene in my mind. 'It was a year or so later. He was in the waiting room in the department of psychotherapy in Manchester. I hardly recognised him: he had lost weight. He looked up, and we exchanged a sad smile and a few words.'

He was slumped in a chair in the corner. I didn't recognise him at first; he seemed much smaller in stature than I remembered. Perhaps he was trying to avoid eye contact with the people who came through the door – he would have known so many of them.

'How are you?' I asked. I wanted to say, *I've missed you.*

'I've been seeing the professor,' E replied. 'He's been trying to help me.'

His eyes told a different story. I could not imagine how E and the professor would ever be able to connect about anything. I felt too awkward to hang around. I didn't stay and talk to him but instead I rushed upstairs to my meeting and let the heavy door of the waiting room clang shut behind me, not looking backwards. When I came down again an hour later, he was gone.

That was the last time I saw E alive.

I wrote to him a few days after that meeting – a short letter, telling him I was in a stable and happy relationship with John. I received a card in the post with a colourful, abstract, oriental design on the front. On the white paper inside, E had written a message in his bold handwriting: *I thought he was important, although you always denied it. I am happy for you and wish you well.*

'I ripped the card up and threw it away a couple of weeks ago,' I told Susan.

'Why?'

'Because I finally found out what he had done... why he was suspended.'

Silence. She waited for me to go on.

'A couple of people apparently complained about him. He was offering them therapy but he suggested they needed to have a relationship with him in order to be fully cured of their problems.'

'I can sense you were very angry?'

'Shocked. Yes, really boiling with rage.' And inside, deep down, although I did not want to admit it and could not bring myself to say it, I knew some of that anger was because he had not wanted to have a relationship with me – and I had wanted him then so very, very much.

I could acknowledge he had transgressed the boundaries of therapy and damaged other people's lives, and I simply couldn't think about him without wanting to scream and shout at him, even though he wasn't there to witness my fury. Such a dammed stupid waste of a talent, such a lot of damage: to his family, to those with whom he had abused his position of trust as a therapist – and to me.

'But I couldn't hate him,' I told her. I could only loathe what he had done and what he had allowed himself to become.

'So you say you couldn't hate him...' Susan continued. 'So there must have been something, somewhere, which prevented you from doing this...'

'It was,' I paused and the tears which ran down my cheeks surprised me, 'because he saved my life.'

It was midnight: a rented apartment and a broken relationship. An open bottle of paracetamol on the table in front of me, whose contents I was considering swallowing. A voice on the telephone piercing the darkness, irritated.

'If you phone me at this time, you have to take me as you find me,' E said.

'I just can't go on. There is nothing worth living for.'

'So you've called me.' A little less irritation in his tone, more exasperation.

'So... I wanted to hear your voice. I needed to talk to you.'

'So talk, tell me what has happened today.'

'Nothing new. Just... I just feel so terribly alone. I can't bear this feeling. I could die in this room and no one would miss me at all.'

'I would. I would miss you very much.' His voice reached out through the night and touched my soul in confirmation. 'I can't stop you, but I don't want you to do this.'

Yes, E had broken the rules, but I also know it was, paradoxically, his lack of respect for some of the rules that kept me alive. This had enabled him to engage me in saving myself, but only with his help. I knew intellectually how grieving for someone involved allowing oneself to 'remember the good as well as the bad', but putting this into practice, getting in touch with the raw emotions linked intimately with the facts, was another matter.

'When I first started to see E,' I said to Susan, 'I remember telling him about all of the awful things that happened in those last few years with Dad: how he used to hit me when he lost his temper and how I felt strangely relieved when he died, because I didn't know how to talk to him any more. How incredibly overbearing he had been and how he used to make me feel.'

She looked up at me with her all-knowing grey-blue eyes. 'Feelings of anger...'

'Yes. Sometimes cold, empty, damaging fury.'

'A bit like you are feeling now.'

I took a deep breath. I realised I wanted to talk with an urgency that I had not experienced in months, to release some pressure through the valve holding back the pure liquid emotion rising inside me, but I was afraid I would lose control of myself as I had done in the past.

'It's not surprising to me that you have such strong feelings about E. He was very important to you. He gave you something that you perhaps never had from your parents, particularly from your mother. But you did get something important from your father, I think, and I suspect this was powerfully reflected and rediscovered in your relationship with E.'

'He believed in me, and I believed in him... But...'

'He let you down. Like your father did?'

We were silent. I was struggling with the memory of an encounter that had taken place in the room down the white corridor in the hospital near the motorway many years before.

'I remember this conversation I had with E, not long before he disappeared. I haven't thought about it for ages...' It all came flooding back to me.

'I wondered for a long time, you know, if your relationship with your father was abusive in some way,' said E.

The thought appalled me. I looked up at him, ready to shake my head.

'How could you think that? Yes, he hit me, but it wasn't abusive in the way I think you mean.'

He put up his hand. 'No, I realise now it wasn't. But it was a painful and complicated relationship.' He paused, and I could read both compassion and a profound sadness in his eyes. 'I suspect now that your father must have loved you very much... But I think, too, that he must have found it impossible ever to tell you.'

'At the end he questioned whether he had been of help to anyone after what happened, after what he had become,' Susan's partner told me much, much later about E, when I dared to ask him. 'But he really thought the work he did with you meant something important; he hoped it had been worthwhile.'

I understand now, more than 20 years later, that those words spoken by E contained the most important gift he ever gave me: the memory of my often angry and sometimes very sad father's troubled, but very tender, love for me.

Through the transference relationship and the powerful feelings we unconsciously develop for a therapist, which really belong with the person we have lost, we can begin to excavate and resolve our difficult relationships with those who have gone but still haunt our dreams.

CHAPTER 14

Communication

Most of us can accept that it is healing to talk. However, talking isn't always easy. We miss opportunities to say what we really need to; sometimes we don't make ourselves as clearly understood as we could or should. We can wait for ages to say something, only to feel frustrated by our failure to share something important; we may be worried about losing control of our emotions and bursting into tears when we try to talk about what really matters to us.

I wonder sometimes how I ended up specialising in teaching communication skills. I grew up in a family where all members seemed unable to talk to each other about things that really mattered or to really listen to what the other person had to say. It's as though I have spent my life trying to solve a problem very personal to me. One of my friends once observed a professor of psychology having trouble parking his car exactly in the space allocated. He reversed backwards and forwards several times. His interest was in obsessional disorders. An expert on the topic of bipolar disorder, Kay Redfield Jamison, wrote a book about her personal experience of it, *An Unquiet Mind*. Researching depression has been my other life's work and I've experienced a fair amount of that too.

From an early age I developed particularly sensitive skills in assessing the emotional temperature of the household in which I grew up. I learned how to judge what mood my father was in, when to try to speak to him, and when to retreat to my room and keep out of the way. Most of the time I avoided confrontation, but unfortunately not always – and particularly not when I was being criticised. But this ability – to pick up on those words, phrases and glances redolent of emotion, for my own survival – has helped me to teach the language of feelings to others.

I was beginning to remember more and more about the past; every now and then a fresh memory would spring into my mind, connecting me back to my teenage years – usually to a conversation with my father, a moment when we were trying to be honest with each other but somehow not succeeding.

We had been sitting in front of the gas fire in the living room at the back of our house. We often sat there together late at night in the years before I left home. Dad would warm his big oil-stained hands. Often we talked about politics: we discussed apartheid in South Africa and how he remembered reading about the Sharpeville massacre. He would tell me about his hatred of fascism in any of its guises and about his unhappy experiences as a rebellious soldier who had been called up just after the war, ready to do something useful, only to spend a couple of years blowing up unwanted explosives in the mists of North Wales. He shared and infused me with his strong sense of social injustice in the world and his views about the future.

We were the only family I knew then who seemed to have its own foreign policy.

'Can you get me some oranges?' my father had asked my mother. She returned home from the greengrocer across the road with ones stamped Outspan. This meant they were from South Africa and a product of the apartheid regime that my father detested.

'I'm not eating those,' he said, then changed his mind when Mum looked as though she was about to cry in exasperation. 'OK, this time, but next time get me Jaffa ones.' Our policy was more favourable towards Israel than South Africa.

'What's the difference?' said my mother.

My father shrugged as though he wouldn't know where to begin.

When I was ten years old, Dad gave me an atlas. It had a blue-and-white cover and was published by the Pergamon Press. We bought it on a trip to Bristol and it was one of my most treasured possessions until it finally fell apart. I could remember tracing, with greaseproof paper, the outline of the People's Republic of China into my school exercise book.

'China will be a world power one day,' Dad said. 'No one believes me, but it will.'

That particular evening I had begun remembering, we had been talking for a while about the election coming up, the one that Heath would lose to Wilson after the miners' strike. We had put up a Labour poster in the front bay window. Our neighbours always hosted the local ward Conservative and Unionist Party Committee Rooms so the poster was intended to irritate them. We laughed about it but then lapsed into silence.

'Dad,' I said finally, 'I'm scared.'

'What about?'

Silence.

'What about?' he repeated.

'Would you... I mean, would it really matter if I didn't go to university?'

'Well, it wouldn't matter to me, really it wouldn't.' He let out a long sigh.

'Would it really not?'

'Don't you want to?' he asked.

'Yes,' I said. I thought I did. 'I just get so frightened. I feel so anxious all the time.'

'You've got to learn how to relax.'

'I can't seem to be able to do it. I'm so wound up.'

'Look, I won't think any less of you if you don't do it.'

'I know.' I was starting to feel angry. I wanted him to care. I thought he wanted me to pass these exams – didn't he? Sometimes I wasn't sure whether I was doing it for me or for him, to show him that I was still his bright-eyed little girl underneath the naïve attempts at sophistication: the make-up, boyfriend and clothes I knew he didn't always approve of. Why didn't he say something helpful or encouraging?

'I don't know what to do,' I said. I could feel the tears coming.

'I really couldn't give a damn whether you go or not! What do you want me to say?'

I started to cry.

'Look, don't get upset about it now...'

He hated it when I burst into tears. I knew that. I wiped my eyes quickly with my fingers until they were sore.

'Ray, do you know what time it is?' my mother interrupted, peering round the living room door.

'I'll be there in a minute.'

He turned towards me as she slammed the door.

We both acted as though nothing had happened. He made no move to get up and go to bed.

'Mash us another cup of tea, will you Linda...' My father was Northern. He always said 'mash' rather than 'brew' or 'make'.

I got up to make his tea while he carried on staring at the fire.

When I returned, we changed the subject back to politics. It was safer ground, with no emotional landmines. But I could not stop thinking about what he had said or, rather, had not said.

My mind was wandering as usual, musing about things, while a member of the audience was speaking at length in Mandarin. It was the winter of 2002, more than a quarter of a century on from the scene at my parents' hearth, and I found myself in a freezing-cold lecture room at the Institute of Mental Health in Beijing. The aim of my visit there was to teach doctors how to talk to people who might be depressed. This was something I did quite often, and still do, in many different countries. Years after my father gave me my first atlas, I began to fulfil my dream of being able to travel all over the world.

Still jet-lagged from the 12-hour journey from London, I was finding it hard to pay attention, as I did not understand a single word of the language. At the side of the room, I could see my colleague nodding off. Outside, through the dusty windows, I glimpsed the outline of grey buildings, with splashes here and there of yellow and red where the banners of new shops and restaurants punctuated the uniformity of the streetscape.

'This is a party functionary,' my interpreter Chen-Li whispered into my left ear, as another man at the back of the room stood up to speak.

'What is he saying?' I asked.

We had just delivered a presentation about depression. The members of the audience, who were not accustomed to interactive sessions, were slow at asking questions. They roughly divided into the younger doctors in the department, sitting at the front – enthusiastic and interested in what we had to say – and the older, more conservative academics and assorted party apparatchiks who were there to keep an eye on all of us seated at the back. It was one of the latter who had risen, not to ask a question but to deliver what seemed, judging by the deferential nods of those seated around him, an important statement.

My interpreter leant towards me. 'He is saying: "Yes, he agrees depression is a truly terrible thing, but we must remember the Communist Party can be a source of great comfort, support and help to people. Doctors need to remind people of this and..."'

'And?'

'Oh I'm not going to bother telling you any more about what he's saying. It's...' He listened for another moment or two and caught the eye of one of the older members of the 'young' group on the front row. Then he turned to me with a defiant glint in his eye and whispered in my ear, 'It is complete rubbish. You don't need to understand it, I promise!'

My father had been right about China becoming powerful, but it was not, as he had predicted, through advancing socialism but by embracing capitalism. I wondered what he would have made of this.

After the session, I took the opportunity to warm my hands on a cup of green tea.

'What are we going to do now?' asked Chen-Li.

'Will you translate for me please?' I checked. It was a slow process. Some of my phrases seemed to take Chen-Li considerably less time than they took me to speak them and some of them far longer. Occasionally, he responded to interjections and I had to ask what the question was about. Chen-Li wasn't a professional interpreter but a doctor: a young and confident member of the department who, I suspected, given his earlier response to the party official, was putting his own spin on things. We turned to the audience.

'I'd like someone who would be prepared to role-play their own patient. You learn a great deal from an exercise like this, finding out what it is like to be on the receiving end of a conversation with a doctor.'

I didn't know what Chen-Li was saying, but it seemed to me from the way he was waving his arms about that he was trying to cajole someone into volunteering.

'I will,' a young woman spoke up in English. She had a shy smile and her name was Soon-Lin. She told us, in a mixture of hesitant English and translated Mandarin, that she was a haematologist in the University Hospital. The case she had in mind was that of a young woman whom she had been treating for leukaemia.

'The consultation upset the patient very much,' explained Chen-Li.

'I tell her treatment, it not work,' added Soon-Lin, in English.

'And is there a person who would be willing to volunteer to play the doctor?'

An attractive, slightly older woman, with a westernised brown-tinted hairstyle and red glossy lipstick, put up her hand. She had already asked one or two questions in English. She told us her name was Michelle.

While the rest of the group had their tea, we retreated into a television studio situated in a small room at the back. We made a recording of the consultation with the help of the technician, a terse creature who seemed more at home in the darkness of his control room than in the daylight. I sat down in front of his two-bar electric heater and watched the consultation on the video monitor.

Soon-Lin was pretending to be her own patient: a 26-year-old university teacher, married and mother of a much-loved only son. She seemed to settle with ease into this role, playing the person she had seen only the day before in the clinic. Michelle's task was to break the news that the leukaemia had relapsed and it was unlikely any more treatment would be effective. Everything had been tried and there was nothing more to be done for her.

Right from the beginning, I didn't need to speak or understand Mandarin to realise all was not going well. Michelle was in full flow. She seemed to be talking a great deal and not giving Soon-Lin a chance to say anything. Chen-Li was providing simultaneous translation directly into my left ear.

'She is saying,' explained Chen-Li, '"This is how it will be. I have to tell you there is nothing we can do. These are the things we have tried so far; we have tried the chemotherapy and..."'

Michelle was very fond of lists. She was very certain of her knowledge. What she was not doing, either in words or actions, was demonstrating that she had any understanding of how her patient might be feeling or whether she was even listening to her.

Suddenly, Soon-Lin erupted into anger. 'I just don't like the way you are telling me this! You are telling me there is no hope for me!' she shouted, grasping the arm of the chair.

'OK, so let me explain it again...' Michelle began. After she had provided the patient with more information, she finally asked, 'Is there anything else I can tell you?'

'No, thank you.'

Soon-Lin put her face into her hands and slumped disconsolately in her chair.

I opened the door into the studio.

'OK, you can come out of role now,' I said to them both.

'Thank you,' Michelle said and smiled confidently.

Soon-Lin still looked on the point of tears.

'Are you OK?' I asked.

'Yes.' She took out a handkerchief and blew her nose.

'I would like you to tell each other how you think this session went, before we join the group. What do you think went well, Michelle, and what might you have done differently? And, Soon-Lin, the same for you: what do you think the doctor did well and what might have been done differently?'

After Chen-Li had ensured they both understood the task, I closed the door of the studio again. 'I think they need to talk about this in private.'

A small group of volunteers assembled at the front of the lecture theatre, keen to see me demonstrate the technique of teaching communication skills using the videotaped role-play exercise. The younger people at the front were keen to participate, whereas the older ones at the back started to look bored. One of them got up and left as we began. I noticed that it was the man who had given us the 'address'. He bowed his head to me, stony-faced, and I reciprocated to show my respect.

'Is this the first time you have seen yourself carrying out a consultation with someone on video?' I asked Michelle.

'Yes,' she replied. I noted that Soon-Lin was sitting at the far side of the group, even though she and Michelle had come into the room together. I took a deep breath. I knew this was going to take all of my diplomatic skills and would be twice as difficult as usual, given the need to wait for a translation. My older colleague smiled at me knowingly from the side of the room, having assumed his previous position. I took this as my own personal challenge.

'The way I approach this is that we use the videotape our colleagues have kindly made for us as a tool for learning. There isn't a right way to communicate with people who are distressed. There are many ways: some helpful, some not so helpful. This is about learning from each other what those alternatives are. Is that clear?'

Several people nodded before Chen-Li had finished translating what I said. I realised the group's grasp of English was better than my understanding of Mandarin.

'We are not here to judge whether this is a good or a bad consultation, only to think of ways in which things might have progressed differently at key points. What could you have done or said differently? What words would you have used? I will stop the tape from time to time and ask you, but if any of you want to stop the interview, please just ask. Michelle, is there anything in particular you would like us to think about while we watch the tape?' I asked.

'No, I was very happy with it,' she replied coolly in English. There was a hint of irritation in her voice.

Over the next three quarters of an hour I had to work hard to protect Michelle from the criticism of some of the more vociferous younger members of the group.

'But see, she isn't listening!' the man who was sitting next to Soon-Lin called out angrily. It seemed as though he had assumed the role of Soon-Lin's protector, whether she wanted it or not.

'OK,' I said. 'At this point, in this interview, what would you have said?'

He paused for a moment. 'I think I would have said, "You look very upset and worried..."'

Soon-Lin turned to face him and smiled.

He smiled back.

'Yes, I think this is one possibility, a good one,' I commented. 'You are aware that she is upset, but she needs to know you can see this. You might have to tell her. Any more suggestions?'

'She used the word "frightened",' Chen-Li said to me in English. 'I would want to know what she meant by "frightened". How was she feeling inside?'

'Yes,' I said, 'can you please tell this to the group in case they did not understand?'

And so we continued, step by step. It wasn't easy teaching through an interpreter, but communicating effectively is often very difficult even at the best of times. Occasionally, I cannot find the right word for what I want to say, even in English. We tried our best to ensure that everyone was able to understand and as the session went on, I saw Soon-Lin begin to relax. Although she had not suggested anything, I could tell she was hearing that her colleagues had not only recognised her distress, but were also demonstrating that they had the skills to respond to it.

'So what have we learned? Soon-Lin, this was your real-life patient. What have you learned from re-enacting this scene about her?'

After a brief hesitation she spoke out, loud and clear, with only a slight quiver. She was impassioned: so very different from the shy young woman who had volunteered for the exercise.

'I learned how it feels not to be listened to. I really felt this so strongly because I realise now I did not listen to the patient, *my patient*, either.' She looked at Michelle, and the members of the group turned around to look at Soon-Lin. I could see the understanding and cautious admiration in their eyes. 'I do not think I listened to her when I saw her. I just told her what I knew, what I thought she needed to know. I did not even ask her whether she needed to know anything else. I had given her a sentence of death, but I didn't think what that must be like. I just kept telling her. Now I know a little more about what I have to do.'

The group was not so much learning a new language as learning how to reconnect with their own humanity. They needed to rehearse the words, to see how they sounded and to try out whether it was possible to say something different – to be different and to communicate in a different way. For Soon-Lin, the learning had been particularly painful but also effective because it had touched her closely. She had experienced real feelings of pain, hopelessness and anger. I hoped it had been a constructive experience for her and that the group had provided a therapeutic, emotionally focused but supportive conversation – one that would, in turn, be of benefit to her own patients.

It was my responsibility to conclude the teaching session with a positive message for the group, and in particular Michelle, who had taken the risk of showing us how she actually consulted with patients.

'Michelle,' I said, 'this session wasn't easy for you, but you have managed the group very well.'

'No,' she shrugged. 'But I want to say I wouldn't really do it this way. This way was better for us to learn something.'

No one challenged her on this, even though I strongly doubted this was true.

I learned something too: the importance in the Asian world of being able to save face and not having to admit, at least in public, that you were wrong.

But this was not only true in the East.

My father and I both possessed the same stubborn, proud streak which prevented us, even in private, from admitting our mistakes and weaknesses to each other and from resolving our differences by talking and listening. We were never able to communicate effectively with each other about those things we disagreed on. Dad and I saved face to the death and even beyond. Reflecting on my visit to Beijing, I could see how growing up in our emotionally repressed household had some parallels to growing up in a repressive regime like the one many members of my audience had experienced.

Being able to talk, being able to hear the views of the other person and being able to negotiate differences are all essential ingredients in relationships. Difficulties in sorting out disagreements with people who are close to us often lie at the heart of depression. Even if they are not the cause, they may slow down or even stall our recovery. Sometimes we cannot communicate as effectively as we want to, but that should not stop us from trying. Just because communication might be imperfect, it isn't any less valuable or necessary.

CHAPTER 15

Grief

In his classic text 'Mourning and Melancholia', Freud linked depression and grief by hypothesising that in unresolved grief the image of the person lost to us becomes fused with our own 'self'. Melancholia, a severe form of depression, comes about when anger is internalised and directed inwards towards this new and changed 'self'.

We can fail to grieve not only for the dead. A similar process occurs when we cannot come to terms with the loss of other things that are important to us: people, ideas, beliefs and hopes. Therapy can be difficult because in beginning to grieve, it can paradoxically feel like the therapist is trying to prize away from you the only thing you have left: the bright, fresh memory you have shut away inside yourself for safe-keeping. The psychoanalyst Darian Leader talks about how in mourning we grieve the dead, but in melancholia we seem to die with them.

'I can teach you about grief.' This was what I told the young doctors as we fried in the summer heat. The aroma of curry from the restaurants a short block away wafted gently in through the windows, streaked by rivulets of rain which had worn through the city grime. There were more than 30 of us in a small, first-floor seminar room, fighting for air. It was an unseasonably warm, late-summer afternoon in Manchester in 2004 and there was no air conditioning, but I could still have managed a lamb rogan josh with a plate of saffron-yellow pilau rice and a cold pint of lager with condensation dripping off the glass.

They were a mixed bunch of students that term. A group of young Pakistani men sat together at a table to my left, laughing and joking with each other. On my right, every week, sat a handsome Spaniard with a long, aquiline nose who looked, judging by the turned-back cuffs of his linen jacket, as if he was more than old enough, like me, to remember the original *Miami Vice*. A slim young Portuguese woman sat on his left and an earthy Northern lass on the other side. At the back, two nervous young women swathed entirely in dark-green robes morally supported each other in the presence of the ample cleavage on display from a lip-glossed beauty nearby, who was chatting away to a tall, blonde German. All of them had something in common: they wanted to become general practitioners in England.

'So,' I asked, 'what are the stages of grief?' I stood next to the flip chart, green marker pen in hand, ready to write.

The German at the back piped up in answer, in a heavily accented monotone, 'Denial, anger, bargaining, depression and acceptance.'

'Well, this is one view of the stages people go through,' I replied, 'but I think it's really important not to take these stages too literally. Not everyone experiences all of them, and not always in that order. I prefer to think in terms of three approximate stages.'

I like things to be in threes – it's simpler.

'There is a first stage of numbness or shock, when you know the person has died but you haven't come to terms with it.' I knew this feeling; I still remembered it well from the first couple of days in Edinburgh after hearing about my father's death. 'That is followed by a period of acute grief, with a desperate sense of yearning, distress and many of the symptoms of what we would otherwise call depression. It may seem just like a depressive illness but some people might hear the voice of the dead person or have moments when they even think they see them. However, it's quite normal.'

'How long does it last for?' asked one of the women.

'Well, it varies. At least three months is normal, but it can last longer, perhaps six months. This is followed eventually by a third stage when the bereaved person begins to take up their life again, to move on, and create new memories in the present instead of only dwelling on their past ones; this is what is sometimes called acceptance.'

'Six months,' someone said quietly at the back of the room. I could not see who it was, as they continued, 'It can take much longer than six months.'

'Indeed it can,' I agreed. 'Grief is a perfectly normal response to loss. For most people it resolves with time but for others it doesn't. What distinguishes normal from abnormal grief?'

'Getting stuck, not moving on,' volunteered someone, 'feeling suicidal.'

'Can anyone tell us about a person they have seen who was failing to grieve?'

Silence.

'OK, let me tell you about someone I treated who was unable to grieve.'

I perched on the edge of a table and struggled to repress the beckoning ice-cold beer in my imagination. 'I saw a couple who had lost their son in a tragic, freak accident. They saw him being killed. Their anger and pain were palpable. It seemed like there was nothing you could say or do because you could not imagine something so awful ever happening to you. You wouldn't wish it on your enemy.' I rose for a moment to ease the cramp in my lower back, and then sat down again. I knew I had their attention with a story. I always did.

'But the thing I will never forget is the pain this guy, the father, would get in his chest when he talked about his son. He didn't cry. He didn't even sound upset. He was perfectly controlled. But when he talked about his despair, he put his fist to his heart and tightened his fingers.'

As I talked, I felt myself putting my own hand to my chest in sympathy.

'He was completely stuck. His emotions were locked inside of him. And the physical pain of loss he felt in his chest, in his heart, was as fresh as the day his son had died. Nothing had changed. It was no better – if anything, it was getting worse.'

'How long before this did it happen?' asked the Spaniard.

'Four or five years before I saw him. I can't remember exactly now.'

'And did it ever get better?' He wanted to understand.

'I hope so, in time, but I don't know. He just didn't believe I could help, so he stopped coming after a while. He thought I was trying to take away from him the memory of his son.'

It's an odd kind of paradox that it can take a lifetime to come to terms with a death. A lifetime spent with pictures which flicker away in the cinema screen of the human mind. The pictures we carry around with us are the images of those we have loved and lost. Letting go of those images can seem like a further insult: the final extinction of a memory, whether painful or pleasant.

I had not been there when my father died. I didn't see what happened, unlike my patient who witnessed the truly horrific death of his child – and I tell myself that this should make it easier. I didn't see him grip his chest in pain, hear him cry out or see him fall. But I have replayed the story of his death, as I imagine it to be, so many times in my head over the years that I believe in some way I was there.

It goes like this.

I am back in the house in which I was brought up and lived until the age of 18. I am in the kitchen, which will always be the first kitchen of my life. It is a big, open-plan room. I can see it furnished in many different ways: with brightly coloured 1960s-style curtains, dusty venetian blinds and cheap laminated furniture or a solid wooden table. I see the dark blue wallpaper in that part of the kitchen that also served as our everyday living room.

I have not seen this room for more than 25 years. I suppose it is still there, back in Skegness where I grew up, but it also exists much closer, suspended in time, somewhere at the heart of me. It will never let go of me, however far I travel away from it in time or space.

It is in this room, in front of the gas fire in the corner where we used to sit and talk about politics into the night, that I see Dad getting dressed on a freezing cold January morning 30 years ago. All is silent apart from the hum of the electric wall clock and the hissing of the kettle on the gas cooker. He has shaved for the first time in a week, in the arctic bathroom he constructed out of an old north-facing pantry, and he stands in his shirt and baggy white underpants, putting on a tie in front of the fish-eye mirror which hangs above the fireplace. He hates wearing a tie, so he is struggling with it, as Mum isn't around to straighten it for him. He pauses to squint at himself in the mirror, too proud to get his eyes tested. He really needs glasses to see at close range but insists on borrowing my mother's specs to read the paper, even though he knows they look quite ridiculous on him, with the little 'fly-away' details on each side. Still deeply tanned after years of working outside, his hair, once black, has suddenly gone grey and he looks older than his 52 years.

On the faded blue studio couch next to him, in the half gloom of the winter morning, I can see his sports jacket and trousers. My mother has put them out for him before going off to work. He has this crazy idea that even if you are sick, you have to dress properly to go and see the doctor. When Mum left home that morning, he was still in bed, where he had been most of the time for the last week. He has had a pain in his upper back which is so severe he sometimes has difficulty in breathing. But he hasn't admitted this to the doctor, who has poked and prodded him and pronounced, despite his history of heart disease, that this is probably a slipped disc. The doctor has told him to rest, which he has done for a week. But today he has got out of bed and is going up to the surgery to see his doctor's partner, as he needs to get a sick note. The kettle is on for the final cup of tea when he has finished getting dressed.

When they found him on the floor in front of the fire, the kettle had long boiled dry.

After my father's death, I was overwhelmed at first with a terrible sense of guilt. I told myself I should have been there to save him. He had a cardiac arrest as he put on his clothes to go and see the doctor. I had spent five years training to be doctor, but at the end of it all, I couldn't save my father's life. So what use was all my education? What use was I? Yet the terrible feeling of guilt and the acute pain of grief did not stay with me for long – I didn't allow them to. I pushed them away, down inside me, and buried them. For a very long time I had failed to grieve properly.

It is 23 miles from Skegness to Boston, the nearest large town. The road winds left and right even though the land is completely flat, as though following some path first trodden flat by a drunken peasant in the Middle Ages, who couldn't find his way home in the dark. This is the route that the hearse took that cold January morning, from the undertakers in Skegness to Boston Crematorium. It was a modern concrete building, devoid of character or history, and entirely suited to the brief service held to mark the passing of my father into the flames. The cremation or funeral is an important part of the ritual of saying goodbye to the dead, of beginning the process of grieving, but this soulless service did not achieve that for me.

'He would have hated this,' I said to my mother, as the Anglican vicar droned on. 'This idiot didn't even know him but is saying what a good man he was. He was an atheist anyway.'

But Mum wasn't listening. She turned round to survey the crowd assembled at the back of the room. 'Who are all these people?' she said. She could barely see, as her eyes were so swollen and red with crying.

'They must be from work,' I said, thinking they must have been from the factory he was working at when he died. 'He never went to work on time and he never had a good word to say about any of them – called them all crawlers and the bosses' toadies – but they're all here.'

'Maybe they respected him,' said Uncle John.

And I knew he was right in a way. Each of them probably owed something to him. He helped people because he knew how to do things. He was immensely practical; the garage was bulging with his tools. But just as he was personally talented, he was equally intolerant of others' failings, including mine.

He was never able to understand how his foreman, Tim, had managed to lose his fingers in a circular saw. He thought it was incredibly funny and very careless.

And there was Tim, standing with his hat in his hands, here to pay his last respects. He raised one hand to us in acknowledgement and I saw where the tops of two of the fingers of his left hand were missing. Oh how Dad would have enjoyed that moment.

'Why don't some people grieve properly? What stops them?'

What I still love about teaching is how young doctors are always so full of questions. They don't let you off the hook. They want to *know*.

'Lots of different reasons,' I replied. 'It could happen if the death is sudden or particularly traumatic; also if, for instance, a body cannot be found or, most usually, if the relationship you have with the dead person was a complicated one.'

That didn't even begin to do justice to the relationship between me and my dad, and I knew it.

'Some people don't begin to grieve, as they are unable to accept that the person is gone, whereas others get stuck in the really acute depressive stage and get more and more distressed, perhaps even wanting to join the dead person. Some get stuck in a phase of idealising the dead person or of feeling very angry with doctors who failed to save them.' I paused and looked around the room to see if what I was saying had a particular resonance. 'Others just stop grieving and bury their feelings because they cannot face dealing with them.'

This was what I knew I had done, for a very long time.

We had come to the end of the session. I made eye contact with Sobia, a young Asian woman who had been sitting at the back of the seminar room, and remembered that she had asked if she could meet with me after the session. Her hair was cut fashionably short and she wore a small diamond stud in her nostril. I wondered whether she was the one who had questioned the validity of the accepted duration of grief earlier.

'You wanted to talk to me? Shall we go to my office? It's just down the corridor.' I gestured towards the door. The ice-cold beer I had been looking forward to receded further into the distance.

I noticed that Sobia's eyes glistened with unshed tears as she looked away from me and out of the window into the summer sunshine. Then she turned back and tried to smile.

'I know what it is like to lose things,' she said. 'My family are back in Pakistan, but I don't hear from them any more.'

'That sounds very sad...'

'My family didn't approve of the person I married,' she paused for a moment and wiped at her eyes. 'They wanted me to marry my cousin. We ran away and left the country... I didn't hear from them except to find out from my sister that my mother had died... It was terrible; I feel so guilty because I wasn't there. It's been three years now, and my father never answers my letters. It's like they are dead to me, and I'm dead to them.'

'That must be very hard.'

She buried her face in her hands and began to weep. We sat in silence for a moment. Then she began to speak again, almost in a whisper. 'I can't bear to think about them; I don't know how to live with it. I've been so depressed. I am dead to them.' As she reiterated this painful thought, I saw her flinch as though she were beating herself, or inviting someone or something else I could not see to punish her.

'I think,' I volunteered, 'that maybe you've not been able to grieve for your mother because of the way in which everything happened?'

It was clear to me that Sobia had lost not only her mother, but also her place within that family. This was particularly difficult to come to terms with: a double loss.

She told me how she was determined to succeed in her career and explained that her husband, who was a researcher at the university, was supporting her, but it had been very difficult to come to terms with her family's rejection. It was too painful to think about the past; I could see that too.

'My GP says I have to try to talk about it...'

'Yes,' I replied, 'talking is important, taking out your photographs, remembering things from the past – the good and the bad. The happy memories as well as the sad ones... But it isn't always easy to do.'

'My childhood was happy... I loved my mother very much; I miss her. I always thought I would see her again. Every day it seems to hurt even more now because I want to have my own child. But I cannot imagine being a mother without my own mother... I have a photograph of her.' Wiping her eyes, she pulled out of her handbag a creased picture of a woman in traditional salwar kameez. I could see the resemblance – she was without doubt her mother's daughter. I said what I usually say in these circumstances: I am not the right person to become involved in treating my students.

'I think you do need to talk, but you need help and support to enable you to do it. Would you consider going to see someone you could talk to? A counsellor? Perhaps talk about it with your doctor first?'

She looked up at me and whispered, 'I know I have to do it. I cannot go on as I am.'

Unlike Sobia, I could go home, although going back was something I had avoided for many years. I know now that I learned to survive losses in my life by never looking back, never saying goodbye. In doing this, I lost even more – not only the things I didn't want to remember, but also the good memories which are interleaved between the bad in my book of recollections. This meant I became a person almost without a past.

John and I had finally driven back to my hometown one autumn afternoon when I felt ready to revisit some of my own memories once more. The place had changed but this was to be expected. We found that the boarding houses and private hotels had been converted into tiny, shabby flats. The town seemed to be fading away, slipping into a deadly slumber. I did not want to be there; there were too many ghosts I was not yet ready to confront and which I could hear chattering between the trees of the avenue where I had lived. They whispered around the corners, '*Are you really ready to come back again?*' We turned away. I could not face the old house and its aura of death. This was something for which I was still not quite prepared.

My favourite place had always been a different land, a few miles to the south of the town, where the fenland surrounding the Wash is completely flat, as far as the horizon and perhaps beyond the curve of the Earth. John and I walked along the roadway towards Gibraltar Point. From a grassy embankment, we watched the sluggish river, brown with silt, which meandered between raised banks – past the old, stone coastguard station with its lonely tower – out towards the distant sea. Tiny farmhouses peppered the fields between rows of poplars, planted to provide respite from the wind that pushed hard against me. Long, straight drainage dykes carved up the landscape into man-made designs. The sky was everywhere, huge, utterly inescapable and full of light. I was caught within it.

We had come here once when I was a teenager, my father and I, carrying a large glass Kilner jar to collect pond water. I can picture Dad striding ahead of me, with his awkward gait, toes pointed outwards and arms barely swinging by his sides. We walked on until we reached the sign announcing the start of the nature reserve at the end of the road. There was a lake there, and Dad reached down into the water and filled the jar half-full. There wasn't very much to see. The water was the colour of weak tea and emanated the putrid organic smell of rotting pondweed, but later, when I examined a drop under the microscope, a whole complex world of living organisms was revealed to exist within a tiny sphere; another universe beyond this one.

'What do you need this for?' he asked.

'It's my biology project.'

'They ask me sometimes, at work you know, how you're doing at the grammar school.' He paused and looked at the ground. 'But I never let on.'

I never asked him why. Perhaps I should have done – I might have learned more about the need he felt to be so reticent about my progress, even though I know it pleased him. Perhaps, despite being an avowed socialist atheist, his Methodist upbringing had instilled this extreme modesty in him. Or perhaps he experienced the same conflicted relationship between risking a sense of pride in achievement well-earned and being dragged down by the negative, relentless internal dialogue which accompanies low self-esteem – a conflict which I inherited from him and have struggled to overcome all my life.

When I went back with John, more than three decades later, a new boardwalk wove towards the dunes, between clumps of blue-grey buckthorn and gorse. When we finally reached the edge of the land where the waves crashed in on the clean sand of the shore, I washed my feet in the water of the Wash. It was cold but cleansing. It might have been harsh and unpredictable but it always restored my spirit. I remembered how I had come to this very place often as a child and teenager with Dad to watch him swim in the sea on summer evenings. Images flooded back into my mind's eye.

'He would sit out there on the sandbank,' I shouted to John. 'He loved it here. He was such a strong swimmer.'

I recalled his sunburned shoulders crawling powerfully out to sea. How safe it felt to be with him then. How I loved him. For a moment I could see Dad there once again, a little way off-shore, in the place he loved too. Completely alive and vital, he was waving to me with his long, brown tanned arm, glistening wet in the evening sunlight, before he set off again to swim back to me against the powerful current trying to drag him away towards the south.

I did not begin to come to terms with losing my father for a long time after his death. And I will always miss him. Grieving means having to let go and move on, and when you are able to, it becomes possible to remember the person you have lost as they really were – not as an idealised saint or vilified target for anger and disappointment, but as a complicated, real and very human being.

I have only one photograph of Dad. It was taken just before I left home to go to university. He stands in his rough shirtsleeves with his arm around my mother, who clasps his hand firmly to her hip. I am standing on his left-hand side, just behind him, scowling into the sun, and my younger brother Ian is in front of us. Alan must have been behind the camera. Dad's smile is slight, enigmatic, as though he knows a secret we do not. Beside him, my mother's grin looks rather forced, as though we had all been having an argument a moment before. As the years pass, the picture, like the intensity of my grief, is gradually fading away to mere shades of grey. I can see now that Dad was ultimately my saving grace; his actions if not his words taught me the enduring power of love and helped to shape the person I have become.

Sobia continued to attend the seminars that summer. At the end of the final session, she hung behind for a moment to speak to me.

'I just wanted to say thank you for telling me to go and seek some help.' She tried to smile, but it did not reach her eyes. The sadness I had seen before was still there, but there was a sense of hope in her voice that I had not detected the last time we spoke. 'I've started to see a therapist. And I have written to my sister and she has been in contact with me again. I could not carry on as I had been. Maybe I will never hear from my father and brother again, but my sister says she misses me. She doesn't want to go against the family... but she is going to keep in touch with me.'

'I am so pleased to hear that,' I replied.

She looked up at me. 'The pain feels a little less than it was... just a little.'

I believe the trajectory of grief is what is important. If it is as fresh and painful to think about the loss today as it was 15 years ago, then it is not progressing. Another significant sign that something is going wrong is when the feelings are becoming more intense, rather than less. Mourning which is thwarted becomes melancholia. If the grief is even just infinitesimally less intense each day on a scale of one to ten, where ten is as awful as it has ever felt, then you are moving on; you are beginning to embrace everyday life again, to look forward to the future, and you are starting to let go of what has passed.

CHAPTER 16

Learning How to Live in the Present

We may need different types of treatment for depression at different points in our life. Coming to terms with the past through psychodynamic therapy might be the right way forwards at one time, but cognitive behavioural therapy aimed at providing us with coping strategies for everyday life may be required at another.

~~~~~~

A patient of mine, Anna, was referred to me after seeing a psychotherapist privately for a couple of years.

'I understand my relationship with my parents much better now, and I would say that things at home with my husband are much easier,' said Anna. 'I understand why I get down.'

'But...'

She stopped examining her bitten fingernails for a moment; they were out of keeping with her otherwise well-groomed appearance. I could see she was taking much better care of herself than she had been only a couple of months before. 'Well, I was going to say I don't feel as hopeless now about the future. Somehow, things make sense now. I can see how my relationship with my father and mother contributed to me being the person I am now. The therapy helped a lot.'

'That's good.'

'I'm sleeping better too since we changed my medication, but I still find just coping with day to day life very difficult... I worry about what people say in the office, coping with my boss and the things she says... And there are times when I find myself drifting downwards again.'

Anna had been quite severely depressed and although she was now considerably recovered, she didn't seem to have regained her previous drive and energy. Despite this, she was an outwardly confident and capable office manager.

'Perhaps this is the point where we review things and try a different approach,' I said. 'What about cognitive behavioural therapy?'

For many people, such as Richard in Chapter 1, the behavioural part of cognitive behavioural therapy (CBT) is the key to helping them begin to feel better and getting them re-engaged with the world. The cognitive part is concerned with challenging the unhelpful thoughts about ourselves, the world and the future, which those of us who suffer from depression seem to have in abundance. These not only trigger our depressed moods, but help to maintain them too.

I was repeatedly ruminating about conversations and interactions I had with other people, going back and replaying them in my head. My new psychiatrist Dr V wanted to refer me to a psychologist, specifically to try to help me with my ruminative thinking. I was less than convinced at first.

'I don't know if I want to see another therapist. I've had a great deal of therapy.'

'But you've never seen a cognitive therapist, have you?' she asked.

'No, that's true.'

I decided it was worth a try. What was there to lose?

And so I saw him at a private hospital. He consulted in a bare, cream-painted room; the carpet was a soft pink colour and I could see well-kept trees through the window. I sat in an upholstered chair and he sat at the desk, taking notes while he asked me questions. It was a very different style of therapy from any kind I had experienced in the past. C, as I will call him, had little in common with E. His approach was immediately friendly, warm and not in any way challenging. I did not feel he wanted to break through my defences to confront the frightened person inside, but rather to invite her out for a chat. He wanted to help.

On my second visit, I returned with the homework that C had asked me to do.

He commented, 'So there were two particular rules you picked out from David Burns's book that we looked at last time...'

I was familiar with the *Feeling Good Handbook* – I had even recommended it to others – but I had never read it. There was a naturally cynical part of me that wanted to rebel against working on something from a book with such a ridiculously optimistic title, but I did not say anything.

'Yes: the one about how it's best to give up your own interests in order to please others... I rated that neutral. And the rule about how criticism will certainly upset the person who will receive it... I was fairly strongly in agreement with that one.'

I listened to myself reciting these statements. Is this what I really believed?

'They are quite hard rules to try to live by...' C looked at me.

I looked down. I could not meet his gaze. Hearing the rules spoken aloud seemed almost silly now, yet on one level I concurred with them perfectly.

'So let's take the second one,' C continued. 'What did you think were the advantages of believing this?'

I paused for a moment, breathed in, and then read aloud, 'Well, I wrote down: *People will like me because I do not upset them. I will be a person with whom people want to spend time. I will not offend other people...*' I went on until I had read out all I had written on the left side of my sheet.

'And the disadvantages?'

Given how strongly I had just supported this statement, I was surprised to see that my list of disadvantages outweighed the advantages. One in particular stood out: *I do not always know whether a person will misinterpret what I say to them as being critical; I worry about it, in case something I said might be viewed as critical. This can take up a lot of my time.* Actually, I ruminated ceaselessly about it.

'So this makes life quite difficult for you, because you worry about upsetting people, but maybe it's really difficult never to offend anyone at all in life?'

'I also have: *It's really hard work censoring everything I say... and I do have a fairly cruel sense of humour*,' which was very true and could be a problem if you did not want to offend, 'and *Sometimes it feels very unfair because people can be very critical of me, and this is hurtful.*'

'Good, you have thought about this quite a lot. But it must be very hard work living to these rules, isn't it? Do you really need to spend so much of your life trying to live up to these lofty aims?' He was challenging me now but in a remarkably non-judgemental way. I could hear my cage rattling softly.

'I have spent a lot of my life doing it, a lifetime even, and worrying about it.' *So much time and energy wasted*, I heard a voice inside me saying.

We shared a smile. We both knew lifelong habits were not easy to break.

'What you are doing when you ruminate is trying to problem-solve, to keep examining the events and to find a solution, but this doesn't happen. It cannot happen. It isn't helpful.'

I nodded. I could see he was right.

He nudged me a little, figuratively speaking. 'Maybe it's time at last to try something different?'

I was growing to like C. I felt safe with him, even though I was well aware that we knew several people in common, because I trusted he would never hint to anyone that I was consulting him.

A few weeks later, C and I were talking about the problems I experienced in meetings.

'I get quite emotional, and try and press my point home, and I seem to scare people. Then I leave and I cannot stop thinking about it.'

'Well, I'm sure you have to deal with some difficult egos at times,' he smiled conspiratorially; I knew he had been an academic too. But he didn't let me off lightly. 'I can see you might come across as quite challenging if you really try to press your point all the way. I mean, don't get me wrong... It's good you can feel very passionate about things, but it has a downside. How could you manage this differently?'

C took me through my preparation for a difficult meeting I had coming up with a colleague. He asked me to think about what I wanted to achieve from it and encouraged me to try to view this as my goal – no more.

'But what about the next couple of days? How are you going to cope with thinking about it?' he enquired.

'I don't know. Trying not to think about, to resist it, just makes things worse.'

And I knew it was the persistent, intrusive and relentless pattern of my ruminative thinking which had always frightened me; it had made me wonder if my brain really was wired up in the same dysfunctional way as my brother Alan's obsessive-compulsive brain.

C wasn't really interested in talking about the past. He didn't pick up much on my comments about my earlier life. However, when I was reflecting on the crazy rules I somehow seemed to have set to live my life within, it wasn't difficult to see how they arose out of my childhood. My father had a similar set of values and, come to think of it, he had the same problems living up to them, something which had never really occurred to me before.

C seemed content that I had gained insight into the origin of my problems in my earlier therapy. Unlike some cognitive therapists I had met over the years – one of whom was determined to argue, when she had had a couple of glasses of wine, about whether there was even such a thing as the 'unconscious mind' – C was willing to acknowledge the value of the work I had done in the past, particularly in the resolution of the grief for my father.

'Sometimes a person isn't ready to do the kind of work we are doing because they are still in crisis or trying to resolve some major issues in their life,' C told me.

'Believe it or not,' I said, 'my mood is much more stable than it was a few years ago.'

'Then it probably is the right time.'

He also wasn't concerned about whether or not I wanted to come off the antidepressants.

'It's up to you and your psychiatrist, but I can fully appreciate how you might want to stay on them.'

And I knew I did, at least for the time being.

However, the thoughts and fears about my brother and his lifelong illness did keep intruding, and I eventually talked to C about Alan. I told him something of my brother's story, and he listened. I thought he realised I needed to talk, to share my worries and fears.

I told him about the problems, which first revealed themselves in my brother's troubled childhood, and how they were not tempered at all by the passage of time. Alan had continued to have difficulties with washing, dressing and undressing each day.

'What treatment did he have?' asked C.

'He was in hospital for a while – a long while as a teenager – but I don't know what treatment he had.' Probably very little, I realised later.

My brother spent several months in an adolescent unit at an old red-brick Victorian asylum in the Lincolnshire marshes in the east of England. It was located somewhere in that place on the map where the contour lines are spaced so far apart it is impossible to find them, and ruler-straight roads run alongside wide drainage ditches, between the edge of the Lincolnshire Wolds and the fringes of the Wash. I went to visit him there once, when I was studying in Edinburgh. When the train stopped at the station, everyone in the carriage peered at you, as they knew exactly where you were going. There was only the hospital estate, surrounded by fields of potatoes as far as you could see, so people assumed you had to be in some way tainted by madness, even if you were not a patient.

After Alan's period there, he didn't return home but spent some time in a residential project for 'maladjusted young people'. He was there when my father died and did not come to the cremation because his social worker advised against it. I know now how much of a mistake that had been. Only rarely would the potential problems which might be caused by attending – for example in someone who was actively psychotic and unable to appreciate exactly what was happening – outweigh the need that a person has to say 'goodbye'.

'I tried to have him to live with me after my divorce,' I told C, 'but it was a disaster. It went OK for a couple of days then he wouldn't come out of his room. He had blocked up the loo with toilet paper too. He wouldn't speak to me... He just wouldn't come out of the room.' I felt my anxiety rising as I remembered the events of that morning.

But I was too ashamed to tell C what had happened after that.

'What's the matter? Why can't you get up?' I had asked Alan.

No reply.

'You've been in there for three days.'

I pushed into the back bedroom. It wasn't easy because a chair was propped against the door handle. In the half-light of a winter morning penetrating through the thin curtains, I could see that my brother was resting on his elbows under the duvet. The room smelled like a stable, and some of his clothes were on the floor next to the bed. They were ripped into several pieces.

'I can't. I just can't face having to go through it.' He sounded weak but I realised for the first time that I felt no sympathy for him any more, only anger. There was simply too much history, too many memories bubbling up from my childhood and clouding my brain, for me to manage the situation with any semblance of reason.

'Alan, please.'

'No, go away and fucking well leave me alone.'

'I just can't take this.'

What happened next still shocks me. I was so incensed with him that I picked up a stool from the corner of the room and brought it down on top of his duvet-covered body. Twice. I don't really think I hurt him, but I know I fully intended to.

'Please get out of this house, now!'

Within minutes he got out of bed, quickly dressed in his remaining clothes and was gone. The bed was soiled. I stripped off the covers, threw them into the dustbin in the garden and arranged for the mattress to be taken to the rubbish tip. It was irreparably soaked with urine.

Then it was all over.

'I eventually got him seen by a professor at an inpatient unit in Yorkshire,' was what I actually told C. 'It's closed now.'

'And did it help?' C asked.

'No, not really, to be honest. I think by then, by the time he had the therapy he needed, it was too late.'

My brother should have had cognitive behavioural therapy when he was young, when he would have been able to respond to treatment before his problems became chronic. But it wasn't widely available then, and by the time he was offered it, his problems were very long-standing. He simply couldn't make use of it. The longer our problems continue before we get the right sort of help, the harder it is for us to change.

Alan was also very stubborn.

He told me even then, 'I should be able to pull myself out of it. I don't need nurses or social workers and I don't want medication.'

I could hear my father, with his rigid non-conformist self-reliance, speaking through him.

'I wanted to help him,' I told C, 'but I couldn't... I cannot. I know he wanted to come and live with me, but I could not cope with him. He frightens me. I still feel very guilty about not being able to change things. Or even cope with him.'

'It sounds very sad indeed...'

'And I still worry if what is wrong with me, if these thinking patterns... I mean, are they the same kind of thing? I have always worried this disorder could still happen to me.'

I knew that in many ways Alan and I were so alike. We both inherited our father's strength of will. Sometimes, however, it seemed as though, in identifying so strongly with Dad's beliefs about health and illness – and his reluctance to see the viewpoint of others – Alan could almost pretend that Dad had never left us. I suspected I would always feel guilty that I could not help him. But I knew I did not have the answers to his problems. If I attempted to carry his burden, I was afraid that I would sink beneath the surface again. Each time we talked, this was one more thing I ruminated about.

'Your brother sounds very disabled by his symptoms,' C began, 'but this is different from what you are experiencing. There are some similarities, yes, but they are not the same thing.'

And deep down I knew he was right. Yes, there were similarities: it did feel as though both Alan and I had some serious problems with our brain circuitry. Indeed, sometimes it just felt like everyday life caused such painful reverberations in my brain that I needed to physically hold my head in my hands to lessen the vibrations brought about by living and to still my thoughts. I *had* experienced obsessions. The thoughts I had about crashing the car had an obsessional quality to them, as they were repetitive, unwanted and intrusive. Obsessional thoughts can occur in depression, and people with obsessional problems can also, understandably, get depressed. But what I experienced most of the time was a replaying of recent conversations and events in a painfully futile attempt to make sense of a problem. And I had no compulsive behaviours like the ones which governed his life.

The weeks passed by, and C began to teach me some specific ways of trying to manage the ruminations when they occurred. He had already demonstrated this to me through an experiment in which he asked me to conjure up in my mind memories, thoughts and images related to a series of fairly neutral words. When I allowed myself to think about and dwell on negative memories or images related to these words, I felt a distinct change in my mood, quite different to when he asked me to conjure up more positive thoughts.

'What was it like?' C asked. 'What did you notice?'

'I started to feel quite down, bleak and empty.'

So the next step was to try not to engage with those thoughts.

'Are you familiar with some of the work on mindfulness?'

I replied in the affirmative. I had become increasingly interested in it, although my first introduction was through reading about Buddhist approaches to managing depression. C asked me to try to work on simply acknowledging the presence of the worrying thoughts and images instead of engaging with them.

'They are there, but you don't have to pull them down and start to think about them,' he told me.

I had tried in the past to meditate and found it helpful in managing my anxiety but it was one of those many things in my life I had put aside because I could never 'find the time' to do it. I knew time was an elastic concept; if I had really wanted to do it, I probably would have found the time. It wasn't difficult for me to understand what C was getting at.

During the following week, every time I found myself ruminating, I tried to let go of the problem I was thinking about. It wasn't easy; I had done this for so long that I didn't notice when it began. I found that having a psychological space in which to deposit the problem seemed helpful; I imagined putting my box of worries on the top shelf of a large walk-in cupboard in the corner of my study. I rarely went in there, although John was always asking me to clear it out to create more space. If I did this, which would make him very happy, perhaps I could begin to fill the top shelf with my worries instead.

My patient Anna began to see a cognitive therapist and, as the weeks went by, she started to feel much more able to cope from day to day.

'I am learning how to challenge the negative thoughts,' she said.

Psychologists call them 'negative automatic thoughts', but there is usually a trigger, a situation, something that will set them off. In Anna's case these triggers generally occurred at work, in her interaction with her boss and other colleagues.

'So the therapy has been helpful?'

'Yes, it has. I don't think I could have been bothered with having to work at it before, when I was going through all the problems with my family; I just felt in too much chaos, but now each day seems a little easier. Sometimes I don't even seem to have to think about how to cope. I just get on with the day like anyone else would, like I used to before the depression really kicked in.'

'And have you done some work on "relapse prevention"?'

There is always a risk that depression will return. However, if we are prepared for the possibility of relapse, and can recognise the early warning signs – such as the increase in our negative thinking and the particular symptoms we know will herald the onset of something more severe – we can act before things get worse. With me, those are still difficulty in sleeping and waking in the night with stomach pains. There is evidence that cognitive therapy can help to prevent relapse.

Anna pulled her notebook out of her handbag. 'Yes, I know with my history there will probably be other times, but I'm prepared. Everything is written down in here. When I feel I need to, I find a moment to take it out and read through what I have learned.'

I saw C for about a year, meeting with him every two or three weeks. At the end, we reviewed what I had achieved. I had not had any relapses during the year, but there had been times when my mood had dipped.

I told him, 'I understand a lot more now about how to manage myself in the present, in everyday life. My other therapy helped too, but this has been entirely different.'

It had also been refreshing to find someone who seemed to understand exactly how my thoughts worked.

After saying goodbye to C, I went out into the car park for the last time and sat in my car for a moment. I took out my diary and read the paragraph that C had asked me to construct for when I feel my thinking getting out of control and my level of anxiety rising in meetings at work.

You are somewhere you don't want to be, with people who make you feel uncomfortable, who you think do not like you; you certainly dislike some of them. They are ambitious and confident, with their own agendas and their own scores to settle.

Pause for a moment. Take a deep breath. Remember why you are here and what you want to achieve. Remember what your goals are. In order to achieve these, you have to spend time with people, but it doesn't mean you have to like them, be liked by them or even attempt to be like them. Imagine your cat is sitting on your lap and you are stroking his ears. Just wait for your moment, take another deep breath and say the minimum you need to say to make your point.

Then shut up.

Conclusion

I've learned a great deal about depression in my life. I know much more about what causes it and its consequences than I did in the past. I can help people who suffer from it.

In the last decade I have experienced a relapse of my depression every couple of years or so. I have now taken one antidepressant or another continuously for more than 20 years. I have experienced some side effects, but I can usually tolerate them. My periods of low mood, which have from time to time been more severe, necessitating a change in my treatment, have almost always been triggered by life events related to my work. My skin is still too thin and I am easily wounded, and I still live my life in a state of perpetual fear of being discovered to be a fraud. I am frequently anxious. Day to day life can still be a struggle. Yet, despite experiencing depression, I have achieved a great deal in my work and been very happy in my second marriage; I think both of these owe something to my extended therapies and medication, and each of these methods of treatment has played an important role.

I am quite sure that depression isn't just the list of symptoms found in the *Diagnostic and Statistical Manual* (*DSM*) of the American Psychiatric Association or in the *International Classification of Diseases*. These are approximations, constructs and guesses as to what 'depression' might be. They are useful for helping us in research and clinical work, but should not be seen as essential truths in their own right. Unfortunately, they are treated as such every day, all over the world. I suspect there is not a single depression, as *DSM* would have us believe, but many different 'depressions', with some features in common and others which are very different.

There are people everywhere who suffer, who feel cut off from the world, who feel life isn't worth living and who kill themselves. They share a lot of experiences – undoubtedly including the symptoms of depression that psychiatrists learn by rote and always ask about – but each person has a different story to tell about their misery, and there are many different reasons why they have become depressed. Their life problems, as I have tried to show in this book, are not simple but complex; they are intertwined with the other realities of the human condition: our vulnerability, fears, losses, wounds, the need to be loved, the pain of loneliness, the difficulty in trusting others, the problems in our past and unresolved grief. It's impossible to really help a person who is depressed without acknowledging and addressing these experiences. This is why medication on its own is never the answer.

I believe, too, that biology plays an important part in how and why we experience depression. I have learned over the last few years about the biological changes that can be seen in the brain in some, but not all, people who are depressed. We inherit the genes that make us vulnerable from our parents. Depression is, for many, an extraordinarily physical experience. The terrible feeling of torpor that psychiatrists call 'psychomotor retardation' is more than simply a psychic phenomenon. Something – although we still do not entirely understand what – happens within our brain functioning and results in the 'epiphenomena' that are the symptoms of depression: low mood, inability to enjoy life, loss of energy, inability to think clearly and feelings of hopelessness. These can be reversed with medication, at least to some degree. But in people who are chronically and severely depressed, there are changes which can be seen in the structure of the brain. When a person has experienced one episode of severe depression triggered by stressful life events, there seems to be some kind of 'kindling' effect in the brain which makes further episodes more likely to occur. Believing this does not mean that I am in any way a biological reductionist, one who only views the causes of illness in simple biological terms – far from it. I don't have any personal sense of whether my 'inflamed' brain (inflammatory theories are the latest in many different biological theories of depression) has structurally changed in some way or if my neurotransmitters – the chemicals which help to relay electrical impulses – are up to full strength (although it can feel like they aren't when I'm not firing on all cylinders).

Severe depression is a singularly awful experience. It saps the life out of the sufferer. It makes each day seem like a lifetime. Indeed, I think that those who seek to explain depression as no more than 'understandable distress' in response to life events are just as guilty of a kind of reductionism as the neuroscientists who pore over the MRI (Magnetic Resonance Imaging) scans and the psychologists who seek to break everything down into instances of 'negative thinking', which can sometimes make the sufferer feel as though it is their own fault for not thinking more 'positively'. Depression is related to all of these factors, and at the same time it is none of them. For each person, the parts that the different dimensions of biology, psychology, life events and difficulties (such as grief, physical ill health and social isolation) play in both precipitating depression and maintaining it will be important to a differing degree.

Depression is a profoundly personal illness. It burrows into the soul and damages our sense of who we are and our reason for living, in the same way a worm makes its way to the core of a ripening apple. We all have to find our own ways of managing the damage it causes, but I know from my own experience that it *can* be done.

Although I am not a religious person, I do know that some people find faith a great support in overcoming depression. Perhaps priests really are the only people who can help us to nourish our souls, but personally I doubt that. I've spent most of my life helping people to patch up their souls in order to keep going and accepting help from others in repairing my own.

Despite what some may say, asking for and receiving help is really nothing to be ashamed of. It demonstrates that you are doing something about how you feel rather than trying to hide it, which only brings more problems. Unfortunately, many societies, including our own, are not yet ready for such a level of honesty, but I know my depression is not something I should be – or am – ashamed of.

I have learned how important it is to be able to really connect with another person in order to be able to understand

and overcome the problems related, in one way or another, to my depressed mood. To be able to have a frank, open and meaningful conversation with another person is, as Bob Hobson (a psychotherapist who supervised my therapy in my early career) said in his book *Forms of Feeling*, crucial in enabling us to explore, learn and modify how we deal with our difficulties, especially those concerned with our significant relationships. I've learned this not just from my work, but from my very own personal journey through depression.

I am beginning to learn the need to nourish my own soul in order to prevent relapse, rather than simply mend it when it is broken. I have survived. I have even been successful in my chosen career. Perhaps my father would have been proud of me, although I suspect he would have never been able to tell me so face-to-face.

As I write this, I am once again in Scotland, sitting at my desk, looking out from my window over moorland on the mainland of Orkney, and planning for the future. The time has finally come to relinquish my work and learn how to take better care of my own 'self', body and mind, and those who are important to me. This is the next challenge, and it is something that we can all do to help ourselves overcome depression.

Glossary

Aetiology: the cause (or causes) of a particular disease or condition. In psychiatry, this means considering underlying vulnerabilities, events or experiences which triggered the current problem and things which perpetuate it.

Bipolar disorder (formerly called manic-depressive illness): a condition in which both depression and mania (feeling high, overactive) occur, and mood can swing from one extreme to the other. Psychotic symptoms (delusions and hallucinations) can also take place. Less severe highs without psychotic symptoms are called hypomania.

Body dysmorphic disorder: a type of anxiety disorder which causes a person to have a distorted view of how they look. They spend such a great deal of time worrying about their appearance, despite reassurance from others, that this interferes with relationships and everyday life.

Cognitive behavioural therapy (CBT): a type of psychotherapy, or talking therapy, which focuses on changing the way a person thinks and behaves. It deals with current problems rather than exploring the past.

Compulsion: repeated action or thought that a person feels the need to carry out in order to relieve or avoid anxiety caused by obsessions.

Delusions: a false personal belief that is not subject to reason or evidence to the contrary and is not explained by a person's cultural or religious background.

Differential diagnosis: the process in medicine of weighing up the probability of one condition versus that of other conditions in explaining a patient's symptoms. In psychiatry this means considering and ruling out other possible diagnoses.

Electroconvulsive therapy (ECT): a treatment for serious mental illness (usually depression) in which an electric current is passed through the brain of a person under general anaesthesia. It is a highly controversial treatment, which can be life-saving but can also cause long-term memory problems.

Hallucination: an experience during which a person hears, sees, feels, tastes or smells something which doesn't exist outside their mind.

Neurotransmitter: a chemical messenger which carries signals across the spaces (synapses) between nerve cells.

Obsession: a repetitive thought, idea or image which a person tries to resist, but which causes anxiety (both because of the obsession and the attempt to resist it).

Obsessive compulsive disorder (OCD): a mental health condition in which a person has obsessive thoughts and carries out compulsive actions.

Procurator fiscal: a public prosecutor in Scotland who investigates all sudden and suspicious deaths (similar to a coroner in other legal systems).

Psychodynamic psychotherapy: a talking therapy in which the therapist helps a person to see how what happened to them in the past influences their present life. It is similar to psychoanalysis (which is based on the work of Sigmund Freud) but much less intense (weekly rather than several times a week).

Psychosis, psychotic: means that the person is experiencing delusions and/or hallucinations.

Schizophrenia: a diagnosis given to people who have a serious and often long-term mental illness with a wide variety of psychotic symptoms, including hallucinations, delusions, difficulties with thinking and changes in behaviour.

Selective serotonin reuptake inhibitor (SSRI): a type of antidepressant, which is thought to increase the activity of serotonin (a neurotransmitter) in the brain (although there is still uncertainty about how these drugs work).

Social phobia: a persistent and overwhelming fear of social situations, such as shopping, meeting strangers and eating in company. It is much more disabling than simply being shy.

Specialing: in mental health nursing means providing constant attendance for an inpatient, in order to protect them from harming themselves or others and to observe their behaviour.

Bibliography

Brown, George W. and Harris, Tirril *Social Origins of Depression: A study of psychiatric disorder in women* (1979, Tavistock)

Burns, David D. *Feeling Good: The new mood therapy* (1980, Avon Books)

Freud, Sigmund 'Mourning and Melancholia' in *The Standard Edition of the Complete Works of Sigmund Freud. Volume XIV (1914–16)*, translated by James Strachey (1957, Hogarth Press and The Institute of Psychoanalysis)

Goffman, Erving *Asylums: Essays on the social situation of mental patients and other inmates* (1961, Anchor Books)

Hobson, Robert F. *Forms of Feeling: The heart of psychotherapy* (1985, Routledge)

Jamison, Kay Redfield *An Unquiet Mind: A memoir of moods and madness* (1995, Alfred A. Knopf)

Kübler-Ross, Elisabeth *On Death and Dying* (1969, Tavistock)

Leader, Darian *The New Black: Mourning, melancholia and depression* (2009, Penguin)

Lott, Tim *The Scent of Dried Roses* (1997, Penguin)

Storr, Anthony *Solitude: A return to the self* (1988, Free Press)

Wurtzel, Elizabeth *Prozac Nation: Young and Depressed in America – A memoir* (1995, Riverhead Books)

Sources of Information and Support

Alcoholics Anonymous supports people who need help with a drinking problem.
www.alcoholics-anonymous.org.uk

Anxiety UK provides support, information and care to people experiencing anxiety.
www.anxietyuk.org.uk

CALM (Campaign Against Living Miserably) is particularly aimed at young men with mental health problems. It provides information and has a daily support line available between 5 p.m. and midnight.
www.thecalmzone.net

Depression Alliance provides information about depression and runs local self-help groups.
www.depressionalliance.org

Living Life to the Full offers free online self-help therapy. Some of this requires you to register and there is also a link to booklets that can be purchased (available in e-book format).
www.llttf.com

Mental Health Foundation provides information about the full range of mental health problems and also downloadable booklets.
www.mentalhealth.org.uk

Mind is the leading voluntary organisation for mental health in England and Wales. It provides downloadable information and support about all mental health problems, and helpful information to navigate your way around services.
www.mind.org.uk

In Scotland, contact the Scottish Association for Mental Health (SAMH).
www.samh.org.uk

NHS Choices has a great deal of useful information about all mental health problems and treatments, including podcasts.
www.nhs.uk

Northumberland, Tyne and Wear NHS Trust publishes downloadable self-help booklets on many topics from anxiety and depression, to domestic violence, anger and shyness. They

can be downloaded free but payment is required for a hard-copy leaflet.
www.ntw.nhs.uk/pic/selfhelp

Rethink Mental Illness provides information for people with mental health problems, and their family and carers. It also runs local groups.
www.rethink.org

There is an advice and information service open from 10 a.m. to 2 p.m., Monday to Friday.

Royal College of Psychiatrists publishes a wide range of free downloadable information on mental health problems, treatment and services.
www.rcpsych.ac.uk/mentalhealthinformation.aspx

Samaritans are contactable 24 hours a day, seven days a week. You do not have to be suicidal to contact them.
www.samaritans.org

Sane provides information and support about all mental health problems.
www.sane.org.uk

UK Council for Psychotherapy holds the national register of accredited psychotherapists and enables you to search for a therapist.
www.ukcp.org.uk

About the Author

Linda Gask (MB ChB, Msc (Psychiatry), PhD, FRCPsych, FRCGP) was born to a Scottish mother and English father, and brought up on the east coast of England, in Lincolnshire. She trained in medicine in Edinburgh and is now Emerita Professor of Primary Care Psychiatry at the University of Manchester. She has worked as a consultant psychiatrist in the North of England over the last 25 years. Now semi-retired, she lives with her husband and cat in a stone house in the Pennines but also spends an increasing part of her time in Orkney.

Linda is highly respected in her field and is the author of several academic textbooks. She has an international reputation for her teaching and research into doctor–patient communication, depression and other common mental health problems. She has also been an advisor to the World Health Organization, served on the board of the World Psychiatric Association, and is the author of more than 180 published articles and book chapters. In 2010 she was awarded Honorary Fellowship of the Royal College of General Practitioners in recognition of her teaching in primary care mental health through her career. She is a director of two social enterprises that she helped to found: one of these, STORM® (www.stormskillstraining. co.uk), provides training in suicide prevention; the other, Six Degrees (six-degrees.org.uk), provides primary care mental health services to Salford, in Greater Manchester.

Since her teenage years, Linda has suffered mental health problems and has first-hand experience of both pharmacological and psychological treatments for depression. She is passionate about challenging the stigma surrounding mental illness by being open about her own problems. She wants to show that her experiences as both a patient and professional question the rigid line that society draws between those who are mentally ill and those who are 'well'.

She blogs about mental health at www.lindagask.com and can be followed on Twitter @suzypuss.

an apple a day

a memoir of *love* and *recovery* from anorexia

emma woolf

AN APPLE A DAY
A Memoir of Love and Recovery From Anorexia

Emma Woolf

£9.99
Paperback
ISBN: 978-1-84953-249-5

I haven't tasted chocolate for over ten years and now I'm walking down the street unwrapping a Kit Kat. It tastes amazing... When I think of the wasted years, the friends lost and evenings spent alone, all those shared meals I've avoided, it strikes me as incredibly sad. But anorexia is a young person's game and I don't have the time or energy to play any more.

At the age of 32, Emma Woolf decided to face the biggest challenge of her life: to overcome her addiction to hunger, exercise and control, and finally beat anorexia. Having met the man of her dreams (and wanting a future and a baby together) she decided it was time to stop starving and start living. And as if that wasn't enough pressure, Emma also agreed to chart her progress in a weekly column for *The Times*.

Honest, hard-hitting and yet romantic, *An Apple a Day* is a compelling and life-affirming memoir of love and recovery.

Have you enjoyed this book?
If so, why not write a review on your favourite website?

If you're interested in finding out more about our books, find
us on Facebook at **Summersdale Publishers** and follow us on
Twitter at **@Summersdale**.

Thanks very much for buying this Summersdale book.

www.summersdale.com